The Annotated Christmas Carol

~~~~~~~~~

Charles Dickens. Portrait by Francis Alexander, 1842.
Courtesy Boston Museum of Fine Arts

W. W. NORTON & COMPANY

New York   London

THE ANNOTATED

CHRISTMAS CAROL

A Christmas Carol in Prose

CHARLES DICKENS

ILLUSTRATED BY JOHN LEECH

Edited with an Introduction, Notes, and Bibliography by

MICHAEL PATRICK HEARN

For information about permission to reproduce selections
from this book, write to Permissions, W. W. Norton & Company, Inc.,
500 Fifth Avenue, New York, NY 10110

Manufacturing by The Courier Companies, Inc.
Book design by JAM Design
Production manager: Andrew Marasia

Library of Congress Cataloging-in-Publication Data

Dickens, Charles, 1812–1870.
[Christmas carol]
The annotated Christmas carol : a Christmas carol in prose / by Charles Dickens ;
illustrated by John Leech ; with an introduction, notes, and bibliography
by Michael Patrick Hearn.
p. cm.
Includes bibliographical references.
ISBN 0-393-05158-7
1. Scrooge, Ebenezer (Fictitious character)—Fiction. 2. Dickens, Charles, 1812–1870.
Christmas carol. 3. London (England)—Fiction. 4. Poor families—Fiction.
5. Sick children—Fiction. 6. Misers—Fiction. I. Hearn, Michael Patrick.
II. Leech, John, 1817–1864. III. Title.

PR4572.C68 2003

823'.8—dc21   2003044493

W. W. Norton & Company, Inc.
500 Fifth Avenue, New York, N.Y. 10110
www.wwnorton.com

W. W. Norton & Company Ltd.
Castle House, 75/76 Wells Street, London W1T 3QT

1 2 3 4 5 6 7 8 9 0

In Memory of

MY FATHER

— M . P . H .

CONTENTS

ACKNOWLEDGMENTS

Due to the complexity of *The Annotated Christmas Carol*, I have relied on a number of people in a variety of ways in the composition and completion of this book: Colin Axon; Georgia B. Barnhill; Susan and David Bloom; June Braun and Robert Leibowits; Mary Margaret Canby; Alice Caulkins; James Cummins; Dennis David; Carol Digel; Lizabeth Dion; Rodney K. Engen; Frank Evina; Lucy, Michael, Celia, and Stephen Evans; Rudy Faust; Martin Gardner; Ruth Gruber; Susan Halpert; Christopher Bruce Hearn; Mary L. Hearn, Malcolm Hillier; Adam Inocent; Jeffrey Kraus; Sasha Lurie; Dan Malan; Rita and Patrick Maund; Jennifer and Dag Mellgren; Herb Moscovitz; David Moyer; David Perdue; John Podeschi; Roger Rees; Emily Richard and Edward Petherbridge; Victoria Sabelli; Jöel Sartorius; Justin G. Schiller; Florian Schweizer; Barbara Seaman; Donna Shepper; Betsy Shirley; Anne Elisabeth Suter; Maria Tatar; Marvin Taylor; Dr. Zelda Teplitz; Michael Weintraub; and Elizabeth Wilson. Kiko Noda, a researcher's researcher, sought and found elusive items in the British Library. Karl Michael Emyrs was especially helpful in the gathering and preparation of the pictures. I have drawn on the rich holdings of the following institutions: American Antiquarian Society; the Beinecke Rare Book and Manuscript Library, Yale University; the Boston Museum of Fine Arts; the British Library; Butler Library, Columbia University; The Charles Dickens Museum, London; Fales Library, New York University; Rare Book Department, the Free Library of Philadelphia; the Houghton Library, Harvard University; the Library of Congress; the New-York Historical Society; and the New York Public Library. I could not have done my work without the vast knowledge and generosity of their staffs. I am also indebted to the recently completed twelve-volume Pilgrim Edition of *The Letters of Charles Dickens* (1965–2002), published by Clarenden Press and edited by Madeline House, Graham Storey, Kathleen Tillotson, and others. Their labors have been herculean, and they have produced a model of fine scholarship that will continue to enrich all other studies of Dickens and his work.

The publication of the annotated books requires a gifted team, and I have been fortunate to work with the best in the business: Andrew Marasia, Director of Production; Nancy Palmquist, Managing Editor; Donald Rifkin, Production Editor; Louise Brockett, Director of Publicity; William Rusin, Sales Director; Elisabeth Kerr, Foreign Rights; and Jeannie Luciano, Publishing Director. Jo Ann Metsch beautifully designed this often difficult and challenging book, and Eileen Cheung was responsible for the handsome jacket. Patient and thorough Ann Tappert in copyediting kept me from making more errors than I might otherwise have made. And I would be remiss not to express my eternal gratitude to my editor, Robert Weil; his assistants, Jason Baskin and Brendan Curry; and my agent, Mitchell Rose. They kept the faith and kept me going.

INTRODUCTION TO

The Annotated Christmas Carol

"No, no," said Mr. Pickwick, "not an end to it,

I assure you; for I must hear how,

and why, and all about it."

—CHARLES DICKENS, from Chapter 28 of
*The Posthumous Papers of
the Pickwick Club* (1837)

A Christmas Carol (1843) is the most popular work of England's most popular novelist, and it has had a remarkable life of its own beyond its author's vast reputation. Should all of Charles Dickens' marvelous creations, from *The Pickwick Papers* (1837) to *The Mystery of Edwin Drood* (1870), be suddenly threatened with extinction, the story of Ebenezer Scrooge would surely survive. It has become a part of Christmas folklore. All misers are Mr. Scrooge, all plum puddings are that devoured by the ravenous Cratchits. Besides having written a thoroughly entertaining narrative, Dickens possessed that special ability of defining better than anyone before or since the spirit of the holiday season. In what he called "the Carol philosophy," he went beyond merely venerating Christmas for "its sacred name and origin" to acknowledging its basic humanism in the words of Scrooge's nephew Fred: "a good time: a kind, forgiving, charitable, pleasant time: the only time I know of, in the long calendar of the year, when men and women seem by one consent to open their shut-up hearts freely, and to think of people below them as if they really were fellow-passengers to the grave, and not another race of creatures bound on other journeys." By the time of his death in 1870, Dickens had already secured so sure a place in the mythology of the holiday that a story cir-culated about a little costermonger's girl in Drury Lane who on hearing the sad news, asked, "Dickens dead? Then will Father Christmas die too?"[1]

Few modern readers realize that *A Christmas Carol* was written dur-ing a decline in the old Christmas traditions. "If Christmas, with its ancient and hospitable customs, its social and charitable observances, were in danger of decay, this is the book that would give them a new lease," declared the English poet and wit Thomas Hood in his review in *Hood's Magazine and Comic Miscellany* (January 1844, p. 68). Dickens has even been credited with almost single-handedly reviving the holiday customs. He knew well a common complaint of his own day.

By the early nineteenth century, there appeared to be little left of the old celebrations that had begun as far back as A.D. 601, when Pope Gre-gory instructed his missionary St. Austin of Canterbury, in converting the Anglo-Saxons, to make the local winter feast a Christmas festival.[2] The result was the often odd adaptation of pagan customs for Christian purposes from Saturnalia, Yule (the Saxon feast for the return of the Sun, in honor of the god Thor), and the Druid holiday.[3] The medieval church saw little conflict between pagan and Christian intentions, and readily absorbed local customs; as Chaucer observed, the Roman god Janus was welcome wherever Christian men sang "Nowel." The festivals grew to twelve days, from Christmas Eve until Epiphany, under the Anglo-Norman kings. As early as 1170, at the command of Henry II, the

[1] See the epigraph to the poem "Dickens Returns on Christmas Day," in Theodore Watts-Dunton, *The Coming of Love* (London: John Lane, 1899), p. 191. Due to the large volume of references, footnotes have been kept to a minimum. Sources for quotations from peri-odicals appear within the body of the text, whenever possible, and page references to often-quoted books appear within the text after the first citation, as noted there. Refer-ences to Dickens' own works are identified primarily by title only within the text; please see the bibliography for further information.

[2] Because the early church fathers feared it came too close to the Roman festival of Sat-urnalia, the seven-day feast celebrating the New Year, December 25 was not proclaimed a holy day until the second century. Not until the fourth century was the birth of Christ cel-ebrated as a public feast.

[3] Holly, for example, originally used in pagan divination, became a Christian symbol: three red berries and three evergreen leaves on a single stalk represent the Holy Trinity. The Druids believed that mistletoe possessed mystical as well as medicinal properties. The early Christians decorated the altars of converted local temples with this remarkable greenery, as Dickens noted in *A Child's History of England* (1852–54), "the same plant we hang up in houses at Christmas Time now—when its white berries grew upon the Oak."

church welcomed the season with plays, masques, and other spectacles that supplied religious instruction with entertainment. The English nobility sponsored many legendary feasts and pageants during the Middle Ages. The magnitude of these celebrations did not decrease when Henry VIII established the Church of England; on the contrary, the king did not merely promote the holiday pageants but performed in them as well.

Everything changed under Oliver Cromwell and the Puritans. Quoting the Scriptures, they attacked the old customs for being no more than pagan superstition; it was blasphemous to celebrate the birth of Christ in the same manner as the Roman feast of Saturnalia. Simple pleasures like mince pies were judged no more than a superstitious and popish abomination. The first blow struck the old holidays with an ordinance of 1642 forbidding the performance of plays. On July 3, 1647, the Roundhead Parliament decreed that the feast of the Nativity of Christ could not be celebrated with the other holy days. The finisher came on December 24, 1652, when it was proclaimed that "no observance shall be had of the five and twentieth of December, commonly called Christmas day; nor any solemnity used or exercised in churches upon that day in respect thereof."

With the Puritan defeat of the Royalists came the conquest of Christmas. *The Arraignment, Conviction, and Imprisonment of Christmas* (1645) described Father Christmas as "much wasted, so that he hath looked very thin, and ill of late." He was now an outcast in England, because his season had formerly been "a time observable for the common People to bring large offerings to the Pope holinesse, to maintaine the Cardinalls, Priests, and Fryers." According to Josiah King's *The Examination and Tryal of Old Father Christmas* (1678), Father Christmas, "of the Town of Superstition, in the County of Idolatry," now stood accused of having "from time to time, abused the people of this Common-wealth, drawing and inticing them to Drunkenness, Gluttony, and unlawful Gaming, Wantonness, Uncleanness, Lasciviousness, Cursing, Swearing, abuse of the Creatures, some to one Vice, and some to another; all to Idleness." The suppression of Christmas became proof of the degeneracy of the age; good fellowship had declined, and along with it the wealthy now neglected the old Christmas spirit of charity. The Puritans believed in honoring its sacred name and origin only in prayer and contemplation.

The Restoration of the English monarchy failed to completely revive the splendor of Christmas past. Yet many of the old customs could still be found in the provinces. "The spirit of hospitality has not quite forsaken us," observed *Round about Our Coal-Fire, or Christmas Entertainments* (1740). "Several of the gentry are gone down to their respective seats in the country, in order to keep their *Christmas* in the old way, and entertain their tenants and trades-folk as their ancestors used to do, and I wish them a merry *Christmas* accordingly." Yet by the end of the eighteenth century many of the old trappings and entertainments had entirely vanished. Such items as plum porridge and peacock pie so common to the old bills of fare were now unknown, and the court demonstrated little interest in celebrating in the lavish former manner.

The Industrial Revolution further discouraged the simple pleasures of the season; employers kept their factories running through Christmas Day. "If a little more success had crowned the Puritan movement of the seventeenth century, or the Utilitarian movement of the nineteenth century," G. K. Chesterton observed in his introduction to the 1924 Charles E. Lauriat edition of *A Christmas Carol*, the old holiday traditions would "have become merely details of the neglected past, a part of history or even of archeology. . . . Perhaps the very word carol would sound like the word villanelle."

Fortunately, a few brave voices rose in praise of the season. A handful of scholars and historians treated the old Christmas customs with a respect and seriousness as if they were of another culture entirely. One of the most important early studies was Thomas K. Hervey's *The Book of Christmas* (1835); it was notable not only for its in-depth history and evaluation of the English holiday but also for its jolly etchings by Robert Seymour (1798–1836), who the following year began embellishing the even more famous *The Pickwick Papers* (1837).[4] Other scholars preserved the old songs associated with the season that were still sung in the country. Davies Gilbert issued *Some Ancient Christmas Carols* in 1822, but the most ambitious collection was *Christmas Carols, Ancient and Modern* (1833), by William Sandys, with a fine long scholarly introduction on the history of Christmas. An expert on Cornish customs who corresponded with Dickens, he knew that preserving these old songs was not an easy task. "In many parts of the kingdom, especially in the northern and western parts," he explained in his introduction, "the festival is still kept up with spirit among the middling and lower classes, though its influence is

---

[4] Charles Dickens must have known Hervey's book well: the old gentleman whom Seymour depicted "Enjoying Christmas" with a copy of Hervey's study in his hand bears a striking resemblance to that other old gentleman drawn by Seymour, Mr. Pickwick.

on the wane even with them; the genius of the present age requires work and not play, and since the commencement of this century a great change may be traced. The modern instructors of mankind do not think it necessary to provide for popular amusements, considering mental improvement the one thing needful."[5]

Remarkably, it was an American who now instructed the English on how best to preserve their Christmas. In describing an old-fashioned Christmas celebrated at the mythical Bracebridge Hall in *The Sketch-Book of Geoffrey Crayon* (1819–20), Washington Irving recognized in "Christmas" that the traditions now "resemble those picturesque morsels of Gothic architecture, which we see crumbling later days." During this holiday, when its "tone and sacred feeling . . . blends with our conviviality and lifts the spirit to a state of hallowed and elevated enjoyment," the Squire of Bracebridge Hall entertained his guests with dances, songs, blindman's buff, an amateur masque, and other amusements in the same good fellowship of country gentlemen of centuries past.[6]

One of Irving's most ardent admirers was Charles Dickens, who was especially fond of the festivities at Bracebridge Hall. He declared in a speech at a banquet in his honor in New York, on February 18, 1842, "I do not go to bed two nights out of seven without taking Washington Irving under my arm upstairs to bed with me."[7] In his very first Christmas

---

[5] William Sandys, *A Selection of Christmas Carols, Ancient and Modern* (London: Richard Beckley, 1833), p. 1.

[6] Another American, Clement Clarke Moore (1779–1863), added to the seasonal mythology the popular conception of Santa Claus, the Yankee version of Father Christmas and the legendary Saint Nicholas. His ballad "An Account of a Visit from St. Nicholas" (1822) is today as much a part of holiday lore as *A Christmas Carol*. By the end of the nineteenth century, largely through this poem and the cartoons of Thomas Nast (1840–1902), this American Ghost of Christmas Presents became as recognizable to English children as their own Father Christmas.

[7] *The Speeches of Charles Dickens*, edited by Kenneth J. Fielding (Oxford: Clarendon Press, 1960), p. 29. All subsequent quotations from Dickens' speeches are also from this book. "There is no living writer, and there are very few among the dead, whose appropriation I should feel so proud to earn," Dickens wrote Irving on April 21, 1841. "I should like to travel with you, outside the last of the coaches, down to Bracebridge Hall" (*The Letters of Charles Dickens*, edited by Madeline House and others, 12 vols. [Oxford: Clarendon Press, 1965–2002], p. 267. This book is the source for all correspondence to and from Charles Dickens and other members of his family, unless otherwise indicated. Due to the enormous reliance on this masterful and definitive edition and in an attempt to limit the number of footnotes, subsequent citations to Dickens' voluminous correspondence are given within the text by date and page number only; the twelve volumes follow the correspondence chronologically).

Charles Dickens. Wood engraving,
The Illustrated London News, April 8, 1843.
Courtesy Library of Congress.

work, the short essay "A Christmas Dinner" in *Sketches by Boz*, a collection similar to the American's *Sketch-Book*, Dickens shared Irving's seasonal sentiments. This brief essay describes an urban Christmas family party ("nothing in nature more delightful!"), celebrated "in a strain of rational good-will and cheerfulness, doing more to awaken the sympathies of every member of the party in behalf of his neighbour, and to perpetuate their good feeling during the ensuing year, than all the homilies that have ever been written, by all the Divines that have ever lived."

This early piece was just a dress rehearsal for another sketch devoted to the "good-humoured Christmas Chapter" in *The Pickwick Papers* (1837). Here, in fiction, Dickens captured all the sentiments and customs honored by Irving in his seasonal essays. The "old-fashioned" drive down to Dingley Dell is as spirited as that to Bracebridge Hall; and when Pickwick and his fellow club members arrive at the ancient country estate, Old Wardle occupies their brief stay with such songs, dances, mistletoe, blindman's buff, and other sports that would have warmed the large, generous heart of old Squire Bracebridge himself. Also, the story within the story, "The Story of the Goblins Who Stole a Sexton," was borrowed from Irving's most famous tale, "Rip Van Winkle," also in *The Sketch-Book*. Although *The Pickwick Papers* opens in 1827, the Christmas at Dingley Dell recalls an even earlier period, a preindustrial England, full of amusements that "are not quite so religiously kept up, in these degenerate times." Here was the traditional English Christmas, "in all his bluff and hearty honesty . . . the season of hospitality, merriment, and open-heartedness; the old year was preparing, like an ancient philosopher, to call his friends around him, and amidst the sound of feasting and revelry to pass gently and calmly away."

Charles Dickens knew how to celebrate the season properly. "Christmas was always a time which in our home was looked forward to with

"Christmas Eve at Mr. Wardle's." Etching by "Phiz"
(Hablôt Knight Browne), *The Pickwick Papers*, December 1836.
Courtesy Library of Congress.

eagerness and delight," his daughter Mamie recalled, "and to my father it was a time dearer than any other part of the year, I think. He loved Christmas for its deep significance as well as for its joys, and this he demonstrates in every allusion in his writings to the great festival, a day which he considered should be fragrant with the love that we should bear one to another, and with the love and reverence of his Saviour and Master." Her brother Henry remembered that Christmas in the Dickens household "was a great time, a really jovial time, and my father was always at his best, a splendid host, bright and jolly as a boy and throwing his heart and soul into everything that was going on."[8]

Inspiration for another Christmas story did not possess Dickens until, like the materialization of Marley's Ghost to Ebenezer Scrooge seven years after Marley's death, seven years after the famous Christmas at Dingley Dell. One could hardly have predicted that so good-humored a tale as *A Christmas Carol* might have been written by the end of 1843. It had been a terrible year for the writer, full of disappointments and seemingly insurmountable pressures, financial, artistic, and personal. For the first time in his phenomenal literary career, Charles Dickens faced a crucial decline in popularity and income.

Charles John Huffam Dickens had come a long way from Portsmouth, a seaport in southwest England, where he was born on February 7, 1812. He was the second of eight children, two of whom died in childhood. From his father, he developed his lifelong fear of poverty. John Dickens (1785–1851) was a poor but convivial clerk with the Navy Pay Office, always in and out of debt. Like Wilkins Micawber in *David Copperfield* (1850), he always believed "that something was sure to turn up." Unfortunately, he did not follow Micawber's maxim in Chapter 11 of the same book: "if a man had twenty pounds a-year, he would be happy, but that of he spent twenty pounds one he would be miserable." The Dickenses moved to Chatham, where the boy was happiest, and then to London. Elizabeth Dickens (1789–1863) tried to rescue the family from her husband's creditors by opening an academy for girls; no one came. At the age of twelve, Charles was taken out of school and sent to work, pasting labels on bottles for Warren's Blacking warehouse; his father landed in debtor's prison. This was the worst period of the child's life, which he

8. Mamie Dickens, *My Father As I Recall Him* (Westminster: Roxburgh Press, 1896), p. 26; and Henry Fielding Dickens, *My Father As I Knew Him* (London: William Heinemann, 1934), p. 44.

later described so vividly in Chapter 11 of *David Copperfield*. Like the climax of a Victorian melodrama or a Dickens novel, the family was saved for the moment when they received a small inheritance. Charles could now attend Wellington House Academy.

Three years later his father was back in debt, and the boy found work as a solicitor's clerk. After mastering shorthand, he became a parliamentary reporter and began selling sketches and stories under the pseudonym "Boz," a family name.[9] These lively studies of London life were collected in two volumes as *Sketches by Boz* (1839) and published with illustrations by the great English caricaturist George Cruikshank. With the launch of Dickens' brilliant literary career, he married Catherine Hogarth (1815–1875), the daughter of one of his editors. They had ten children.

Dickens was already engaged on another far more lucrative literary project in early 1836. Robert Seymour, a designer of comic sporting prints in the Cruikshank manner, proposed a new series about a club of comic sportsmen, and the publishers Chapman and Hall suggested that Dickens supply a story. But instead of restricting it to the sporting theme, Dickens developed the idea into the first of his serial novels issued in monthly parts, in which he wove all sorts of scenes and characters into the "perambulations, perils, travels, adventures" of the Pickwick Club. Seymour felt threatened by the ambitious young writer: when Dickens asked him to redo a picture for the second number, the deeply troubled artist shot himself. The next illustrator, Robert Buss, did not work out and was dropped after the third number. He was replaced by Hablôt Knight Browne (1815–1882), who signed his work "Phiz" compatibly with Boz.

With the appearance of the Cockney manservant Sam Weller in the fourth part in July 1836, *The Posthumous Papers of the Pickwick Club* became a literary phenomenon. "In less than six months, from the appearance of the first number of *The Pickwick Papers*," reported Abraham Hayward in *The Quarterly Review* (October 1837), "the whole reading public were talking about them—the names of Winkle, Wardle,

---

9. "Boz,'" Dickens explained in the preface to the 1867 Charles Dickens Edition of *The Pickwick Papers*, "was the nickname of a pet child, a younger brother [Augustus, 1827–1866], whom I had dubbed Moses, in honour of the Vicar of Wakefield; which being facetiously pronounced through the nose, became Boses, and being shortened, became Boz. Boz was a very familiar household word to me, long before I was an author, and so I came to adopt it."

Charles Dickens. Caricature by "Phiz"
(Hablôt Knight Browne), prospectus for the
magazine *Master Humphrey's Clock*, 1840.
Private collection.

Weller, Snodgrass, Dodson and Fogg, had become familiar in our mouths as household terms; and Mr. Dickens was the grand object of interest to the whole tribe of 'Leo-hunters,' male and female, of the metropolis. Nay, Pickwick chintzes figured in linendrapers' windows, and Weller corduroys in breeches-makers' advertisements; Boz cabs might be seen rattling through the streets, and the portrait of the author of *Pelham* or *Crichton* was scraped down or pasted over to make room for that of the new popular favourite in the omnibusses" (p. 484).[10]

Here was a new and distinctive voice in English letters. Some readers, according to Hayward, while acknowledging "a remarkable fact that his writings are most popular amongst the women of the higher circles," agreed that Dickens' "class of subject are such as to expose him at the outset to the fatal objection of vulgarity" (pp. 506, 484). No one before had depicted the lower strata of English society so affectionately and vividly. "The fact is, Mr. Dickens writes too often and too fast," Hayward concluded. "In too many instances he has been compelled to . . . put forth, in their crude, unfinished, undigested state, thoughts, feelings, observations, and plans which it required time and study to mature—or supply the allotted number of pages with original matter of the most common-place description, or hints caught from others and diluted to make them pass for his own. If he persists much longer in this course, it requires no gift of prophecy to foretell his fate—he has risen like a rocket, and he will come down like the stick" (p. 518).

10. He is referring to two popular novels, *Pelham, or The Adventures of a Gentleman* (1828), by Sir Edward Bulwer-Lytton (1803–1873), and *Crichton* (1837), by William Harrison Ainsworth (1805–1882).

But Boz would not keep silent. His energy and invention seemed unstoppable. He wrote in rapid succession *Oliver Twist* (1838), *Nicholas Nickleby* (1839), *The Old Curiosity Shop* (1841), and *Barnaby Rudge* (1841). He was now the most successful English novelist of his age. He was the "Inimitable Boz" (as he called himself), living comfortably at No. 1 Devonshire Terrace and tossing off monthly and later weekly numbers of his eagerly awaited stories. Dickens was not yet entirely sure of his powers. "I am trying to enjoy my fame while it lasts," he said in 1840, "for I believe I am not so vain as to suppose that my books will be read by any but the men of my own times."[11]

He was also an outspoken social critic. He attacked the Poor Law in *Oliver Twist*, Yorkshire schools in *Nicholas Nickleby*. "My past history and pursuits have led me to a familiar acquaintance with numerous instances of extreme wretchedness and deep-laid villainy," Dickens confessed in *The Glory and Shame of England*. "In the haunts of squalid poverty I have found many a broken heart too good for this world" (pp. 8–9).

The rush for copies of *Master Humphrey's Clock* at Chapman and Hall's. Drawing by Richard Doyle, *A Journal by Dick Doyle*, 1840. *Courtesy Library of Congress.*

[11.] Charles Edwards Lester, *The Glory and Shame of England*, vol. 2 (New York: Harper and Bros., 1841), p. 11.

His work was as popular in the United States as it was in England, and this was due largely to the absence of a strong international copyright law to prevent his books from being printed by anyone anywhere in America without compensation to the author. Some Yankees resisted Dickens. "There were many persons in our country who could not be prevailed upon to read his works for a long time after the publication of *The Pickwick Papers*," admitted the American writer and abolitionist Charles Edwards Lester. "So many vulgar representations of Sam Weller had appeared on the theatre bills at every corner of the street, that the name of 'Boz' became associated with all that was offensive in the burlesque and low farce of the American stage."[12]

But America fascinated Dickens, and he decided he must study modern democracy in action and write about it. He was not interested in a novel about his experiences abroad. He had been writing fiction steadily for five years now; and he was ready to try another form. There were already two hundred European travel books about the United States, the most famous being Frances Trollope's *Domestic Manners of the Americans* (1832), Harriet Martineau's *Society in America* (1837), and Frederick Marryat's *Diary in America* (1839). And they sold well. It seemed like the English could not read enough about how backward and bad mannered their American cousins were.

The young republic readily welcomed the most distinguished English literary figure ever to visit its shores. When Dickens and his wife arrived in Boston Harbor on January 22, 1842, after an eighteen-day passage on the steam packet *Britannia*, reporters greeted them on the pier and escorted them to a hotel. Boston had become "Boz-town." Dickens proudly wrote his great friend and future biographer John Forster from America on January 29, "of the crowds that pour in and out the whole day; of the people that line the streets when I go out; of the cheering when I went to the theatre; of the copies of verses, letters of congratulation, welcomes of all kinds, balls, dinners, assemblies without end" (p. 34). Though he was traveling as a private citizen, the American public treated him like a visiting dignitary. Boston played specially composed Boz Waltzes at a banquet in his honor, and New York topped them with the famous "Boz Ball."

---

12. *The Glory and Shame of England*, vol. 2, p. 4. Nevertheless, Lester told Irving, "I believe there is no English author now living who is so much admired and read by our countrymen as Mr. Dickens" (p. 3).

The SS *Britannia*. Frontispiece by Clarkson Stanfield, *American Notes*,
"Cheap Edition," 1850.
Private collection.

Thomas Carlyle was surprised by "*all* Yankee-doodle-dom, blazing up like one universal soda-bottle round so very measurable a phenomenon."[13]

All the adulation was eventually wearying. Like that of a modern movie or rock star, this celebrity disrupted his comfort. Crowds pressed to get a glimpse of Dickens wherever he went, even while he posed for a portrait in Frances Alexander's studio. Mobs cheered him in the streets. When he agreed to attend a reception in Philadelphia, he had to shake hands with five hundred people for two hours to avoid a riot. He was

[13] Sir Charles Gavan Duffy, *Conservations with Carlyle* (New York: Charles Scribner's Sons, 1892), p. 245.

forced to quickly hire a secretary to help him with his voluminous mail that came in from all parts of the country. He never refused to sign an autograph, but denied young ladies locks of his pretty hair. He could not possibly accept all the invitations that came in from all over the country. "I can do nothing that I want to do, go nowhere I want to go, and see nothing that I want to see," he wrote Forster on February 24. "If I turn into the street, I am followed by a multitude. If I stay at home, the house becomes, with callers, like a fair." He could not find peace even in a church: "there is a violent rush to the neighbourhood of the pew I sit in, and the clergyman preaches *at* me" (p. 87). He felt like a prisoner in this strange land.

The handsome young dandy appeared to the ex-mayor of New York Philip Hone to be "a small, bright-eyed, intelligent-looking young fellow, thirty years of age, somewhat of a dandy in his dress, with 'rings and things and fine array,' brisk in his manner and of a lively conversation. If he does not get his little head turned by all this, I shall wonder at it."[14] Boston Brahmins found him vain and vulgar: he combed his hair at the dinner table and wore a flaming red vest or a brilliant green one when the fashion there was black. Many thought he was also ungrateful to his American hosts. He made the big mistake of publicly calling for international copyright protection while in Boston, Hartford, and New York. While he argued that it would protect American literature as much as foreign, the popular press was furious that Boz should insult his generous American hosts.

He went as far south as Richmond, as far west as St. Louis. He even went up into Canada. He saw Niagara Falls and Looking Glass Prairie. He visited the mill town of Lowell, Massachusetts, the Parkinson Institute for the Blind in Boston, Five Points and the Tombs Prison in New York City. He talked with many of the country's important literary figures, Washington Irving, Henry Wadsworth Longfellow, William Cullen Bryant, and Edgar Allan Poe. He was introduced to politicians like Daniel Webster and John C. Calhoun. He met with President John Tyler at the White House. But he came back disappointed with America. "This is not the Republic I came to see," he confessed to his friend the actor

14. *The Diary of Philip Hone*, edited by Alan Nevins, vol 2 (New York: Dodd, Mead, 1927), p. 588. All subsequent quotations of Hone are also from this book, unless otherwise indicated.

William Macready in a letter of March 22. "This is not the Republic of my imagination" (p. 156). He sincerely loved the men and women of America, but there were certain things he just could not abide. "In the respects of not being left alone, and of being horribly disgusted by tobacco chewing and tobacco spittle, I have suffered considerably," he explained. "The sight of Slavery in Virginia; the hatred of British feeling upon that subject; and the miserable hints of the impotent indignation of the South, have pained me very much—on the last head, of course I have felt but mingled pity and amusement; on the others, sheer distress. But however much I like the ingredients of this great dish, I cannot but come back to the point from which I started, and say that the dish itself goes against the grain with me, and that I don't like it" (p. 158).

On his return to London, he wrote about it all, the good and the bad, in *American Notes for General Circulation* (1842). Unfortunately, many Americans could only see the bad. He did not paint a pretty picture: Americans were too familiar with strangers and obsessed with money. He hated that great American pastime, tobacco spitting, which took place even on the floor of Congress. He also dared to write unsentimentally about the great American shame, slavery. He saved the big ammunition for the American press, which had so hounded him while he was there.

The response to *American Notes* among America's foremost literary men varied considerably. "It is jovial and good-natured, and at times very severe," Longfellow wrote Charles Sumner on October 16, 1842. "He has a good chapter on Slavery."[15] Emerson thought that as an account of America, "it is too short, and too narrow, too superficial, and too ignorant, too slight, and too fabulous, and the man totally unequal to the work. . . . As a picture of American manners nothing can be falser."[16] William Cullen Bryant was likewise offended. "Mr. Dickens was but four months in the United States," he wrote in the New York *Evening Post* (November 9, 1842), "and, allowing him to make the best use of his opportunity, must have gone back without knowing much of the country or its people."

[15.] *The Letters of Henry Wadsworth Longfellow*, edited by Andrew Hilen, vol 2 (Cambridge, Mass: Harvard University Press, 1966), p. 473.

[16.] *The Heart of Emerson's Journals*, edited by Perry Bliss (Boston: Houghton Mifflin, 1928), p. 192.

Caricature of Charles Dickens by "Alfred Crowquill" (Alfred Henry Forrester).
Song sheet cover, "Yankee Notes for English Circulation,
or Boz in a-Merry-Key," 1842. *Courtesy Library of Congress.*

Perhaps no one else in America was more offended by *American Notes* than James Gordon Bennett of the *New York Herald*. "Of all the travellers that ever visited this land," he wrote on November 8, 1842, "Dickens appears to have been the most flimsy—the most childish—the most trashy—the most contemptible. He has neither common grammar, sense, arrangement, nor generalization." Bennett believed he surpassed even Trollope and Marryat, "and seems to be the essence of balderdash reduced to the last drop of silliness and inanity." None of this prevented the *New York Herald* from publishing excerpts on its front page on November 7, the day after sheets arrived from England. The paper proudly reported the next day in an editorial, "there was a rush among the newsboys and newspaper venders generally, that would have made Dickens stare. We probably sold 15,000 additional copies before *The New World* or *Brother Jonathan* appeared."

Ten thousand copies of the complete book that was issued as an extra number of *The New World* were quickly grabbed up after two o'clock; and at four, *Brother Jonathan* released the product of its piracy. "All the principal streets were full of newsboys, bawling out at the top of their lungs—'Dickens' work'—'Boz's Notes'—'Here goes Boz—only a shilling!'" said the *Herald*. "Probably more copies of Boz's *Notes* were sold yesterday in New York than will be sold in England in 10 years. Yet we are an ignorant, barbarous people in literary taste. So we are when we can relish such trash." Within days, Harper and Brothers of New York and Lea and Blanchard of Philadelphia issued the bound book. Of course, Dickens did not receive a farthing from all these American sales.

Catherine and Charles Dickens with Mary Hogarth, his sister-in-law. Drawing by Daniel Maclise, 1843.
Courtesy Library of Congress.

Southern reaction was especially swift and fierce. His attack on slavery threatened their very economic existence. "The work . . . is pervaded by a captious, sneering spirit," said the *Southern Quarterly Review* of Charleston, South Carolina, in January 1843; "taking the work as a whole, we have seldom read a more fault-finding, discourteous, bitter, shallow production. . . . It has excited by its meanness, scurrility and trivial character, the scorn of the whole country, including even those adoring parasites and sycophants who were most ready to bend the knee to their idol, while he was among us" (pp. 167–68).

In the meantime, Dickens began to serialize another novel, but *Martin Chuzzlewit* (1844) failed to catch on like the author's previous work. The public never warmed up to the story as they had with the other novels. Perhaps readers did not care for the theme. Dickens explained in his preface to the 1852 Cheap Edition that his purpose in writing *Martin Chuzzlewit* was "to exhibit in a variety of aspects the commonest of all the vices; to show how Selfishness propagates." This time he tried "to keep a steadier eye upon the general purpose and design" than in previous work.

Then Dickens made a rash move to recapture his public and fortune: *American Notes* had been so successful, four printings in two months, that Dickens sent Martin Chuzzlewit to America in Chapter 16 to cover some of the same ground he himself had the year before and to reiterate complaints expressed in his controversial travel book. "Here's this morning's New York Sewer!" the newsboys greet Martin from the docks. "Here's this morning's New York Stabber! Here's the New York Family Spy! Here's the New York Private Listener! Here's the New York Peeper! Here's the New York Plunderer! Here's the New York Keyhole Reporter! Here's the New York Rowdy Journal! Here's all the New York papers!" Dickens instructed his illustrator H. K. Browne in a letter of August 1843 to draw Martin Chizzlewit in the thriving city of Eden on the Mississippi, as "the picture of hopeless misery" and "everything else dull, miserable, squalid, unhealthy, and utterly devoid of hope: diseased, starved and abject" (p. 543).

With some pride Dickens reported to Forster on August 15, 1843, "Martin has made them all stark raving mad across the water" (p. 541). *Brother Jonathan* reported on July 29, 1843, that everyone in America "is also waiting in a sort of smouldering but inwardly raging fever of curiosity and impatience for the resumption of the history of Martin's adventures among us." The paper took offense to "the rather dull, vapid, and feeble tone which pervaded the attempted sketches in these last chapters" as well as the author's "narrow and bitter spirit of prejudice" that marred its pages (pp. 379–80). *Brother Jonathan* serialized *Martin Chuzzlewit* anyway from February 8 through August 26, 1843. Another journal, *The Rover,* shrewdly predicted in August 1844 that the book's "being well seasoned with abuse of this country will only make our people the more eager to read it" (p. 368).

Everyone felt compelled to comment on Dickens on the Americans. *The New World* complained on February 3, 1844, that "the whole novel, as far as it has yet proceded, is founded upon . . . the mistake of supposing that a tale can be perfectly successful without the impersonation of a single character worthy of, or capable of exciting, the reader's sympathy. In *Martin Chuzzlewit* we are introduced to a world of knaves and fools, destitute of any one quality that could command respect" (p. 145). None of this prevented the publisher from advertising *Martin Chuzzlewit* in the May 1844 *Repository of Romance* as "DICKENS FOR NOTHING."

"Dickens has shown that a man may have great talents, and great benevolence, without being a gentleman," scolded New York's *Magazine for the Million* (February 14, 1844). "To use one of his own vulgar but expressive phrases—he is a snob" (p. 33). Dickens was even denounced in the pulpit of the Methodist Chapel on Madison Street in New York City, to loud applause. Friends wondered about the wisdom of his recent actions. "I wish you had not made such an onslaught on the Americans," wrote Lord Francis Jeffrey, founder of *The Edinburgh Review*. "Even if it were all merited, it does mischief, and no good. Besides, you know that there are many exceptions; and if ten righteous might have saved a city once, there are surely innocent and amiable men and women, and besides boys and girls, enough in that vast region, to arrest the proscription of a nation."[17] It mattered little with the Americans that Dickens in *Martin Chuzzlewit* was just as rough with his own countrymen. After all, Pecksniff is an Englishman, not a Yankee.

Sending Martin Chuzzlewit to America proved to be a boost, but not a cure. Sales in England remained so disappointing that William Hall of Chapman and Hall clumsily suggested that £50 be deducted from Dickens' monthly £200 stipend and applied against the debt he owed the firm. Dickens was furious. "I am so irritated," he wrote Forster on June 28, 1843, "so rubbed in the tenderest parts of the eyelids with bay-salt, by what I told you yesterday, that the wrong kind of fire is burning in my head, and I don't think I *can* write [more of *Martin Chuzzlewit*]" (pp. 516–17). He, more than anyone else, knew that Chapman and Hall would have been nothing without him. Dickens believed now, "A printer is better than a bookseller" (p. 517). He was ready to look for other ways of issuing his work.

His financial troubles were now the talk of the town. "With the usual fickleness of fashion," reported *The Critic* in January 1844, "it is just now the rage to decry Dickens, by pronouncing his *Chuzzlewit* a failure, and his writings vulgar, and whispering 'Boz is going down,' and such-like drawing-room gossip" (p. 62). The rumors swiftly sped across the Atlantic. "In the literary circles of England, and indeed throughout all classes," reported a London correspondent to the *New York Herald* (January 24, 1844) on December 14, "Dickens's work upon America is universally condemned. It has done an injury to his fame which only some new and successful effort of his undoubted genius can redeem. *Martin Chuzzlewit* is certainly not such an effort." *The New World* gloated on February 3, 1844, on hearing that Dickens "is now bankrupt, not only in character, but in estate: it is easy to perceive that his motives for urging a law of international copyright must have been strong, and that the calumnies which he has published against America, were dictated by bitterness of spirit aris-

[17.] Quoted in Henry Cockburn, *Life of Lord Jeffrey*, vol. 2 (Edinburgh: Adam and Charles Black, 1852), pp. 381–82.

ing from disappointments of a pecuniary character" (p. 145). Dickens finally denied it, but that did nothing to silence the gossip.

Yes, he had to come up with "some new and successful effort of his undoubted genius." He was feeling the strain of the new novel, referring to the writing as his "*Chuzzlewit* agonies." He thought of moving his family to the Continent, where it was cheaper to live than in London; the change of scene might also supply plenty of material for a new series of travel sketches. But another story to recapture the public jaded by *Martin Chuzzlewit* seemed more immediately needed. If he was unsure of his public, he was sure of his abilities. He wrote Forster on November 2, 1843, "That I feel my power now, more than I ever did. That I have a greater confidence in myself than I ever had. That I *know*, if I have health, I could sustain my place in the minds of thinking men, though fifty writers started up to-morrow. But how many readers do *not* think!" (p. 590).

His mind was full of possibilities. Dickens was preoccupied with the child labor question; and the first report of the Commission for Inquiring into the Employment and Condition of Children in Mines and Manufactures, released in 1842, so enraged him that he went to Cornwall that autumn to see for himself how appalling conditions were. He thought of writing a cheap pamphlet himself to be called "An Appeal to the People of England, on behalf of the Poor Man's Child" (pp. 459). But, distracted with other obligations, Dickens never wrote it and went on to other projects.

Baroness Angela Georgina Burdett-Coutts, a wealthy friend and philanthropist (to whom Dickens dedicated *Martin Chuzzlewit*), sought his counsel in regard to a request to sponsor the Ragged Schools of Field Lane, Holborn. He responded by visiting these free institutions for the poor, located in a dismal part of London he thought worthy of Fagin from *Oliver Twist* (1838). "The school is held in three most wretched rooms on the first floor of a rotten house," he reported back to her by letter on September 16, 1843. "I have very seldom seen, in all the strange and dreadful things I have seen in London and elsewhere, anything so shocking as the dire neglect of soul and body exhibited in these children . . . To find anything within them—who know nothing of affection, care, love, or kindness of any sort—to which it is possible to appeal, is, at first, like a search for the philosopher's stone" (pp. 562–64).

Dickens was determined now to help educate the poor in his own small way. He approached Macvey Napier, editor of *The Edinburgh Review*, on September 16, 1843, with the idea of an article on "certain voluntary places of instruction, called 'The Ragged Schools' . . . and of the schools in Jails—and of the ignorance presented in such places . . . I could shew these people in such a state so miserable and so neglected, that their very nature rebels against the simplest religion—and that to convey to them the faintest outlines of any system of distinction between Right and Wrong, is in itself a Giant's task, before which Mysteries and Squabbles for Forms, *must* give way" (p. 565).

By year's end, Dickens had found another form in which to express his deep concern for the conditions of the poor. The Athenaeum, a charitable institution that served the Manchester poor, approached the novelist on speaking at its first annual fund-raising soirée of October 5. His sister Fanny urged him to come so he could also visit her and her family in the city, and he happily accepted the invitation. Sharing the platform with Benjamin Disraeli and other prominent Tories, Dickens spoke passionately on the need for educational reform within the lower classes. He had little patience for those who still clung to the old maxim, "A little learning is a dangerous thing": "Why, a little hanging was considered a very dangerous thing, according to the same authorities, with this difference, that because a little hanging was dangerous, we had a great deal of it; and because a little learning was dangerous, we were to have none

"The Ragged School." Etching by George Cruikshank, *Our Own Time*, 1846.
Private collection.

at all." To instruct such ill-informed people as to which was their "estimate of the comparative danger of 'a little learning' and a vast amount of ignorance," as well as "the most prolific parent of ignorance," he offered to take them "into certain jails and nightly refuges . . . where my own heart dies within me when I see thousands of immortal creatures condemned, without alternative or choice, to tread, not what our great poet calls 'the primrose path to the everlasting bonfire,' but one of jagged flints and stones, laid down by brutal ignorance, and held together like the solid rocks by years of this most wicked axiom." The Athenaeum provided a refuge where the working man, who though not yet able to keep "the wolf of hunger from his door," might still "but once have chased the dragon of ignorance from his hearth" (pp. 47–48).

The speaker was deeply touched by the enthusiastic applause, and something about "the bright eyes and beaming faces" before him that night inspired him to try to recapture the warmer feelings of the people at large. He recognized who his true audience was now. "In the literary point of view—in their bearings upon literature," he saw that through institutions like the Athenaeum, "the more intelligent and reflective society in the mass becomes, and the more readers there are, the more distinctly writers of all kinds will be able to throw themselves upon the truthful feeling of the people, and the more honoured and the more useful literature must be" (pp. 45–49).

Dickens had other business to take care of during his three-day visit to Manchester and hurried about the streets. One evening while on such a journey, his mind still burning with thoughts of Want and Ignorance and the necessity of throwing himself "upon the truthful feeling of the people," he conceived the plot of *A Christmas Carol in Prose*. When he returned to Devonshire Terrace, this "Ghost Story of Christmas" so possessed him that during the writing, as he confessed to his American friend C. C. Felton in a letter of January 2, 1844, he "wept, and laughed, and wept again, and excited himself in a most extraordinary manner, in the composition; and thinking whereof, he walked about the black streets of London, fifteen and twenty miles, many a night when all sober folks had gone to bed" (p. 2).

Dickens drew freely from earlier work in developing the story and the characters. The rudimentary plot came from the winter's tale at Dingley Dell, "The Story of the Goblins Who Stole a Sexton." The germ of that had come from Washington's "Rip Van Winkle": the visitation of spirits to a man who has imbibed too many spirits himself. The surly grave dig-

"The Goblin and the Sexton."
Etching by "Phiz" (Hablôt Knight Browne),
The Pickwick Papers, December 1836.
Courtesy Library of Congress.

ger Gabriel Grub served as the prototype for Ebenezer Scrooge. He can
think of nothing better to do on Christmas Eve than dig a grave and
indulge in a bottle of Hollands. Bent on reforming the old sinner, a band
of goblins appear to the sexton and spirit him away to their enchanted
cavern to view panoramas of Christmas life. Gabriel views both the rich
and the poor and the proper way that they and he should celebrate the
season. Through this supernatural medium, Grub, like Scrooge, converts
to a new and sober life.

What distinguishes *A Christmas Carol* from all previous holiday
work is its conscious recognition that this festive season, as Scrooge is
reminded in Stave 1, "is a time, of all others, when Want is keenly felt,

and Abundance rejoices." In writing this seasonal ghost story, Dickens upheld his noble purpose as a writer, one he had adhered to in previous works, as he declared at that Boston banquet in his honor on February 1, 1842, to be "an earnest and true desire to contribute, as far as in me lies, to the common stock of healthful cheerfulness and enjoyment. I have always had, and always shall have, an invincible repugnance to that mole-eyed philosophy which loves the darkness, and winks and scowls in the light" (p. 19). He had another goal in the new story. "I have a great faith in the poor," he explained in a letter of April 4, 1844. "To the best of my ability I always endeavor to present them in a favourable light to the rich; and I shall never cease, I hope, until I die to advocate their being made as happy and as wise as the circumstances of their condition, in its utmost improvement, will admit of their becoming" (p. 95).

As he told that august assembly in Boston on February 1, 1842, he believed that "these creatures have the same elements and capacities of goodness as yourselves, they are moulded in the same form, and made of the same clay; and though ten times worse than you, may, in having retained anything of their original natures amidst the trials and distresses of their condition, be really ten times better." Charles Dickens himself had come from such beginnings. "Virtue shows quite as well in rags and patches as she does in purple and fine linen," he said in Boston; "she and every beautiful object in external nature, claim some sympathy in the breast of the poorest man who breaks his scanty loaf of daily bread." He was certain that virtue "dwells rather oftener in alleys and by-ways than she does in courts and palaces, and that it is good, and pleasant, and profitable to track her out, and follow her" (pp. 19–20).

Now he had the proper means in which to make his "Appeal to the People of England, on behalf of the Poor Man's Child." He may have already had a suspicion of what he might do when he warned a friend in a letter of March 10, 1843, that by the end of the year "you will certainly feel that a Sledgehammer has come down with twenty times the force—twenty thousand times the force—I could exert by following out my first idea. Even so recently as . . . the other day, I had not contemplated the means I shall now, please God, use. But they have been suggested to me, and I have girded myself for this seizure—as you shall see in due time" (p. 461).

The form and themes having been resolved, Dickens drew on the life around him as well as his own experiences to give verisimilitude to his fantastic tale. In particular, he depended greatly on his childhood for telling details. The boy Scrooge, left alone in the schoolroom at holiday, finds solace in children's books, as young Charles Dickens did. The warmth and exuberance of the Cratchit Christmas dinner he knew first-hand when his family lived in Camden Town. The pathos of Tiny Tim's death was real to him as well, for he lost a brother and a sister when he was a child himself. "It is from the life, and I was there," he wrote to Forster on November 4, 1846, of an episode in *Dombey and Son* with an assurance also true to *A Christmas Carol*; "I remember it all as well, and certainly understood it as well, as I do now. We should be devilish sharp in what we do to children" (p. 653).

His concern for the children of the poor found further expression in the demon girl and boy, Want and Ignorance. In defending them, the Ghost of Christmas Present pleads for all lost children, "wretched, abject, frightful, hideous, miserable," who labored in England's factories and the Cornish mines and who attended the Ragged Schools. Here Dickens acted as a prophet, warning the public of the consequences of their indifference. Want and Ignorance were the legacy of a country that neglected its young.

With all elements falling into place, Dickens still had little time to complete the story for the holidays. He locked himself up in his house; and while struggling through the next two installments of "*Chuzzlewit* agonies," he feverishly worked on the manuscript. "I was very much affected by the little Book myself," he admitted to the writer Charles Mackay on December 19, 1843; "in various ways, as I wrote it; and had an interest in the idea, which made me reluctant to lay it aside for a moment" (p. 610). All other projects had to be abandoned, he wrote Napier on October 24, 1843, because "I plunged headlong into a little scheme . . . set an artist at work upon it; and put it wholly out of my own power to touch the *Edinburgh* subject until after Christmas is turned. For carrying out the notion I speak of, and being punctual with *Chuzzlewit*, will occupy every moment of my working time, up to the Christmas Holidays" (pp. 585–86). He worked all hours of the day and late into the night. He sent his regrets to Cruikshank on November 21, 1843, that they could not get together, "for I am finishing a little Book for Christmas, and contemplate a Bolt, to do so in peace" (p. 601). He broke appointments, such as that with his solicitor Thomas Mitton; he asked to be forgiven on November 25, 1843, because his friend's "note found me in the full passion of a roaring Christmas scene!" (p. 602). He could not take time out to receive his friends when they stopped by. "At the time when

Charles Dickens. Wood engraving by
W. J. Linton after an 1843 miniature by
Margaret Gilles, *The People's Journal*,
January 3, 1846.
Courtesy The Charles Dickens Museum, London.

you called, and for many weeks afterwards," he apologized to Edward Bulwer-Lytton on January 25, 1844, "I was so closely occupied with my little *Carol* (the idea of which had just occurred to me), that I never left home before the owls went out; and led quite a solitary life" (p. 30).

He was an inspired but also a disciplined writer. "No city clerk was ever more methodical or orderly than he," insisted his eldest son Charley in a supplement to *Windsor Magazine* (Christmas 1934); "no humdrum, monotonous, conventional task could ever have been discharged with more punctuality or with more businesslike regularity, than he gave to the work of his imagination and fancy. At something before ten he would sit down—every day with very, rare exceptions—to his desk . . . and would there remain until lunch time— sometimes, if he were much engrossed with any particular point or had something in hand which he was very anxious to finish there and then, until later" (p. 24). His sister Mamie said in *My Father As I Recall Him*, "His 'studies' were always cheery, pleasant rooms, and always, like himself, the personification of neatness and tidiness." The one at Devonshire Terrace was "a pretty room, with steps leading directly into the garden from it, and with an extra baize door to keep out all sounds and noise" (p. 49). So diligently did he labor on the new story that within six weeks (by the second one in November), Dickens delivered the finished manuscript to the printers. "To keep the *Chuzzlewit* going, and to do this little book, the *Carol*, in the odd times between two parts of it," he confessed to Felton on January 2, 1844, "was, as you may suppose, pretty tight work. But when it was done I broke out like a Madman" (p. 3).

The Christmas fervor continued to burn within him, as he celebrated the holidays with an exuberance that his friends had never witnessed before. "Such dinings, such dancings, such conjurings, such blindman's-buffings, such theatre-goings, such kissings-out of old years and kissingsin of new ones, never took place in these parts before," he proudly reported to Felton. "And if you could have seen me at a children's party at [actor William] Macready's the other night, going down a Country dance something longer than the Library at Cambridge with Mrs. M. you would have thought I was a country Gentleman of independent property, residing on a tip-top farm, with the wind blowing straight in my face every day" (pp. 2–3). These giddy activities seemed perfectly justified, because from all early indications, *A Christmas Carol* would be a glorious success, both artistically and financially.

His publishers, however, had not immediately seen much value in the book. There was talk of issuing instead either a cheap edition of his works up to that time or a new magazine edited by Dickens. The writer rejected both suggestions: as he explained to Forster in a letter of November 1, 1843, the cheap edition was premature and might damage himself and the titles then in print; he feared that the magazine might suggest to the public that he was "writing tooth and nail for bread, headlong, after the close of a book taking so much out of one as *Chuzzlewit*" (p. 587). He was not yet ready to forgive and forget them; but through Forster's negotiations, Chapman and Hall gingerly agreed to bring out *A Christmas Carol* on commission terms. Under this proposal, which Dickens himself made, the author was charged the full cost of production and thus was entitled to the entire profits from the sales; the publishers

No. 1 Devonshire Terrace, London. Wood engraving
after a drawing by Daniel Maclise.
Courtesy Library of Congress.

Title page and first page of text of the manuscript of *A Christmas Carol*, 1843.
Courtesy Pierpont Morgan Library.

Stave I.

Marley's Ghost.

Marley was dead: to begin with. There is no doubt whatever, about that. The register of his burial was signed by the clergyman, the clerk, the undertaker, and the chief mourner. Scrooge signed it; and Scrooge's name was good upon 'change, for anything he put his hand to. Old Marley was as dead as a door-nail.

Mind! I don't mean to say that I know, of my own knowledge, what there is particularly dead about a door-nail. I might have been inclined, myself, to regard a coffin-nail as the deadest piece of ironmongery in the trade. But the wisdom of our ancestors is in the simile; and my unhallowed hands shall not disturb it, or the country's done for. You will therefore permit me to repeat, emphatically, that Marley was as dead as a door-nail.

Scrooge knew he was dead? Of course he did. How could it be otherwise? Scrooge and he were partners for I don't know how many years. Scrooge was his sole executor, his sole administrator, his sole assign, his sole residuary legatee, his sole friend and sole mourner. And even Scrooge was not so dreadfully cut up by the sad event, but that he was an excellent man of business on the very day of the funeral, and solemnized it with an undoubted bargain.

The mention of Marley's funeral brings me back to the point I started from. There is no doubt that Marley was dead. This must be distinctly understood, or nothing wonderful can come of the story I am going to relate. If we were not perfectly convinced that Hamlet's Father died before the play began, there would be nothing more remarkable in his taking a stroll at night, in an easterly wind, upon his own ramparts, than there would be in any other middle-aged gentleman rashly turning out after dark in a breezy spot, say Saint Paul's Churchyard for instance, literally to astonish his son's weak mind.

Scrooge never painted out old Marley's name. There

retained only a fixed commission on the total number of copies sold. Dickens rationalized that under these terms he would finally receive the largest possible earnings he deserved. He treated Chapman and Hall no better than printers, but he was a novice in the ways of the English publishing trade.

It was a risky proposition. This "Ghost Story of Christmas" was unlike the other holiday books then the fashion, the Christmas Annuals, those "literary butterflies of winter, in all their taking garments of crimson, sand scarlet, and gold."[18] But the people were wearying of these lachrymose keepsakes, dedicated to love and friendship and illustrated with heavy engravings of languid maidens in Oriental costume but rarely containing any direct reference to the season during which they were put on the market.

Dickens devised an elaborate new scheme for his little book's production. As he was paying all costs, he could do whatever he wanted. But he also insisted that the price of the book be low, only five shillings, to encourage as many buyers as possible. Dickens personally oversaw every aspect of the volume's manufacture. He approved the russet cloth binding (blind stamped with the title in gold on front and spine), the color endpapers, the gilt edges, and the title page printed in green and red. He discussed with Forster the cover design and advertising; as late as December 6, 1843, he had the title page "materially altered" to blue and red, admitting to Mitton that these leaves "always look bad at first" (p. 605). The title page was originally postdated "1844"; but Dickens wanted it to reflect the year in which it was published, and changed it back. The endpapers became yellow when it was discovered that the green ink easily rubbed off. The result was a beautifully designed volume that far exceeded anything else then being sold for a mere five shillings.

To illustrate the book, Dickens chose the popular *Punch* cartoonist John Leech (1817–1864). Author and artist became acquainted as far back as 1836, when at Seymour's suicide, Leech (along with many other designers) applied to Dickens to continue the illustrating of *The Pickwick Papers*. The young man, through Cruikshank's introduction, submitted a drawing, "Tom Smart and the Chair," taken from Chapter 14 of the novel. The writer cordially replied in August 1836, "I have to acknowledge the receipt of your design for the last *Pickwick*, which I think extremely well-received, and executed." But he was reluctant to

18. See *Punch's Snap-dragons for Christmas* (London: Punch Office, 1845), p. 43.

commit himself, for the publishers had already engaged another artist, Hablôt Knight ("Phiz") Browne, "a gentleman of very great ability, with whose designs I am exceedingly well satisfied, and from whom I feel it neither my wish, nor interest, to part" (p. 168). Leech pressed for another commission from Chapman and Hall, but Dickens evidently wanted to be rid of him. No commission was forthcoming.

Within three years, Leech had established himself as one of the leading cartoonists in that grand age of comic artists in the pages of *Punch*, published by Dickens' printers Bradbury and Evans. Leech was not only one of the first contributors to the famous satiric magazine, but he soon dominated it with his sly satires on modern manners. His work was easily identified by his totem, a visual pun on his name—a physician's leeching bottle. This was an era when doctors still used leeches for bloodletting in treating various illnesses and relieving fevers by supposedly ridding the patient of poisons in the body. When the monthly parts of *Martin Chuzzlewit* were announced for publication the autumn of 1842, Leech once more approached Dickens as a collaborator. "I have never forgotten the having seen you some years ago," Dickens more energetically wrote the artist on November 5, 1842, "or ceased to watch your progress with much interest and satisfaction. I congratulate you heartily on your success; and myself on having had my eye upon the means by which you have obtained it." Dickens could now seriously consider Leech if not for *Martin Chuzzlewit* (on which H. K. Browne was already engaged as illustrator), then for some other project.

By the third week in October Dickens had something for him. As Phiz

John Leech.
*Courtesy Rare Book Department,
Free Library of Philadelphia.*

"Tom Smart and the Chair." Sketch by
John Leech for *The Pickwick Papers*, 1836.
Courtesy Library of Congress.

was preoccupied with *Martin Chuzzlewit*, Dickens offered Leech *A Christmas Carol*. Dickens must have decided that the book should contain four wood engravings and four hand-colored etchings and which incidents should be depicted.[19] As with every other aspect of the book's design, Dickens went over each preliminary sketch with Leech. This was before the photographic age, so Leech had to draw each picture directly on the wood block to be engraved by William James Linton.[20]

Leech etched the four full-page plates himself, two to a steel plate as was the fashion at the time. He also made color sketches to guide the hand-colorers. Leech was a nervous, easily offended artist, and Dickens must have taken pains to please and appease him. Apparently, he asked Leech to change the color of the robe worn by the Ghost of Christmas Present: it is red in the original watercolor (now in the Pierpont Morgan Library), but green in the book, in accordance with the text. Leech was disappointed with the final hand-coloring. "This was a primitive process," explained Edgar Browne, Phiz's son. "Leech of course set the pattern, the copyist would

[19] The scheme of *A Christmas Carol* resembles that of another book illustrated by Leech, *The Wassail Bowl* (1842), a small volume bound in russet cloth with a Christmas device stamped in gold on the cover and illustrated with inserted steel etchings and textual wood engravings. Dickens owned a copy of this book by his friend Albert Smith, and it may have influenced his decision to hire Leech for *A Christmas Carol*.

[20] Although they were advertised as "woodcuts," these pictures are technically wood engravings. W. J. Linton (1812–1897) was one of the most skilled of Victorian wood engravers. He was often responsible for the pictures for *The Illustrated London News*, but he also

spread out a number of prints all round a large table, having a number of saucers ready prepared with the appropriate tints, . . . and then would start off and tint all the skies, then all the coats, and so on, till every object was separately coloured, and the work was done. The effect was certainly gay, but generally too crude to be pleasant."[21] Leech must have complained to Dickens about the quality of the hand-colored proofs. "I do not doubt, in my own mind," Dickens tried to console him in a letter of December 14, "that you unconsciously exaggerate the evil done by the colourers. You can't think how much better they will look in a neat book, than you suppose. But I have sent a Strong Dispatch to C[hapman] and H[all], and will report to you when I hear from them. I quite agree with you, that it is a point of

"The Christmas Bowl." Preliminary pen-and-ink drawing by John Leech for *A Christmas Carol*, 1843. *Courtesy Beinecke Rare Book and Manuscript Library, Yale University.*

great importance" (p. 608). Leech really had no reason for despair: the hand-colored plates remain as fresh and charming as the day they were produced.

Dickens was pleased with Leech's contribution to *A Christmas Carol*, the only one of the five Christmas Books that Leech illustrated solely on his own. Perhaps he was too busy with other commitments, particularly with *Punch*, to take on the other books by himself. He was the only artist to appear in all of them. Daniel Maclise, Edwin Landseer, Richard Doyle, and John Tenniel and others contributed one or more drawings to the series; but Leech defined the spirit of the Christmas

---

worked on the Moxon Tennyson of 1857 with designs by Dante Gabriel Rossetti, John Everett Millais, William Holman Hunt, and others. Linton emigrated to the United States in 1866 and established the Appledore Press in Hamden, Connecticut; he received an honorary degree from Yale University in 1891. Linton did not care much for Charles Dickens. "Warm-hearted and sentimental, but not unselfish," he wrote in his memoirs, *Threescore and Ten Years, 1820–1890* (New York: Charles Scribner's Sons, 1894), Dickens "was not the gentleman. There was no grace of manner, no soul of nobility in him" (p. 161).

[21.] Edgar Browne, *Phiz and Dickens* (London: John Nisbet, 1913), p. 21.

"The Spirit of Christmas Present." Political cartoon
by John Tenniel, *Punch*, December 30, 1893.
Courtesy Library of Congress.

Books with his lively pictures in the very first volume. Leech never illustrated anything else by Dickens. The last drawing he ever did for a Dickens work was the frontispiece to the Cheap Edition of *Christmas Books* (1852), the first collected edition of the holiday series. He reworked the frontispiece of the 1843 edition, "Mr. Fezziwig's Ball," as a bold wood engraving.

Leech was a pivotal figure in English caricature. John Ruskin recognized his importance in an 1883 lecture "The Fireside: John Leech and John Tenniel" where he praised "the kind and vivid and genius of John Leech, capable in its brightness of finding pretty jest in everything, but capable in its tenderness also of rejoicing in the beauty of everything, softened and illumined by its loving wit the entire scope of English social scene."[22] Dickens shared his admiration for the artist and social critic. "In all his drawings, whatever Mr. Leech desires to do, he does," Dickens wrote in a review of Leech's book *The Rising Generation* in *The Examiner* (December 30, 1848). "The expression indicated, though indicated by the simplest means, is exactly the natural expression, and is recognized as such immediately. . . . Into the tone as well as into the execution of what he does, he has brought a certain elegance which is altogether new, without involving any compromise of what is true." His gentle but pointed wit fell somewhere between

22. John Ruskin, *The Art of England* (Orpington, Eng.: George Allen, 1884), p. 122.

the grotesque energy of George Cruikshank's satiric etchings and the more stolid, naturalistic wood engravings of John Tenniel, his successor at *Punch*.[23] As his career progressed, Leech went beyond comedies of manners to sporting subjects in the spirit of Thomas Rowlandson and James Gillray and carried on by Randolph Caldecott after Leech's death.

Leech was as prolific as he was eclectic. Dickens called him the "great popular artist of the time, whose humour was so delicate, so nice, and so discriminating, and whose pencil like his observation was so graceful and so informed with the sense of beauty that it was mere disparagement to call his works 'caricatures.'"[24] His most enduring work remains his pictures for *A Christmas Carol*. The charming suite of eight pictures beautifully captures the settings and sentiments of Dickens' famous story. Whether it be in a representation of the Fezziwig ball or in the depiction of Marley's Ghost and the other spirits, every other illustra-

"And Tiny Tim upon his shoulder."
Wood engraving after Gustave Doré,
Journal pour tous, June 29, 1861.
Courtesy Library of Congress.

tor of the story must pay respects to Leech's original concepts. Oddly, Leech never depicted Bob Cratchit with Tiny Tim on his shoulder. Almost every subsequent illustrator of *A Christmas Carol* has been sure to draw father and son.[25] Phiz provided a charming little engraving of

23. Tenniel, famous as the original illustrator of Lewis Carroll's *Alice's Adventures in Wonderland* (1865), paid homage to his predecessor at *Punch* in a parody of Leech's famous picture "Scrooge's Third Visitor," with William Gladstone as the miser, published on December 30, 1893.

24. Speech given at the second anniversary dinner of the Newsvendor's Benevolent Institution, held at Albion Tavern, on January 27, 1852 (p. 136).

25. The Frenchman Gustave Doré was apparently the very first artist to depict the pair, in *Journal pour tous* (June 29, 1861); not surprisingly, the two Cratchits here look more Gal-

Scrooge and Marley's Ghost on the title page of *Christmas Books* in the 1859 Library Edition of Dickens' works, but the illustrator who will always be associated with *A Christmas Carol* is John Leech.

With the illustrations engraved, etched, and colored, and the manuscript at the printers, it was only a few weeks before the finished volume was in the booksellers' hands, just in time for Christmas. The earliest reaction to the story was enthusiastic. "I have shewn the book to two or three Judges of very different views and constitutions," Dickens assured Mitton in a letter of December 4. "I have never seen men, personally and mentally opposed to each other, so unanimous in their predictions, or so hot in their approval" (p. 605). He must have sent Mitton proofs for his opinion. "I am extremely glad you *feel* the *Carol*," Dickens wrote him on December 6, "for I knew I meant a good thing. And when I see the effect of a little *whole* as that, on those for whom I care, I have a strong sense of the immense effect I could produce with an entire book. Bradbury predicts Heaven knows what. I am sure it will do me a great deal of good; and I hope it will sell, well" (p. 605).

The author sent out the first of his presentation copies on December 17. The official publication date was December 19, and he was all out of books by December 22. Among the fortunate few to receive copies was the poet Samuel Rogers. "If you should ever have inclination and patience to read the accompanying little book," Dickens wrote him that day, "I hope you will like the slight fancy it embodies" (p. 608). He did not: Rogers told his nephew that "the first half hour was so dull it sent him to sleep, and the next hour was so painful that he should be obliged to finish it to get rid of the impression. He blamed Dickens's style very much."[26]

The bilious Rogers was the exception among those honored with

lic than Cockney. The first "newly illustrated" edition of *A Christmas Carol*, issued with Dickens' approval, was published by Ticknor and Fields of Boston in 1868, with amusing wood engravings by Sol Eytinge Jr. (1833–1905). See Appendix. He and the writer became friends through their publisher. Dickens thought that Eytinge's illustrations "are remarkable alike for a delicate perception of beauty, a lively eye for character, a most agreeable absence of exaggeration, and a general modesty and propriety which I greatly like" (quoted in Frederic G. Kitton, *Dickens and His Illustrators* [London: George Routledge, 1899], p. 232). Edwin A. Abbey, Fred Barnard, Reginald Birch, Francis D. Bedford, Quentin Blake, Charles E. Brock, Henry M. Brock, Warren Chappell, F. O. C. Darley, Charles Dana Gibson, Trina Schart Hyman, Roberto Innocenti, Fritz Kredel, John R. Neill, Arthur Rackham, Philip Reed, Norman Rockwell, Ronald Searle, Everett Shinn, Jessie Willcox Smith, and Lisbeth Zwerger are among the many artists of varying skill who have depicted the famous characters of *A Christmas Carol*.

[26.] Henry Sharpe quoted in P. W. Clayden, *Rogers and His Contemporaries*, vol. 2 (London: Smith Elder, 1889), pp. 239–40.

author's copies just in time for the holidays. "Blessings on your kind heart, my dear Dickens!" wrote Lord Francis Jeffrey, "and may it always be as light and full as it is kind, and a fountain of kindness to all within reach of its beatings! We are all charmed with your *Carol,* chiefly, I think, for the genuine *goodness* which breathes all through it, and is the true inspiring angel by which its genius has awakened. . . . Well, you should be happy yourself, for you may be sure you have done more good, and not only fastened more kindly feelings, but prompted more positive acts of benevolence, by this little publication, than can be traced to all the pulpits and confessionals in Christendom, since Christmas 1842."[27]

Even dour Thomas Carlyle was touched by the book's spirit. "A Scotch philosopher, who nationally does not keep Christmas," William Makepeace Thackeray reported in *Fraser's Magazine* (February 1844), "on reading the book, sent out for a turkey, and asked two friends to dine—this is a fact!"(p. 169). This was confirmed by the philosopher's wife, Jane Carlyle, who wrote her sister on December 23 that "the visions of *Scrooge*—had so worked on Carlyle's nervous organization that he has been seized with a perfect *convulsion* of hospitality, and has actually insisted on *improvising two* dinner parties with only a day between."[28] She herself thought it was "really a kind-hearted, almost poetical little thing, well worth any Lady or gentleman's perusal—somewhat too much imbued with the Cockney-admiration of *The Eatable,* but as Dickens writes 'for the greatest happiness of the greatest number' (of Cockneys) he could not be expected to gainsay their taste in that particular" (p. 167). Carlyle happily passed the copy Dickens sent him on to his father-in-law, noting on the flyleaf, "Read with satisfaction; presented with satisfaction, and many Christmas wishes."[29]

[27.] Quoted in Cockburn, *Life of Lord Jeffrey,* vol. 3, pp. 380–81. Dickens was so fond of him that he named his fifth child Francis Jeffrey Dickens (1844–1886) and dedicated the third Christmas Book, *The Cricket on the Hearth* (1845), to Lord Jeffrey.

[28.] *Jane Welsh Carlyle: Letters to Her Family, 1839–1863,* edited by Leonard Huxley (London: John Murray, 1924), p. 169.

[29.] "Carlyle's *Carol,*" *The Dickensian,* summer 1938, p. 154. Dickens was eager that his friend like the new book. After all, as Kathleen Tillotson suggested in "The Middle Years from the *Carol* to *Copperfield,*" in *Dickens Memorial Lectures 1970* (London: Dickens Fellowship, 1970), he may have recalled both the title and the structure of Carlyle's *Past and Present* (1843) while composing *A Christmas Carol.* The Scottish philosopher was not famous for his Christmas cheer. Years later Carlyle was harsh in his appraisal of Dickens' philosophy. "His theory of life was entirely wrong," he told Sir S. G. Duffy in *Conservations with Carlyle.* "He thought men ought to be buttered up, and the world made soft and accommodating for them, and all sorts of fellows have turkey for their Christmas dinner" (p. 75).

New Christmas Book by Mr. Dickens.

Shortly will be Published, in small 8vo, Price Five Shillings,

With Four Coloured Etchings and Woodcuts by Leech,

A CHRISTMAS CAROL.

IN PROSE.

BEING

A GHOST STORY OF CHRISTMAS,

By CHARLES DICKENS.

LONDON: CHAPMAN AND HALL, 186, STRAND.

Advertisement for *A Christmas Carol*,
The Athenaeum, December 9, 1843.
Courtesy Library of Congress.

Dickens was praying for *A Christmas Carol* to succeed. His finances were so bad, as he admitted to Mitton on December 4, 1843, "I must anticipate the Christmas Book, by the sum I mention, which will enable me to keep comfortable." Understandably, he was anxious about how the book was being handled by the publishers and received by the public. "Can you believe that with the exception of *Blackwood's, the Carol is not advertized in One of the Magazines!*" he complained to his lawyer. "Bradbury would not believe it when I told him on Saturday last. And he says that nothing but a tremendous push can possibly atone for such fatal negligence" (pp. 604–5). Announcements did appear in *The Examiner* and other weeklies (but no other monthlies), beginning on November 18, that a "New Christmas Book by Mr. Dickens" was coming in December. A full page was devoted to *A Christmas Carol* in the thirteenth number of *Martin Chuzzlewit* in December. But Dickens had little faith that Chapman and Hall knew what they were doing to promote the book. "Consequently," he told Mitton, "I have written to the Strand [Chapman and Hall], and said—Do this—Do that—Do the other—keep away from me—and be damned" (p. 605).

From the first day of publication, sales were tremendous. He happily wrote his lawyer that Chapman and Hall reported on December 24, "that the Carol was then in its Sixth Thousand; and that as the orders were coming in fast from town and country, it would soon be necessary to reprint" (pp. 615–16). There were nine thousand in print at the first of the year; and, as he wrote Forster on January 3, 1844, "two thousand of the three printed for second and third editions are already taken by the trade" (p. 9). The English loved the little book. "Its success is most prodigious," its author bragged to Felton on January 2. "And by every post, all manner of strangers write all manner of letters to him about their homes and hearths, and how this same *Carol* is read aloud there, and kept on a very little shelf by itself. Indeed it is the greatest success as I am told, that this Ruffian and Rascal has ever achieved" (p. 2).

"Faithfully yours, Charles Dickens." Wood engraving after a drawing by Charles Martin, *Pictorial Times*, April 20, 1844. *Private collection.*

Some proper English ladies had trouble with the ghostly nature of the story. "The *Christmas Carol* strikes me much as it does you," poet Elizabeth Barrett Browning admitted to Dickens' friend Lady Blessington on December 27. "I don't like the machinery—which is entangled with allegory and ghostery—but I like and admire the mode of the working out—and the exquisite scenes about the clerk and little Tiny [Tim]; I thank the writer in my heart of hearts for them." Poet and novelist Mary Russell Mitford agreed, "I like Dickens's *Christmas Carol*, too, very much—not the ghostly part, of course, which is very bad; but the scenes of the clerk's family are very fine and touching."[30]

[30.] *The Brownings' Correspondence*, edited by Philip Kelley and Ronald Hudson, vol. 8 (Winfield, Kans.: Wedgestone Press, 1990), p. 113; and Mitford quoted in *The Life of Mary Russell Mitford*, edited by Rev. A. G. K. L'Estrange, vol. 2 (London: Richard Bentley, 1869), p. 286.

It could not but affect all classes of English society. "Its cheery voice of faith and hope, ringing from one end of the island to the other, carried pleasant warning alike to all," recalled Forster in his biography of Dickens, "that if the duties of Christmas were wanting no good could come of its outward observances; that it must shine upon the cold hearth and warm it, and into the sorrowful heart and comfort it; that it must be kindness, benevolence, charity, mercy, and forbearance, or its plum pudding would turn to bile, and its roast beef be indigestible."[31] Predictably, the aristocracy did not so easily warm up to this cozy little economic parable. Novelist Sir Edward Bulwer-Lytton dismissed it as overrated and said it owed its popularity solely to the "agreeable feelings" that it generated. "There never was such an age in the World in which the Poor have been the subject of such tender anxious interest, both from the Public and individuals," he sighed; "and the fierce tone of menace to the rich is unreasonable and ignorant."[32] Dickens' friend Douglas Jerrold touched on contemporary English prejudice against Dickens and his work among the upper classes when he described a fictitious mistress who has just discharged a governess for reading a novel instead of attending to her children. "What book, think you, was it?" asks the lady in "Punch's Complete Letter-Writer" in *Punch* in 1844. "*A Christmas Carol*. I have never read the thing; but knowing it to be aimed at the best interests of good society, all the feelings of a mother rushed upon me, and I believe I *did* read her a pretty lesson" (p. 149).

The reviews were generally favorable. After all, Dickens was fortunate in having so many friends and acquaintances write laudatory ones just in time for Christmas. Charles Mackay, subeditor of the London *Morning Chronicle*, declared on December 19, "It is impossible to read this little volume through, however hastily, without perceiving that its composition was prompted by a spirit of wide and wholesome philanthropy—a spirit to which selfishness in enjoyment is an inconceivable idea—a spirit that knows where happiness can exist, and ought to exist, and will not be happy itself till it has done something towards promoting its growth there." Mackay therefore recommended "this little volume as an amusing companion, and a wholesome monitor, to all who would enjoy in truth and in spirit 'A merry Christmas and a happy New Year.'"

[31]. John Forster, *The Life of Charles Dickens*, vol. 2 (London: Chapman and Hall, 1873), p. 67. All subsequent references to Forster's biography are also from this edition.

[32]. Quoted in Sibylla Jane Flower, "Charles Dickens and Edward Bulwer-Lytton," *The Dickensian*, May 1973, p. 84.

The Athenaeum's music critic Henry Fottergill Chorley said on December 23 that it was "a tale to make the reader laugh and cry—open his hands, and open his heart to charity even towards the uncharitable,—wrought up with a thousand minute and tender touches of the true 'Boz' workmanship." He concluded that "such a noble meal" was "most capitally *carolled* in prose by Mr. Dickens; and will call out, we hope, a chorus of 'Amens,' in the shape of kindly sympathies and bounteous deeds, from the Land's End to John o' Groat's House" (pp. 1127–28). The poet Leigh Hunt predicted in the London *Examiner* (December 23) that "the little book will soon be in every one's hand. . . . Such is this *Song of Joy* to Christmas; such the vivid and hearty style, which thousands on thousands of readers as we trust, will raise a glorious Christmas Chorus."[33]

Another friend, Laman Blanchard, suggested in *Ainsworth's Magazine* (January 1844) that this new story about Christmas was "illustrative of its true spirit, descriptive of its glowing features, and helping to bring closer together hundreds and hundreds of readers—all shaking with laughter, and some sprinkling a few tears over their ripe pleasure—in the enjoyment of a common sentiment." He thought that "it was a carol not for age or for youth alone, but for both—not for Christmas only, but for every season, whether the sun shines, or the snow drifts." He shrewdly predicted that *A Christmas Carol* would be "as surely heard and remembered a hundred Christmases to come. And may the wise and merry author of it live to see that we are not false prophets" (pp. 84, 88).

"It was a blessed inspiration that put such a book into the head of Charles Dickens," said Thomas Hood in *Hood's Magazine* (January 1844); "a happy inspiration of the heart, that warms every page. It is impossible to read, without a glowing bosom and burning cheeks, between love and shame of our kind, with perhaps a little touch of misgiving" (p. 68). That was high praise, indeed, from the man who had just published in *Punch* the powerful "The Song of the Shirt," about the harsh life of a poor seamstress.[34] Another colleague, William Layton Sammons, in his Cape Town

---

[33] The *Reading Mercury, Oxford Gazette, Newbury Herald, and Berks County Paper* in "Mr. Charles Dickens's Reading of the *Christmas Carol*" (December 23, 1854) attributed this unsigned review to Hunt. See also Alec W. Brice, "Reviewers of Dickens in the *Examiner*: Fonblanque, Forster, Hunt, and Morley," *Dickens Studies Newsletter*, September 1972, pp. 74–76.

[34] And Dickens greatly appreciated their generous words. "I cannot thank you enough for the beautiful manner, and the true spirit of friendship, in which you noticed my *Carol*," he gushed in a letter to Blanchard on January 4, 1844. "But I must thank you, because you have filled my heart up to the brim, and it is running over. You meant to give me pleasure,

paper *Sam Sly's African Journal* (August 15, 1844), suggested that *A Christmas Carol* "will turn out to be the *young man's* and the *boy's*, if not the *'best companion,'*—a very useful and delightful one, and next to their bibles, prove a valuable text book for old age."

Some readers were surely baffled: this was not what one expected from a Christmas book at the time. "Instead of preaching a homily," said *The Spectator* on December 23, "he tells a 'ghost story,'—not a blood-freezing tale of horror, but a serio-comic narrative, in which the ludicrous and the terrible, the real and the visionary, are curiously jumbled together, as in the phantasmagoria of a magic lantern" (p. 1216). "It is not comedy, nor tragedy," said the London *Morning Post* on December 26, "nor simple narrative, nor pure allegory, nor sermon, nor political treatise, nor historical sketch; but it is a strange jumbling together of all these, so that one knows not what to make of it. It has all Mr. Dickens's mannerisms, and is so far (to us) displeasing and absurd; but it has touches of genius too, mixed up with its huge extravagance, and a few of those little happy strokes of simple pathos, to which . . . the author has been indebted for his great popularity." *The Atlas* warned on December 23 that anyone "who perhaps, took it up in the expectation of finding some careless trifle thrown off for the occasion without premeditation, like the contribution to an annual, will find himself agreeably mistaken. A glance at the first page or two will convince him that only Boz in his happier vein could have penned it." "Read it then, gentle reader, with attention," suggested *The Sun* on December 22; "and do not suppose, because it is a ghost-story, that it is a mere frivolous exercise of the fancy."

The London *Observer* (December 31) did not believe it was "a ghost story in the usual acceptance of the term. There is nothing of the superstitious in it." This paper thought this "very tiny and tastefully got up volume" was really "intended for the juvenile portion of the community." The December *Dublin Review* suggested that perhaps Dickens' ghosts "are too earthly to be real visitors from another world. They seem to think too much of the creature comforts of Christmas, and to have for-

---

my dear fellow, and you have done it. The tone of your elegant and fervent praise has touched me in the tenderest place. I cannot write about it; and as to talking of it, I could do no more than a dumb man. I have derived inexpressible gratification from what I know and feel was a labour of love on your part. And I can never forget it" (p. 13). He likewise sent Hood in January 1844 "a thousand thanks for your kind and charming notice of the *Carol*" (p. 1).

gotten altogether the higher and holier influences of the season—to place the enjoyment of the Christmas time in the mirth and jollity which accompany it;—in the beef, and poultry, and pudding—the games and puzzles and forfeits of the evening fireside,—without once advertising to the Christian character of the festival, or the joy of spirit and peace of conscience which constitute its true and genuine happiness." But the journal also confessed, "It is long since we read prose or poetry which pleased us more" (p. 529).

Bell's Weekly Messenger said on December 30, "Nothing can be more absurd than the fable itself and the whole of its groundwork: it is the veriest brick and mortar, puerility and absurdity, of the idlest fairy tale; but his fancy no sooner comes to some perch upon some beam or rafter of this vile scaffolding, than his imagination waves his magic wand, and all the gorgeous splendour of poetry is called up and produced before the eye of his reader." Dickens was like a Cockney Dante, who "has here converted an incredible fiction into one of the strongest exhibitions of religious and moral truth, and into one of the most picturesque poetical allegories which we possess in our language" (p. 426). "If ever a writer deserved public honours for the service he has rendered to his kind," said *The Magazine of Domestic Economy and Family Review* in January, "that man is Charles Dickens, and the *Christmas Carol* should be read and reverenced in all time to come as a glorious manual of Christian duties" (p. 326).

Some considered *A Christmas Carol* a vast improvement over the writer's other recent efforts. "Mr. Dickens has here made a decided hit," announced *Tait's Edinburgh Magazine* in February 1844; "and as the fickle and, perhaps, unreasonable public appear to think that, for sometime back, he has been making nothing but blots, we rejoice the more the better fortunes of the story of the regeneration of Mr. Scrogges [*sic*], as well as in the acquirement of a happy, enlivening, and kindly-spirited book, which will be equally apt for many a Merry Christmas, as for that which has just passed" (p. 135). The Unitarian *Inquirer* agreed on December 23, "Mr. Dickens has made the world a Christmas present, which will increase its merriment at this festive season of the year, and, which is far better, teach it an important lesson, . . . every one will read the book; and, if they will take our advice, as quickly as they can" (p. 808).

"This volume, small as it is, will probably add very much to Mr. Dickens's reputation," predicted the London *Sunday Times* (January 7, 1844). "It is, in fact, an exquisite gem in its way. The whole economy of the work is perfectly delightful, and its moral purpose deserving of the highest praise. Nowhere do we remember to have seen a more cheerful or a more instructive picture of Christmas, or a truer interpretation of the useful purposes to which its festivities may be applied. Generally the tone of the story is sweet and subdued, but occasionally it soars, and becomes altogether sublime." *Pictorial Times*, in its roundup of holiday publications on December 23, had only praise for this "small and cheerfully illustrated book" about "an old hunks, a skinflint, a selfish, money-grubbing, lucre lover—a creature of living flesh and blood, yet destitute of living feelings and sympathies. . . . May this book work as happy a change upon some, at least, of the thousands who sacrifice virtue, honour, honesty, and all human feelings and sympathies at the shrine of Mammon. Commend we the *Christmas Carol, in Prose* to all Christmas book buyers" (p. 282).

The London *Weekly Dispatch* (December 24) thought that the new book, "exceedingly amusing, and of the most beneficial tendency," was a vast improvement on "a certain class of trash, which is so copiously poured out at the Christmas season. . . . We should fail very much in our duties to our readers if we did not recommend this clever and benevolent work. It is a rich Christmas offering." The London *Globe and Traveller* (December 30) called it "the most attractive book of the season. Most cordially do we wish it an extensive circulation . . . for the lessons of benevolence it conveys, and the *seasonable virtues* inculcated by its pages." *The Critic* in February 1844 suggested that this story "cannot fail to serve the cause of charity, and to carry its moral to the bosoms of the many Scrooges of this money-seeking age and money getting country" (p. 62). "Let the Christmas of 1843 yield what store of good things it may," proclaimed *The Britannia* on December 23, "it will bring nothing more valuable of its kind than Mr. Dickens's *Christmas Carol*" (p. 807).

The Illustrated London News (December 23) did not know where to begin to describe "the surpassing beauty with which the accomplished author of this seasonable little volume has worked out" the scheme of the story, whether to start with "some of its *spirituel* yet substantial truths—its impressive eloquence, or its unfeigned lightness of heart—its playful and sparkling humour, or its under currents of thought—its gems of world knowledge, or its gentle spirit of humanity—all which light up every page, and, of a truth, put us in good humour with ourselves, with each other, with the season, and with the author" (p. 410).

Theodore Martin, under the pseudonym "Bon Gaultier" in *Tait's Edinburgh Magazine* (February 1844), explored attitudes toward the new book "that all the people are raving about" in Scotland. He quoted an Irish observer, "What is it, but an apoplectic farrago of chuckling and cramming?" This observer summarized in verse what he thought was Dickens' peculiar concept of the holy day:

> What's Christmas, indeed.
> But a season to feed:
> Why should it be more in the Christian's eye?
> 'Twas made but for this;
> But to revel and kiss,
> And spoil one's digestion with brandied mince-pie.

But the Irishman admitted that he knew the book from "extracts only. Some trash about a Mr. Fezziwig's ball, and dinner of the Cratchit family, and so forth." So Martin countered, "It is a noble book, finely felt, and calculated to work much social good. Indeed, Dickens has produced nothing which gives me so high an idea of his powers. It may contain too much, perhaps, about the mere Cockneyish delights of roast goose and plum-pudding; but these are trifles" (p. 129).

As was the fashion of the day, most of the reviews printed vast excerpts from the story to tantalize the readers. "The best recommendation of the book," insisted the London *Globe and Traveller* (December 30), "is a selection from its contents." The most quoted passages were the famous set pieces, the shops on Christmas morning, the Fezziwig ball, the Cratchit Christmas, the wild festivities in Scrooge's nephew's parlor. "These various scenes," said *The Spectator* on December 23, "are depicted with vivid force and humorous pleasantry, dashed with pathos, but not unalloyed by exaggeration. The more lively scenes are the truest, as well as the most agreeable: not that they are altogether free from the fault of excess, but mirthful exuberance has a license that is not allowable in graver moods" (p. 1216). *The Mirror of Literature, Amusement, and Instruction* (January 6, 1844) never got around to publishing a proper review; instead, it reprinted the description of the London market from Stave 3 as a little self-contained essay, "Christmas Morning" by Mr. C. Dickens (pp. 6–7), without disclosing its source. *The Noncomformist* (December 27) likewise extracted part of the same section as "Christmas Shops," without further commentary. Instead of a conventional review, Douglas Jerrold's *The Illuminated Magazine* (February 1844) published a poetic tribute, "To Charles Dickens, on His *Christmas Carol*":

> Honour to Genius! when its lofty speech
> Stirs through the soul, and wakes its echoing strings:
> But honour tenfold! when its day-words reach
> The selfish heart, and there let loose the springs
> Of pity, gushing blood-warm from a breach
> Rent in its close-bound, stony coverings.
> Yea! tenfold honour, and the love of men,
> The kind, the good, attend on Genius then,
> And bless and sanctify those words divine.
> Such words, Charles Dickens, truly have been thine;
> And thou hast earn'd true glory with all love:
> Long may the torch of Christmas gladly shine
> Upon thy home, while voices from above
> Music thy Carol, and again impart
> Mirth and good tidings to the poor man's heart. (p. 170)

After the severe trouncing *American Notes* and *Martin Chuzzlewit* had recently received, the complaints against *A Christmas Carol* were relatively mild. "We would almost quarrel with Mr. Dickens indeed, for having delayed its publication so long," said *John Bull* (December 25). "Had it appeared a month ago . . . it would have been the means of producing many a 'merry Christmas' where now there will be none" (p. 812). *The New Monthly Magazine* in January offered its own quibble, "We have no objection to its gilt leaves, its gay cover, and its genteel typography; but these form a *chevaux-de-frise* about it that keeps it from the poor. Let it be published (by public subscription if need be) on 'poorman's' paper, at the price of a few pence, and its mission will be complete" (p. 149).

Some critics did note "some instances of bad taste" in *A Christmas Carol*. T. Cleghorn in his overview, "Writings of Charles Dickens" (*North British Review*, May 1845), said that the "little story abounds with mannerism, but with the best as well as the less pleasing characteristics of the author. We have, no doubt, his carelessness and incorrectness of style—but then all his copiousness and variety; his tendency to overstrained and extravagant imagery—but then, his unrivalled exuberance of life and animation" (p. 86). The religious press generally ignored the little Christmas parable, apparently for being too secular in nature. The conservative *Christian Remembrancer*, however, in January 1844, rather grudgingly acknowledged *A Christmas Carol* to be "a very acceptable present at this season. A very old and hackneyed subject is treated in a very original way, and the story displays all its author's eminent powers of combining humour with pathos" (p. 119).

A Christmas Carol so captured the public's fancy that references to its characters began appearing in unexpected places. Douglas Jerrold spoke in "To Governesses of 'Decided Piety,'" in *Punch* (July 6, 1844, p. 11), of "the worldly wisdom of the excellent Scrooge," which pleased Dickens exceedingly. In 1845, *Punch's Snap-dragons for Christmas* (which Leech illustrated) mentioned "a fine, hale, octogenarian . . . with a heart overflowing with benevolence, and a countenance in which it was as incontrovertibly written, as in every line of Charles Dickens' *Carol*" (p. 23). The little story was already a part of Christmas lore.

Perhaps Thackeray said it best in his holiday roundup "A Box of Novels," in *Fraser's Magazine* (February 1844). He thought Dickens' new story was the most important book of the lot. "I do not mean that the *Christmas Carol* is quite as brilliant or self-evident as the sun at noonday," he explained; "but it is so spread over England by this time, that no sceptic, no *Fraser's Magazine*,—no, not even the god-like and ancient *Quarterly* [*Review*] itself . . . could review it down." And, he admitted, "I am not sure the allegory is a very complete one, and protest, with the classics, against the use of blank verse in prose; but here all objections stop." Thackeray was favorably impressed with the profound effect the little book already had on the British public. "Many men," he reported, "were known to sit down after perusing it, and write off letters to their friends, not about business, but out of their fulness of heart, and to wish old acquaintances a happy Christmas." He confessed, "The last two people I heard speak of it were women; neither knew the other, or the author, and both said, by way of criticism, 'God bless him!'" Thackeray concluded, "What a feeling this is for a writer to be able to inspire, and what a reward to reap!" (pp. 168–69).

Reviewers so caught up with the infectious good humor of the story generally ignored Leech's contribution to the book. And yet he still received his fair share of praise. "Mr. Leech has illustrated it most happily," said Blanchard in *Ainsworth's Magazine* (January 1844); "his ghosts and shadows are as true as any of the choice corporeal pleasantries that figure in his brilliant scenes; and nothing could be more like life than these" (p. 88). *The Magazine of Domestic Economy* (January 1844) agreed that the book "is very pleasingly adorned with capital woodcuts and coloured etchings by Leech, whose 'quality' is sufficiently known to carry with it its own recommendation" (p. 328). *The Morning Post* (December 26, 1843) thought that "the frontispiece is the best, being a very merry little sketch, at which we hope many children will laugh." Many did.

Scene from *A Christmas Carol, or The Miser's Warning,* at the Strand Theater. Etching by Findlay, 1844. *Courtesy British Library Board.*

"All the world and his wife know the plot of the *Christmas Carol,*" declared *Age and Argus* on February 10, 1844. It was no surprise then that at least eight different stage versions of the story opened in London in early 1844; at least twelve ran in England by year's end. Three entirely different productions opened on February 5, at the Adelphi Theatre, the Strand Theatre, and the Royal Surrey Theatre.[35] As there was at the time no copyright protection of dramatic versions of one's work, Dickens could not stop these unauthorized uses. *A Christmas Carol,* with its clever dialogue, unique characters, and unusual plot, was ideal for the London stage. Playwrights Charles Zachary Barnett with the Surrey Theatre and Charles Webb at the Strand Theatre effortlessly lifted great sections almost verbatim from the original. Their work was hasty but adequate; playwrights at the time were generally paid a pound an act. Not all of the changes were improvements: Barnett, in *A Christmas Carol, or The Miser's Warning,* introduced a new character, "Dark Sam," whose purpose was to pick Bob Cratchit's pocket so that Fred could befriend the poor clerk by offering him a sovereign for his Christmas dinner; and Webb was the only one

[35.] See Malcolm Morley, "Curtain Up on *A Christmas Carol,*" *The Dickensian*, June 1951, pp. 159–64; and H. Philip Bolton, *Dickens Dramatized*, vol. 1 (Boston: G. K. Hall, 1987). All plays had to be submitted to the Examiner of Plays prior to performance, and scripts of *A Christmas Carol* by C. Z. Barnett, Charles Webb, and Edward Stirling survive in the Lord Chamberlain's Collection in the Manuscript Division of the British Library. William Barth of London published Stirling's script in 1844, but Barnett's was the most enduring of these early dramas. J. Duncombe published it in London in 1844, and it was later added to Dicks' Standard Plays and kept in print by Samuel French. In 1874, the Theatre Comique in New York put on an odd reworking of Barnett's script, *Santa Claus, or Poverty's Holiday*, in which not only Santa and a band of fairies but also Mormon leader Brigham Young, suffragist Victoria Woodhull, and businessman Jim Fisk were in the huge cast of characters. Barbarian Press of Mission, British Columbia, issued a limited edition of Barnett's *A Christmas Carol, or The Miser's Warning* in 1984, with an introduction by Joel H. Kaplan and wood engravings by E. N. Ellis.

Scene from *A Christmas Carol; or, Past, Present, and Future,* at the
Adelphi Theatre. Wood engraving, *The Illustrated London News,*
February 17, 1844. *Courtesy Library of Congress.*

who conveniently reunited Scrooge with his long lost sweetheart in the
final scene.

Webb was particularly ambitious: *A Christmas Carol; or, The Past,
Present, and Future* was apparently used in at least five different productions that year, including those at Sadler's Wells, the Strand Theatre,
and the Queen's Theatre. They were not identical, however; for example,
*Old Scrooge, or The Miser's Dream and the Past, the Present, and the
Future* at Sadler's Wells turned into a Christmas pantomime when the
three Ghosts appeared onstage with Puck, Punch, Pan, Apollo, Mirth,
and other stock whimsical characters, all speaking in bad verse.

"The only dramatic version sanctioned by C. Dickens, Esq.," as the
advertisements made clear, was *A Christmas Carol; or, Past, Present, and
Future,* written by Edward Stirling, which opened at the Adelphi Theatre
on February 5, 1844. The Adelphi had a higher standing as a theater at
the time than either the Surrey or the Strand. Richard John Smith, famous
for his villains under the stage name "O. Smith," had also made a specialty
of playing in dramatizations of Dickens' novels and was now Scrooge.

Dickens could not prevent anyone from putting on a production of his story, but at least he had a hand in Stirling's. As triple bills were the fashion of the day, *A Christmas Carol* was followed here by the dubious entertainment *Judith of Geneva* and the obligatory Christmas pantomime *Harlequin Blue Beard, or The Fairy of the Silver Crescent*, replaced later in the run by a burlesque of *Richard III*. Some of the comedy was crude. (For example, Mrs. Cratchit's favorite part of the goose is "the parson's nose"; and she accuses Scrooge of working her husband "more than a blackamoor nigger.") The Ghost of Christmas Present sang a gratuitous and mundane ditty, "The Song of Christmas," with words by E. Fitzball and music by G. Herbert Rodwell:

> Tho' the wind blow; tho' the snow fall,
> We laugh at old care to-day;
> They're dancing and singing in bower and hall;
> And we'll be as merry as they.
> The mistletoe hangs on the rafters high—
> Fill, fill every bosom with cheer;
> For Christmas was meant for jollity,
> And cometh but once a year.
>   Then deck up your houses with holly.

> Bring in the haunch, let the hearth blaze.
> Eat, drink, and chase every pain;
> With joyous old carol of bygone days
> We seem to live over again.
> Then what care we for a wintry sky,
> Who dream but of sunshine here?
> Why, Christmas was made for jollity,
> And cometh but once a year.
>   Then deck up your houses with holly.

Dickens later granted Rodwell permission to reproduce Leech's picture "Scrooge's Third Visitor" on the sheet music.[36] In June 1844, D'Almaine and Company, London, who published "The Song of Christmas," also issued "The Christmas Carol Quadrilles" by Edwin Meriott, "dedicated to Charles Dickens Esq.," with "Mr. Fezziwig's Ball" on the front wrapper, again with the author's permission.

[36.] In a letter to G. H. Rodwell, February 6, 1844, *Letters*, p. 40.

"The Song of Christmas." Words by E. Fitzball and music by
G. Herbert Rodwell, lithograph after John Leech, 1844.
Courtesy British Library Board.

Albert Smith reported in *The Illustrated London News* on February
10 that the play "dramatised by Mr. Stirling in a most *sterling* manner . . .
was produced . . . with most decided success" (p. 83). But while enjoying
the Fezziwig ball and the Cratchit Christmas dinner, as well as Marley's
Ghost and the other spirits and O. Smith as Scrooge and Edward Richard
Wright as Bob Cratchit, *The Sentinel* nevertheless admitted on February
10, "much that is truly and touchingly pathetic, as well as exquisitely
humorous, in the original, is unavoidably left out." The London *Morning
Herald* (February 6), however, would "hardly have thought this tale, so

"The Christmas Carol Quadrilles." Music by Edwin Merriott,
hand-colored lithograph after John Leech, 1844.
Courtesy Music Division, Library of Congress.

pleasant in reading, would have shown so well in a dramatic dress, but we
were agreeably surprised to find so little of the spirit, the feeling, and, we
may add, the moral of the tale lost in its representation on the boards of
a theatre." The public loved it.

Dickens himself was not so favorably impressed when he and Mitton
went to the Adelphi on February 20. "Better than usual, and Wright
seems to enjoy Bob Cratchit, but *heart-breaking* to me," he wrote Forster
the next day. "Oh Heaven! if any forecast of *this* was ever in my mind! Yet

O. Smith was drearily better than I expected. It is a great comfort to have that kind of meat underdone; and his face is quite perfect" (p. 50). At least the play advertised the book.[37] When compared with the author's other works, *A Christmas Carol* was never a popular theatrical attraction in the nineteenth century, perhaps because the public's interest was satiated with the annual Public Readings Dickens did of the famous Christmas story from 1858 until his death. Today a Christmas cannot pass without countless productions of *A Christmas Carol* being staged all over the world. It is impossible to estimate how many schools, church groups, and other amateur as well as legitimate companies have put on plays based on the famous book over the last century.[38]

Foreign interest in the new work by Charles Dickens was also keen. On a visit to London the previous summer, Bernhard Tauchnitz of Leipzig secured from the writer the rights to issue authorized versions of his books in English for distribution on the Continent for British and other tourists. Provided with advance proofs of *A Christmas Carol*, he was able to publish his "edition sanctioned by the author" simultane-

---

[37.] Stirling's play was eventually produced in New York City, at the Park Theatre, on Christmas Day 1844. It was successfully revived at the Adelphi on Christmas Eve 1859, with J. L. Toole as Bob Cratchit.

[38.] The entertainment industry has greatly exploited *A Christmas Carol*. The first movie was a British production of 1901, called *Scrooge, or Marley's Ghost*. Essanay made a silent picture in 1908, Thomas A. Edison another in 1910. Bransby Williams had an unusual career as Scrooge: having played him on the stage, he made the earliest sound recording for British Edison in 1905 and did the same for Columbia Records in 1912; he also appeared in the first sound picture in 1928 from British Sound Film, as well as the first BBC television version in 1946. Seymour Hicks, once the most famous stage Scrooge in England, repeated the role in the 1935 Twickenham talkie *Scrooge*. Lionel Barrymore played Scrooge on the radio beginning in 1934; but Reginald Owen filled in when Barrymore was too ill to appear in the 1938 MGM picture. The first American television version was aired in 1941. Ronald Colman, Ralph Richardson, Alec Guinness, Frederick March, Basil Rathbone, Emlyn Williams, Albert Finney, Lawrence Olivier, Bill Murray, Michael Caine, Mr. Magoo, Mickey Mouse, the Muppets, even Eleanor Roosevelt have all been involved in one form or another with *A Christmas Carol*. There have been ballets and operas, and Benjamin Britten composed *Men of Goodwill: Variations on "A Christmas Carol"* in 1947. The strangest production was either "Rich Little's Christmas Carol" of 1963, in which the impersonator took all the parts, or Marcel Marceau's "mime" BBC Television version of 1973. There was an all-Black Broadway musical, *Comin' Uptown*, which opened in 1979 with Gregory Hines. The Alan Menken musical has been a popular annual holiday production at Madison Square Garden since 1994. There have been admirable television productions with George C. Scott in 1984 and Patrick Stewart (who also did an excellent one-man stage version) in 1999. Perhaps the best live-action dramatization was the classic 1951 British movie with Alistair Sim as Scrooge. The finest animated cartoon remains Richard Williams' 1970 Academy Award–winning picture, which beautifully brought John Leech's pictures to life with Sim providing the voice of Scrooge.

"Master Fezziwig's bal." Lithograph after John Leech
in Dutch edition of *A Christmas Carol*, 1844.
*Courtesy Special Collections, Fales Library,
New York University.*

ously with Chapman and Hall's. The little book contained only one plate, a crudely redrawn and hand-colored "Marley's Ghost" as the frontispiece. Reportedly, Dickens was well paid for this courtesy. *A Christmas Carol* in English was also available in Paris through Beaudry's European Library in 1844. "I'm not sure what impression this tale would cause if it were translated," wondered the French critic Paul Émile Daurand Forgues in *Révue Britannique* (January 20, 1844). "A large part of its prowess resides in certain idioms, and certain descriptions that are utterly local." Nevertheless, he believed it was "a little bourgeois poem that touches the heart through elegant and delightful scenes, honest feelings, and a sweet and melancholy moral. In short, by everything that is becoming so rare in the midst of the exaggerations of novels, tales and short stories, as they are made today" (p. 220–21). Amédée Pichot published the earliest translation, his own *Les Apparitions de Noël* ("The Ghosts of Christmas"), in his *Révue Britannique* (May and June 1844) and in book form in 1847. Pichot considered "the little masterpiece" to be "the model of the moral novel." He admitted in the June issue, "One feels better after such reading. No detail blemishes the picture; not a risky scene, not a vulgar word deny the novelist's legitimate ambition of assisting the moralist" (p. 446). It was translated into German, Dutch, and Russian in 1844, into Czech in 1846, into Danish in 1852, and into Serbo-Croatian in 1868. The great French illustrator Gustave Doré provided wood engravings for a translation in *Journal pour tous* (June 16–July 6, 1861). Unfortunately, these

"There stood a solitary lighthouse." Wood engraving after Gustave Doré,
Journal pour tous, July 3, 1861.
Courtesy Library of Congress.

magazine illustrations were never republished in book form in Doré's lifetime and were then forgotten. Some of his Parisian scenes went widely
afield of Dickens' intentions; some were probably done for reasons other
than "Cantique de Noël en prose." For example, Scrooge and the Ghost
of Christmas Present look remarkably like Dante and Virgil exploring
the rings of Hell in Dante's *Inferno*, which Doré was also illustrating in
1861.

William Layton Sammons did not think that the story would sell
more than one hundred copies in Cape Town, South Africa, in 1844.
"Africa is the wrong quarter to chant *A Christmas Carol* in," he sug-

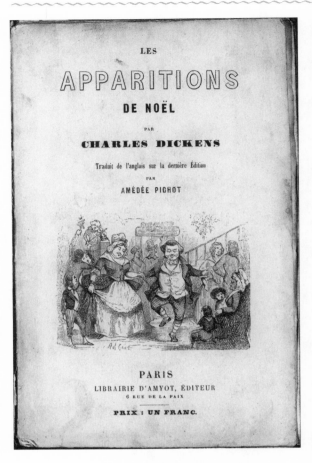

"Le bal de Fezziwig." Cover of French
edition of *A Christmas Carol*, 1847.
Courtesy Rare Book Department,
Free Library of Philadelphia.

gested in *Sam Sly's African Journal* (August 15, 1844); "we have neither the season on point of cold, and but few of the characteristics that distinguish that merry-making period." But he was wrong: *A Christmas Carol* is now known all over the world. In January 1990, while traveling through northwest India, American novelist John Irving played a videotape of *A Christmas Carol* to a group of young circus acrobats he knew. "They were illiterate Hindu children," he recalled in his introduction to the 1995 Modern Library edition of *A Christmas Carol and Other Stories*, "but they were riveted to the story, which was as fascinating to them as it remains to our children." He was later told that though they knew nothing of the English Christmas it depicted, *A Christmas Carol* became their favorite ghost story. "I remember thinking that Charles Dickens would have been pleased," Irving added.

The United States Magazine and Democratic Review reported in January 1844 that "a new Christmas Gift Book, by Dickens, will be over by the next steamer." The first copies bound for the United States left Liverpool on January 4, 1844, on the *Britannia*, the very boat that brought Dickens to America in 1842. After a rough passage, she pulled into East Boston on Sunday, January 21, at 4:15 P.M. The pirates must have been waiting at the dock. "An English copy of Dickens' *Christmas Carol* was received by the Harpers on Monday, in the shape of a beautiful book with exquisite illustrations," a New York correspondent told the Boston *Bay State Democrat* (January 31), "and on Wednesday morning it was on the wings of every wind all over the country."

They moved fast. Harper and Brothers of New York, then among the most aggressive of the American pirates, advertised in the *Sun*, the *True Sun*, the *Plebian*, and other New York papers that at 10 o'clock the morning of January 24, 1844, their edition of *A Christmas Carol*, the very first ever printed in the United States, would be published for six cents. It was a cheap production, just a pamphlet with the text in double columns, no illustrations, and bound in blue wrappers that made it look like an old chapbook or a religious tract. The edition was quickly exhausted, and the book went back to press in March.

Then the pirates stole from the pirates. The New York *True Sun* evidently took the Harper book and serialized it on the front page of the daily paper from January 29 to February 2. Then they reprinted it complete in their weekly edition,

"Fezziwig's Weihnachtsball."
Autolithograph after John Leech in German edition of *A Christmas Carol*, 1844.
Courtesy Special Collections, Fales Library, New York University.

charging only three cents to undercut the Harpers. *The Boston Daily Advertiser* of January 24 had room on its front page for only two extracts, the Cratchit Christmas and the nephew Fred's party. "Take it all in all, we look upon [*A Christmas Carol*] as inferior to no former production of its Author," said *The New World* on February 17. "It is beautiful exceedingly, full of kind and tender thoughts, delicate fancies, happy witticisms, pleasant illustrations. It is one of those stories, the reading of which makes every one better, more contented with life, more resigned to misfortune, more hopeful, more charitable" (p. 211). But it did not make *The New World* any more charitable toward Charles Dickens: it

A CHRISTMAS CAROL.

STAVE I.

MARLEY'S GHOST.

MARLEY was dead: to begin with. There is no doubt whatever about that. The register of his burial was signed by the clergyman, the clerk, the undertaker, and the chief mourner. Scrooge signed it: and Scrooge's name was good upon 'Change, for anything he chose to put his hand to. Old Marley was as dead as a door-nail.

Mind! I don't mean to say that I know, of my own knowledge, what there is particularly dead about a door-nail. I might have been inclined, myself, to regard a coffin-nail as the deadest piece of ironmongery in the trade. But the wisdom of our ancestors is in the simile; and my unhallowed hands shall not disturb it, or the Country's done for. You will therefore permit me to repeat, emphatically, that Marley was as dead as a door-nail.

Scrooge knew he was dead? Of course he did. How could it be otherwise? Scrooge and he were partners for I don't know how many years. Scrooge was his sole executor, his sole administrator, his sole assign, his sole residuary legatee, his sole friend and sole mourner. And even Scrooge was not so dreadfully cut up by the sad event, but that he was an excellent man of business on the very day of the funeral, and solemnised it with an undoubted bargain.

The mention of Marley's funeral brings me back to the point I started from. There is no doubt that Marley was dead. This must be distinctly understood, or nothing wonderful can come of the story I am going to relate. If we were not perfectly convinced that Hamlet's Father died before the play began, there would be nothing more remarkable in his taking a stroll at night, in an easterly wind, upon his own ramparts, than there would be in any other middle-aged gentleman rashly turning out after dark in a breezy spot—say Saint Paul's Churchyard for instance—literally to astonish his son's weak mind.

Scrooge never painted out Old Marley's name. There it stood, years afterwards, above the warehouse door: Scrooge and Marley. The firm was known as Scrooge and Marley. Sometimes people new to the business called Scrooge Scrooge, and sometimes Marley, but he answered to both names: it was all the same to him.

Oh! But he was a tight-fisted hand at the grindstone, Scrooge! a squeezing, wrenching, grasping, scraping, clutching, covetous old sinner! Hard and sharp as flint, from which no steel had ever struck out generous fire; secret, and self-contained, and solitary as an oyster. The cold within him froze his old features, nipped his pointed nose, shrivelled his cheek, stiffened his gait; made his eyes red, his thin lips blue; and spoke out shrewdly in his grating voice. A frosty rime was on his head, and on his eyebrows, and his wiry chin. He carried his own low temperature always about with him; he iced his office in the dog-days; and didn't thaw it one degree at Christmas.

External heat and cold had little influence on Scrooge. No warmth could warm, nor wintry weather chill him. No wind that blew was bitterer than he, no falling snow was more intent upon its purpose, no pelting rain less open to entreaty. Foul weather didn't know where to have him. The heaviest rain, and snow, and hail, and sleet, could boast of the advantage over him in only one respect. They often "came down" handsomely, and Scrooge never did.

Nobody ever stopped him in the street to say, with gladsome looks, "My dear Scrooge, how are you? when will you come to see me?" No beggars implored him to bestow a trifle, no children asked him what it was o'clock, no man or woman ever once in all his life inquired the way to such and such a place, of Scrooge. Even the blindmen's dogs appeared to know him; and when they saw him coming on, would tug their owners into doorways and up courts; and then would wag their tails as though they said, "no eye at all is better than an evil eye, dark master!"

But what did Scrooge care? It was the very thing he liked. To edge his way along the crowded paths of life, warning all human sympathy to keep its distance, was what the knowing ones call "nuts" to Scrooge.

Once upon a time—of all the good days in the year, on Christmas Eve—old Scrooge sat busy in his counting-house. It was cold, bleak, biting weather: foggy withal: and he could hear the people in the court outside go wheezing up and down, beating their hands upon their breasts, and stamping their feet upon the pavement-stones to warm them. The city clocks had only just gone three, but it was quite dark already: it had not been light all day: and candles were flaring in the windows of the neighbouring offices, like ruddy smears upon the palpable brown air. The fog came pouring in at every chink and keyhole, and was so dense without, that although the court was of the narrowest, the houses opposite were mere phantoms. To see the dingy cloud come drooping down, obscuring everything, one might have thought that Nature lived hard by, and was brewing on a large scale.

The door of Scrooge's counting-house was open that he might keep his eye upon his clerk, who in a dismal little cell beyond, a sort of tank, was copying letters. Scrooge had a very small

First page of the Harper and Brothers piracy
of *A Christmas Carol*, 1844.
Courtesy Rare Book Department,
Free Library of Philadelphia.

serialized the story in full between February 3 and 17, at the same time denouncing Dickens' treatment of the United States.

Americans immediately embraced *A Christmas Carol*. "It is a perfect jewel," noted Philip Hone in his diary on January 27, "an opal with light beaming from every part; one of those quaint, simple, affecting things which make you laugh and cry to your heart's content, and then wonder how you could laugh and cry so much over thirty pages of nothing at all. But this is a miniature *Oliver Twist*, fresh from the same casket which produced *The Pickwick Papers*, and sparkling with the same mild radiance" (p. 684). New York lawyer and diarist George Templeton Strong picked up "Dickens's clever (and mighty absurd) extravaganza" when he was feeling blue on the evening of January 26 and noted, "I've been very comfortable and strong ever since. . . . Delightful book is Mr. Dickens's. He's not dead yet, though *Martin Chuzzlewit* is flat and the *American Notes* a libel on this model republic of enlightened freemen."[39] Fanny Longfellow, the poet's wife,

[39] *The Diary of George Templeton Strong*, edited by Allen Nivens and Milton Halsey Thomas, vol. 1 (New York: Macmillan, 1952), p. 115.

said *A Christmas Carol*, "in its English garb, with capital woodcuts and a nice clear type," was "a most admirable production, I think, and has had a great success in England, comforting people for the tediousness of [*Martin*] *Chuzzlewit*. It is evidently written at a *heat* and from the *heart*, and has a Christmas crackle of glow about it, besides much pathos and poetry of conception, which form a rich combination. The sketch of the poor clerk's dinner is in his best manner, and almost consoles one for the poverty it reveals."[40]

The American press was surprisingly generous in praising the new story. The lengthiest review was supplied by the author's friend Lewis Gaylord Clark in the March 1844 *Knickerbocker*.[41] Much of what he said paraphrased the review in *The Britannia*. However, he did call *A Christmas Carol* "the most striking, the most picturesque, the most truthful, of all the limnings which have proceeded from its author's pen" (p. 276). He had three words of advice: "READ THE WORK" (p. 281). Other journals merely reprinted notices from the British press.[42] Many other American reviews were brief, often referring in some way to *American Notes* and *Martin Chuzzlewit*. "It is printed as a children's book," insisted *The Boston Daily Advertiser* (January 24, 1844), "but is more calculated for 'children of a larger growth.' In its simplicity and quiet depth of expression, it has much of its author's earlier style, before he had wasted that simplicity and expression, by applying it to subjects beyond the reach of his judgment or his information." The paper highly recommended the book to its readers, "if there are any copies within their reach." The New York *Sun* noted on January 25 that "as 'Boz's' ghosts always have something peculiar about them, no doubt there will be much curiosity to see how the ghosts in the little work get along." The 1844 *Mirror of Fashion* found it to be "a pleasant as well as pathetic sketch in Boz's best manner . . . plain, natural and vivid" and predicted that the little book "bids fair to become as popular as the best of Dickens's writings" (pp. 12–13).

[40.] *Mrs. Longfellow: Selected Letters of Fanny Appleton Longfellow (1817–1861)*, edited by Edward Wagenknecht (New York and London: Longmans, Green, 1956), p. 105.

[41.] More needs to be done on the initial critical response to *A Christmas Carol* in the United States. Ruth F. Glancy's ambitious but inadequate and inaccurate *Dickens's Christmas Books, Christmas Stories, and Other Short Fiction: An Annotated Bibliography* (New York and London: Garland Publishing, 1985) lists only one American review.

[42.] For example, the London *Morning Chronicle* review appeared on the front pages of the Philadelphia *United States Gazette* (January 24, 1844) and the *New York American* (January 26); *The Anglo American* (February 3) reprinted the notice from *The Britannia*.

"An amusing affair—go and buy it," *The Boston Bee* simply advised on January 25.

"How easily do we forgive the vagaries of genius, and the occasional failings of a character generally good!" observed *The Magazine for the Million* on February 24. "Mr. Dickens by his *Christmas Carol*, has made up for the abuse and vulgarities of his *American Notes* and *Martin Chuzzlewit*. . . . More like the *Carol* and less of the *Chuzzle*, will be better for his fame, and what he thinks so much of, his purse" (p. 33). The New York *Evening Post* (January 25) was at first dismissive of the little volume for being "short and simple, and marked throughout by the characteristic defects and excellencies of Mr. Dickens's manner. . . . The story is pleasantly told, with some exaggeration, but a good deal of interest." But Bryant had to admit in an editorial on Dickens on February 3, that "such a delightful work" as "his last composition, and we almost said his best," was "overflowing with good nature and good will towards the humblest and most friendless of our race."

Some who had opposed Dickens' other recent work gave in to the little Christmas tale. "This is worthy of the better days of Boz," admitted the *Southern Literary Messenger* in March, "although it does come to us baldly printed on 'whity brown paper.' There is many a Scrooge in the world, who might see his picture here, and be better by imitating the reformation of the hero of the tale" (p. 188).[43] "If Dickens had never written anything but this little pamphlet of thirty-two pages, he would still be immortal," declared *The Lady's Companion* in March. "It is, without doubt, one of the choicest and most sparkling gems in the language; and if Mr. Dickens will forget to abuse the Americans—who are beginning to care nothing about it; and, in good sooth, for him either—and give us a good, long substantial SOMETHING, as good or any where near as good as this, he will speedily get out of bankruptcy and on his legs again." *A Christmas Carol* "is as joyous and resounding as if the heart whence it proceeded never had known or dreamed of care and sorrow" (p. 270).

Americans, still smarting from the Englishman's attacks, at first resisted the new book. "How do you like the *Christmas Carol* of Dickens!" wondered an observer in *The Anglo American* of February 10. "Frequently have I put this question to many of my friends and how very few will allow it any merit" (p. 382). "It is, indeed, a work possessing much

43. Whity brown paper was a cheap, not fully bleached stock, used for wrapping and toilet paper.

merit," insisted *The Lady's Companion* in August, "although by many *would-be* critics, it has been condemned" (p. 202). They had difficulty with the paradox of a man who could write so vicious a book as *American Notes* and something so kind and generous as *A Christmas Carol.* "If so be some persons, despising Dickens for his ingratitude and for his having been possessed with the spirit of lies when he wrote about this country, have refused to read *A Christmas Carol*, let them do so without delay," advised *The New World* on February 17. "Turn back, oh, reader . . . and make yourself oblivious of all evil things for many delightful hours spent in perusing this heart-softening story. It is hard enough to imagine how its author can be malignant, slanderous, and very fond of brandy and water; one would think that the latter beverage might curdle the milk of human kindness, which seems to flow so copiously through his nature" (p. 211).

But it was not enough for *The New World* to steal from Dickens; it had to chastise him as well. On December 28, 1844, it published Lincoln Ramble's "Sequel to *The Christmas Carol*," a further assault on the author of *American Notes* and *Martin Chuzzlewit* in the most purplish of prose. In it, Dickens has just completed his Christmas story and has good reason to feel proud of himself: "Yes, thousands—millions would read the *Carol*. Throughout the Old World, it would be seized with avidity to relieve a dull hour, and even in the wilds of the Far West, the hardy backwoodsman would linger over its incidents with sincere and heartfelt pleasure" (p. 803).

And just as he is feeling most smug about himself, the Spirit of Truth transports Dickens, like Scrooge, to apocryphal scenes of his past life to remind him of his humble origins and the wrong course he has taken in pursuit of fortune and fame. The Spirits of Ingratitude and Sycophancy stand guard as he writes about America. "Thou has permitted a mean impulse to direct thy pen, and a malevolent feeling to rankle in thy heart," Truth scolds him. "Thou hast gratified malevolence at the expense of justice, and poured out gall and wormwood to appease an offended vanity. No generous emotion, no lofty purpose, called forth your comments on America. . . . Blush, 'Boz,' when thou art compelled to admit and to feel, in the silence of thy heart, the unworthy impulse that has dictated some of thy poor ebulitions of spleen against America. . . . Let thy face crimson in deepest dye, when thou placest in contrast the black current which deluged thy breast during the preparation of thy American articles, with the kindly stream of sympathies which poured over it during the creation of that *Christmas Carol*" (p. 807). Just as Truth disappears, another vision unfolds, a magnificent banquet attended by some of his most popular characters to remind Dickens of his better qualities as a writer.

Carey and Hart of Philadelphia did not get around to issuing the first *illustrated* piracy until April 15. This fairly good imitation of the original London edition was far more elaborate than the Harper pamphlet, with all of Leech's pictures, both the steel etchings and wood engravings, being freely reengraved on metal and highly colored. The pictures were a bit crude. Nevertheless, the 1843 *Ladies' Mirror* said they were done "in the true George Cruikshank style" (p. 12). On April 27, *The New World* once again took notice of *A Christmas Carol*, adding that "the edition before us is by far the handsomest that has appeared in this country" (p. 535). *Godey's Lady's Book* declared in June that this elegantly embellished edition was "an unexceptionable gift book, as it is about the best of Dickens's shorter stories" (p. 292).

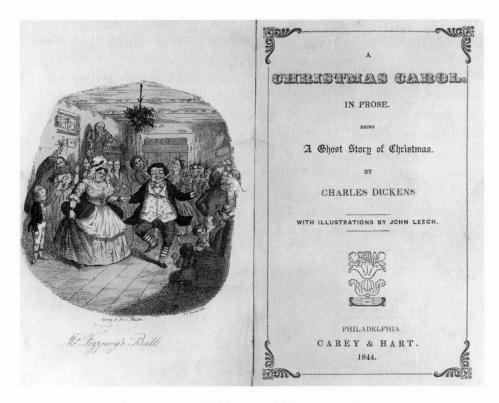

Frontispiece and title page of the Carey and Hart
piracy of *A Christmas Carol*, 1844.
Courtesy Beinecke Rare Book and Manuscript Library, Yale University.

Dickens could do nothing about the pirated editions abroad, but he was determined to get those at home. From the unprecedented success of *The Pickwick Papers*, Dickens was plagued with domestic theft of his work. A year before *A Christmas Carol* came out, Dickens sought legal advice about a cheap publication, *Parley's Penny Library; or, Treasury of Knowledge, Entertainment, and Delight*, "containing every incident in *The Old Curiosity Shop* and *Barnaby Rudge*" as well as an extensive extract from *American Notes* without the author's permission.[44] "The fellow who publishes these Piracies hasn't a penny in the world," he admitted in a letter to his old friend Thomas Noon Talfourd on December 30, 1842; "but I shall be glad to know, at your convenience, whether the Law gives us any means of stopping him short" (p. 411). Apparently the jurist advised that there was little that could be done, because Dickens took no legal action against plagiarism at that time.

He felt differently when the same gentleman with a band of cheap booksellers offered the sixteenth number of *Parley's Illuminated Library* (January 6, 1844), containing "A Christmas Ghost Story, re-originated from the original by Charles Dickens, Esq., and analytically condensed expressly for this work," for twopence. Through his solicitor Mitton, Dickens filed an affidavit to obtain an injunction to stop them from "printing, publishing, selling, or otherwise disposing of the said publication, or any continuation thereof."[45] As he had paid for the publication of *A Christmas Carol*, he was especially interested in the financial fate of his investment and could not ignore this flagrant abuse of his rights. "I

[44.] Not to be confused with the original "Peter Parley," American children's book writer Samuel Griswold Goodrich (1793–1860). The two met in the United States, but Dickens wrote Thomas Hood on October 13, 1842, that Goodrich was "a scoundrel and a Liar; and if he would present himself at my door, he would, as he very well knows, be summarily pitched into the street" (p. 341). He thought the American betrayed him on the copyright question. They had spoken cordially in Washington, D.C., on the need for a strong international copyright law; the "Peter Parley" books were as widely pirated in England as Dickens' works were in the United States. But while presiding at a meeting back in Boston, Goodrich argued that there was no need to change the law. Dickens was so furious when he heard this that he vowed to "ever proclaim said Parley to be a Scoundrel" (p. 342). Goodrich complained in the second volume of *Recollections of a Lifetime* (New York: Miller, Orton and Mulligan, 1856) that Dickens, in *American Notes*, "plucked out the feathers of the American Eagle, and then called it a very unclean bird" (p. 358). Although Goodrich had nothing to do with *Parley's Illuminated Library*, some of Dickens' resentment toward him must have colored his fury at the London pirates.

[45.] Quoted in E. T. Jaques, *Charles Dickens in Chancery* (London: Longmans, Green, 1914), p. 16. All quotations from the affidavits and other legal papers concerning the plagiarism case are from this source.

"A Christmas Ghost Story." Wood engraving by George Stiff, *Parley's Illuminated Library*, *The Dickensian*, Winter 1937–38.
Courtesy Library of Congress.

have not the least doubt that these Vagabonds can be stopped, they must be," he wrote Mitton on January 7, 1844. "So let us go to work in such terrible earnest that everything tumble down before it. . . . Let us be *sledge-hammer* in this, or I shall be beset by hundreds of the same crew, when I come out with a long story" (p. 16). Mitton immediately registered the book's copyright in Dickens' name on January 8 and awaited further instructions from the enraged writer.

Dickens was deeply offended by what the scoundrels had done to his book. He informed Mitton on January 7 that this "colourable imitation" was "precisely the same and the characters the same and the names the same with the exception of the name Fezziwig, which is printed F*u*zziwig. That the incidents are the same, and follow in the same order. That very frequently indeed . . . the language is the same. That where it is not, it is weakened, degraded; made tame, vile, ignorant, and mawkish" (p. 17). One need only quote the pedestrian opening to see exactly what Dickens meant:

Everybody, as the phrase goes, knew the firm of "Scrooge and Marley"; for, though Marley had "long been dead" at the period we have chosen for the commencement of our story, the name of the deceased partner still maintained its place above the warehouse door; somewhat faded, to be sure, but there it was. . . .[46]

46. Dickens and Mitton's action was most effective, for no copy of *Parley's Illuminated Library* is known to have survived. The opening page was reproduced in *The Dickensian* (winter 1937–38, p. 41). The pirated version may have circulated prior to its publication in

The incidents are indeed the same, but the pitiful paraphrasing has none of the distinctive character, none of the abundant wit of the original. It is obvious that any alteration was made (as Dickens' affidavit claimed) "for the purpose of endeavoring to conceal the fact that the deponent's work has been copied, or imitated" (p. 17). It contained only the first two-thirds of the story, however, stopping abruptly with the goose on the Cratchit table and the pudding yet to come: "All was eager expectation." The conclusion was promised for the next issue of *Parley's Illuminated Library*, on January 13. It was never published.

Boz *was* inimitable. As he wrote Clarkson Stanfield on January 9, he was fully justified in "swearing affidavits against a Gang of Robbers who have been pirating the *Carol*; and against whom the most energetic vengeance of the Inimitable B, is solemnly (and lawfully) denounced" (p. 18). As he wrote Talfourd on January 7, he could not bear that his book was "made to appear a wretched, meagre, miserable thing; and is still hawked about with my title and my name—with my characters, my incidents, and whole design" (p. 17). But the defendants immediately moved to dissolve the injunction.

Plagiarists have no shame. "They are the damnedest rascals in the World, one and all," Dickens wrote Mitton on January 13. "If we do not trounce them, all I can say is, that the English Law in these matters is even worse than I can take it to be" (p. 20). Richard Egan Lee of Lee and Haddock replied to the suit that the purpose of *Parley's Illuminated Library* was "to impart in a familiar style synoptical sketches of all works of value, both ancient and modern" (p. 30). He said that the novelist never objected to *Parley's Library* with the new versions of *The Old Curiosity Shop* and *Barnaby Rudge*; the volume was even dedicated to Dickens. Why did not the writer take legal action at that time? "When I got injunctions in the *Carol* case," Dickens recalled in a letter of May 3, 1854, "I almost lost them because I had quietly submitted to be robbed in like manner before" (p. 324). Dickens denied in his response that he had ever seen or read the volume.

Parley's Illuminated Library, for *Bell's Weekly Messenger* (December 30, 1843) in its review of *A Christmas Carol* prints extracts not taken from the original text, as in the following: "Scrooge and Marley was a City firm, whose names stood high upon 'Change; wealthy, hard dealing, and always in business. Old Marley died, leaving Scrooge his sole executor, sole residuary legatee, sole friend, and sole mourner. And oh what a tight-fisted hand at the grindstone was this old Scrooge! a squeezing, wrenching, grasping, covetous old sinner. Hard and sharp as flint, giving nothing and keeping everything, secret and self-contained, and solitary as an oyster" (p. 426).

Lee said that "A Christmas Ghost Story" contained "very considerable improvements and large original additions, as well as condensations." For an example, he said that Dickens mentioned only that Tiny Tim sang a song while Henry Hewitt, the author of "A Christmas Ghost Story," provided "a song of sixty lines, such song being admirably adapted to the occasion and replete with pathos and poetry." Lee further insisted that "numerous incongruities in the *Carol*, involving the unhinging of the whole plot, have been tastefully remedied by Mr. Hewitt's extended critical experience of dramatic effect, and his ready perception of harmonies" (p. 30).

While claiming to "hold in utter disdain the meanness of copying and employing as his own the ideas and modes of expression of any author, living or dead," Henry Hewitt, "a gentleman of considerable experience and talent," replied that he had "in numerous particulars wholly abandoned the plot of the *Christmas Carol*, in order to improve the tale and render the same the more consistent, and to give greater effect to the leading incidents therein." There were so many defects in the writing that Hewitt was forced to "substitute what he verily believes to be a more artistical style of expression and of incident." He even had the gall to accuse Dickens of being "more indebted to Washington Irving for the materials of his *Christmas Carol* than the deponent is to Dickens as regards the *Christmas Ghost Story*."[47] He said the author of *A Christmas Carol* even stole from Hewitt, having "however unconsciously, been indebted to the critical remarks made by the deponent from time to time in *Parley's Library*, for the germ of more than one of his productions" (pp. 31–32). George Stiff, "an artist of great reputation and distinguished talent," said that he never read *A Christmas Carol* and never looked at Leech's work when he illustrated "A Christmas Ghost Story." Having "carefully compared these plates with his illustrations," he believed "that there is no figure, character, scene, or personage in the *Christmas*

[47.] An obscure playwright, George Soane, accused Dickens of plagiarizing a story in his book *The Last Ball and Other Tales* (1843). "A little tale of mine, 'The Three Spirits,' was thought by many to be in its general scope and subject exceedingly like Boz's *Christmas Carol*," Soane slyly noted in his preface to his long forgotten Christmas Book *January Eve* (1847); "yet the *Carol* was not published until some years after it. If then there be any imitation in the case at all, it is Boz—glorious Boz—who has taken a hint from my writings." Three phantoms, the Past, the Present, and the Future, do haunt a man on a winter's eve in this otherwise unremarkable Christmas tale; the last spirit takes him on a nightmarish journey that includes a storm at sea. But the story hardly resembles and possesses none of the wit and grandeur of *A Christmas Carol*. There is no evidence to suggest that Dickens was ever familiar with Soane's work.

Carol at all resembling any figure, character, scene or personage in his pictures." He argued in his deposition "that by the abridged reproduction of the *Christmas Carol* in the candid manner set forth in the title of the 'Christmas Ghost Story,' a positive benefit, instead of injury as charged, would be conferred on Dickens's copyright and reputation" (pp. 32–33).[48]

But the vice-chancellor, Sir J. Knight Bruce, would have none of this nonsense. As *The Times* reported on January 19, the defense argued that "a fair application of mind and talent had been made to the labours of another by a new author, so to render the publication a new thing." "A man is not the less robbed because you tell him you rob him," replied the judge. He finally demanded, "Show me any incident in *Parley's Magazine* [*sic*] different from one in Mr. Dickens's book." Dickens reported back to Forster on January 18, that "at every successive passage, he cried, 'That is Mr. Dickens' case. Find another!' He said that there was not a shadow of a doubt upon the matter. That there was no authority which would bear a construction in their favour; the piracy going beyond all previous instances." Dickens was ecstatic at the court's decision. "The Pirates are beaten flat," he wrote Forster. "They are bruised, bloody, battered, smashed, squelched, and utterly undone" (p. 24).

Actually they had hardly been scratched. Dickens plunged into six chancery suits to catch all the guilty parties and demanded £1,000 in damages from the publishers and plagiarists; he thought of printing the petitions in a number of *Martin Chuzzlewit* to acquaint the public with the injustice he had suffered. But Lee and Haddock declared bankruptcy, and Dickens was forced to take action against the assignees. He was being pressed from all sides; one defendant sent an associate to threaten Dickens with publishing a damaging advertisement as well as further legal complications. But the writer stood firm. The booksellers who hawked the cheap pirated copies finally gave up, but the publishers persisted with further legal entanglements.

Nothing had been settled by May 1844, and Dickens withdrew his suits in the hope he would be charged only the expense for bringing them

---

[48.] Among the documents filed in favor of the defendants was one filed by Edward Laman Blanchard, who should not be confused with Dickens' friend Samuel Laman Blanchard (1804–1845). The other Blanchard testified that "the '[Christmas] Ghost Story' will materially contribute to the popularity of and consequent demand for the *Carol*, which work, as well as others of the plaintiff's books, are very similar in many parts and passages to Washington Irving's writings" (p. 36).

before the court. As the pirates had no assets, he was legally responsible for their costs as well. "I have dropped—dropped!—the action and the Chancery Suit against the Bankrupt Pirates," he wrote Talfourd on May 5. "We have had communication with the assignees, and find their case quite desperate." As for "the vagabonds," Lee and Haddock, he lost "all my expenses, costs and charges in those suits." In the end, he blamed the judge for being "a pragmatical donkey—judicially speaking" (p. 119). It has been estimated that Dickens lost £500, a sum he could ill afford at the time. Despite his being right to protect his legal rights, Dickens learned, as he wrote Forster around November 1846, "that it is better to suffer a great wrong than to have recourse to the much greater wrong of the law." He confessed to having "a morbid susceptibility of exasperation, to which the meanness and badness of the law in such a matter would be stinging in the last degree." Again beset with pirates, he chose not to pursue the culprits to trial. "I shall not easily forget," he reminded Forster, "the expense, and anxiety, and horrible injustice of the *Carol* case, wherein, in asserting the plainest right on earth, I was really treated as I were the robber instead of the robbed. . . . And I know of nothing that could come, even of a successful action, which would be worth the mental trouble and disturbance it would cost" (p. 651). Some of this bitterness toward the court is evident in the Jardyce and Jardyce case of *Bleak House* (1853).

At the height of the chancery action, Dickens was dealt another blow. "Prepare yourself for a shock!" he wrote Mitton on February 12. "I never was so knocked over in my life, as when I opened this *Carol* account on Saturday Night. And though I had got over it by yesterday and could look the thing good-humouredly in the face, I have slept as badly as Macbeth ever since—which is, thank God, almost a miracle with me" (pp. 42–43). Although he "had set my heart and soul upon a Thousand clear," the profit on the first six thousand copies was a paltry £230: after all the production costs had been accounted for, Dickens was left with enough money to cover only a fraction of his many debts. He dared not predict much of a gain on the next four thousand. "Such a night as I have passed!" he wrote Forster on February 11. "I really believed I should never get up again, until I passed through all the horrors of a fever. I found the *Carol* accounts awaiting me, and they were the cause of it." He fully recognized the irony of the situation. "What a wonderful thing it is," he had to admit to Forster, "that such a great success should occasion me such intolerable anxiety and disappointment!" The weight of his debts was so heavy that "all the energy and determination I can possibly exert will be required to clear me before I go abroad." He vowed to reduce his expenses, because "if I do not, I shall be ruined past all mortal hope of redemption" (p. 42). Perhaps he exaggerated his dilemma: by March, with the encouraging midyear accounts in, he was safe from bankruptcy.

The blame for this disastrous report lay with the author himself. Dickens had demanded an expensive, luxurious production while insisting on a relatively low selling price. The gilt edges, elaborate binding, eight wood engravings and steel etchings, and the enormously expensive hand-coloring all ate into his profits. Nothing could sway Dickens now from believing that Chapman and Hall were entirely at fault. He was convinced that they had dragged their feet in promoting the book during the flurry of Christmas business while charging him with every production expense from the cost of paper to that of the two steel plates for Leech's etchings. "I have not the least doubt," he wrote Mitton on February 12, "that they have run the expenses up, anyhow, purposely to bring me back, and disgust me with charges. If you add up the different charges for the plates [£190], you will find that they cost more than I get" (p. 43). There is no proof that they overcharged him, but it was a shame that the publishers did not instruct the innocent writer in the realities of printing costs. And he probably would not have listened.

The only recourse he saw was to change publishers. Perhaps Bradbury and Evans were better for him after all. *A Christmas Carol* proved not to be seasonal: it continued to sell well into the new year, but his entire earnings on the sales of *A Christmas Carol*, from January through December 1844, were a modest £726, for seven thousand copies. Bradbury and Evans offered him £2,800 down on assignment for a fourth share of everything he might write in the next eight years, and they agreed to pay Chapman and Hall the remainder of the writer's debt to that company.[49] Ironically, the feelings of good fellowship and forgiveness that pervade *A Christmas Carol* could not dissuade its author from hard dealing with pirates and publishers. It is sad that the publication of so joyous a book should have caused its creator such anxiety and disappointment in his fellowmen.

The book eventually lived up to the author's expectations. Dickens could boast in a letter of June 10, 1844, that *A Christmas Carol* "has been

---

[49.] Dickens returned to Chapman and Hall after a dispute with Bradbury and Evans in 1858; they remained his publishers until his death in 1870.

a most extraordinary success; and it sells, quite rapidly. It has been reprinted eight times" (p. 145). And another two before the year was up. "Dickens may ring the old year out and the new year in," reported *The Literary Gazette* on December 21, 1844; "but if we may judge from the popularity of his *Christmas Carol*, now in its tenth edition, or very nearly an edition for every month of the departing 1844, he, in point of fact, continues to sing and ring all the years through" (p. 818). Writing in a letter of April 12, 1845, Dickens proudly referred to himself as "the author of *A Christmas Carol in Prose* and other works" (p. 294).

In spite of all his recent headaches, Dickens did not hesitate to follow *A Christmas Carol* with a second Christmas Book. He promised Forster on October 8, 1844, that it would be " a great blow for the poor": it would be powerful, yes, "but I want it to be tender too and cheerful; as like the *Carol* in that respect as may be, and as unlike it as much as a thing can be. The duration of the action will resemble it a little, but I trust to the novelty of the machinery to carry that off; and if my design be anything at all, it has a grip upon the very throat of the public" (p. 200).

The Chimes (1844) set the pattern for all subsequent Christmas Books. Dickens had learned his lesson. Although a companion volume to *A Christmas Carol, The Chimes* was published in a less elaborate format; all the pictures were wood engravings, and there was no hand-coloring. "I believe I have written a tremendous Book," he wrote Mitton from Genoa on November 5, 1844; "and knocked the *Carol* out of the field. It will make a great uproar, I have no doubt" (p. 211). *The Cricket on the Hearth* (1845), *The Battle of Life* (1846), and *The Haunted Man* (1848) soon followed. (He was so preoccupied with *Dombey and Son* that there was no Christmas Book in 1847.) Each tended to do better than the last. "*The Christmas Carol*, the first and the best, has reached only a *tenth* edition," reported *Tait's Edinburgh Magazine* in January 1847. "*The Chimes* was said to be inferior to its predecessor, and is up to the twelfth edition. *The Cricket on the Hearth* had the worst character of the three, and has, therefore attained its twenty-second edition. . . . On the ratio of increase in the previous publications, *The Battle of Life* will run into forty-four editions" (p. 55). There was only a slight falling off in sales with *The Haunted Man*.[50]

Dickens introduced a new sort of Christmas Annual in his Christmas

[50.] According to Robert L. Patten, *A Christmas Carol* sold 20,930 in its first year; *The Chimes* at least 20,000 within the same period; *The Cricket on the Hearth* twice that; *The Battle of Life*, 24,450; and *The Haunted Man*, 17,776. See *Dickens: The Critical Heritage*, edited by Philip Collins (London: Routledge and Kegan Paul, 1971), pp. 618–19.

Books. They all derived from what Dickens defined in a letter to Forster on July 7, 1845, as his "*Carol* philosophy—cheerful views, sharp Anatomization of humbug, jolly good temper . . . and a vein of glowing, hearty, generous, mirthful, beaming references in everything to Home, and Fireside" (p. 328). Thackeray in his review of *The Cricket on the Hearth* in the London *Morning Chronicle* (December 24, 1845) defined Dickens' aim in his Christmas Books as "to startle, to keep on amusing his reader; to ply him with brisk sentences, rapid conceits, dazzling pictures, adroit interchange of pathos and extravaganza." He admitted that Dickens "has such a kindly, friendly hold upon every one of us as perhaps no writer ever had before." The writer merely reclothed the same story in some new holiday dress: each tells of a change of heart; only the love story *The Battle of Life* (1846) does not rely on a supernatural agency. None of these has ever succeeded in knocking *A Christmas Carol* out of the field. They are among the most neglected of the famous author's many works and seldom read today, while the story of Scrooge is known everywhere.

The lucrative series ended only when Dickens took up the editorship of the weekly *Household Words* and later *All the Year Round*, but he continued to write for the Christmas Numbers of these periodicals. He published a selection of these magazine pieces as *Christmas Stories* (1859) to distinguish them from his *Christmas Books*. They are almost all forgotten now. "They began by caroling merrily," said the London *Times* (December 25, 1847), "then they chimed less cheerfully, then they chirped dismally, and lastly they died on a battlefield." Only *A Christmas Carol* has become a perennial holiday classic.

The holidays were soon inundated with countless imitations, many illustrated by artists associated with Dickens, such as Cruikshank and Leech. Every publisher had to have something new and seasonal on its Christmas list, every magazine had to have a special Christmas Number filled with holiday stories, poems, and pictures of dubious skill. "Mr. Dickens need not fear a comparison with his imitators," declared *Douglas Jerrold's Weekly Newspaper* (December 12, 1846). "They must, one and all, be content to stand back, respectfully recognizing the supremacy of Boz" (p. 513). Even Thackeray, who wrote his own series of Christmas Books, including the fine comic fairy tale *The Rose and the Ring* (1855), conceded in the *Morning Chronicle* (December 24, 1845) that Dickens was "the great monopoliser" of the Christmas Book, the "chief literary master of the ceremonies for Christmas . . . who best understands the kindness and joviality and withal the pathos of the season."

Everyone seemed to be writing one, and not everyone could. "A

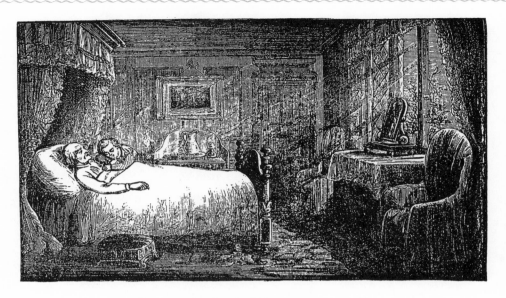

"Even in death—God bless us every one."
Frontispiece, *Christmas Eve with the Spirits,* 1870.
Courtesy Library of Congress.

Christmas story, in the proper sense," Anthony Trollope argued, "should be ebullition of some mind anxious to instil others with a desire for Christmas religious thought, or Christmas festivities,—or, better still, with Christmas charity. Such was the case with Dickens when he wrote his two first Christmas stories."[51] Hans Christian Andersen dedicated a collection of seven fairy tales, *Christmas Greetings to My English Friends* (1847), to Charles Dickens.[52] The Dane's use of Christmas is often as touching as Dickens': "The Little Fir Tree" and "The Snow Queen" deserve their status as international holiday classics, and the tragedy of the Little Match Girl possesses a pathos worthy of Tiny Tim's sad history. Oscar Wilde was in part a direct descendant of both Dickens and Andersen with "The Young King" in *The House of Pomegranates* (1891). This remarkable seasonal fairy tale was Wilde's reworking of *A Christmas Carol* to embody his own aesthetic principles and theory of Christian martyrdom: like Scrooge and his three spirits, a vain, young, sensual

[51.] Anthony Trollope, *An Autobiography* (Edinburgh and London: William Blackwood and Sons, 1883), p. 213.

[52.] "A Thousand Thanks, my dear Andersen," Dickens wrote in late January 1848, "for your kind and dearly-prized remembrance of me in your Christmas book. I am very proud of it, and feel deeply honoured by it, and I cannot tell you how much I esteem so generous a mark of recollection from a man of such genius as you possess" (pp. 242–43).

prince reforms through the agency of three dreams. There was at least one shameless plagiarism of *A Christmas Carol*, the anonymously published *Christmas Eve with the Spirits . . . with Some Further Tidings of the Lives of Scrooge and Tiny Tim* (1870), published in the year of Dickens' death and purporting to tell what happened after the miser reformed and up to his own death.[53]

There have been a few modern stories, O. Henry's "The Gift of the Magi" (1911), Valentine Davies' *Miracle on 34th Street* (1947), Dylan Thomas's *A Child's Christmas in Wales* (1954), and Truman Capote's *A Christmas Memory* (1957), worthy of a place on the same shelf as the Dickens classic. *How the Grinch Stole Christmas* (1957) by Dr. Seuss is a whimsical modern retelling of how Scrooge found Christmas.

A Christmas Carol (both as a single volume and in the collected *Christmas Books*) continued to sell so well that Charles Dickens, Jr., could declare in his introduction to the 1892 Macmillan edition of the collected works that it "shares with *Pickwick* and *David Copperfield* the distinction of being the most universally popular of all the books of Charles Dickens." Dickens himself did much to keep the story before the public through his Public Readings of *A Christmas Carol*. It was the first of his works he read for charity and one of the last he performed for his own profit. It did not matter whether it was in July or December; he almost always opened a new series of appearances with *A Christmas Carol*. Its popularity has long surpassed that of either *The Pickwick Papers* or *David Copperfield*. Even people who have never even heard of Charles Dickens know Scrooge and Tiny Tim. *A Christmas Carol* is as much a part of Christmas today as plum pudding and mistletoe.

Although the public has always loved the book, the critical response to *A Christmas Carol* has been mixed. "It is a little book not to be talked or written of according to ordinary rules," Blanchard insisted in *Ainsworth's Magazine* (January 1844, p. 86). "Who can listen to objec-

---

[53] The author of this unauthorized "sequel" elusively explained his reasons in his preface for not signing this work as being "for any Author who, having written and published many works with his name attached, wishing to test whether his writing deteriorates or improves, published one anonymously, and consequently without any *prestige* attaching to his name" and "for any Author publishing his first work and wishing it to be fairly tested by its own merits alone." Obviously, the real reason was that latter one. He must have had two other reasons for this defense: he wanted naive readers to think it was written by Dickens himself, and he sought to protect himself from a possible lawsuit from the estate. Recently, there has been a subgenre of Scrooge books: *Carol for Another Christmas* (1996) by Elizabeth Ann Scarborough, *A Midnight Carol* (1999) by Patricia K. Davis, *The Trial of Ebenezer Scrooge* (2001) by Bruce Bueno de Mesquita, and *Lost* (2001) by the ubiquitous Gregory Maguire.

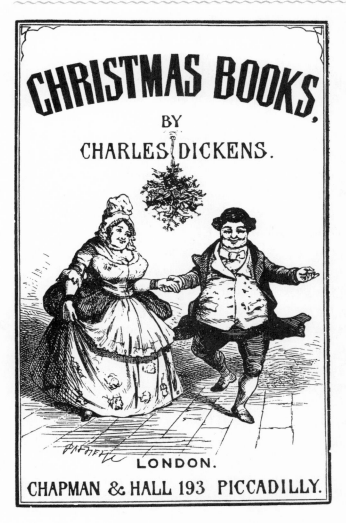

Cover with wood engraving after John Leech,
Christmas Books, 1865.
Courtesy British Library Board.

tions regarding such a book as this?" wondered Thackeray in *Fraser's* in February 1844. "It seems to me a national benefit, and to every man or woman who reads it a personal kindness" (p. 169). He, like Blanchard, believed that as far as a book like this was concerned, "the individual critic had best hold his peace" (p. 168).

Others disagree. Some people have dismissed it as minor Dickens. "To the majority of readers it seems—and perhaps still seems—that Dickens achieved his best pathos in the Christmas books," admitted the once highly influential critic George Gissing. "Two of those stories answered their purpose admirably; the other two [*sic*] showed a flagging spirit; but not even in the *Carol* can we look for anything to be seriously compared with the fine features of his novels."[54] Still others have found it downright offensive. "For a confession, I dislike them," said Sir Arthur Quiller-Couch, "grossly sentimental and as grossly overcharged with violent conversions to the 'Christmas Spirit.'"[55] Even *The Dickensian* (winter 1937–38), the organ of the Dickens Fellowship, published Norman Berrows' "Some

[54] George Gissing, *Charles Dickens, A Critical Study* (New York: Dodd, Mead, 1898), p. 234.

[55] Arthur Quiller-Couch, *Charles Dickens and Other Victorians* (Cambridge: Cambridge University Press, 1925), pp. 16–17. The American novelist William Dean Howells shared much the same opinion of Dickens and *A Christmas Carol*. "The pathos appears false and strained," the realist groused; "the humor largely horse-play; the character theatrical; the joviality pumped; the psychology commonplace; the sociology alone funny" (*Criticism and Fiction* [New York: Harper and Bros., 1891], pp. 175–76).

Candid Opinions on *A Christmas Carol*," which accused the book of being "saturated with exaggerated Christmas fervour" and "larded with soggy and indigestible lumps of sickly sentiment" (p. 21).

Dickens had been falling out of literary fashion by the time of his death in 1870. "He knew nothing of the nobler power of superstition," complained John Ruskin, "was essentially a stage manager, and used everything for the effect on the pit. . . . it is Dickens' delight in the grotesque and rich exaggerations which has made him, I think, nearly useless in the present day. I do not believe he has made *any* one more good-natured."[56]

The Scottish novelist Margaret Oliphant sarcastically referred to Dickens in *Blackwood's Edinburgh Magazine* (June 1871) as "the first to find out the immense spiritual power of the Christmas turkey" (p. 677). She recalled that *A Christmas Carol*, that

Drawing after John Leech for the cover of the "Copyright Edition" of *A Christmas Carol*.
Private collection.

"apotheosis of turkey and plum-pudding," "produced an effect which at this distance we find very difficult to account for. Dickens was then at the highest pinnacle of his fame, and everything that fell from his lips was eagerly received by an admiring public." The little book was embraced like "a new gospel" while it "addressed perhaps the widest

56. *The Works of John Ruskin*, edited by E. T. Cook and Alexander Wedderburn, vol. 37 (London: George Allen; New York: Longmans, Green, 1909), pp. 7, 10.

audience that is capable of being moved by literature." She conceded that the story "retains a certain vigour still, but not by right of any vivid character or striking scene. Its interest is almost entirely forced, and its power quite artificial. Goose and stuffing are its ethereal influences; and the episode of Tiny Tim is . . . only touching because of the personal recollections which any allusion to a feeble or dying child inevitably recall." She also blamed the book for "the flood of terrible joviality and sentimentality which since that time has poured upon us with every Christmas, which detracts from our gratitude; but its effect at the time of its publication was extraordinary, and it must, we presume, have been attended by good practical results" (pp. 689–90).

But he was still beloved by poets. "If Dickens had never in his life undertaken the writing of a long story," argued Algernon Swinburne in *The Quarterly Review* (July 1902), "he would still be great among the immortal writers of his age by grace of his matchless excellence as a writer of short stories. His earlier Christmas Books might well suffice for the assurance of a lasting fame" (p. 36). They also had a profound effect upon the young Robert Louis Stevenson: he wrote a friend in 1874, "they are too much perhaps. I have only read two of them yet, and feel so good after them and would do anything, yes and shall do anything, to make it a little better for people. . . . I want to go out and comfort some one; I shall never listen to the nonsense they tell one about not giving money— I *shall* give money; not that I haven't done so always, but I shall do it with a high hand now."[57] Despite such praise for these little books, it became conventional not merely to underrate Dickens' powers as an artist but also to deride his popularity. "In literature as in dress," the French writer André Maurois, explained, "there are fashions. Certain books are deemed beautiful or graceless, certain authors admirable or damnable, not because the reader experiences pleasure or unpleasant emotions, but because he ought to experience them."[58] Dickens would not have cared. Once, when Hans Christian Andersen was so hurt by a review of one of his books, Dickens tried to comfort him by advising, "Don't ever let yourself be upset by the newspapers; they're forgotten in a week and your

[57.] *The Letters of Robert Louis Stevenson*, edited by Sidney Colvin, vol. 1 (New York: Charles Scribner's Sons, 1911), p. 178. Elliot L. Gilbert suggested in "The Ceremony of Innocence: Charles Dickens' *A Christmas Carol*" (*PMLA*, January 1975) that Stevenson's short story "Markheim" contains "the basic philosophic structure of Dickens' tale" (p. 29).

[58.] André Maurois, *Dickens*, translated by Hamish Miles (London: John Lane, 1934), p. 107.

book will live on! God has given you so very much; follow your own lead and give what you have in you; go your own way; you're above all those petty things!" He then made a mark with his foot in the sand. "That's criticism," he said, rubbing it out, "and it's gone just like that!"[59]

During the twentieth century, Dickens slowly came back into fashion; by the centenary of his death in 1970, he was universally recognized as one of the great figures not only in Victorian but in English literature. Yet some still agree with Richard Aldington's complaint that one must be a "ruthless" Dickensian to deny that the death of Tiny Tim is "an unwarrantable hitting below the sentimental belt" and "the conversion of Ebenezer Scrooge is as full of cant as it is improbability."[60] *A Christmas Carol* has also been the victim of eccentric critical interpretation. For example, Michael Steig argued in "Dickens' Excremental Vision" (*Victorian Studies*, March 1970) that *A Christmas Carol* was worthy of Jonathan Swift in its scatological references: for example, a "stool" in Scrooge's office cannot be just a stool but must bear deep unconscious symbolic meaning to the ghost story. Such dubious observations say far more about the critic's obsessions than they do anything pertinent about the author's.

A few modern critics have found the courage to acknowledge *A Christmas Carol* as an important work within the artistic development of Dickens the novelist. "The mystery of Christmas is in a manner identical with the mystery of Dickens," insisted G. K. Chesterton. "If ever we adequately explain the one we may adequately explain the other."[61] Likewise, Edmund Wilson in his pivotal study, "Dickens: The Two Scrooges," in *The Wound and the Bow* (1941), interpreted the story of the miser's conversion as a metaphor for the author's entire career. "If we try, after re-reading the whole of Dickens, to forget the detail of this immense mass of people and scenes, and to isolate the two or three essential impressions which dominate the rest and in a way give the general tone," suggested Maurois in his study of Dickens, "I feel for my part that I should be left first and foremost with certain scenes from the Christmas Books" (p. 156). Edgar Johnson, the best of the novelist's biographers, believed

[59.] Quoted in *The Diaries of Hans Christian Andersen*, translated by Patricia L. Conroy and Sven H. Russel (Seattle and London: University of Washington Press, 1990), pp. 254–55.

[60.] Richard Aldington, *Four English Portraits, 1801–1851* (London: Evans Bros., 1948), p. 148.

[61.] G. K. Chesterton *Appreciations and Criticisms of the Works of Charles Dickens* (London: J. M. Dent; New York: E. P. Dutton, 1911), p. 103.

that *A Christmas Carol* was "indeed the very core of Dickens' vision of what the relations between men should be, a warm and glowing celebration of sympathy and love."[62]

Many popular misconceptions about the story still persist, no doubt arising from the countless dramatic versions of varying authenticity that arrive annually with the fruitcake and mistletoe. Trollope said in *The St. Paul's Magazine* (July 1870) that the faults most commonly attributed to Dickens in his day were "want of art in choice of words and want of nature in the creation of character" (p. 373). Most people still tend to think as the actor Lionel Barrymore said in his introduction to the 1938 John C. Winston edition of *A Christmas Carol*, that Scrooge is no more than "the cringing symbol of the earth's greatest encumbrance, Greed." The miser is merely a puppet whose strings are being adroitly tugged by the author toward an unconvincing conversion. But this is a too simplistic conclusion, unsupported by a reading of the original story.

To understand Scrooge, one must comprehend the nature of Dickens' characters. Chesterton tried to defend Dickens by arguing that all his figures are caricatures and then tried to prove that there is a great art in exaggeration. George Orwell was more astute in his his analysis of Dickens' creations. He recognized that the novelist "did not consider himself a caricaturist, and was constantly setting in action characters who ought to be static." Orwell added, "The monstrosities that he created are still remembered as monstrosities, in spite of getting mixed up in would-be probable melodramas. Their first impact is so vivid that nothing that comes afterwards effaces it."[63] Trollope admitted that "his characters, if unnatural, have made a second nature by their own force" (p. 374). Many have become types and entered the language.

That cantankerous humbug, Ebenezer Scrooge, is a fine example of Orwell's argument. There is nothing of the classical hero about this old screw. He is painted in such broad strokes when first met that he could easily be the ogre of any household, not just the Cratchits'. Dickens' method is caricature in describing him as "a squeezing, wrenching, grasping, scraping, clutching, covetous old sinner!" His very name

[62.] Edgar Johnson, "Dickens: The Dark Pilgrimage," in *Charles Dickens 1812–1870, A Centenary Volume*, edited by E. W. F. Tomlin (London: Weidenfeld and Nicolson, 1969), p. 50.

[63.] George Orwell, *A Collection of Essays* (San Diego: Harcourt, Brace, 1993), pp. 97–98. Dickens told Charles Edwards Lester in *The Glory and Shame of England* that his characters "are real likenesses" and that he had not "attempted anything more than to arrange my story as well as I could, and give a true picture of scenes I have witnessed" (p. 8).

reflects these characteristics. He exudes a dreary atmosphere of "his own low temperature always about . . . him," as prevalent as the London fog itself or as engulfing as the "infernal atmosphere" of his dead partner's ghost. In his words as in his actions, he fully lives up to his first physical description. At first glimpse, Dickens seems to have created a man without qualities. So strong and unyielding is this introduction that the name "Scrooge" has entered the language to describe the most hard-hearted of misers.

Yet he is not so simple a character as he first appears. One characteristic that offers some hope to his eventual redemption is his twisted sense of humor. Dickens made this point even clearer in his Public Readings: one member of the audience noted that "it has always seemed as if the one chink through which Scrooge's sympathies are got at and his heart-strings are eventually touched, is discernable in his keen sense of humour from the outset." That absurd attack on Christmas with its wild threat of boiling in Christmas puddings and driving stakes of holly through hearts suggests that "he were laughing in his sleeve from the very commencement."[64] The tone is unctuous sarcasm: he tells his nephew in Stavel, "You're quite a powerful speaker. . . . I wonder you don't go into Parliament."

This odd sense of humor returns during the interview with Marley's Ghost. Scrooge's flippancy and lack of fearful

"Scrooge." Drawing by Charles Dana Gibson, *People of Dickens*, 1899. *Courtesy Christopher Bruce Hearn.*

---

[64] Charles Kent, *Charles Dickens as a Reader* (London: Chapman and Hall, 1872), pp. 99–100.

" 'What Do You Want with Me?' " Wood engraving after Edwin A. Abbey,
Christmas Books, Harpers' "Household Edition," 1876.
Courtesy Special Collections, Fales Library, New York University.

respect jar the reader. There may be some reluctance in his jokes, but they are there nonetheless. He has quite a quick tongue for an "old screw." Dickens slowly reveals the man's character. He first appears as he does in public, how he wishes to be seen by the rest of the world. As he has no friends, no confidants, and "nobody ever stopped him in the street," his personality must be revealed by the way he interacts in his office, how he treats the few people who will do business with him. The "squeezing, wrenching, grasping, scraping, clutching, covetous old sinner" is the public Scrooge.

When Marley's Ghost appears, the reader first glimpses the private Scrooge. Dickens as the omnipresent author can reveal the unknown man, in his dressing gown, behind the apartment door, in a vulnerable state none of his associates has had an opportunity to observe. Even the initial signs of a ghost cannot disturb his sense of self. "Humbug!" he replies. Marley's Ghost is no more than illusion, a phantom of his own creation, not of imagination through fancy but created by the cold hard facts of indigestion; he accuses the specter of being not more than a bit of beef, a blot of mustard, a crumb of cheese, a fragment of an underdone potato. His joke that there is more of gravy than the grave about Marley's Ghost is a macabre jest.

Dickens does not want the reader to think there is anything contradictory here. He demands sympathy for his antihero. At first, Scrooge sounds more like the villain than the hero of this drama. Scrooge's reactions during the interview with Marley's Ghost are as shocking as any of the phantom's. When the apparition screams, Scrooge falls to his knees, something one does not expect from a man as "hard and sharp as flint, from which no steel had ever struck out generous fire." Good! He feels fear! His aggressively callous indifference to the poor gives one the impression that nothing can affect his cold exterior. But Dickens strips him of all his emotional armour during his intercourse with Marley's Ghost behind the closed door of his apartment. That he can sense terror makes him human and then sympathetic. He shows humility and seeks comfort from the spirit, just like other men. He even betrays a touch of tenderness for his departed partner: he asks why he is now fettered and admits that they always were good friends. The Scrooge revealed in his own chambers is far more psychologically complex than the old skinflint back in the countinghouse.

Orwell complained that "Dickens' characters have no mental life. They say perfectly the thing they have to say, but they cannot be conceived as talking about anything else. They never learn, never speculate" (p. 99). That is not true of Ebenezer Scrooge: he *does* learn, he *does*

"Marley's Ghost." Wood engraving after Fred Barnard, *Christmas Books*, Chapman and Hall's "Household Edition," 1876.
Courtesy Simmons College.

"Scrooge and the Ghost of Christmas Past."
Wood engraving after F. O. C. Darley,
Christmas Books, 1867.
Courtesy Dan Malan.

speculate as he heads toward his inevitable redemption. The story's purpose is to record the regeneration of a lost soul; it is a one-character narrative revealed through the mind of this individual. Dickens meticulously charts the secret inner workings of the man's brain and heart.

The possibility of salvation is first suggested on the journey with the Ghost of Christmas Past. Returned to the home of his boyhood, the pitiful creature cries out in joy, and a tear of happiness falls down his cold cheek. When the spirit confronts him with the reality of this sentiment, Scrooge shrugs it off as no more than a pimple, not as the true reflection of a melting heart. But this crustiness soon passes: as the Norfolk coach sweeps by, crammed with laughing boys all on their way home for the holidays, Dickens asks, "Why did his cold eye glisten, and his heart leap up as they went past! Why was he filled with gladness when he heard them give each other Merry Christmas"? Why had he failed to notice the life around him as it passed him by? How could such deep feelings be aroused in the same man who advised, "If I could work my will, every idiot who goes about with 'Merry Christmas' on his lips, should be boiled with his own pudding, and buried with a stake of holly through his heart"?

Dickens reveals through the visitations of the three spirits the repressed emotions of this once seemingly unredeemable person. At first his gentler sentiments are purely selfish: he weeps for the pitiful boy he once was, the one child left behind in a dismal schoolhouse not to celebrate the holidays at home like his classmates. Slowly his heart opens to others. Scrooge atones for the three sins committed earlier in the day. On seeing himself once more, a lonely forgotten wretch, he reflects on the abuse he administered to a poor caroler in the snow. When the phantom of his long-dead beloved sister appears, Scrooge remembers her son, his nephew Fred, and becomes "uneasy in his mind," no doubt recalling his harsh words to the ebullient young man on Christmas Eve. And finally, during the heady gaiety of the Fezziwig ball, he takes a moment to consider his own cruel treatment of his poor clerk, expressing a glint of remorse for his callousness.

His awakening consciousness of the fate of others is evident when the Ghost of Christmas Present takes him to the modest Cratchit home on Christmas Day. Scrooge expresses true concern for the future of Tiny Tim:

> "Spirit," said Scrooge, with an interest he had never felt before, "tell me if Tiny Tim will live."
>
> "I see a vacant seat," replied the Ghost, "in the poor chimney corner, and a crutch without an owner, carefully preserved. If these shadows remain unaltered by the Future, the child will die."
>
> "No, no," said Scrooge, "Oh no, kind Spirit! say he will be spared."

The remorse he feels as he views scenes of joy and sorrow at Christmas is sincere. He weeps on seeing himself as a child; on hearing a tune known to his sister and played by his niece by marriage, whom he does not know, "he softened more and more; and thought that if he could have listened to it often, years ago, he might have cultivated the kindness of life for his own happiness with his own hands, without resorting to the sexton's spade that buried Jacob Marley." He realizes what he has missed, the lost possibilities due to his avarice, when he gazes on the daughter of his former sweetheart Belle. In the sad scene where the thwarted girl breaks off their engagement, she says he demanded release "in a changed nature; in an altered spirit; in another atmosphere of life; another Hope as its great end."

Another atmosphere is revived within him as he journeys with the three spirits. That cold, hard exterior melts away just as the dismal fog gives way to the glorious golden sunshine of Christmas Day. It is apparent that despite his bilious cant, Scrooge was not completely free of the Christmas spirit; it just lay dormant within him. So little was needed to revive it: the old miser is so caught up in the game of forfeits (which he somehow knew how to play) at his nephew's party that "wholly forgetting in the interest he had in what was going on, that his voice made no sound in their ears, he sometimes came out with his guess quite loud, and very often guessed right, too." So carried away with the Fezziwig festivities,

Scrooge seems to be "speaking unconsciously like his former, not his latter, self." He had just denied it all these years. Chesterton's supposition that Scrooge must have been secretly dispersing Christmas turkeys all along is pure fancy, but the old man did retain within him, like the flame of memory that could not be entirely "bonneted," the possibility of resurrecting his old holiday spirit.

His choice to isolate himself from the joys and nuisances of daily life resulted in the repression of the sentiments that were once a vital part of his personality. The process of Scrooge's return to his former self is long and carefully constructed. He discovers the example for his later life as well as the medium for his salvation in pictures of the humble Cratchit household. When he poignantly asks that the Ghost of Christmas Yet To Come show him "some tenderness connected with a death," he is taken back to Bob Cratchit's, this time on the first Christmas immediately following the death of Tiny Tim. Scrooge at this point is ready to alter his life; he will accept whatever lessons the spirit will teach him. He is unconcerned when he finds his accustomed corner at the 'Change empty now, "for he had been revolving in his mind a change of life, and thought and hoped he saw his new-born resolutions carried out in this." But he is just deluding himself. The spirit shows him his true fate: death. The only mark he has left on the world is the briefest inscription on a cold, gray stone in some forgotten graveyard. Confronted with this seemingly hopeless vision lacking any apparent means to absolve himself, Scrooge desperately vows to alter the future, not only his own but that of his fellowmen.

This epiphany is not so sudden (as Chesterton said in *Appreciations and Criticisms*) "as the conversion of a man at a Salvation Army meeting" (p. 112). Thomas Hood, who had little hope in the rich, suggested in his review in *Hood's Magazine* (January 1844) that it was "a moral trick of metamorphosis as astounding as any mechanical one in the Christmas Pantomimes!—the parish cage into a Refuge for the Destitute—Newgate [Prison] into the Philanthropic—a Pawnbroker into a Samaritan—a Scrooge into a Samaritan!—a Nero overnight, a Titus in the morning!" (p. 74). But they exaggerate. The process that Dickens unfolds in his story is long, precise, and subtle. Scrooge learns through the recollection of his former self, the example of his clerk and nephew, and a warning of what *may* happen should he continue to follow the same path in life.

As shown through the slow stages toward the miser's change of heart, Scrooge's failure as a human being began early, in suppressing the kindly sentiments of his childhood. "If we can only preserve ourselves from growing up," Dickens wrote in "When We Stopped Growing" (*Household Words*, January 1, 1853), "we shall never grow old, and the young may love us to the last. Not to be too wise, not to be too stately, not to be too rough with innocent fancies, or to treat them with too much lightness—which is as bad—are points to be remembered that may do us all good in our years to come." He was speaking of mental, not physical, age. Scrooge's life reflects that of his creator: the boy Scrooge is the boy Dickens, the Cratchits of Camden Town were the Dickenses of Bayham Street. "Here was a child who had suffered," Maurois said of Dickens, "who was to keep all through his life that sympathy with the poor which cannot easily be attained by those who have not lived the life of the poor. . . . From now on he would have a war to wage against the hard of heart who exploit children, against the hypocrites who style themselves religious and yet lack charity, against bullying schoolmasters, against prisons and poverty and insolence, and he would wage it victoriously" (p. 20).

Unlike the pitiful Scrooge, Dickens never forgot what it felt like to be a child. "No one, at any rate no English writer," wrote Orwell, "has written better on childhood than Dickens. In spite of the fact that children are now comparatively sanely treated, no novelist has shown the same power of entering into the child's point of view" (p. 60). Dickens exercised this rare ability in retracing Scrooge's youth and recording both the joyous and sorrowful scenes in the Cratchit home. The first sign of retribution for Scrooge lies in his return to the schoolroom. Here, as a boy, his emotions are raw, naked, unashamed, and unfettered by the avaricious experiences of his grown life. The spirit touches him deeply in resurrecting his sweet long forgotten past. The old man cries out "with fervour" on spotting the old, familiar road; he proclaims the name Ali Baba "in ecstasy" on recognizing the storybook character. These memories are not all pleasant, for nostalgia demands a touch of pain along with the joy.

For Dickens, it is not enough just to recollect what it was like to be a child; one must also *be* like a child. What distinguishes Bob Cratchit from Scrooge is that the clerk has never forgotten how to be childish. Even the hard reality of his poverty cannot make him think it beneath his dignity to go down a slide with a band of boys, and twenty times, or to play blindman's buff at Christmas. Fred may be neglected by his uncle, apparently his only relative in the world, but he too retains the soul of a boy as he fills his holiday party with children's games. This same spirit awakens within Scrooge as he goes from Past to Present to Future.

The metaphor that Dickens most often employs to describe Scrooge

"Bob Cratchit and Tiny Tim."
Wood engraving after Sol Eytinge Jr.,
A Christmas Carol in Four Staves, 1867.
Private collection.

at his most joyous and uninhibited is like a child. When the Ghost of Christmas Present motions the two of them to leave Fred's house, Scrooge begs "like a boy to be allowed to stay until the guests departed." Scrooge confesses on the dawn of his conversion to being "as merry as a school-boy." This childish spirit even affects the narrator himself, when he admits on viewing Belle's children, "What would I not have given to be one of them! . . . I should have liked, I do confess, to have had the lightest license of a child, and yet been man enough to know its value."

Scrooge will find his salvation in another boy. He gave up Belle and never had any children of his own. He has neglected his nephew. Yet he has one more chance to redeem himself by being "a second father" to the poor cripple Tiny Tim, his clerk's son. "Were there no poor homes to which [that blessed Star] would have conducted *me*!" laments Marley's Ghost. Scrooge's second visitor, neither man nor child and yet both, arouses in the miser through glimpses of childhood past remorse for his abuse of another boy, the caroler he threatened with a ruler.

There lies a paradox in Dickens' conception of childhood and what constitutes the childlike spirit. What is most sympathetic about adults, Fred, Bob Cratchit, and finally Scrooge, is their ability to act childishly; what is most remarkable about Dickens' children is how mature, how unchildlike they can be. Pip in Chapter 8 of *Great Expectations* is surprisingly aware for his tender years. He confesses, "I had known, from the time when I could speak, that my sister . . . was unjust to me." Paul Dombey is even odder in Chapter 8 of *Dombey and Son*; he was "never so distressed as by the company of children. . . . 'Go away, if you please,' he would say to any child who came to bear him company. 'Thank you, but I don't want you.'" This ambivalence toward other children is shared by Judy Smallweed in Chapter 21 of *Bleak House*, who "never owned a doll, never heard of Cinderella, never played at any game. She once or twice fell into children's company when she was about ten years old, but the children couldn't get on with Judy, and Judy couldn't get on with them. She seemed like an animal of another species, and there was instinctive repugnance on both sides." She is but one branch on the great family tree of adult children. "There has been only one child in the Smallweed family for several generations," Dickens sardonically describes her lineage. "Little old men and women there have been, but no child, until Mr. Smallweed's grandmother, now living, became weak in her intellect, and fell (for the first time) into a childish state."

Among these mature children must be included Tiny Tim. He is remarkably reflective, with almost a supernatural power of observation that baffles his loving father. "Somehow he gets thoughtful, sitting by himself so much," says Bob, "and thinks the

"Bob Cratchit and Tiny Tim." Wood engraving after Fred Barnard, *Christmas Books*, Chapman and Hall's "Household Edition," 1876.
Courtesy Simmons College.

strangest things you ever heard." This wretched child possesses the wisdom old Scrooge so sorely lacks. While everyone is having a good time at the Cratchits' on Christmas, he takes time to sing a song "about a lost child travelling in the snow." "A Merry Christmas to us all, my dears," cries Bob. "God bless us!" And Tiny Tim adds a wiser corollary to his father's toast, "God bless us every one!" This doomed boy of, like David Copperfield, "excellent abilities, . . . quick, eager, delicate" even in death possesses a "childish essence . . . from God." "If these shadows remain unaltered," the fate of children like Tiny Tim is the grave.

Other individuals robbed of their childhoods, like Scrooge and Tom Gradgrind of *Hard Times*, become social monsters. Dickens offered a

horrifying vision of the consequences of child neglect in the ragged boy
in Chapter 3 of *The Haunted Man*:

> All within this desolate creature is barren wilderness. All within the
> man bereft . . . is the same barren wilderness. . . . From every seed of evil
> in this boy, a field of ruin is grown that shall be gathered in, and gar-
> nered up, and sown again in many places in the world, until regions are
> overspread with wickedness enough to raise the waters of another Del-
> uge. Open and unpunished murder in a city's streets would be less guilty
> in its daily toleration, than one such spectacle as this. . . . He is the
> growth of man's indifference; you are the growth of man's presumption.
> The beneficent design of Heaven is, in each case, overthrown, and from
> the two poles of the immaterial world you come together.

Because the old miser Scrooge recognizes his folly, Tiny Tim does *not*
die. Scrooge must save him from that other idol, Gain. He views the warning in the demon children Want and Ignorance. His care for Tiny Tim
will serve as an example to others in preventing the approaching Deluge.

Dickens' view of the child goes beyond his personal experience and a
model for action to condemnation of a society that ignores its responsibility to the young. *A Christmas Carol* may be seen as, in the words of
Edgar Johnson in "The Dark Pilgrimage," "a serio-comic parable of
social redemption: the miserly Scrooge is the embodiment of the pursuit
of material gain and indifference to human welfare represented by both
the businessmen and the nineteenth century economists, and his conversion is a symbol of that change of heart in society on which Dickens had
set his own heart" (p. 50). Scrooge is the archetypal "economic man," the
utilitarian who exists only for the accumulation of money; he prays to
that other idol, Gain, because he is a convert to what Carlyle called the
cult of Mammonism. Scrooge's soul is weighed down like Marley's by
"cash-boxes, keys, padlocks, ledgers, deeds, and heavy purses wrought in
steel." His is a profession that demands precision, exactness, and has no
place for human sentiment or frailty of any kind that might unbalance
the strict laws of mathematics and economics; appropriately, he threatens a caroler with a ruler. There is no place for nonsense, for humbug, in
his narrow little world.

His callous opinions are merely the economic cant of the political
theorists of his day. The poor are poor because they have made themselves so, and Scrooge cannot be bothered to provide the means "to make
idle people merry." The only refuges he is willing to provide for them are

the prisons and the workhouses, which he already funds through no choice of his own. His debt to society has been paid through compulsory taxation; there is no need to waste any more of his money providing charity at Christmas or any other day of the year. He loses nothing in supporting these institutions, because the Treadmill and the Poor Law are supposed to protect men such as him from being cheated by their creditors. Whatever might be the proper solution to the social problem is of no concern to Scrooge. He does not care whether the poor live or die so long as they do not threaten his own utilitarian ends.

Scrooge does not just parrot political cant; he embodies these principles. All sentiment is humbug; any emotion that might hinder business must be avoided. On the day of his partner's funeral, he does not grieve: he makes a nice bargain. He lacks imagination, as it might distract him from making money. Any flight of fancy he shrugs off as the result of indigestion or a cold in the head. He comprehends nothing beyond his "factious purposes." His senses cannot be trusted when something so wondrous as Marley's Ghost materializes. Although he sees it with his own two eyes, it does not conform to his utilitarian purpose, so it must be humbug.

Another utilitarian, Jacob Marley, challenges this economic man. He tries to warn his former partner of the false path they both have tread and what road he should now take. "The common welfare was my business," cries Marley's Ghost; "charity, mercy, forbearance, and benevolence, were, all, my business." All he needed to have done to save himself from the incessant nocturnal wanderings after death was to improve the condition of one, just one poor family. The true defender of the poor is the Ghost of Christmas Present. This visionary Father Christmas is the only truly active spirit in the story. The Ghost of Christmas Past has the ability to present only "shadows of the things that have been"; it does not judge, it cannot alter what has been. The Ghost of Christmas Yet To Come lacks the power of reflection; this grim reaper can only move forward, and nothing can divert it from its inevitable course. Only the Ghost of Christmas Present comments on the events and offers Scrooge a chance for redemption. It offers examples of the happy life as alternatives to Scrooge's miserable little existence.

The phantom early establishes its position. It explains that the light of its torch falls most of all upon a poor man's dinner "because it needs it most." It bears no patience for the narrow Puritanism that would deny the common man his simple pleasures in the name of God. The jolliest of the Christmas scenes in the book are those of the less fortunate. Working people running to the bakeries for their holiday meals are just as festive as "the Lord Mayor, in the stronghold of the mighty Mansion House." The Ghost finds its way to the hovel of a Cornish miner and his family as well to a ship in a storm at sea. They have time for Christmas carols, which transcend their condition. The most memorable seasonal scenes in English literature are the Fezziwig ball, the Cratchit Christmas, and Fred's Christmas party. There is nothing extravagant about the way they honor the day except in their shared exuberance. Even in their genteel poverty, the Cratchits have much to celebrate.

There may be tenderness in these humble scenes, but the Ghost has none for Scrooge. At the close of the holiday season, after a children's Twelfth Night party, it bluntly confronts Scrooge with a boy and a girl who know nothing about twelfth-cake and conjuring. The Ghost of Christmas Present, in a voice like Thomas Carlyle's, introduces the monster children, Ignorance and Want, sheltered by the folds in its robe. These little wretches represent Dickens' most powerful indictment of the utilitarian mind. Without the Ghost of Christmas Present to comfort and protect these children, narrow Puritanism and Mammonism would unleash them upon the world. They swiftly fade into that dismal figure, the Ghost of Christmas Yet To Come. Society has a responsibility to find some way to solve the problems of poverty and misery before these children grow up. When Scrooge asks if they have any refuge, he is struck with his own words, "Are there no prisons? Are there no workhouses?" The answer seems to be the dreaded Ghost of Christmas Yet to Come, the Doom which must be erased from the children's brows.

"It seems," said Orwell, "that in every attack Dickens makes upon society he is always pointing to a change in spirit rather than a change in structure" (p. 64). Dickens does not offer specific directions. Only the Christmas spirit protects these children; no one else is aware of their existence. Dickens never reveals *how* Scrooge was a second father to Tiny Tim. It is all a matter of faith. He avoids details; for example, when Scrooge tries to make up for his past sins, he whispers in the gentleman's ear the amount of his gift to charity away from the narrator's and the reader's hearing.

A Christmas Carol fails dismally as a political tract. "From one angle," noted Marxist critic T. A. Jackson, "the *Christmas Carol* appears as propaganda in favour of pathetic resignation. Bob Cratchit . . . has little to be thankful for, and yet is presented as still finding excuses for his wretched old screw of an employer. . . . For Bob Cratchit a miserly boss was, in a time of economic depression such as prevailed in 1843, just one more of those ills which, since it could not be cured, must be endured."[65] The change in consciousness must come from the employer, not the employed; Bob Cratchit never demands what Carlyle thought every working man deserved, "a fair day's wages for a fair day's work." Scrooge would probably just tell him to look for another position if he did ask. Dickens saw nothing wrong in Bob's character; there was no reason to blame the victim. He believed that the ideal relationship between boss and worker was one of mutual trust and benevolence. Fezziwig was the perfect employer. "He has the power to render us happy or unhappy," Scrooge explains; "to make our service light or burdensome; a pleasure or a toil. Say that his power lies in words and looks; in things so slight and insignificant that it is impossible to add and count 'em up: what then? The happiness he gives, is quite as great as if it cost a fortune." He is the example that Scrooge must and will follow in his future dealings with Bob Cratchit.

Scrooge must change, not Bob Cratchit. The purpose of the book was, as Dickens stated in his preface to the original 1843 edition, "in a whimsical kind of masque which the good humour of the season justified, to awaken some loving and forbearing thoughts, never out of season in a Christian land." He was addressing the Scrooges, not the Bob Cratchits. The solution was psychological, not political. The individual can correct injustice. Why wait for society to do it? While others believed that if one changed society, one changed the individual, Dickens saw no need to overhaul the system until there were better people to live in it. Utilitarians have never been fond of *A Christmas Carol*. It appeals more to the poet than to the political scientist. "Who could not be happy in his world?" wondered the philosopher George Santayana. "Yet there is nothing essential to it which the most destructive revolution would be able to destroy.[66] It is no surprise Lenin walked out on a production of *The Cricket on the Hearth* at the Moscow Art Theatre in 1922.[67]

[65]. T. A. Jackson, *Charles Dickens: The Progress of a Radical* (New York: International Publishers, 1938), p. 293.

[66]. George Santayana, *Soliloquies in England and Later Soliloquies* (London: Constable, 1922), p. 58.

[67]. "Ilyich was already bored after the first act," his widow Nadezhda Krupskaya wrote in *Memories of Lenin* (London: Lawrence and Wishart, 1942). "Dickens' middle-class sentimentality began to get on his nerves and when the dialogue commenced between the old toy-seller and his blind daughter, Ilyich could stand it no longer and walked out in the middle of the scene" (p. 299).

While considering the social content of this *Christmas Carol in Prose*, one is struck with how nonreligious a Christmas story it is. Andrew Lang, in the 1897 Gadshill Edition of *Christmas Books*, thought it was merely "Christianity illuminated by the flames of punch." English children's book writer Eleanor Farjeon suggested in her introduction to the 1954 University Press edition of *Christmas Books*, "It is a Christmas in which hobgoblins are more appropriate than the Holy Spirit, a Christmas which may seem to glorify the Altar less than the Hearth; and, since more households have hearths than they have altars, a Christmas which has dominated the home-festival for well over a century." Dickens rejected the dogmas of the established church and had little interest in questions of miracles. "There was more piety in being human than in being pious," Santayana explained. "In reviving Christmas, Dickens transformed it from the celebration of a metaphysical mystery into a feast of overflowing simple kindness and good cheer; the church bells were still there—in the orchestra; and the angels of Bethlehem were still there—painted on the back-curtain" (p. 60). When he first mentions biblical characters in *A Christmas Carol*, they appear on the old fireplace tiles; they belong more to storybooks than to the Holy Scriptures. Remarkably, no scene in this Christmas story takes place in a church, no clergyman plays a role in the drama. "His Christmas," explained Ruskin, "meant mistletoe and pudding—neither resurrection from the dead, nor rising of new stars, nor teaching of wise men, nor shepherds" (p. 7). This domestic sermon is free of clerical cant.

Dickens believed in good works, not just good words. His was an active Christianity that had no place for pious hypocrites. "There are some upon this earth of yours who lay claim to know us," says the Ghost of Christmas Present, "and who do their deeds of passion, pride, ill-will, hatred, envy, bigotry, and selfishness in our name; who are as strange to us and all our kith and kin, as if they had never lived." As he wrote Napier back in 1843, he could do without "Mysteries and Squabbles for Forms" when there were people "in such a state so miserable and so neglected, that their very nature rebels against the simplest religion" (p. 565). Dickens' *Christmas Carol* offered a popular religion that he thought would be of benefit to all people. He believed it was being Christian to celebrate the holiday with all its traditions. "In fighting for Christmas," G. K. Chesterton argued, Dickens "was fighting for the old European festival, Pagan and Christian, that trinity of eating, drinking, and praying which to moderns appears irreverent, for the holy day which is really a holiday.[68] Thackeray recognized that this "charity sermon" is free of theological discussion, but full of simple holiday pleasures and feelings. "I believe it occasioned immense hospitality throughout England," said Thackeray; "was the means of lighting up hundreds of kind fires at Christmas time; caused a wonderful outpouring of Christmas good feeling; of Christmas punch-brewing; an awful slaughter of Christmas turkeys, and roasting and basting of Christmas beef."[69] Dickens' "charity sermon" was preached not in the pulpit at Westminster, but by the hearth of the common man.

Yet Dickens did not entirely ignore the Christmas story in his story. There are biblical references here and there, but what Dickens emphasized were the good works of Christ. He sympathized with the Unitarian doctrine "Believe in the supremacy of God the Father, and in the humanity and divine mission of Jesus of Nazareth." It has been suggested that the theme of *A Christmas Carol* parallels an axiom of the popular Protestant theologian Thomas Arnold, "The salvation of man's soul is effected by Christ's spirit."[70] Dickens taught his children about the humanity of Christ. "No one ever lived, who was so good, so gentle, and so sorry for all people who did wrong, or were in any way ill or miserable, as He was," he wrote in 1849 in *The Life of Our Lord* (1934). He stressed the poverty of his Lord, and that He chose His disciples from the poor. "Heaven was made for them as well as for the rich," Dickens preached in his new Gospel, "and God makes no difference between those who wear good clothes and those who go barefoot and in rags. The most miserable, the most ugly, deformed, wretched creatures that live, will be bright Angels in Heaven if they are good here on earth." And it is through the active Christ, his good works and example, that Dickens derived his religious beliefs. As Tiny Tim observed, one should reflect during this season of merrymaking on he "who made lame beggars walk and blind men see."

Central to Dickens' interpretation of Christ's life was Christ's attitude toward children. "It is good to be children sometimes," he wrote in *A Christmas Carol*, "and never better than at Christmas, when its mighty Founder was a child himself." On his return to the Cratchit home at the

[68] G. K. Chesterton, *Charles Dickens* (London: Methuen, 1906) p. 161.

[69] William Makepeace Thackeray, *The English Humourists of the Eighteenth Century* (New York: Harper and Bros., 1853), p. 292.

[70] See N. C. Peyrouton, "The Life of Our Lord," *The Dickensian*, May 1963, p. 106.

time of Tiny Tim's death, Scrooge overhears one line of the Gospel, "And He took a child, and set him in the midst of them." Herein lies the lesson Scrooge must follow in his new life. He must be as Christ in the treatment of children. "Why," moans Marley's Ghost, "did I walk through crowds of fellow-beings with my eyes turned down, and never raise them to that blessed Star which led the Wise Men to a poor abode?" The Ghosts of Christmas Past, Present, and Yet To Come are the new Wise Men. And just as these kings were led to a poor abode, Scrooge makes a pilgrimage to the humble home of Tiny Tim. Through the grace of the Ghost of Christmas Present, Scrooge finds salvation in this Christ child–like boy. It seems true for Scrooge that "Spirit of Tiny Tim, thy childish essence was from God!" One should indeed be devilish sharp in what one does to children.

All these intentions, personal, social, religious, are well meaning, but they would be sought in other places if *A Christmas Carol* did not work as a compelling work of literature. Chesterton argued in his introduction to the 1924 Charles E. Lauriat edition that "the historical and moral importance is really even greater than the literary importance." But that is too glib. Why should this little story survive while all the earnest pamphlets and sermons over the last century and a half have disappeared? *A Christmas Carol* is a work of art, an important work of literature, which must be considered as such to be granted its proper place within Dickens' entire body of work.

Despite its subtitle, *A Christmas Carol* is not a traditional ghost story. "For all his moral Christmas ghosts, and his interest in the ghostly," wrote Andrew Lang in his introduction to the 1897 Gadshill Edition of *Christmas Books*, "Dickens never . . . wrote a good ghost story *au naturel*. He brought in the fantastically grotesque: he had not the success in this province, because he had not the seriousness, of De Foe, of Scott, and Bulwer-Lytton." He had other purposes in mind. After all, his spirits are benevolent; they come not to haunt but to help the old sinner. "Your welfare!" the Ghost of Christmas Past tells Scrooge why he is there. *A Christmas Carol* is closer to a fable, which demands a strict structure that his previous novels did not require. Edgar Johnson suggested that in this seriocomic parable of social redemption, Marley's Ghost symbolizes divine grace with the three Christmas ghosts serving as the agencies of memory, example, and fear.[71] There is one false note in

[71.] Edgar Johnson, "The Christmas Carol and the Economic Man," *American Scholar*, winter 1951–52, p. 98.

this Christmas carol: if the Ghost of Christmas Past acts as the agent of Scrooge's memory, the picture of domestic bliss seven years before in Belle's house is amiss; unless he were a Peeping Tom in his past, Scrooge was never a witness to this pleasant Christmas scene. The tone and all the details put this scene more in character with the journey of the Ghost of Christmas Present. Dickens may have sensed the problem; he dropped it from his Public Readings. The scene has rarely been retained in other adaptations of the story.

As Lang further observed in the Gadshill Edition, Dickens created "a ghost with a purpose." His structure remains strong and clear. Chesterton, in *Charles Dickens*, saw no scheme in it at all. He found the story to be "everywhere irregular" with "the same kind of artistic unity that belongs to a dream" (p. 169). That may be true of *Alice in Wonderland*: it is not true of *A Christmas Carol*. Chesterton thought "it is a kind of philanthropic dream, an enjoyable nightmare, in which the scenes shift bewilderingly and seem as miscellaneous as the pictures in a scrapbook, but in which there is one, constant state of the soul, a state of rowdy benediction and a hunger for human faces" (p. 170). Every one of Chesterton's "bewildering" scenes has a place within the tight structure of the parable. Although the technique of wildly and widely shifting scenes may appear erratic at first glance, the line of argument moves as intrepidly on as does the Ghost of Christmas Yet To Come itself. Every sin committed, every callous remark spoken in the beginning of the story, literally comes back to haunt Scrooge. Through the revelations of his distant past, he regrets recent cruelties to the boy singing a carol, to his nephew, to his clerk. The Ghost of Christmas Present plays devil's advocate in challenging Scrooge's vicious political cant. And through the Ghost of Christmas Yet To Come, Scrooge views the consequences of these acts: each scene is one more step to his ultimate end, forgotten and unloved in death.

Dickens borrows for his seasonal ghost story the traditional opening of the fairy tale, "Once upon a time . . ." Here was a different kind of winter's tale. "No one was more intensely fond than Dickens of old nursery tales," Forster wrote regarding *A Christmas Carol* in his biography of Dickens, "and he had a secret delight in feeling that he was here only giving them a higher form. The social and manly virtues he desired to teach, were to him not less the charm of the ghost, goblin, and the fairy fancies of his childhood; however rudely set forth in those earlier days. What now were to be conquered were the more formidable dragons and giants which had their places at our own hearths" (pp. 68–69). From the fairy tale, he took his supernatural medium: Marley's Ghost serves Scrooge in the same manner as do the fairy godmother in the French *conte de fées* and the benevolent animals in the German *Hausmärchen*. Scrooge must be tested three times, just like a hero in a folktale, before he receives his reward. And Dickens' story ends "happily ever after" with a line as effective and memorable as that old phrase, "God Bless Us, Every One!"

The fairy tale influence is also apparent in the literary style of the story. Dickens enchants his descriptions with a vivid animism endemic to the tales of Grimm and Andersen. Inanimate objects are as colored with the grotesque as the living, breathing characters. Even when depicting a typical marketplace or the interior of a dismal rag-and-bottle shop, his style cannot be called naturalistic. "The elements of the fairy tale are superimposed on the everyday world, and the deep symbolic truths of myths gleam through the surface," observed Johnson.[72] Personification is everywhere. The clock in the bell tower strikes the hours "as if its teeth were chattering in its frozen head," and Scrooge's house plays hide-and-seek with the other buildings; Spanish onions wink and French plums blush in the produce stalls; the fog and frost transform into "the Genius of the Weather." "His imagination," said Orwell, "overwhelms everything, like a weed" (p. 94). The effect is ironic: life around Scrooge in London is so animated in all its details that this utilitarian, who "had as little of what is called fancy about him as any man in the City of London," does not see the strange forces all about him until he is startled by his dead partner's face on the door knocker.

The style is at its liveliest in these descriptions. It is not for everyone. "But," Trollope added in *The St. Paul's Magazine* (July 1870), "his words have been so potent, whether they be right or wrong according to any fixed rule, that they have justified themselves by making themselves into a language which is itself popular" (pp. 373–74). Thackeray and others objected to the liberal use of free verse in these passages; Dickens' prose does rely heavily on poetic elements such as alliteration, assonance, apostrophe, simile, and internal rhyme. He knew what he was doing in his Christmas Books: he warned Forster in regard to *The Battle of Life* in a letter of November 13, 1846, "If in going over the proofs you find the tendency to blank verse (I *cannot* help it, when I am very much in

---

[72.] Edgar Johnson, *Dickens Criticism: Past, Present, and Future* (Cambridge, Mass.: A Charles Dickens Reference Center Publication, 1962), pp. 10–11.

earnest) too strong, knock out a word's brains here and there" (p. 656). And Dickens was never more in earnest than in *A Christmas Carol*. Phrases that could scan as verse abound throughout the text:

> Beat on the table with the handle of his knife,
> And feebly cried Hurrah!

and

> Beware them both, and all of their degree,
> But most of all beware this boy, for on his brow I see . . .

The author *cannot* help himself. His presence is felt so strongly throughout the writing that Dickens does indeed seem to be constantly "standing in the spirit at your elbow." Taking down everything he can think of, the sentences become great lists of all the marvels he sees. He stimulates the senses: he fills individual passages with odors, tastes, sights, or sounds. "Every thing is piled up and up, detail on detail, embroidery on embroidery," wrote Orwell. "It is futile to object that this kind of thing is roccoco—one might as well make the same objection to a wedding-cake. Either you like it or you do not like it" (p. 97). They are on occasion overwhelming, like too much punch or fruitcake at Christmas; it is excess fully in keeping with the spirit of the season. Not everyone reacts the same to such intoxicating passages; they may either delight the reader with their festive abundance and Christmas cheer or sicken him. Not everyone reacts the same to his humor: puns and jests and other jokes abound, and in the oddest unexpected places and from the unlikeliest characters. Dickens knew there are many kinds of laughter, as different as Fred's hearty outburst and the unsettling cackling of Mrs. Dilber and her cronies.

The style is at its most characteristic in the great scenes of Christmas revelry enjoyed by Fezziwig, Bob Cratchit, and Fred. "As you read any of the passages where Dickens is at his happiest," suggested Maurois, "there are certain words that perpetually recur: there is *brisk*, there is *jolly*, there are all the adjectives expressive of open-heartedness, cheerfulness, sympathy, zeal" (pp. 156–57). Their spirit is infectious; here must lie the passages he said possessed him when he was writing the story.

No matter how emotionally involved the writer is in his material, Dickens never steers clear of his intended purposes. Often when the action is at its most giddying and exuberant, when "Abundance rejoices," he jars the reader with a scene of abject poverty. He noted in Chapter 17 of *Oliver Twist* that it was stage custom "in all good murderous melo-dramas, to present the tragic and comic scenes, in as regular alternation, as the layers of red and white in a side of streaky bacon." He insisted, "Such changes appear absurd; but they are not so unnatural as they would seem at first sight. The transitions in real life from well-spread boards to death-beds, and from mourning weeds to holiday garments, are not a whit less startling; only, there, we are busy actors, instead of pas-sive lookers-on, which makes a vast difference." He could just as well have been writing about his "Ghost Story of Christmas" when he added that "sudden shiftings of the scene, and rapid changes of time and places, are . . . by many considered as the great art of authorship."

A Christmas Carol is a tale of contrasts. The Ghost of Christmas Past, intent on its mission to teach Scrooge its lesson, takes the miser without warning from the jolly Fezziwig ball to the pitiful interview with the rejected sweetheart. The Ghost of Christmas Present buffets the old man about from the bustling London streets to the misery of a Cornish miner's hut and a storm at sea and then back to the cozy but lively domes-ticity of Fred's party; the blasts of the gale transform into the nephew's boisterous laughter. Stave 4 sustains an atmosphere of scattered gloom and mystery, but contrast is crucial here as well. The horror of the for-gotten man's corpse is followed by "some tenderness connected with a death" in the Cratchit household, now dressed in mourning when last it was alive with Christmas cheer. Some critics have objected to the ways Dickens manipulates the reader, but they cannot criticize him for care-lessness in the writing. Nothing is arbitrary, nothing gratuitous in these frantic shifts in time and place. *A Christmas Carol* is a tightly con-structed and painstakingly executed story.

Dickens wrote the story in a few weeks of impassioned inspiration. But a glance at the manuscript (now in the Pierpont Morgan Library) demonstrates with what craft and care he constructed the tale.[73] Unlike

---

[73.] Dickens presented "my own, and only MS of the Book" to his solicitor Thomas Mitton, perhaps out of gratitude for the work he did on the chancery suit against the piracy of *A Christmas Carol*. Five years after Dickens' death, Mitton sold the manuscript to a London bookseller, Francis Harvey, reportedly for £50. An autograph collector, Henry George Churchill, quickly snatched it up in 1882 and later sold it to the bookseller Bennett in Birmingham. The transaction caused enormous excitement in the area, with crowds of people begging for a glimpse at the famous manuscript. Robson and Kerslake of London bought it from Bennett for £200 and quickly turned it over to Stuart M. Samuel, a Dick-

his bulkier, meatier novels, *A Christmas Carol* was not issued in monthly parts; it came into the world whole. Here was the author's first important attempt at a sustained, complete work from its inception. The critic John Butt recognized the full significance of this new approach to composition for Dickens: *A Christmas Carol* was "the first time he had attempted to direct his fertile imagination within the limits of a carefully constructed premeditated plot . . . the first occasion of Dickens discovering a plot sufficient to carry his message, and a plot conterminous with his message, a plot, that is to say, the whole of which bears upon his message and does not overlap." Here he combined "healthful cheerfulness and enjoyment" with his "great Faith in the Poor." Through *A Christmas Carol,* Butt explained, Dickens "had at last kept a steadier eye on the purpose and design of his work which was to characterize his novels from *Dombey and Son* onwards."[74] This, the first Christmas Book, defined not only the holiday itself, but the direction of the author's subsequent work.

A Christmas Carol was always a personal favorite of his many books, and he recognized its importance within his entire output. Yet he seems never to have been entirely satisfied with the writing. From the early galleys to the final authorized version in *Christmas Books,* of the Charles Dickens Edition, published the year of his death, the writer was constantly revising the text. The numerous changes between manuscript and first printing, both little and big, demonstrate his struggle to get every word and every phrase just right. Many alterations are minor: punctuation and spelling corrections (he had a particular difficulty in putting "u" in "parlour," "honour," and "favour"); and toning down exclamations ("Good God" becomes "Good Heaven," "Lord bless me" merely "Bless me"). But often he greatly improved a passage; for example, the awkward "why do spirits come on earth, and only to me" in the manuscript became the more polished and dramatic "why do spirits walk the earth, and why do they come to me" in the finished book. The most radical remodeling

---

ens collector, for £300. It was from Samuel that J. Pierpont Morgan secured the manuscript for an undisclosed price. Before it left England, apparently for good, a facsimile was published in 1890 by Eliot Stock in London and Brentano's in New York. The Pierpont Library published its own edition in 1967 and again in 1993 with a new introduction by John Mortimer. See Frederic G. Kitton, "Some Famous Christmas Books," *The Library Review,* January 1893, pp. 707–8.

[74.] John Butt, *Pope, Dickens, and Others* (Edinburgh: Edinburgh University Press, 1969), p. 137.

"Want and Ignorance." Wood engraving
after Sol Eytinge Jr., *A Christmas Carol*, 1868.
Private collection.

of the text was done for his Public Readings, discussed in the introduction to the appendix.

Another common misapprehension is that Dickens was the most unliterary of men of letters. "In all his works," insisted George Stott in *Contemporary Review* (January 1869), "there is hardly a quotation or an illusion except occasionally from Shakespeare and the best known parts of the Bible" (pp 222–23). In even so brief a story as *A Christmas Carol,* Dickens refers to Irving, Wordsworth, Tennyson, Juvenal, *Joe Miller's Jest Book, Jack and the Giant-Killer, Robinson Crusoe, Valentine and Orson, The Arabian Nights,* in addition to Shakespeare and the Bible. There are numerous references to some now forgotten nineteenth-century phenomena, such as temperance and phrenology. Some of the Christmas customs are now obscure, surely to American readers. London has changed and the language has changed. All of these must be explained or there is no understanding of the subtlety of the puns, metaphors, analogies, and allusions.

Over a century and a half have passed since *A Christmas Carol* was first published, and there is no indication that the light in the torch carried by the Ghost of Christmas Present will ever go out. The message is as pertinent today as it was in the London of the 1840s. Many people still react to its philosophy with a good resounding "Bah! Humbug!" Scrooge can still be found everywhere. The new economic man works his way but with a different vengeance. The current utilitarian does not view the season as "a poor excuse for picking a man's pocket every twentieth-fifth of December." Instead, he rejoices in it, because its current commercialism pays homage to that other idol, Gain. Many people are known to solemnize it with an undoubted bargain . . . or two. Christmas has become the businessman's season, so dependant is the economy on its success or failure. It is now a vast phenomenon far beyond Dickens' wildest dreams. And he must take some of the blame for what it has become. The old Christmas spirit, apparent in a Salvation Army Santa or a poor caroler in the slush, still carries its torch, however feebly, to combat both Ignorance and Want. The secular sentiments of the season survive because of Dickens' *Carol.* Despite the intrepid machinations of industrialization, with its inevitable brutalities that cling to any progressive society, Christmas remains "a kind, forgiving, charitable, pleasant time . . . when men and women seem by one consent to open their shut-up hearts freely." For Dickens to have added even a little to this common good makes his contribution to the world of letters unique and enduring. As Thackeray advised, "God bless him!"

"He seized the extinguisher-cap, and by a sudden motion
pressed it down in its head." Wood engraving after
Gustave Doré, *Journal pour tous,* June 29, 1861.
Courtesy Library of Congress.

Charles Dickens. Portrait by Daniel Maclise, 1839.
Courtesy Free Library of Philadelphia.

The Annotated Christmas Carol

Mr. Fezziwig's Ball.

A CHRISTMAS CAROL

IN PROSE

A Ghost Story of Christmas

PREFACE.[1]

I have endeavoured in this Ghostly little book, to raise the Ghost of an Idea, which shall not put my readers out of humour with themselves, with each other, with the season, or with me. May it haunt their houses pleasantly, and no one wish to lay it.

Their faithful Friend and Servant,

C. D.

December, 1843.

1. *Preface.* Charles Dickens provided "a very short preface" for Chapman and Hall's Cheap Edition of his *Christmas Books* (1852), the first collection of all five volumes in one:

> I have included my little Christmas Books in this cheap edition, complying with a desire that has been repeatedly expressed to me, and hoping that they may prove generally acceptable in so accessible a form.
>
> The narrow space within which it was necessary to confine these Christmas Stories when they were originally published, rendered their construction a matter of some difficulty, and almost necessitated what is peculiar in their machinery. I never attempted great elaboration of detail in the working out of character within such limits, believing that it could not succeed. My purpose was, in a whimsical kind of masque, which the good-humour of the season justified, to awaken some loving and forbearing thoughts, never out of season in a Christian land. I have the happiness of believing that I did not wholly miss it.

He wrote the printer William Bradbury on September 9, 1852, that it was "short—because I really have nothing to say!" (*The Letters of Charles Dickens,* edited by Madeline House and others, 12 vols. [Oxford: Clarendon Press, 1965–2002], p. 758. Unless otherwise indicated, all subsequent citations of Dickens' and his family's correspondence are from this source and are given by date and page number only). He retained only the second paragraph in the definitive Charles Dickens Edition of 1868, as there was no need to refer to the earlier edition. (Dickens also supplied descriptive running heads for this edition, which have been added to the contents page of *The Annotated Christmas Carol*.) Except for the apparent slip of the pen in his 1852 preface, Dickens made a distinction between his five novella-length Christmas Books and the Christmas Stories (sometimes written in collaboration with Wilkie Collins) that appeared annually in his magazines, *Household Words* (1850–58) and *All the Year Round* (1859–67). *Christmas Stories* appeared in the Charles Dickens Edition of 1871.

A Christmas Carol.[1]

STAVE[2] ONE.

MARLEY'S GHOST.

Marley[3] was dead: to begin with. There is no doubt whatever about that. The register of his burial was signed by the clergyman, the clerk, the undertaker, and the chief mourner. Scrooge[4] signed it: and Scrooge's name was good upon 'Change,[5] for anything he chose to put his hand to. Old Marley was as dead as a door-nail.[6]

Mind! I don't mean to say that I know, of my own knowledge, what there is particularly dead about a door-nail.[7] I might have been inclined, myself, to regard a coffin-nail as the deadest piece of ironmongery in the trade. But the wisdom of our ancestors[8] is in the simile; and my unhallowed hands shall not disturb it, or the Country's done for. You will therefore permit me to repeat, emphatically, that Marley was as dead as a door-nail.

Scrooge knew he was dead? Of course he did. How could it be otherwise? Scrooge and he were partners for I don't know how many years. Scrooge was his sole executor, his sole administrator, his sole assign,[9] his sole residuary legatee,[10] his sole friend and sole mourner. And even Scrooge was not so dreadfully cut up by the sad event, but that he was an excellent man of business[11] on the very day of the funeral, and solemnised it with an undoubted bargain.

The mention of Marley's funeral brings me back to the point I started from. There is no doubt that Marley was dead.[12] This must be distinctly understood, or nothing wonderful can come of the story I am going to

1. *A Christmas Carol. The Critic* reported in January 1844 that since publication, this "title has occasioned much perplexity" (p. 62). The London *Morning Advertiser* (December 25, 1843) likewise complained in its review, "We scarcely consider the title of this pretty volume altogether a correct one." A carol is a song or ballad of joy celebrating the birth of Christ. Dickens wrote at least one Christmas carol in verse—that sung in Chapter 29 of *The Pickwick Papers* (1837); Henry Russell set it to music in 1838. While the title of Dickens' first Christmas Book may not be entirely accurate, the tone is perfect. "The story sings from end to end like a happy man going home," argued G. K. Chesterton in *Charles Dickens* (London: Methuen, 1906); "and, like a happy and good man, when it cannot sing it yells. It is lyric and exclamatory, from the first exclamatory words of it. It is strictly a Christmas Carol" (p. 170).

2. *Stave.* An archaic form of "staff," a stanza of a poem or song. Dickens here extended the pretense of his story being "a Christmas carol in prose" by calling its chapters verses. He maintained the conceit in the two subsequent Christmas Books by setting off their chapters in accordance with the stories' titles: *The Chimes* (1844) is divided into four "quarters," like the tolling of a clock, and the divisions of *The Cricket on the Hearth* (1845) are called "chirps."

3. *Marley.* According to "Marley Alive" in *The Dickensian* (summer 1938, p. 154), Dickens took the name of Scrooge's partner from Dr. Miles Marley, an Irishman who practiced medicine on Cork Street, Piccadilly. Dickens was a guest of his at a St. Patrick's Day party, and when the subject of the novelist's interest in unusual names came up, Dr. Marley mentioned that he thought his own surname quite remarkable. Dickens reportedly replied, "Your name shall be a household word before the year is out" (p. 154).

4. *Scrooge.* From the colloquial or vulgar word "scrooge": to crowd or squeeze. This meaning is apparent in the miser's being "a squeezing, wrenching, grasping, scraping, clutching, covetous old sinner!" Other variants of the word's spelling are scroodge, scrowdge, scrowge, skrouge; in Chapter 39 of *The Old Curiosity Shop* (1841), "Kit [at the theater] had hit a man on the head with the handkerchief of apples for 'skrowdging' his parent with unnecessary violence." See Stave 4, note 26.

So powerful is his introduction that "Scrooge" has entered the language as a synonym for "miser." "The character of the old miser we were, at the outset, disposed to consider extravagant," said the London *Sunday Times* (January 7, 1844); "but when we paused to recollect what has been revealed by the annals of real life, we perceive that Mr. Dickens's fancy had not done any outrage to nature, which has produced monsters quite as hardened, quite as griping and penurious as Mr. Scrooge. That a total change should be affected in the moral economy of such a person is, no doubt, somewhat improbable, but not by any means so improbable as to be past belief." *The Atlas* (December 23, 1843) admitted that Scrooge is "the type of thousands in England." They believed in what Thomas Carlyle called the "Gospel of Mammonism."

Success was now determined by how much wealth one accumulated. Hell, Carlyle lamented in Chapter 2 of *Past and Present* (1843), had become in nineteenth-century industrial England "the terror of 'Not succeeding'; of not making money, fame, or some other figure in the world—chiefly of not making money!" "This," said *The Atlas*, "is what the modern Englishman hates and fears—what he shrinks from with all his soul and with all his strength. . . . The true test of a social or political philosophy, after all, is not what riches or material wealth it tends to produce, but what sort of men." Thomas Hood may have been the first to use the name as an adjective when he wondered in his review of *A Christmas Carol* in *Hood's Magazine* (January 1844) "whether we have not grown *Scroogey?*" He worried that, like Scrooge's, "our own heads have not become more inaccessible, our hearts more impregnable, our ears and eyes more dull and blind, to sounds and sights of human misery" (p. 68).

5. *Scrooge's name was good upon 'Change.* Meaning that he was financially sound and his credit would be honored. 'Change is the Royal Exchange, the financial center of London, lying between Threadneedle Street and Cornhill; opposite, on the northwest, lies the Bank of England, and on the south-

New Royal Exchange,
The Illustrated London News, April 6, 1844.
Courtesy Library of Congress.

west the Mansion House. The inscription over the doorway reads, "The earth is the Lord's and the fullness thereof." The building burned down in 1838, and a new one was under construction at the time of the story. It was opened by Queen Victoria in 1845.

6. *Old Marley was as dead as a door-nail.* This popular simile is often credited to William Langland (c. 1330–c. 1400), who used it in *The Vision of Piers Plowman* (1362) as "ded as a dore-nayle"; but it may well be of an earlier date. F. H. Ahn in his notes to an 1871 edition of *A Christmas Carol* reported finding it in an ancient British ballad "St. George for England":

> But George he did the dragon kill,
> As dead as any door-nail. (p. 143)

Dickens, however, likely knew the expression from Shakespeare, in *2 Henry IV* 5.3.111–12 and *2 Henry VI* 4.9.37.

The phrase may have come to Dickens in a dream just two months before he began *A Christmas Carol*. "Apropos of dreams," he wrote his American friend C. C. Felton on September 1, 1843, "is it not a strange thing if writers of fiction never dream of their own creations: recollecting I suppose, even in their dreams, that they have no real existence? *I* never dreamed of any of my own characters. . . . I had a good piece of absurdity in my head a night or two ago. I dreamed that somebody was dead. I don't know whom, but it's not to the purpose. It was a private gentleman and a particular friend; and I was greatly overcome when the news was broken to me (very delicately) by a gentleman in a cocked hat, top boots, and a sheet. Nothing else. 'Good God,' I said. 'Is he dead!' 'He is as dead, Sir,' rejoined the gentleman, 'as a door-nail . . . ' " (p. 550).

7. *I don't mean to say that I know . . . what there is particularly dead about a door-nail.* Shakespearean scholar George Steevens

explained in a note to *Second Part of Henry IV*, in *The Plays and Poems of William Shakespeare*, edited by Edmond Malone (vol. 17, London: R. C. and J. Rivington, 1821), a book Dickens owned, "This proverbial expression is oftener used than understood. The *door nail* is the *nail* on which in ancient *doors* the knocker strikes. It is therefore used as a comparison to any one irrecoverably dead, one who has fallen (as Virgil says) *multâ morte*, i.e. with abundant death, such as reiteration of strokes on the head would naturally produce" (p. 225). "I was perfectly aware of Steevens's note in reference to the door-nail," Dickens admitted to a reader in a letter of March 25, 1844. "My meaning in observing gaily, in the *Carol*, that I don't know what there is particularly dead about a door-nail, is, that I don't know why a door-nail is more dead (if I may use the expression) than anything else that never had life" (pp. 84–85).

8. *the wisdom of our ancestors.* Sarcastic reference to a cant political phrase, said to originate with the conservative Irish philosopher and statesman Edmund Burke (1729–1797). In his famous "Speech on Conciliation with the American Colonies," delivered in the House of Commons on March 22, 1775, Burke admitted to "a profound reverence for the wisdom of our ancestors, who have left us the inheritance of so happy a Constitution and so flourishing an empire, and, what is a thousand times more valuable, the treasury of the maxims and principles which formed the one and obtained the other." Dickens and other nineteenth-century reformers thought otherwise. Dickens further expressed his contempt for this phrase by installing in his library at Gad's Hill a series of dummy book backs under the title *The Wisdom of Our Ancestors*, comprising *Ignorance, Superstition, The Block, The Stake, The Rack, Dirt,* and *Disease*.

9. *assign.* Or assignee, one to whom the property and affairs of the deceased are transferred. Scrooge, being Marley's sole partner and sole friend, inherited the whole of the estate. Dickens was well acquainted with these legal terms after having been apprenticed to the law firm of Ellis and Blackmore in 1827–28.

10. *residuary legatee.* One to whom the remainder of an estate after payment of debts and charges is bequeathed.

11. *an excellent man of business.* G. E. Stembridge in "What Was Scrooge's Business?" (*The Dickensian,* April 1924) reported that Scrooge was a "financier," "something in the nature of a company promoter or a moneylender" (p. 100). Scrooge thus does not provide any actual services or goods; he deals solely in the exchange of money.

12. *There is no doubt that Marley was dead.* "I think we get the idea," groused American novelist John Irving in his introduction to the 1995 Modern Library edition of *A Christmas Carol and Other Stories* of the four times Dickens states in the first four paragraphs that Marley is dead. "An editor of today's less-is-more school of fiction would doubtless have found this repetitious, but Dickens never suffered a minimalist's sensibilities; in Dickens's prose, the refrain is as common as the semicolon."

relate. If we were not perfectly convinced that Hamlet's Father[13] died before the play began, there would be nothing more remarkable in his taking a stroll at night, in an easterly wind, upon his own ramparts, than there would be in any other middle-aged gentleman rashly turning out after dark in a breezy spot—say Saint Paul's Churchyard[14] for instance—literally to astonish his son's weak mind.[15]

Scrooge never painted out Old Marley's name. There it stood, years afterwards, above the warehouse door: Scrooge and Marley. The firm was known as Scrooge and Marley. Sometimes people new to the business called Scrooge Scrooge, and sometimes Marley, but he answered to both names. It was all the same to him.[16]

Oh! But he was a tight-fisted hand at the grindstone, Scrooge![17] a squeezing, wrenching, grasping, scraping, clutching, covetous old sinner! Hard and sharp as flint, from which no steel had ever struck out generous fire; secret, and self-contained, and solitary as an oyster. The cold within him froze his old features, nipped his pointed nose, shrivelled his cheek, stiffened his gait; made his eyes red, his thin lips blue; and spoke out shrewdly in his grating voice. A frosty rime[18] was on his head, and on his eyebrows, and his wiry chin. He carried his own low temperature always about with him; he iced his office in the dog-days;[19] and didn't thaw it one degree at Christmas.

External heat and cold had little influence on Scrooge. No warmth could warm, nor wintry weather chill him.[20] No wind that blew was bitterer than he, no falling snow was more intent upon its purpose, no pelting rain less open to entreaty. Foul weather didn't know where to have him.[21] The heaviest rain, and snow, and hail, and sleet, could boast of the advantage over him in only one respect. They often "came down"[22] handsomely, and Scrooge never did.

Nobody ever stopped him in the street to say, with gladsome looks, "My dear Scrooge, how are you? when

13. *Hamlet's Father.* To foreshadow the coming of Marley's Ghost, Dickens alludes to the most famous ghost in English literature. Reference to this spirit is especially appropriate here, because on the disappearance of the ghost of Hamlet's father, the officer Marcellus reflects on a Christmas legend:

> It faded on the crowing of a cock.
> Some say that ever 'gainst that season comes
> Wherein our saviour's birth is celebrated
> The bird of dawning singeth all night long;
> And then, they say, no spirit can walk abroad. (1.1.138–42).

This "legend" may have been entirely Shakespeare's invention.

14. *Saint Paul's Churchyard.* An irregular street encircling St. Paul's Cathedral and burial ground in the heart of London. "The actual graveyard has long since been closed up," noted F. H. Ahn in his 1871 edition. "The narrowness of the way here, and the many small outlets into Paternoster Row, render it a place peculiarly susceptible to draft" (p. 144). It is eminently appropriate that Dickens should mention this breezy area, for it was once chiefly inhabited by booksellers who were the first to publish *Hamlet* and Shakespeare's other plays.

15. *his son's weak mind.* In the manuscript (now in the Pierpont Morgan Library), Dickens digressed from the narrative in discussing Hamlet's character: " . . . although perhaps you think that Hamlet's intellects were strong, I doubt it. If you could have such a son tomorrow, depend upon it, you would find him a poser. He would be a most impracticable fellow to deal with; and however creditable he might be to the family after his decease, he would prove a special encumbrance in his lifetime, trust me."

Dickens wisely crossed out this amusing but distracting passage before the story went to the printers.

16. *he answered to both names. It was all the same to him.* Dr. Zelda Teplitz in her paper "*The Christmas Carol* in Relation to Dickens," delivered at the American Psychoanalytical Association, in New York, on December 13, 1974, pointed to several curious correspondences within this double image of Scrooge and Marley. Dr. Teplitz argued that the relationship between the

"Old Scrooge sat busy in his counting-house." Wood engraving after Gustave Doré, *Journal pour tous*, June 16, 1861.
Courtesy Library of Congress.

living and dead partners was reminiscent of that between Dickens' two sisters-in-law, Georgina Hogarth, who joined his household in 1842, and Mary, who died in 1837. "I trace in many respects a strong resemblance between her [Mary's] mental features and Georgina's," Dickens wrote his mother-in law on May 8, 1843, "so strange a one, at times, that when she [Georgina] and Kate [his wife] and I are sitting together, I seem to think that what has happened is a melancholy dream from which I am just awakening. The perfect like of what she was, will never be again, but so much of her spirit shines out in this sister, that the old time comes back again at some seasons, and I can hardly separate it from the present" (p. 483). Likewise, Scrooge and Marley are so similar that the latter's ghost returns to the other miser at the Christmas season in a vision, Scrooge's melancholy dream. Dickens developed the double as "the living man, and the animated image of himself dead" in *The Haunted Man* (1848), in which the chemist Redlaw, like Scrooge, is redeemed by the visitation of a ghost—not that of a dead partner, but a replica of himself.

17. *Scrooge!* Dickens drew the miser's character in part from that of Gabriel Grub, the melancholy grave digger in "The Story of the Goblins Who Stole a Sexton," in Chapter 29 of *The Pickwick Papers* (1837): "an ill-conditioned, cross-grained, surly fellow—a morose and lonely man, who consorted with nobody but himself . . . and who eyed each merry face as it passed him by, with such a deep scowl of malice and ill-humor, as it was difficult to meet without feeling something the worse for."

The change from sexton to miser may have been suggested to Dickens by an actual carol, "Old Christmas Returned, or Hospitality Revived," included in William Sandys' collection *A Selection of Christmas Carols, Ancient and Modern* (London: Richard Beckley, 1833). It is described as "being a Looking-glass for rich Misers, wherein they may see (if they be not blind) how much they are to blame for their penurious house-keeping, and likewise an encouragement to those gentry, who lay out a great part of their estates, in hospitality, relieving such persons as have need thereof." The song includes the maxim:

> Who feasts the poor, a true reward shall find,
> Or helps the old, the feeble, lame, and blind. (p. 53)

And Scrooge does just that and more when he reforms.

18. *A frosty rime.* Dickens is being redundant: rime is hoarfrost, or frozen mist; this refers to Scrooge's grayness as well as to his cold spirit.

19. *the dog-days.* July 3 to August 11, often the hottest days of the year, when the Dog Star, Sirius, rises and sets with the sun and adds its heat to the weather. Popular belief says that dogs often go mad at this season, called by the Romans "caniculare dies."

20. *nor wintry weather chill him.* Dickens changed this phrase to "no cold could chill him" in the 1867 Ticknor and Fields Public Reading edition, as a stronger echo of "no warmth could warm."

21. *didn't know where to have him.* Didn't know how to get at him, how to affect him; as in *1 Henry IV* 3.3.115–16: "Why? She's neither fish nor flesh; a man knows not where to have her."

22. *"came down."* A pun: to come down as applied to the weather is to fall freely, but in its slang sense it means to be liberal with money or to make a generous contribution. Americans too got the joke: the Buffalo *Commercial Advertiser* (March 13, 1868), on reviewing Dickens' reading of *A Christmas Carol*, reported that "when the reader, with his peculiar look and intonation repeated the sentence declaring that the snow and sleet often 'came down' handsomely, and that Scrooge never did, the applause broke forth from all parts of the house."

23. *what it was o'clock.* Colloquial, what time it was.

24. *an evil eye.* "An eye which charms," explained James Orchard Halliwell-Phillipps in *A Dictionary of Archaic and Provincial Words* (1847). "Superstitious people suppose that the first morning glance of him who has an evil eye is certain destruction to man or beast, if not immediate, at least eventually." The supernatural power to cause great harm with a glance is a superstition known to all peoples from ancient times to the present. Romans passed laws against it; witches have been accused throughout history for blighting crops, causing storms, and even killing with just a stare. The person possessing this power is not necessarily evil; one cannot always control it and should be pitied more than persecuted for this dangerous affliction. Dickens attaches a moral significance to this power in Stave 2: "There was an eager, greedy, restless motion in the eye, which showed the passion [Gain] that had taken root, and where the shadow of the growing tree would fall."

25. *"nuts."* This current interjection of disdain meant in its original sense agreeable or gratifying, here used as "good luck."

26. *old Scrooge.* Although Dickens never specifies how old the miser is, Charles Webb suggested in his 1844 play *A Christmas Carol; or, The Past, Present, and Future* that Scrooge is fifty-seven years old, hardly ancient by today's standards but a good age in that day.

27. *his counting-house.* Business office for carrying out correspondence and keeping accounts. In "A Visit to Newgate," in *Sketches by Boz* (1839), Dickens gave the usual fixtures of a merchant's counting-house as "a wainscotted partition, a shelf

will you come to see me?" No beggars implored him to bestow a trifle, no children asked him what it was o'clock,[23] no man or woman ever once in all his life inquired the way to such and such a place, of Scrooge. Even the blindmen's dogs appeared to know him; and when they saw him coming on, would tug their owners into doorways and up courts; and then would wag their tails as though they said, "no eye at all is better than an evil eye,[24] dark master!"

But what did Scrooge care! It was the very thing he liked. To edge his way along the crowded paths of life, warning all human sympathy to keep its distance, was what the knowing ones call "nuts"[25] to Scrooge.

Once upon a time—of all the good days in the year, on Christmas Eve—old Scrooge[26] sat busy in his counting-house.[27] It was cold, bleak, biting weather: foggy withal: and he could hear the people in the court outside go wheezing up and down, beating their hands upon their breasts, and stamping their feet upon the pavement-stones to warm them. The city clocks had only just gone three, but it was quite dark already: it had not been light all day: and candles were flaring in the windows of the neighbouring offices, like ruddy smears upon the palpable brown air. The fog came pouring in at every chink and keyhole,[28] and was so dense without, that although the court was of the narrowest, the houses opposite were mere phantoms. To see the dingy cloud come drooping down, obscuring everything, one might have thought that Nature lived hard by, and was brewing on a large scale.

The door of Scrooge's counting-house was open that he might keep his eye upon his clerk,[29] who in a dismal little cell beyond, a sort of tank, was copying letters. Scrooge had a very small fire, but the clerk's fire was so very much smaller that it looked like one coal. But he couldn't replenish it, for Scrooge kept the coal-box in his own room; and so surely as the clerk came in with the shovel, the master predicted that it would be necessary for them to part. Wherefore the

or two, a desk, a couple of stools, a pair of clerks, an almanack, a clock, and a few maps." They are generally dreary places in Dickens' works, as in Chapter 5 of *The Old Curiosity Shop* (1841), Chapter 10 of *Bleak House* (1853), Chapter 22 of *Great Expectations* (1861), and Book 2, Chapter 5, of *Our Mutual Friend* (1865). Only the Cheeryble Brothers' countinghouse, run by Timothy Linkinwater in Chapter 37 of *Nicholas Nickleby* (1839), is a model of efficiency and comfort.

For his play *A Christmas Carol; or, The Past, Present, and Future,* produced in London in 1844, Charles Webb located Scrooge's place of business in Tokenhouse Yard, Cornhill, not far from the London Exchange. Edwin Chancellor Beresford in *The London of Charles Dickens* (London: Grant Richards, 1924) thought that Scrooge's business was either "in Cross Lane, leading out of St. Dunstan's Hill, on the east side, or Idol Lane" (p. 280). But Gwen Major suggested in "Scrooge's Chambers" (*The Dickensian*, winter 1932–33, p. 11) that his office was in St. Michael's Alley, a financial center in the same area since the mid-seventeenth century.

28. *The fog came pouring in at every chink and keyhole.* The New York correspondent to the Boston *Bay City Democrat* (January 31, 1844) challenged Dickens on the meteor-

"Sees-unable Weather" by George Cruikshank, *The Comic Almanac*, 1841.
Courtesy Library of Congress.

ological soundness of his representation of the London weather: "In the commencement of the book he describes the city as being shrouded in a dense fog, which streamed through the keyhole of Scrooge's office, *while the thermometer was at zero!* In our country, vapor vanishes at the approach of frost. But perhaps a London fog may be less easily 'scared up.'"

29. *clerk.* Pronounced "clark." Bob Cratchit (whose name is not revealed until Stave 3) is one of those good-natured middle-aged men, described by Dickens in "The Streets—Morning" (*Sketches by Boz*, 1839), "whose salaries have by no means increased in the same proportion as their families," and who "plod steadily along, apparently with no object in view but the counting-house; knowing by sight almost every body they meet or overtake, for they have seen them every morning (Sundays excepted) during the last twenty years, but speaking to no one. If they do happen to overtake a personal acquaintance, they just exchange a hurried salutation, and keep walking on, either by his side, or in front of him, as his rate of walking may chance to be. As to stopping to shake hands, or to take a friend's arm, they seem to think that as it is not included in their salary, they have no right to do it." The writer's father, John Dickens (1785–1851), was a clerk in the Navy Pay Office and shared some characteristics with not only Wilkins Micawber of *David Copperfield* (1850) but Bob Cratchit as well.

In Chapter 31 of *The Pickwick Papers* (1837), Dickens describes the various ranks of clerks in a legal firm: " . . . the Articled Clerk, who has paid a premium, and is an attorney in perspective, who runs a tailor's bill, receives invitations to parties, knows a family in Gower Street, and another in Tavistock Square: who goes out of town every Long Vacation to see his father, who keeps live horses innumerable; and who is, in short, the very aristocrat of clerks . . . the salaried clerk—out of door, or in door, as the case may be—who devotes the major part of his thirty shillings a week to his personal pleasure and adornment, repairs half-price to the Adelphi Theatre at least three times a week, dissipates majestically at the cider cellars afterwards, and is a dirty caricature of the fashion, which expired six months ago." Bob Cratchit's position at Scrooge and Marley is similar to that of "the middle-aged copying clerk, with a large family, who is always shabby and often drunk." (The latter detail does not apply here.) These men were little more than scriveners who made multiple copies of documents, so their jobs were precarious. Dickens himself, when employed at the age of fifteen by Ellis and Blackmore, solicitors, was one of "the office lads in their first surtouts, who feel a befitting contempt for boys at day-schools, club as they go home at night, for saveloys [sausages] and porter: and think there's nothing like 'life.' "

30. *A merry Christmas, uncle!* Compare the arrival of the nephew with that of the young man's mother Fan in Stave 2; each tries to cheer up Scrooge in honor of the holiday.

31. *God save you!* Oddly, this statement as well as perhaps the most famous line in the story, "God bless us every one!" could not be spoken on the London stage at the time. Up until 1968, every script had to be submitted to the Lord Chamberlain's examiner of plays, who decided whether or not it could be publicly performed. This censor had to check for indecency, impropriety, blasphemy, libel, and sedition. However, it was perfectly fine to say "Heaven save you!" in the London theater in 1844.

32. *this nephew of Scrooge's.* Charles Kent, who managed the 1867–68 Public Reading

clerk put on his white comforter, and tried to warm himself at the candle; in which effort, not being a man of a strong imagination, he failed.

"A merry Christmas, uncle![30] God save you!"[31] cried a cheerful voice. It was the voice of Scrooge's nephew, who came upon him so quickly that this was the first intimation he had of his approach.

"Bah!" said Scrooge, "Humbug!"

He had so heated himself with rapid walking in the fog and frost, this nephew of Scrooge's,[32] that he was all in a glow; his face was ruddy and handsome; his eyes sparkled, and his breath smoked again.

"Christmas a humbug, uncle!" said Scrooge's nephew. "You don't mean that, I am sure."

"I do," said Scrooge. "Merry Christmas! what right have you to be merry? what reason have you to be merry? You're poor enough."

"Come, then," returned the nephew gaily. "What right have you to be dismal? what reason have you to be morose? You're rich enough."

Scrooge having no better answer ready on the spur of the moment, said, "Bah!" again; and followed it up with "Humbug."

"Don't be cross, uncle," said the nephew.

"What else can I be" returned the uncle, "when I live in such a world of fools as this? Merry Christmas! Out upon merry Christmas! What's Christmas time to you but a time for paying bills without money; a time for finding yourself a year older, and not an hour richer; a time for balancing your books and having every item in 'em through a round dozen of months presented dead against you? If I could work my will," said Scrooge, indignantly, "every idiot who goes about with 'Merry Christmas,' on his lips, should be boiled with his own pudding, and buried with a stake of holly through his heart.[33] He should!"[34]

"Uncle!" pleaded the nephew.

"Nephew!" returned the uncle, sternly, "keep Christmas in your own way, and let me keep it in mine."

tour, insisted in *Charles Dickens as a Reader* (London: Chapman and Hall, 1872) that to "anyone who ever had the happiness of grasping Charles Dickens's hand in friendship," this "description of Scrooge's Nephew was, quite unconsciously but most accurately, in every word of it, a literal description of himself, just as he looked upon any day in the blithest of all seasons, after a brisk walk in the wintry streets or on the snowy high road. . . . The Novelist himself was depicted there to a nicety" (p. 99).

33. *buried with a stake of holly through his heart.* Like Quilp in the last chapter of *The Old Curiosity Shop* (1841), who, once he is declared a suicide, "was left to be buried with a stake through his heart in the centre of four lonely roads." Carol L. Bernhardt explained in her notes to the 1922 Loyola University Press edition of *A Christmas Carol* that this was a custom in medieval times in disposing of a murderer. The practise was discontinued after 1623. This procedure is perhaps better known as a way of quelling a vampire. Evidently Scrooge views anyone who would waste good money on celebrating Christmas no better than a murderer or at least a bloodsucking vampire.

34. *He should!* "I'm sick of Christmas!" Scrooge added in the manuscript; but recognizing that that was a bit much, Dickens deleted it before the text went to the printers.

35. *fellow-passengers.* Changed to "fellow-travellers" in the 1867 Ticknor and Fields Public Reading edition of *A Christmas Carol.* That word served an important part in *Little Dorrit* (1857), the novel that Dickens completed just prior to his reworking of *A Christmas Carol* for his 1858 reading tour. Dickens employs the metaphor of man as a blind tourist traveling through life as an important theme in that story; life is seen as a journey, with every person either a brother or sister to every other human being, every one of whom should think, as Scrooge's nephew does, that those below one "really were fellow-passengers to the grave, and not another race of creatures bound on other journeys," each one affecting every other life, on this path toward death. He called both the second chapter of Book 1 and the first chapter of Book 2 of *Little Dorrit* "Fellow Travellers," explaining to John Forster in a letter on August 19, 1855, that he wanted to show "people coming together, in a chance way . . . being in the same place, ignorant of one another, as happens in life" (pp. 692–93). "And thus ever," he concluded Chapter 2 of Book 1, "by day and by night, under the sun and under the stars, climbing the dusty hills and toiling along the weary plains, journeying by land, and journeying by sea, coming and going so strangely, to meet and to act and react on one another, move all we restless travellers through the pilgrimage of life."

36. *he would see him.* He would see him damned or in Hell first; as in "Plague on't, an I thought he had been valiant and so cunning in fence I'd have seen him damned ere I'd have challenged him" (*Twelfth Night* 3.4.252–54). Of course, the full expression could not be uttered on the London stage the year *A Christmas Carol* came out: O. Smith as Scrooge at the Adelphi said, "I'll see you—hem! first!"; George Bennett at the

"Keep it!" repeated Scrooge's nephew. "But you don't keep it."

"Let me leave it alone, then," said Scrooge. "Much good may it do you! Much good it has ever done you!"

"There are many things from which I might have derived good, by which I have not profited, I dare say," returned the nephew: "Christmas among the rest. But I am sure I have always thought of Christmas time, when it has come round—apart from the veneration due to its sacred name and origin, if anything belonging to it can be apart from that—as a good time: a kind, forgiving, charitable, pleasant time: the only time I know of, in the long calendar of the year, when men and women seem by one consent to open their shut-up hearts freely, and to think of people below them as if they really were fellow-passengers[35] to the grave, and not another race of creatures bound on other journeys. And therefore, uncle, though it has never put a scrap of gold or silver in my pocket, I believe that it *has* done me good, and *will* do me good; and I say, God bless it!"

The clerk in the tank involuntarily applauded: becoming immediately sensible of the impropriety, he poked the fire, and extinguished the last frail spark for ever.

"Let me hear another sound from *you*" said Scrooge, "and you'll keep your Christmas by losing your situation. You're quite a powerful speaker, sir," he added, turning to his nephew. "I wonder you don't go into Parliament."

"Don't be angry, uncle. Come! Dine with us to-morrow."

Scrooge said that he would see him[36]—yes, indeed he did. He went the whole length of the expression, and said that he would see him in that extremity first.

"But why?" cried Scrooge's nephew. "Why?"

"Why did you get married?"[37] said Scrooge.

"Because I fell in love."

"Because you fell in love!" growled Scrooge, as if

Strand and Henry Marston at Sadler's Wells exclaimed, "I'll see you hanged first!" while R. Honner replied merely, "No, no—" at the Royal Theatre Surrey. By the time Dickens returned to America, censorship had gotten somewhat more liberal on the use of profanity on the stage, but not everyone approved this change. "If any pieces deserve to be 'damned,' as the profane-phrase goes, it is those in which the base word 'damn,' occurs so often," scolded the *Boston Post* (December 2, 1867). "It appears to be a favorite with many authors, and actors multiply its use with reckless looseness. It is an insult to an audience, and is in the worse possible taste."

Dickens himself was not afraid to use the full expression at times. The Washington, D.C., *Evening Star* reported on February 4, 1868, that on the night before, Dickens grew "exceedingly wrathful behind the scenes" when the gas lights could not be adjusted properly for his opening reading of *A Christmas Carol* at Carroll Hall, and he refused to perform under such conditions. When his business manager George Dolby tried to get him to reconsider and suggested he "make the best of it," "Mr. Dickens, in the language of his own Scrooge, said to Mr. Dolby that he would see him—, yes indeed he did. He went the whole length of the expression and said that he would see him in that extremity first." Dickens finally relented and went on exactly as scheduled.

37. *"Why did you get married?"* Scrooge agrees with contemporary English econo-mists who did not approve of anyone's marrying until one had sufficient income to support a family. To wed for love was sentimental nonsense; as revealed in Stave 2, Scrooge himself agrees to break his engagement to a dowerless girl because it disagrees with his financial ambitions. Obviously, the miser expected his nephew to follow his example. "Early marriages are the surest prelude among the lower orders to early deaths," insisted *The Union Magazine* (February 1846) in "Charles Dickens's Christmas Books." "The bursting swarms of the courts, alleys, and cellars, wherever a labouring population abounds and labour is scarce, receive their manifold increase from no cause more signally than from the rash precipitancy of marrying" (p. 233). Dickens, of course, had no sympathy for such utilitarian theories of marriage.

Dickens explored the theme further in the First Quarter of *The Chimes* (1844): Mr. Filer, a political economist, complains in regard to young couples that there is "no more hope to persuade 'em that they have no right or business to be married." Critics of the second Christmas Book tended to agree with Mr. Filer and accused Dickens of irresponsibly encouraging poor people to marry. They agreed with Alderman Cute's absurd prediction, "You'll have children—boys. Those boys will grow up bad of course, and run wild in the streets without shoes and stockings. . . . Perhaps your husband will die young, (most likely,) and leave you with a baby. Then you'll be turned out of doors, and wander up and down the streets."

38. *fifteen shillings a-week.* This was not a terrible wage at the time for single, salaried workers; laborers were generally paid eight shillings a week. Dickens himself, at age sixteen, got fifteen shillings weekly in the last three months of his employment as office boy at Ellis and Blackmore, solicitors, in 1828. (See William J. Carlton, "Mr. Blackmore Engages an Office Boy," *The Dickensian,* September 1952, p. 164.) However, fifteen shillings a week was far too little for a married man with a large family to support.

39. *Bedlam.* A corruption of "Bethlehem," the most famous of all lunatic asylums and consequently a synonym for "madhouse." It was originally the Hospital of St. Mary of Bethlehem in London; founded as a priory in 1247, it was first used to house the insane as early as 1402. In 1547, after Henry VIII dissolved church property, it was incorporated as a royal foundation as a madhouse; it was relocated in St. George's Fields, Lambeth, in 1814. "Bedlam" was used as far back as the sixteenth century, as in *2 Henry VI,* 5.1.129: "To Bedlam with him! Is the man grown mad?"

40. *two other people.* Edward Stirling in his 1844 play *A Christmas Carol; or, Past, Present, and Future* identified these gentlemen as overseers and churchwardens with petitions for the poor.

41. *seven years.* Originally Dickens had Marley die "ten years ago, this very day," but halfway through the story he decided on the far more effective "seven years, this very night." Traditionally the number seven has extraordinary magical powers. Note that the name "Scrooge" contains seven letters, a number said to be fatal to men. Coincidentally, it was exactly seven years before that Dickens wrote his last Christmas Story, "The Story of the Goblins Who Stole a Sex-

that were the only one thing in the world more ridiculous than a merry Christmas. "Good afternoon!"

"Nay, uncle, but you never came to see me before that happened. Why give it as a reason for not coming now?"

"Good afternoon," said Scrooge.

"I want nothing from you; I ask nothing of you; why cannot we be friends?"

"Good afternoon," said Scrooge.

"I am sorry, with all my heart, to find you so resolute. We have never had any quarrel, to which I have been a party. But I have made the trial in homage to Christmas, and I'll keep my Christmas humour to the last. So A Merry Christmas, uncle!"

"Good afternoon!" said Scrooge.

"And A Happy New Year!"

"Good afternoon!" said Scrooge.

His nephew left the room without an angry word, notwithstanding. He stopped at the outer door to bestow the greetings of the season on the clerk, who, cold as he was, was warmer than Scrooge; for he returned them cordially.

"There's another fellow," muttered Scrooge; who overheard him: "my clerk, with fifteen shillings a-week,[38] and a wife and family, talking about a merry Christmas. I'll retire to Bedlam."[39]

This lunatic, in letting Scrooge's nephew out, had let two other people[40] in. They were portly gentlemen, pleasant to behold, and now stood, with their hats off, in Scrooge's office. They had books and papers in their hands, and bowed to him.

"Scrooge and Marley's, I believe," said one of the gentlemen, referring to his list. "Have I the pleasure of addressing Mr. Scrooge, or Mr. Marley?"

"Mr. Marley has been dead these seven years,"[41] Scrooge replied. "He died seven years ago, this very night."

"We have no doubt his liberality is well represented by his surviving partner," said the gentleman, presenting his credentials.

It certainly was; for they had been two kindred spirits. At the ominous word "liberality," Scrooge frowned, and shook his head, and handed the credentials back.

"At this festive season of the year,[42] Mr. Scrooge," said the gentleman, taking up a pen, "it is more than usually desirable that we should make some slight provision for the Poor and destitute, who suffer greatly at the present time. Many thousands are in want of common necessaries; hundreds of thousands are in want of common comforts, sir."

"Are there no prisons?"[43] asked Scrooge.

"Plenty of prisons," said the gentleman, laying down the pen again.

"And the Union workhouses?"[44] demanded Scrooge. "Are they still in operation?"

"They are. Still," returned the gentleman, "I wish I could say they were not."

"The Treadmill[45] and the Poor Law are in full vigour, then?" said Scrooge.

"Both very busy, sir."

"Oh! I was afraid, from what you said at first, that something had occurred to stop them in their useful course," said Scrooge. "I'm very glad to hear it."

"Under the impression that they scarcely furnish Christian cheer of mind or body[46] to the multitude,"[47] returned the gentleman, "a few of us are endeavouring to raise a fund to buy the Poor some meat and drink, and means of warmth. We choose this time, because it is a time, of all others, when Want is keenly felt, and Abundance rejoices. What shall I put you down for?"

"Nothing!" Scrooge replied.

"You wish to be anonymous?"

"I wish to be left alone," said Scrooge. "Since you ask me what I wish, gentlemen, that is my answer.[48] I don't make merry myself at Christmas, and I can't afford to make idle people merry. I help to support the establishments I have mentioned: they cost enough: and those who are badly off must go there."

"Many can't go there; and many would rather die."[49]

ton," serialized as part of *The Pickwick Papers* in December 1836. Dr. Teplitz in her paper (cited in note 16, above) pointed to other events in the author's life of seven years before that seemed to correspond to the composition of *A Christmas Carol*. She also noted that the number seven is mentioned exactly seven times in reference to Marley's death in the book.

42. *At this festive season of the year.* This portly gentleman speaks in the philanthropic rhetoric of the time. He could easily have written the report "Celebration of Christmas-Day in the Metropolitan Workhouses" that appeared in the London *Morning Advertiser* (December 23, 1843):

> At this season of the year, when the mind of the Christian is cheered and chastened by the recollection of the sacred occasion of which the joyousness of the period is commemorative, a detailed account of the good fare afforded to our poorer brethren, on the anniversary of the nativity of Him who, while on this earth, so beautifully pointed out our duty to the poor, cannot but be gratifying to all who feel an interest in the treatment of the halt, the aged, the helpless, and the blind. The publication, at such a season, of these details, serves as an annual acknowledgement of the claims of the poor to our sympathies, while it reminds us of the duties we owe to those whose comforts we are perhaps too prone to forget.

They did not expect too much from their subscribers. "And oh! how little is required to throw the sunshine of happiness around some miserable abode," wrote Thomas Miller in *A Holiday Book for Christmas and the New Year* (London: Ingram, Cook, 1852); "and to know that, instead of a sorrowful group, huddling around the all but fireless grate, the little pudding is boiling in the pot, and the small joint turning on its worsted jack, from the fork stuck into the mantlepiece above the fire—that there is a happy light dancing in the children's eyes— a clapping of little hands every time the saucepan lid is uplifted—and that five paltry shillings purchased all this happiness" (p. 19). Five paltry shillings was the cost of *A Christmas Carol*.

43. *"Are there no prisons?"* Scrooge's callous response to providing additional charity rephrases the sarcastic retort in Chapter 6 of Thomas Carlyle's *Chartism* (1840): "Do we not pass what Acts of Parliament are needful; as many as thirty-nine for the shooting of partridges alone? Are there not treadmills, gibbets; even hospitals, poorrates, New-Poor Laws? So answers . . . Aristocracy, astonishment in every feature."

44. *the Union workhouses?* Oliver Twist (1838) opens with the remark that among public buildings in England at the time, there was one "common to most towns, great or small, to wit, a workhouse." The story begins with the birth of Oliver Twist in one of these shameful institutions. The Poor Law Amendment Act of 1834, or New Poor Law, created unions through the consolidation of parishes (several parishes were consolidated to form each union), each of which had its own workhouse, run by its own board of directors. The public hoped that this legislation might reduce the cost of looking after the poor, keep beggars off the street, and force the destitute to work hard for their charity. The able-bodied were worked in penury, and their dependents were kept in the house, where as little as possible was spent on food, clothing, and shelter. They were little more than prisons characterized by strict discipline; the poor were punished simply for being poor. It was considered a disgrace to go to such a place.

The London *Times* and other newspapers carried regular reports of abuses in the workhouses, and Dickens was one of their most vocal critics. "I believe there has been in England, since the days of the Stuarts," he wrote in a postscript to *Our Mutual Friend* (1865), "no law so often infamously administered, no law so often so openly violated, no law habitually so ill-supervised. In the majority of the shameful cases of disease and death from destitution, that shock the Public and disgrace the country, the illegality is quite equal to the inhumanity— and known language could say no more of their lawlessness." Not until 1871 was the law more humanely administered through the establishment of local Boards of Guardians and Guardians' Committees. Modern social welfare finally replaced the law in the 1940s.

45. *The Treadmill.* A mill operated by persons walking on steps fastened to the circumference of a great and wide horizontal wheel. This form of criminal punishment was introduced as hard labor in 1817, at Brixton Prison. Dickens, in the last chapter of *The Old Curiosity Shop* (1841), spoke sarcastically of how it was required of a prisoner "that he should partake their exercise of constantly ascending an endless flight of stairs, and lest his legs, unused to such exertion, should be weakened by it, that he should wear upon on ankle an amulet or charm of iron." Jane Carlyle noted that "a person in a tread-mill . . . must move forward or be crushed to death!" (*Jane Welsh Carlyle: Letters to Her Family,* edited by Leonard Huxley [London: John Murray, 1924], p. 171). It remained in operation until 1898.

46. *they scarcely furnish Christian cheer of mind or body.* Typical Christmas dinner provided by these institutions was that described by the London *Morning Advertiser* (December 23, 1843) as supplied to the 2,130 inmates of St. Marleybone Workhouse: "Half a pound of roast beef (free from bone), 1lb. of potatoes, 1lb. of plum-pudding, with 1oz. of tea, 4oz. of sugar, together with tobacco, snuff, etc. in the evening to those who make choice of it. The children allowed the same fare, at discretion, with fruit and sweetmeats in the evening." According to the London *Times* (December 27, 1843), the Refuge for the Destitute, Playhouse Yard, Whitecross Street, supplied its inmates with plum cake in addition to the usual bread and cheese on Christmas Day; and Whitbread and Company, brewers, donated a hogshead of beer. Many others received less for the holidays.

47. *multitude.* "Unoffending multitude" in the 1867 Ticknor and Fields Public Reading edition, perhaps to distinguish them from the undeserving poor.

48. *that is my answer.* Dickens originally added, "I pay for the Treadmill, and I pay for the workhouses," but crossed it out before the manuscript when to the printer. Conservative prime minister Robert Peel (1788–1850) revived the income tax on all incomes above £150 in March 1842, providing for public financial support of these institutions.

49. *many would rather die.* For example, old Betty Higden in Book 3, Chapter 8, of *Our Mutual Friend* (1865), whose "highest sublunary hope" was "patiently to earn a spare bare living, and quietly to die, untouched by workhouse hands." She finally dies by the side of the road in Lizzie Hexam's arms. "No, I have earned no money today," an old woman told Henry Mayhew in vol. 2 of his *London Labour and the London Poor* (London: George Woodfall and Son, 1851), "I have had a piece of dried bread that I steeped in water to eat. I haven't eaten anything else today; but, pray, sir, don't tell anybody of it. I could never bear the thought of going into the 'great house' [workhouse]; I'm so used to the air, that I'd sooner die in the street, as many I know have done. . . . I'd sooner die like them than be deprived of my liberty, and be prevented from going about"(p. 145).

50. *the surplus population.* As Michael Slater noted in his 1971 edition of *A Christmas Carol*, Thomas Robert Malthus (1766–1834), one of the laissez-faire political economists Dickens despised, predicted in his famous *An Essay on the Principle of Population* (1803) that population, if left unchecked, would inevitably increase more readily than the supply of food. *He* knew exactly "What the surplus is, Where it is": "A man who is born into a world possessed, if he cannot get subsistence from his parents, on whom he has a just demand, and if society do not want his labour, has no claim of *right* to the smallest portion of food, and, in fact, has no business to be where he is. At Nature's mighty feast there is no vacant cover for him. She tells him to be gone"(p. 531)

Mr. Filer, a student of Malthus in the First Quarter of *The Chimes* (1844), shares the opinion that the poor "have no earthly right or business to be born. And *that* we know they haven't. We reduced it to a mathematical certainty long ago!" Dickens harbored no sympathy for such political economical cant; in *Hard Times* (1854), his most scathing attack on these philosophers, he named two of the younger Gradgrinds Malthus and Adam Smith, the latter named after another British political economist (1723–1790) who supported laissez-faire economic policies and self-interest.

51. *flaring links.* Torches made of tow with pitch or tar, from the word "lint," frayed linen; these were carried about the city before the introduction of street lamps. "In Dickens's days," noted E. Gordon Browne in his 1907 edition of *A Christmas Carol*, "the link-boy was a common sight especially when the fog, or 'London particular,' as it was sometimes called, wrapped the whole city in darkness. There are still to be seen outside the houses in and around Mayfair and Belgravia the torch extinguishers,

"If they would rather die," said Scrooge, "they had better do it, and decrease the surplus population.**50** Besides—excuse me—I don't know that."

"But you might know it," observed the gentleman.

"It's not my business," Scrooge returned. "It's enough for a man to understand his own business, and not to interfere with other people's. Mine occupies me constantly. Good afternoon, gentlemen!"

Seeing clearly that it would be useless to pursue their point, the gentlemen withdrew. Scrooge resumed his labours with an improved opinion of himself, and in a more facetious temper than was usual with him.

Meanwhile the fog and darkness thickened so, that people ran about with flaring links,**51** proffering their services to go before horses in carriages, and conduct them on their way. The ancient tower of a church,**52** whose gruff old bell was always peeping slily down at Scrooge out of a gothic window in the wall, became invisible, and struck the hours and quarters in the clouds, with tremulous vibrations afterwards, as if its teeth were chattering in its frozen head up there. The cold became intense. In the main street, at the corner of the court, some labourers were repairing the gas-pipes, and had lighted a great fire in a brazier,**53** round which a party of ragged men and boys were gathered: warming their hands and winking their eyes before the blaze in rapture. The water-plug**54** being left in solitude, its overflowings sullenly congealed, and turned to misanthropic ice. The brightness of the shops where holly sprigs and berries crackled in the lamp-heat of the windows, made pale faces ruddy as they passed. Poulterers' and grocers' trades became a splendid joke: a glorious pageant, with which it was next to impossible to believe that such dull principles as bargain and sale had anything to do. The Lord Mayor, in the stronghold of the mighty Mansion House,**55** gave orders to his fifty cooks and butlers to keep Christmas as a Lord Mayor's household should; and even the little tailor, whom he had

which were attached to each side of the doorways. These extinguishers were in the shape similar to those attached to candlesticks, and were made of iron" (p. 97).

52. *a church.* According to Edwin Chancellor Beresford's *The London of Charles Dickens* (London: Grant Richards, 1924, p. 280), this church was either St. Dunstan's in the east with its Gothic tower, between Tower Street and Upper Thames Street, or St. Mary Aldermary, between Bow Street and what is now Queen Victoria Street. Frank S. Johnson in "About *A Christmas Carol*" (*The Dickensian*, winter 1931–32, p. 9) identified this as St. Michael's Church, near the Royal Exchange, London.

53. *a brazier.* A large flat pan for holding coals.

54. *water-plug.* Fireplug, or hydrant.

55. *Mansion House.* The official residence of the Lord Mayor of London, built in 1739–53, and giving its name to the immediate neighborhood, the eastern end of Cheapside, in the heart of the city. The impression that this elegant building was an intimidating fortress went back to Dickens' childhood, when he was lost in the City and looked in the window. "There was a dinner preparing at the Mansion House," he recalled in "Gone Astray" (*Household Words*, August 13, 1853), "and when I peeped in at a grated kitchen window, and saw the men cooks at work in their white caps, my heart began to beat with hope that the Lord Mayor, or the Lady Mayoress, or one of the young Princesses their daughters, would look out of an upper apartment and direct me to be taken in. But, nothing of the kind occurred. It was not until I had been peeping in some time that one of the cooks called to me (the window was open) 'Cut away, you sir!' which frightened me so, on account of his black whiskers, that I instantly obeyed." Dickens did not exaggerate the lavishness of the banquets often held in the Mansion House.

The Right Hon. Lord Mayor, *The Illustrated London News*, April 22, 1843.
Courtesy Library of Congress.

Banquet at the Mansion House, *The Illustrated London News*, April 22, 1843.
Courtesy Library of Congress.

56. *the beef.* Dickens originally gave them a goose, but changed it in the manuscript, perhaps recognizing that a poor tailor at the time would more likely have beef for his holiday dinner. According to "Christmas Preparations" (London *Times*, December 23, 1843), beef cost six to nine pence a pound for prime parts; a goose was four to eight shillings. Jane Carlyle defined "the most approved fashion" of keeping Christmas in England in December 1843 as "gormandizing over roast-beef and plumpudding"—and drink (*Jane Welsh Carlyle: Letters*, 1924, p. 166). One of the two charitable gentlemen lectured Scrooge in Charles Webb's 1844 play *A Christmas Carol; or, The Past, Present, and Future* that the poor had "no chance, Sir, unless the really wealthy do something for them, of their regaling on roast beef and plum pudding, this year."

57. *Saint Dunstan.* An English monk (924–988), who was also a painter, a jeweler, a blacksmith, and the patron saint of goldsmiths. And he was skilled in politics: he became chief advisor to King Edred, and later King Edgar, who made Dunstan archbishop of Canterbury. In Chapter 4 of *A Child's History of England* (1852–54), Dickens credited him with being "the real king, who had the real power" and "a clever priest; a little mad, and not a little proud and cruel." He was also the subject of legends. "[Dunstan] was an ingenious smith," Dickens recounted, "and worked at a forge in a little cell . . . and he used to tell the most extraordinary lies about demons and spirits, who, he said, came there to persecute him. For instance, he related that, one day when he was at work, the devil looked in at the little window, and tried to tempt him to lead a life of idle pleasure; whereupon, having his pincers in the fire, red-hot, he seized the devil by the nose, and put him in such pain, that his bellowings were heard for miles and miles. Some people are

fined five shillings on the previous Monday for being drunk and blood-thirsty in the streets, stirred up to-morrow's pudding in his garret, while his lean wife and the baby sallied out to buy the beef.[56]

Foggier yet, and colder! Piercing, searching, biting cold. If the good Saint Dunstan[57] had but nipped the Evil Spirit's nose with a touch of such weather as that, instead of using his familiar weapons, then indeed he would have roared to lusty purpose. The owner of one scant young nose, gnawed and mumbled[58] by the hungry cold as bones are gnawed by dogs, stooped down at Scrooge's keyhole to regale him with a Christmas carol: but at the first sound of

"God bless you merry gentleman!
May nothing you dismay!"[59]

Scrooge seized the ruler[60] with such energy of action, that the singer fled in terror,[61] leaving the keyhole to the fog and even more congenial frost.

At length the hour of shutting up the counting-house arrived. With an ill-will Scrooge dismounted from his stool, and tacitly admitted the fact to the expectant clerk in the Tank, who instantly snuffed his candle out, and put on his hat.

"You'll want all day to-morrow, I suppose?"[62] said Scrooge.

"If quite convenient, Sir."

"It's not convenient," said Scrooge, "and it's not fair. If I was to stop half-a-crown[63] for it, you'd think yourself ill used,[64] I'll be bound?"

The clerk smiled faintly.

"And yet," said Scrooge, "you don't think *me* ill—used, when I pay a day's wages for no work."

The clerk observed that it was only once a year.

"A poor excuse for picking a man's pocket every twenty-fifth of December!"[65] said Scrooge, buttoning his great-coat to the chin. "But I suppose you must have the whole day. Be here all the earlier next morning!"

inclined to think this nonsense a part of Dunstan's madness . . . but I think not. I observe that it induced the ignorant people to consider him a holy man, and that it made him very powerful. Which was exactly what he always wanted."It is quite proper that Dickens should mention Saint Dunstan here, as Scrooge will soon be visited by spirits himself.

"London Carol Singers." Etching by Robert Seymour, *The Book of Christmas* by Thomas K. Hervey, 1836.
Private collection.

"The Most Approved Way of Pulling a Man's Nose (as practised by St. Dunstan)." Etching by George Cruikshank, *Vol. 1 of My Sketch Book*, 1834.
Private collection.

58. *mumbled.* Bit gently with the mouth mostly closed.

59. *May nothing you dismay!* Dickens has slightly misquoted the opening lines of this famous song, preserved by William Sandys in *Christmas Carols, Ancient and Modern* (1833):

> God rest you merry gentlemen,
> Let nothing you dismay. (p. 102)

This was probably the most widely sung Christmas carol at the time. "In the metropolis," wrote Sandys, "a solitary itinerant may be occasionally heard in the streets, croaking out 'God rest you merry gentlemen,' or some other old carol, to an ancient

and simple tune" (p. cxxv). Apparently to satisfy the censors, Edward Stirling changed the first line of the carol in his 1844 play *A Christmas Carol; or, Past, Present, and Future* to "Bless, bless you merry gentlemen. . . ."

60. *the ruler.* Scrooge, a man of mathematics and precise measurements, appropriately threatens the boy with this essential tool of his trade, used in making charts and graphs to record his monetary gains and losses.

61. *the singer fled in terror.* For this episode, Dickens adapted a more brutal attack on a young caroler from "The Story of the Goblins Who Stole a Sexton," in Chapter 29 of *The Pickwick Papers* (1837):

> Now, Gabriel . . . was not a little indignant to hear a young urchin roaring out

some jolly song about a merry Christmas, in this very sanctuary. . . . As Gabriel walked on, and the voice drew nearer, he found it proceeded from a small boy. . . . So Gabriel waited until the boy came up, and then dodged him into a corner and rapped him over the head with his lantern five or six times, just to teach him to modulate his voice. And as the boy hurried away with his hand to his head, singing quite a different sort of tune, Gabriel Grub chuckled very heartily to himself.

The cross old grave digger must atone for this sin, just as Scrooge must for his, before the story is up.

62. *"You'll want all day to-morrow, I suppose?"* Closing a business in London on Christmas Day was left up to the discretion of the employer at the time. However, it was customary for some employers to entertain lavishly their workers at the holidays. Laman Blanchard disclosed in "My Christmas Dinner" (*Sketches from Life*, vol. 2 [New York: Wiley and Putnam, 1846]) how a friend "makes it a rule, at all these festivals, to empty the entire contents of his counting-house into his little dining-parlor; and you consequently sit down to dinner with six white-waistcoated clerks, let loose upon a turkey" (p. 179).

The same was true in the United States. Among those who saw Dickens read *A Christmas Carol* in Boston on Christmas Day 1867 was Franklin Fairbanks, owner of Franklin Scale Company in St. Johnsburg, Vermont. He later told his wife, "I feel that after listening to Mr. Dickens's reading of *A Christmas Carol* to-night I should break the custom we have hitherto observed of opening the works on Christmas Day." The next year he introduced a new tradition of giving every employee a turkey in the spirit of the reformed Ebenezer Scrooge. (See Gladys Storey, *Dickens and Daughter* [London: Frederick Muller, 1939], pp. 120–21.) It was not until June 26, 1870, that the United States Congress declared Christmas Day a federal holiday.

63. *half-a-crown.* Or "half a bull"; this English coin (once worth two shillings and a sixpence, or one eighth of a pound, but now out of circulation) was anciently stamped with a crown. It is one-sixth of the clerk's weekly salary; he, like most people at the time, works six days a week, Monday through Saturday.

64. *ill used.* Strengthened to "mightily ill-used" in the 1867 Ticknor and Fields Public Reading edition.

65. *every twenty-fifth of December!* Here Scrooge cannot even say the name "Christmas"; he, unlike his nephew, refuses to acknowledge "the veneration due to its sacred name and origin." It is just another day of the year to the old miser.

The clerk promised that he would; and Scrooge walked out with a growl. The office was closed in a twinkling, and the clerk, with the long ends of his white comforter dangling below his waist (for he boasted no great-coat), went down a slide on Cornhill,[66] at the end of a lane of boys, twenty times, in honour of its being Christmas-eve, and then ran home to Camden Town[67] as hard as he could pelt, to play at blindman's-buff.[68]

Scrooge took his melancholy dinner in his usual melancholy tavern;[69] and having read all the newspapers, and beguiled the rest of the evening with his banker's-book, went home to bed. He lived in chambers which had once belonged to his deceased partner. They were a gloomy suite of rooms, in a lowering pile of building[70] up a yard, where it had so little business to be, that one could scarcely help fancying it must have run there when it was a young house, playing at hide-and-seek with other houses, and have forgotten the way out again. It was old enough now, and dreary enough, for nobody lived in it but Scrooge, the other rooms being all let out as offices. The yard was so dark that even Scrooge, who knew its every stone, was fain to grope with his hands. The fog and frost so hung about the black old gateway of the house, that it seemed as if the Genius of the Weather[71] sat in mournful meditation on the threshold.

Now, it is a fact, that there was nothing at all particular about the knocker on the door, except that it was very large. It is also a fact, that Scrooge had seen it night and morning during his whole residence in that place; also that Scrooge had as little of what is called fancy[72] about him as any man in the City of London,[73] even including—which is a bold word—the corporation, aldermen, and livery.[74] Let it also be borne in mind that Scrooge had not bestowed one thought on Marley, since his last mention of his seven-years' dead partner that afternoon. And then let any man explain to me, if he can, how it happened that Scrooge, having

66. *Cornhill.* A well-known thoroughfare in Cheapside, London; it derived its name from the corn market that once was held there.

"Innocent Mirth—the Slide on the Pavement." Wood engraving after John Leech, *Punch's Almanack for 1848.*
Courtesy Library of Congress.

67. *Camden Town.* Once a suburb, now a part of London. " Camden Town lies to the north-east of Regent's Park on London clay," explained Charles Dickens, Jr., in *Dickens's Dictionary of London* (London: Charles Dickens, 1879), "and is a moderately rented neighbourhood, with, as a rule, very moderate sized houses. Quite small houses of six, eight, and ten rooms each can here be found, and it is, relatively to its distance

"Home to Camden Town." Wood engraving after Gustave Doré, *Journal pour tous,* June 29, 1861.
Courtesy Library of Congress.

from Charing Cross, the cheapest neighbourhood, so far as rent is concerned, in London." His father, who was a boy there, recalled it in "An Unsettled Neighbourhood" (*Household Words*, November 11, 1854) as being "as shabby, dingy, damp and mean a neighbourhood, as one would desire not to see. Its poverty was not of a demonstrative order." See Stave 3, note 34.

68. *blindman's-buff.* A popular parlor game, not originally associated with Christmas, in which the contestant is blindfolded and then must catch another guest and guess whom he or she has caught. It is said to be of ancient origin, having been played by the Greeks; in the Middle Ages, it was known as "hoodman blind" because a hood was worn instead of a blindfold. Joseph Strutt in Book 4, Chapter 4, of *The Sports and Past-times of the English People* (1801) described that medieval game as played much the way it is today: "a player is blinded and buffeted by his comrades until he can catch one of them, which done, the person caught is blinded in his stead." A 1740 chapbook, *Round about Our Coal-Fire*, reported that "it is lawful to set anything in the way for Folks to tumble over, whether it is to break Arms, Legs, or Hands." By the nineteenth century, the blindman had the right to kiss his captive if it was a young lady. Today this boisterous game is almost solely played at Christmas.

One of the most memorable games of blindman's buff in English literature is that played by Mr. Pickwick at Dingley Dell, in Chapter 28 of *The Pickwick Papers* (1837):

> ... it was a still more pleasant thing to see Mr. Pickwick, blinded shortly afterwards with a silk-handkerchief, falling up against the wall, and scrambling into corners, and going through all the mysteries of blindman's buff, with the utmost relish for the game, until at last he caught one

of the poor relations; and then had to evade the blind-man himself, which he did with a nimbleness and agility that elicited the admiration and applause of all beholders.

Oddly, Dickens makes no further reference to blindman's buff at the Cratchit Christmas in Stave 3; instead, Scrooge's nephew and his guests play it. Edward Stirling, however, returned the game to the Cratchits in his dramatization *A Christmas Carol; or, Past, Present, and Future*, staged at the Adelphi in February 1844; and he added the following exchange between Bob and his daughter Martha to send the blindman on his way:

> *Martha.* How many horses has your
> father got?
> *Bob.* Three.
> *Martha.* What color are they?
> *Bob.* Black, white, and grey.
> *Martha.* Turn round three times and
> catch who you may.

69. *his usual melancholy tavern.* Gwen Major suggested in "Scrooge's Chambers" (*The Dickensian*, winter 1932–33, p. 11) that this place was Garraway's Coffee House, in 'Change Alley, between Cornhill and Lombard Street. Tea was first sold here; and Defoe, Swift, and Steele all frequented it. In Dickens' day, it was popular with brokers and other businessmen and known for its pale ale, punch, sherry, and sandwiches. Dickens mentions it in *The Pickwick Papers* (Chapter 34, 1837), *Martin Chuzzlewit* (Chapter 27, 1844), and *Little Dorrit* (Book 1, Chapter 29, 1857). It was demolished in 1878.

70. *a lowering pile of building. Bell's Weekly Messenger* (December 30, 1843) identified the place as "one of those lone large houses in some court on Dowgate-hill, the remains of the grandeur and opulence of the old city, but which are now deserted and converted into warehouses" (p. 426). Major suggested in "Scrooge's Chambers" (*The Dickensian*, winter 1932–33, p. 11–13) that it was a house that once stood at 46 Lime Street, in the Langborn Ward. Her description of this house closely follows that in the story: by the nineteenth century, it had become offices for many firms (including three wine merchants), and it stood far back and alone up a narrow courtyard, known for its old gates; the building had once been a private residence, and most of the rooms were said to have been left in much the same condition as in the time of Charles I. After the building was demolished in 1875, it was appropriately replaced by a bank.

71. *the Genius of the Weather*. A guardian or attendant spirit, at the time more commonly called "the clerk of the weather."

72. *fancy*. Scrooge is a man of measurements and calculations who lacks any imagination or romance. Dickens believed that one must cultivate fancy as the best weapon against the oppressions and injustices of contemporary English society. In "A Preliminary Word" (*Household Words*, March 30, 1850), Dickens defined the purpose of his new magazine as to "tenderly cherish that light of Fancy which is inherent in the human breast. . . . To show to all, that in all familiar things, even in those which are repellant on the surface, there is Romance enough, if we will find it out.:— to teach the hardest workers at this whirling wheel of toil, that their lot is not

necessarily a moody, brutal fact, excluded from sympathies and graces of imagination." There would be "no mere utilitarian spirit, no iron binding the mind to grim realities" to soil its pages. It would fight men like Thomas Gradgrind of *Hard Times* (1854), who, like Scrooge, demanded only facts in life, no fancy. (See also Stave 3, note 68.)

73. *the City of London*. That part of the old metropolis, about a square mile in size, which comes under the jurisdiction of the Lord Mayor and the City Corporation. It has its own police force and courts of justice. It is still the business heart of London, where the Royal Exchange, the Mansion House, Cornhill, and St. Paul's Cathedral are all located.

74. *the corporation, aldermen, and livery*. "The corporation of every city or incorporated borough, consists of a mayor, alderman, and common-councilmen," F. H. Ahn explained in his 1871 edition of *A Christmas Carol*. "The mayors, who in London, York, and Dublin, have the title of Lord, are chosen annually by the livery out of the court of aldermen, who in their turn are chosen and elected for life by freemen. Each alderman represents a ward, of which in London there are 26, and 206 common-councilmen. None but freemen (burgesses) can engage in trade in London, and all must belong to some of the guilds or companies, many of the members of which are entitled to wear its distinguished dress or livery— hence livery-men" (p. 147).

75. *not a knocker, but Marley's face.* "The various expressions of the human countenance afford a beautiful and interesting study," Dickens observed in "Our Next-door Neighbour," in *Sketches by Boz* (1839); "but there is something in the physiognomy of street-door knockers, almost as characteristic, and nearly as infallible. Whenever we visit a man for the first time, we contemplate the features of his knocker with the greatest curiosity, for we well know, that between the man and his knocker, there will inevitably be a greater or less degree of resemblance and sympathy." Richard Hengist Horne insisted in *A New Spirit of the Age* (vol. 1, London: Smith Elder, 1844), "The knocker which changes into Marley's dead-alive face, and yet remains a knocker, is taken from Hoffmann's 'Golden Pot'" (p. 51).

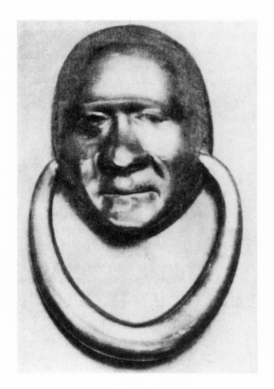

The Marley door knocker,
The Dickensian, October 1924.
Courtesy Library of Congress.

his key in the lock of the door, saw in the knocker, without its undergoing any intermediate process of change: not a knocker, but Marley's face.[75]

Marley's face. It was not in impenetrable shadow as the other objects in the yard were, but had a dismal light about it, like a bad lobster in a dark cellar.[76] It was not angry or ferocious, but looked at Scrooge as Marley used to look: with ghostly spectacles turned up upon its ghostly forehead. The hair was curiously stirred, as if by breath or hot-air; and though the eyes were wide open, they were perfectly motionless. That, and its livid colour, made it horrible; but its horror seemed to be, in spite of the face and beyond its control, rather than a part of its own expression.

As Scrooge looked fixedly at this phenomenon, it was a knocker again.

To say that he was not startled, or that his blood was not conscious of a terrible sensation to which it had been a stranger from infancy, would be untrue. But he put his hand upon the key he had relinquished, turned it sturdily, walked in, and lighted his candle.

He *did* pause, with a moment's irresolution, before he shut the door; and he *did* look cautiously behind it first, as if he half-expected to be terrified with the sight of Marley's pigtail sticking out into the hall. But there was nothing on the back of the door, except the screws and nuts that held the knocker on; so he said "Pooh, pooh!" and closed it with a bang.

The sound resounded through the house like thunder. Every room above, and every cask in the wine-merchant's cellars below, appeared to have a separate peal of echoes of its own. Scrooge was not a man to be frightened by echoes. He fastened the door, and walked across the hall, and up the stairs: slowly too: trimming his candle as he went.

You may talk vaguely about driving a coach-and-six up a good old flight of stairs, or through a bad young Act of Parliament;[77] but I mean to say you might have got a hearse up that staircase, and taken it broadwise,

"Not a knocker, but Marley's face." Wood
engraving after Gustave Doré, *Journal
pour tous*, June 16, 1861.
Courtesy Library of Congress.

Thomas Carlyle translated E. T. A. Hoffmann's "Der goldene Topf" (1814) in *German Romance* (1827), and Dickens may well
have recalled the episode in the Second
Vigil from this version of the famous German Romantic tale: The student Anselmus
"was looking at the large, fine bronze
knocker; but now when, as the last stroke
tingled through the air with loud clang
from the steeple-clock of the Kreuzkirche,
or Cross-church, he lifted his hand to grasp
this same knocker, the metal visage twisted
itself, with horrid rolling of its blue-
gleaming eyes, into a grinning smile."

Dickens may have had in mind the striking knocker that once graced the front door
of No. 8 Craven Street, when it was occupied by Dr. David Rees. (Was Dr. Rees a colleague of Dr. Marley mentioned in note 3,
above?) It was finally removed in 1899 for
safekeeping from curiosity seekers. See
Ernest H. Rann, "The Story of Dickens's
Christmas Carol," *Cassell's Magazine*,
December 1907, p. 77; and T. W. Tyrell, "The
'Marley' Knocker," *The Dickensian*, October 1924, pp. 202–3. William Makepeace
Thackeray introduced a similarly odd one in
Chapter 4 of his Christmas Book *The Rose
and the Ring* (1855): the Fairy Blackstick
transforms the porter Jenkins Gruffanuff
into a brass door knocker for being "*brazen,
brass!*" with her.

76. *a bad lobster in a dark cellar.* "We may
think the writer is only indulging in comic
incongruity until we realize that he is
invoking the idea of a face after burial, with
the stench and phosphorescent glow of
decay," noted Alfred B. Harbage in *A Kind
of Power: The Shakespeare-Dickens Anthology* (Philadelphia: American Philosophical
Society, 1975, p. 34). Rotting crayfish do
seem to glow in the dark.

77. *driving a coach-and-six . . . through a
bad young Act of Parliament.* English laws
were often so loosely worded and filled with
so many loopholes that an accused person
could easily escape prosecution. "The late
Irish agitator Daniel O'Connell used to
boast," noted Dr. L. Riechelmann in his
notes to the 1864 B. G. Teubner edition of *A
Christmas Carol*, "that he could drive a
coach-and-six through an Act of Parliament,
that is to say, that he knew how to contrive
its being rejected or repealed" (p. 13).

78. *the splinter-bar.* The crossbar in front of the carriage, attached to the leather traces and supporting the springs.

79. *dip.* According to "A Visit to Charles Dickens" (*Temple Bar*, December 1870, pp. 31–32), Dickens once explained to Hans Christian Andersen that a dip is a candle. It is made by simply dipping a wick several times in melted tallow and is cheaper than a wax candle, which is moulded.

80. *that.* Dickens changed this for clarity's sake to "it's being very dark" in the prompt copy of *A Christmas Carol* that he used in his Public Readings; the volume is now in the Berg Collection of the New York Public Library. Philip Collins edited a facsimile that the library published as *A Christmas Carol: The Public Reading Version* in 1971.

81. *lumber-room.* A storeroom, sometimes for firewood, but more often for unused household items.

82. *gruel.* Oatmeal or other cereal boiled in lots of water. This meager fare was the staple diet in prisons and workhouses at the time. The workhouse in Chapter 2 of *Oliver Twist* (1838) is well provided with "an unlimited supply of water" and "small qualities of oatmeal" and issues "three meals of thin gruel a day, with an onion twice a week, and half a roll on Sunday." It is for this slop that Oliver asks the master, "Please, sir, I want some more." Small wonder Scrooge thinks such institutions are sufficient for the poor: the old miser's diet is not much better than theirs.

83. *Scrooge had a cold in his head.* According to the notes in a French edition of *A Christmas Carol*, published by Charles Poussielgue in Paris in 1893, gruel was a folk remedy in England against head colds

with the splinter-bar[78] towards the wall, and the door towards the balustrades: and done it easy. There was plenty of width for that, and room to spare; which is perhaps the reason why Scrooge thought he saw a locomotive hearse going on before him in the gloom. Half a dozen gas-lamps out of the street wouldn't have lighted the entry too well, so you may suppose that it was pretty dark with Scrooge's dip.[79]

Up Scrooge went, not caring a bottom for that:[80] darkness is cheap, and Scrooge liked it. But before he shut his heavy door, he walked through his rooms to see that all was right. He had just enough recollection of the face to desire to do that.

Sitting room, bed-room, lumber-room.[81] All as they should be. Nobody under the table, nobody under the sofa; a small fire in the grate; spoon and basin ready; and the little saucepan of gruel[82] (Scrooge had a cold in his head)[83] upon the hob.[84] Nobody under the bed; nobody in the closet; nobody in his dressing-gown, which was hanging up in a suspicious attitude against the wall. Lumber-room as usual. Old fire-guard, old shoes, two fish-baskets, washing-stand on three legs, and a poker.

Quite satisfied, he closed his door, and locked himself in; double-locked himself in, which was not his custom. Thus secured against surprise, he took off his cravat; put on his dressing-gown and slippers, and his night-cap; and sat down before the fire to take his gruel.

It was a very low fire indeed; nothing on such a bitter night. He was obliged to sit close to it, and brood over it, before he could extract the least sensation of warmth from such a handful of fuel. The fire-place was an old one, built by some Dutch merchant long ago,[85] and paved all round with quaint Dutch tiles,[86] designed to illustrate the Scriptures. There were Cains and Abels; Pharaoh's daughters, Queens of Sheba, Angelic messengers descending through the air on

as well as other complaints. "It's very likely it *will* be troublesome," warns the surgeon of the newborn baby in the opening of *Oliver Twist* (1838). "Give it a little gruel if it is."

84. *the hob.* An old-fashioned fire grate: a raised stone or iron shelf on either side of an open fireplace, where things were placed to keep warm. Hobs were added after the fireplace was converted from wood to coal burning.

85. *built by some Dutch merchant long ago.* The fireplace was likely installed during the emigration of Dutch merchants after the revolution of 1688–89, when William III, stadtholder of the Netherlands, became William of Orange of Great Britain; his wife was Mary, daughter of James II, the last of the Stuart kings.

86. *Dutch tiles.* According to Johnson's "About *A Christmas Carol*" (*The Dickensian*, winter 1931–32, p. 8), the fireplace in the house on the Brook at Chatham, where Dickens was a boy, was decorated with Dutch tiles, depicting scenes from the Scriptures. Most of the figures and incidents depicted are from the Old Testament: Cain and Abel, Genesis 4; Pharaoh's daughter, Exodus 2; the Queen of Sheba, 2 Chronicles 9; Abraham, Genesis 11–26; and Belshazzar, Daniel 4–5. Oddly, in an early stage of his readings of *A Christmas Carol*, Dickens dropped only "Queens of Sheba" from this lengthy list of biblical characters in the Berg prompt copy.

87. *butter-boats.* Serving dishes for melted butter or butter sauces; Dickens is comparing the size and shape of these vessels to those of the crudely painted apostles' ships on the Dutch tiles.

88. *the ancient Prophet's rod . . . swallowed up the whole.* Exodus 7.8–12 describes how Aaron's staff, after being transformed into a snake by God, swallows up all the rods transformed into serpents by the Pharaoh's magicians.

89. *each smooth tile had been a blank at first, with power to shape some picture on its surface from the disjointed fragments of his thoughts.* Scrooge's ability to see all sorts of shapes and pictures on amorphous surfaces, revealing images of his troubled subconscious, is the same psychological process exploited by Rorschach tests, in which the individual is asked to describe unexpected objects suggested by inkblots. Leonardo da Vinci described this form of free association in his notebooks as "the way to stimulate and arouse the mind to various inventions":

> if you look at any walls spotted with various stains or a mixture of different kinds of stones, if you are about to invent some scene you will be able to see in it a resemblance to various different landscapes adorned with mountains, rivers, rocks, trees, plains, wide valleys, and various groups of hills. You will also be able to see diverse combats and figures in quick movement, and strange expressions of faces, and outlandish costumes, and an infinite number of things which you can reduce into separate and well conceived forms. (*Leonardo Da Vinci's Note-Books,* edited by Edward McCurdy [New York: Empire State Book, 1923])

Da Vinci further observed that this process not only affected the eyes but the

clouds like feather-beds, Abrahams, Belshazzars, Apostles putting off to sea in butter-boats,[87] hundreds of figures, to attract his thoughts; and yet that face of Marley, seven years dead, came like the ancient Prophet's rod, and swallowed up the whole.[88] If each smooth tile had been a blank at first, with power to shape some picture on its surface from the disjointed fragments of his thoughts,[89] there would have been a copy of old Marley's head on every one.

"Humbug!" said Scrooge; and walked across the room.

After several turns, he sat down again. As he threw his head back in the chair, his glance happened to rest upon a bell, a disused bell, that hung in the room, and communicated for some purpose now forgotten with a chamber in the highest story of the building. It was with great astonishment, and with a strange, inexplicable dread, that as he looked, he saw this bell begin to swing. It swung so softly in the outset that it scarcely made a sound; but soon it rang out loudly, and so did every bell in the house.

This might have lasted half a minute, or a minute, but it seemed an hour. The bells ceased as they had begun, together. They were succeeded by a clanking noise, deep down below; as if some person were dragging a heavy chain over the casks in the wine-merchant's cellar. Scrooge then remembered to have heard that ghosts in haunted houses were described as dragging chains.[90]

The cellar-door flew open with a booming sound, and then he heard the noise much louder, on the floors below; then coming up the stairs; then coming straight towards his door.

"It's humbug still!" said Scrooge. "I won't believe it."

His colour changed though, when, without a pause, it[91] came on through the heavy door, and passed into the room before his eyes. Upon its coming in, the dying

ears as well, "as it does with the sound of bells in whose clanging you may discover every name and word that you can imagine" (p. 173). Dickens, likewise, plays with the ringing of bells in Scrooge's chambers on the approach of Marley's Ghost and in his second Christmas Book, *The Chimes* (1844), in which the clanging invokes the Goblin of the Great Bell.

90. *dragging chains.* Andrew Lang observed in his introduction to the 1897 Gadshill edition of *Christmas Books* that this "old-fashioned phenomenon of clanking chains derived from classical superstition." Dickens noted in "A Christmas Tree" (*Household Words*, September 21, 1850) that the number of ghosts in haunted houses are "reducible to a very few general types and classes; for, ghosts have little originality, and 'walk' in a beaten track"; among their common pursuits is "the rattling of a chain." Not all scholars have accepted this tradition. "Dragging chains is not the fashion of English Ghosts," insisted Francis Grose in *A Provincial Glossary* (1787); "chains and black vestments being chiefly the accoutrements of foreign spectres, seen in arbitrary governments: dead or alive, English Spirits are free."

91. *it.* Traditionally ghosts are believed to be sexless, no matter what they might have been in life; Dickens, likewise, refers to each of Scrooge's other unearthly visitors only as "it."

92. *the dying flame leaped up.* "If, during the time of an Apparition, there is a lighted candle in the room," wrote Grose in *A Provincial Glossary*, "it will burn extremely blue: this is so universally acknowledged, that many eminent philosophers have busied themselves in accounting for it, without once doubting the truth of the fact." Dickens likely knew this superstition from Shakespeare: Brutus observes at the appearance of Caesar's ghost, "How ill this taper burns!" (*Julius Caesar* 4.2.326). Dickens may also have known this phenomenon from the appearance of the ghost in Canto 16 of Lord Byron's unfinished *Don Juan* (1819–24):

> The door flew open, not swiftly, but as
>   fly
> The sea-gulls, with a steady, sober
>   flight,
> And then swung back, nor close, but
>   stood awry,

Preliminary pencil and wash drawing by John Leech for "Marley's Ghost," 1843.
Courtesy Houghton Library, Harvard University.

flame leaped up,[92] as though it cried "I know him! Marley's Ghost!"[93] and fell again.

The same face: the very same. Marley in his pig-tail, usual waistcoat, tights, and boots;[94] the tassels on the latter bristling, like his pigtail, and his coat-skirts, and the hair upon his head. The chain he drew was clasped

Marley's Ghost.

about his middle.[95] It was long, and wound about him like a tail; and it was made (for Scrooge observed it closely) of cash-boxes, keys, padlocks, ledgers, deeds, and heavy purses wrought in steel. His body was transparent: so that Scrooge, observing him, and looking through his waistcoat, could see the two buttons on his coat behind.

Half letting in long shadows on the
    light,
Which still in Juan's candlesticks
    burned high,
For he had two, both tolerably bright,
And in the doorway, darkening dark-
    ness, stood
The sable Friar in his solemn hood.

Dickens referred to this ghost in "The Bloomsbury Christening," in *Sketches by Boz* (1839), and again in Chapter 8 of *Martin Chuzzlewit* (1844).

93. *"I know him! Marley's Ghost!"* The illustrator John Leech read this simile literally and amusingly depicted the flame with a face and crying, "Marley's Ghost!"

94. *Marley in his pig-tail, usual waistcoat, tights, and boots.* Francis Grose insisted in *A Provincial Glossary*, "Ghosts commonly appear in the same dress they usually wore whilst living." He also noted that a ghost, like Marley's, "is supposed to be the spirit of a person deceased, who is either commissioned to return for some especial errand . . . or, having committed some injustice whilst living, cannot rest till that is redressed." Just as the ghost of Hamlet's father appears "in the very clothes that he wore on work-a-days" (as Dickens noted in Chapter 49 of *The Old Curiosity Shop*, 1841), Marley dresses in death exactly as he had in life. He obviously belonged to an earlier generation than Scrooge: although common in the eighteenth century, pigtails had gone out of fashion for men by the time of the story. The London *Era* (February 18, 1844) facetiously objected that a ghost, like Marley's, "should come to

"Scrooge fell on his knees, and clasped his hands before his face." Wood engraving after Gustave Doré, *Journal pour tous*, June 16, 1861.
Courtesy Library of Congress.

us in anything but the proper habiliments of the grave. We could forgive having our privacy intruded on by our friends were they properly shrouded; but to trouble them to walk out of their coffins, and make free with their wardrobes, after having willed them to their friends, or left them to their heirs,—heaven defend us from such a monstrous injustice! We should take a ghost which would condescend to penetrate such an act to be anything but a choice spirit, for your choice spirit should be an honest fellow."

95. *The chain he drew was clasped about his middle.* The London *Era* (February 18, 1844) sarcastically suggested that "in life it had probably hung round his neck an emblem of civic dignity."

96. *Marley had no bowels.* Certain parts of the body were at one time believed to be the seats of human affections; the bowels were thought to be the center of compassion, as mentioned in 1 John 3.17: "But whoso hath this world's goods, and seeth his brothers have need, and shutteth up his bowels of compassion from him, how dwelleth the love of God in him?" Thus Marley, like Scrooge, lacked in life any pity for his fellowmen. Dickens is, of course, also reasserting that "Marley was dead to begin with": from the time of ancient Egypt, corpses have been disemboweled before burial, to retard the body's deterioration.

97. *marked.* Clarified as "noticed" in the 1867 Ticknor and Fields Public Reading edition.

98. *"for a shade"* . . . *"to a shade."* Another pun: "For a shade," for a ghost; "to a shade," to a degree.

Half-title vignette by "Phiz" (Hablôt Knight Browne), *Christmas Books*, "The Library Edition of Charles Dickens's Works," 1859.
Courtesy British Library Board.

Scrooge had often heard it said that Marley had no bowels,**96** but he had never believed it until now.

No, nor did he believe it even now. Though he looked the phantom through and through, and saw it standing before him; though he felt the chilling influence of its death-cold eyes; and marked**97** the very texture of the folded kerchief bound about its head and chin, which wrapper he had not observed before; he was still incredulous, and fought against his senses.

"How now!" said Scrooge, caustic and cold as ever. "What do you want with me?"

"Much!"—Marley's voice, no doubt about it.

"Who are you?"

"Ask me who I *was.*"

"Who *were* you then?" said Scrooge, raising his voice. "You're particular—for a shade." He was going to say "*to* a shade,"**98** but substituted this, as more appropriate.

"In life I was your partner, Jacob Marley."

"Can you—can you sit down?" asked Scrooge, looking doubtfully at him.

"I can."

"Do it then."

Scrooge asked the question, because he didn't know whether a ghost so transparent might find himself in a condition to take a chair; and felt that in the event of its being impossible, it might involve the necessity of an embarrassing explanation. But the ghost sat down on the opposite side of the fireplace, as if he were quite used to it.**99**

"You don't believe in me," observed the Ghost.

"I don't," said Scrooge.

"What evidence would you have of my reality, beyond that of your senses?"

"I don't know," said Scrooge.

"Why do you doubt your senses?"

"Because," said Scrooge, "a little thing affects them.**100** A slight disorder of the stomach makes them cheats. You may be an undigested bit of beef, a blot of

99. *as if he were quite used to it.* The ghost's familiarity with this spot anticipates its later statement, "I have sat invisible beside you many and many a day."

100. *a little thing affects them.* As Lang observed in his introduction to the 1897 Gadshill edition of *Christmas Books*, "Mr. Scrooge vainly pleads the popular theory of hallucinations," that ghosts and other specters are caused by indigestion. Interpreters of dream psychology, from Aristotle to Sigmund Freud, have argued that nightmares are the result of natural disorders or other stimuli on the sleeping mind. "A disordered state of the stomach and liver will often produce dreams," argued Robert Macnish in *The Philosophy of Sleep* (Glasglow: W. R. M'Phun, 1838), a book Dickens owned. "Persons of bad digestion, especially hypochondriacs, are harassed with visions of the most frightful nature" (p. 53). He argued, "Those whose digestion is healthy, whose minds are at ease, and who go supperless to bed, will seldom be troubled with it." Nightmares might be brought on by food "such as cheese, cucumbers, almonds and whatever is hard to be digested" (p. 148–49)

Just the suggestion of something during the waking hours may create phantoms at night: that Marley should suddenly appear to Scrooge after all these years may have been suggested by the portly gentleman's simple question of whether he was addressing Mr. Scrooge or Mr. Marley. As Thomas De Quincey (one of Dickens' favorite authors) explained in his introductory remarks to *Suspiria De Profundis* (1845), "He whose talk is of oxen will probably dream of oxen." One is often aroused from sleep by some outside sound or other influ-ence that finds representation within the dream. It is a psychological metaphor. Writers have often explored this bridging between dream objects and actual ones: in Alice's dreams in *Alice's Adventures in Wonderland* (1865) and *Through the Looking-Glass* (1872), a pack of playing cards is only falling leaves, the Red Queen merely a kitten after all.

In a letter to Forster written about September 30, 1844, Dickens described a recent dream he had had in Italy. Like Scrooge with his indigestion, Dickens suffered from "a return of rheumatism in my back, and knotted round my waist like a girdle of pain." He saw a female figure dressed in a robe. At first he could not tell who the woman was, but soon he was certain it was the spirit of his dead sister-in-law, Mary Hogarth. He questioned her about the true religion, and she replied that Catholicism would be best for him. When he awoke he tried to unravel "the fragments of reality" that may have inspired the vision. He reasoned that the figure may have been suggested by a space on the wall where a religious picture must have once hung; he had been speculating what it might have been, perhaps a madonna. Before retiring, he had heard the convent bells, which made him think of the Catholic services. All these random sounds and thoughts must have determined the spirit's reply. "And yet," he concluded in the letter, "for all this, put the case of that wish being fulfilled by any agency in which I had no hand; and I wonder whether I should regard it as a dream, or an actual Vision!" (p. 196). Scrooge shares this doubt in Stave 2, when he contemplates what he has seen, "Was it a dream or not?"

101. *taking off the bandage round its head.* The dead were often bound round the chin and head to keep the mouth closed and from making some ghastly expression. Sir John Everett Millais drew Dickens on his deathbed after the bandage had been put round his head. He arrived the day after

Dickens on his deathbed by John Everett Millais, 1870.
Courtesy The Charles Dickens Museum, London.

Dickens died, with the sculptor Thomas Woolner, who made a death mask from which he fashioned a bust of the famous novelist. Mamie Dickens thought the sketch "is, like all Sir John's drawings, most delicate and refined, and the likeness absolutely faithful to what my father looked in death" (*My Father As I Recall Him*, [Westminster: Roxburgh Press, 1896], p. 125).

mustard, a crumb of cheese, a fragment of an underdone potato. There's more of gravy than of grave about you, whatever you are!"

Scrooge was not much in the habit of cracking jokes, nor did he feel, in his heart, by any means waggish then. The truth is, that he tried to be smart, as a means of distracting his own attention, and keeping down his terror; for the spectre's voice disturbed the very marrow in his bones.

To sit, staring at those fixed, glazed eyes, in silence for a moment, would play, Scrooge felt, the very deuce with him. There was something very awful, too, in the spectre's being provided with an infernal atmosphere of its own. Scrooge could not feel it himself, but this was clearly the case; for though the Ghost sat perfectly motionless, its hair, and skirts, and tassels, were still agitated as by the hot vapour from an oven.

"You see this toothpick?" said Scrooge, returning quickly to the charge, for the reason just assigned; and wishing, though it were only for a second, to divert the vision's stony gaze from himself.

"I do," replied the Ghost.

"You are not looking at it," said Scrooge.

"But I see it," said the Ghost, "notwithstanding."

"Well!" returned Scrooge. "I have but to swallow this, and be for the rest of my days persecuted by a legion of goblins, all of my own creation. Humbug, I tell you; humbug!"

At this, the spirit raised a frightful cry, and shook its chain with such a dismal and appalling noise, that Scrooge held on tight to his chair, to save himself from falling in a swoon. But how much greater was his horror, when the phantom taking off the bandage round its head,**101** as if it were too warm to wear in-doors, its lower jaw dropped down upon its breast!

Scrooge fell upon his knees, and clasped his hands before his face.

"Mercy!" he said. "Dreadful apparition, why do you trouble me?"

"Man of the worldly mind!" replied the Ghost, "do you believe in me or not?"

"I do," said Scrooge. "I must. But why do spirits walk the earth, and why do they come to me?"

"It is required of every man," the Ghost returned, "that the spirit within him should walk abroad among his fellow-men, and travel far and wide; and if that spirit goes not forth in life, it is condemned to do so after death. It is doomed to wander through the world—oh, woe is me!—and witness what it cannot share, but might have shared on earth, and turned to happiness!"

Again the spectre raised a cry, and shook its chain, and wrung its shadowy hands.

"You are fettered," said Scrooge, trembling. "Tell me why?"

"I wear the chain I forged in life," replied the Ghost. "I made it link by link, and yard by yard; I girded it on of my own free will, and of my own free will I wore it. Is its pattern strange to *you*?"

Scrooge trembled more and more.

"Or would you know," pursued the Ghost, "the weight and length of the strong coil you bear yourself? It was full as heavy and as long as this, seven Christmas Eves ago. You have laboured on it, since. It is a ponderous chain!"

Scrooge glanced about him on the floor, in the expectation of finding himself surrounded by some fifty or sixty fathoms of iron cable: but he could see nothing.

"Jacob," he said, imploringly. "Old Jacob Marley, tell me more. Speak comfort to me, Jacob."

"I have none to give," the Ghost replied. "It comes from other regions, Ebenezer Scrooge, and is conveyed by other ministers,[102] to other kinds of men. Nor can I tell you what I would. A very little more, is all permitted to me. I cannot rest, I cannot stay, I cannot linger anywhere.[103] My spirit never walked beyond our counting-house—mark me!—in life my spirit never

102. *It comes from other regions . . . and is conveyed by other ministers.* From Heaven and by the heavenly host. Like the spirit of Virgil in the fourth canto of Dante's *Inferno*, Marley's Ghost must speak in "veiled speech," because Christ is unknown and cannot be named in the infernal world. In the same manner, Marley in life failed to follow Christ's teachings by not choosing to raise his eyes "to that blessed Star which led the Wise Men to a poor abode."

Early reviewers of *A Christmas Carol* suspected that Dickens must have been influenced by the great Italian poet. "Kindred spirits," literally and figuratively, serve as guides in both works: Marley plays Virgil to Scrooge's Dante. Theoretically, both journeys take place over three days and on holy days, Easter in the *Inferno* and Christmas in *A Christmas Carol*. Dickens' view of the Invisible World retains much of the atmosphere of Dante's. Marley would have been sent to the fourth circle of Hell, that of the avaricious; just as the condemned in Dante's Inferno must roll great weights, so must Marley and his fellow specters drag chains, cash boxes, and other heavy symbols of their former trade. Note that both authors give their works technically inaccurate titles: Dante calls his epic poem a comedy, Dickens names his story a carol.

103. *I cannot rest, I cannot stay, I cannot linger anywhere.* Dickens in the galleys carefully changed this lamentation from "I may not rest, I may not stay, I may not linger anywhere," thereby removing any chance of choice for the spirit.

104. *the Ward.* An officer or watchman of the ward, one of twenty-six parishes, or divisions, of London, here likely Langborn Ward. It was in 1829 that the modern metropolitan police force was formed under Sir Robert Peel; policeman are called "bobbies" after him.

105. *captive, bound, and double-ironed.* Dickens had trouble with this line: he changed it to "man, cruel man" in the Berg prompt copy and then "blind man, blind man" in the 1867 Ticknor and Fields Public Reading edition.

106. *Yet such was I! Oh! such was I!* "Yet I was like this man! I once was like this man!" in the 1867 Ticknor and Fields Public Reading edition.

roved beyond the narrow limits of our money-changing hole; and weary journeys lie before me!"

It was a habit with Scrooge, whenever he became thoughtful, to put his hands in his breeches pockets. Pondering on what the Ghost had said, he did so now, but without lifting up his eyes, or getting off his knees.

"You must have been very slow about it, Jacob," Scrooge observed, in a business-like manners, though with humility and deference.

"Slow!" the Ghost repeated.

"Seven years dead," mused Scrooge. "And travelling all the time?"

"The whole time," said the Ghost. "No rest, no peace. Incessant torture of remorse."

"You travel fast?" said Scrooge.

"On the wings of the wind," replied the Ghost.

"You might have got over a great quantity of ground in seven years," said Scrooge.

The Ghost, on hearing this, set up another cry, and clanked its chain so hideously in the dead silence of the night, that the Ward[104] would have been justified in indicting it for a nuisance.

"Oh! captive, bound, and double-ironed,"[105] cried the phantom, "not to know, that ages of incessant labour by immortal creatures, for this earth must pass into eternity before the good of which it is susceptible is all developed. Not to know that any Christian spirit working kindly in its little sphere, whatever it may be, will find its mortal life too short for its vast means of usefulness. Not to know that no space of regret can make amends for one life's opportunities misused! Yet such was I! Oh! such was I!"[106]

"But you were always a good man of business, Jacob," faultered Scrooge, who now began to apply this to himself.

"Business!" cried the Ghost, wringing its hands again. "Mankind was my business. The common welfare was my business; charity, mercy, forbearance, and benevolence, were, all, my business. The dealings of my trade were but a drop of water in the comprehensive ocean of my business!"

It held up its chain at arm's length, as if that were the cause of all its unavailing grief, and flung it heavily upon the ground again.

"At this time of the rolling year," the spectre said, "I suffer most. Why did I walk through crowds of fellow-beings with my eyes turned down, and never raise them to that blessed Star which led the Wise Men to a poor abode? Were there no poor homes to which its light would have conducted *me!*"

Scrooge was very much dismayed to hear the spectre going on at this rate, and began to quake exceedingly.

"Hear me!" cried the Ghost. "My time is nearly gone."

"I will," said Scrooge. "But don't be hard upon me! Don't be flowery, Jacob! Pray!"

"How it is that I appear before you in a shape that you can see, I may not tell. I have sat invisible beside you many and many a day."

It was not an agreeable idea. Scrooge shivered, and wiped the perspiration from his brow.

"That is no light part of my penance," pursued the Ghost. "I am here to-night to warn you, that you have yet a chance and hope of escaping my fate. A chance and hope of my procuring, Ebenezer."

"You were always a good friend to me," said Scrooge. "Thank'ee!"

"You will be haunted," resumed the Ghost, "by Three Spirits."

Scrooge's countenance fell almost as low as the Ghost's had done.

"Is that the chance and hope you mentioned, Jacob?" he demanded, in a faultering voice.

"It is."

"I—I think I'd rather not," said Scrooge.

"Without their visits," said the Ghost, "you cannot hope to shun the path I tread. Expect the first to-morrow, when the bell tolls One."[107]

107. *when the bell tolls One.* The ghost of Hamlet's father, too, enters when the bell tolls one in *Hamlet* 1.1.

"Scrooge followed to the window."
Wood engraving after
Gustave Doré, *Journal pour tous*, June 16, 1861.
Courtesy Library of Congress.

108. *Every one of them wore chains.* Marilyn P. Hollinshead speculated in "Dickens in Pittsburgh: A Stereoscopic View" (*The Dickensian*, January 1978, p. 35) that "a horrible thought" that troubled Dickens after he visited the Western Pennsylvania Penitentiary in Pittsburgh may have suggested this association of ghosts with prisoners. *"What if ghosts be one of the terrors of these jails?"* he wrote John Forster on April 3, 1842. "The utter solitude by day and night; the hours of darkness; the silence of death; the mind for ever brooding on melancholy themes, and having no relief; sometimes an evil conscience very busy; imagine a prisoner covering up his head in the bedclothes and looking out from time to time, with a ghastly dread of some inexplicable silent figure that always sits upon his bed, or stands (if a thing can be said to stand, that never walks as men do) in the same corner of his cell. The more I think of it, the more certain I feel that not a few of these men (during a portion of their imprisonment at least) are nightly visited by spectres" (p. 181).

109. *linked together.* The manuscript added "some were monstrous dogs, for their noses were attached to them," but Dickens crossed this out before it went to the printers.

"Couldn't I take 'em all at once, and have it over, Jacob?" hinted Scrooge.

"Expect the second on the next night at the same hour. The third upon the new night when the last stroke of Twelve has ceased to vibrate. Look to see me no more; and look that, for your own sake, you remember what has passed between us!"

When it had said these words, the spectre took its wrapper from the table, and bound it round its head, as before. Scrooge knew this, by the smart sound its teeth made, when the jaws were brought together by the bandage. He ventured to raise his eyes again, and found his supernatural visitor confronting him in an erect attitude, with its chain wound over and about its arm.

The apparition walked backward from him; and at every step it took, the window raised itself a little, so that when the spectre reached it, it was wide open. It beckoned Scrooge to approach, which he did. When they were within two paces of each other, Marley's Ghost held up its hand, warning him to come no nearer. Scrooge stopped.

Not so much in obedience, as in surprise and fear: for on the raising of the hand, he became sensible of confused noises in the air; incoherent sounds of lamentation and regret; wailings inexpressibly sorrowful and self-accusatory. The spectre, after listening for a moment, joined in the mournful dirge; and floated out upon the bleak, dark night.

Scrooge followed to the window: desperate in his curiosity. He looked out.

The air was filled with phantoms, wandering hither and thither in restless haste, and moaning as they went. Every one of them wore chains[108] like Marley's Ghost; some few (they might be guilty governments) were linked together;[109] none were free. Many had been personally known to Scrooge in their lives. He had been quite familiar with one old ghost, in a white waistcoat, with a monstrous iron safe attached to its ancle, who cried piteously at being unable to assist a

Preliminary pencil and wash drawing by
John Leech for "The Phantoms," 1843.
Courtesy Houghton Library, Harvard University.

wretched woman with an infant, whom it saw below, upon a door-step. The misery with them all was, clearly, that they sought to interfere, for good, in human matters, and had lost the power for ever.

Whether these creatures faded into mist, or mist enshrouded them, he could not tell. But they and their spirit voices faded together; and the night became as it had been when he walked home.

Scrooge closed the window, and examined the door by which the Ghost had entered. It was double-locked, as he had locked it with his own hands, and the bolts

110. *dull.* Here meaning in monotonous tones. Kate Field in *Pen Photographs of Charles Dickens's Readings* (Boston: James R. Osgood, 1871) considered the one failure in Dickens' characterizations to be his making the spirits "perhaps too monotonous,— a way ghosts have when they return to earth. It is generally believed that ghosts, being 'damp, moist, uncomfortable bodies,' lose their voices beyond redemption and are obliged to pipe through eternity on one key. . . . Solemnity and monotony are not synonymous terms, yet every theatrical ghost insists that they are, and Dickens is no exception to the rule" (p. 36).

were undisturbed. He tried to say, "Humbug!" but stopped at the first syllable. And being, from the emotion he had undergone, or the fatigues of the day, or his glimpse of the Invisible World, or the dull[110] conversation of the Ghost, or the lateness of the hour, much in need of repose; went straight to bed, without undressing, and fell asleep upon the instant.

STAVE TWO.

THE FIRST OF THE THREE SPIRITS.

When Scrooge awoke, it was so dark, that looking out of bed, he could scarcely distinguish the transparent window from the opaque walls of his chamber. He was endeavouring to pierce the darkness with his ferret eyes,[1] when the chimes of a neighbouring church[2] struck the four quarters. So he listened for the hour.

To his great astonishment the heavy bell went on from six[3] to seven, and from seven to eight, and regularly up to twelve; then stopped. Twelve! It was past two when he went to bed. The clock was wrong. An icicle must have got into the works. Twelve!

He touched the spring of his repeater,[4] to correct this most preposterous clock. Its rapid little pulse beat twelve; and stopped.

"Why, it isn't possible," said Scrooge, "that I can have slept through a whole day and far into another night. It isn't possible that anything has happened to the sun, and this is twelve at noon!"

The idea being an alarming one, he scrambled out of bed, and groped his way to the window. He was obliged to rub the frost off with the sleeve of his dressing-gown before he could see anything; and could see very little then. All he could make out was, that it was still very foggy and extremely cold, and that there was no noise of people running to and fro, and making a great stir, as there unquestionably would have been if night had beaten off bright day, and taken possession of the world. This was a great relief, because "three

1. *ferret eyes.* The ferret, a member of the weasel family, has sharp, red eyes; in England, these animals are used to drive rabbits and rats from their lairs. Scrooge thus has a penetrating gaze.

2. *a neighbouring church.* Gwen Major in "Scrooge's Chambers" (*The Dickensian*, winter 1932–33, p. 14) identified this place as St. Andrew's Undershaft, at the corner of Leadenhall Street and St. Mary Avenue.

3. *six.* Apparently Scrooge usually rose at six in the morning; this was the usual hour of waking for Londoners of the time.

4. *his repeater.* Repeating watch or clock, invented about 1767, able to strike the hour and quarter hour when a button is pushed. Not all of these timepieces were as cheap as Scrooge's must be. Ralph Nickleby keeps a gold one in his pocket in Chapter 2 of *Nicholas Nickleby* (1839); Wemmick tells Pip in *Great Expectations* (vol. 2, Chapter 6, 1861) that his benefactor has a gold repeater "worth a hundred pound if it's worth a penny."

5. *"three days after sight of this First of Exchange pay to Mr. Ebenezer Scrooge or his order."* This quotation is slightly different from that in the manuscript (now in the Pierpont Morgan Library): "sixty days after sight pay to me or my order." This is the technical form in which a bill of exchange is worded; each one, drawn up for a debt or credit without an actual exchange of money, is prepared in three sets as the first, second, and third exchange, so that if one is lost, the others will be available; once one is accepted, the bill becomes worthless. Scrooge is worried because, if not presented by the date assigned in writing, the bill is worth nothing. Dickens likely changed the payment date from sixty to three days to increase the miser's distress. Scrooge has already lost one day by the clock, so he has little time to settle his accounts. No wonder he is so troubled.

6. *United States' security.* Dickens originally wrote "a questionable security," but soon came up with this more distinctive and controversial comment. A United States' security at that time seemed no security at all to the English. In the 1830s, individual states, without backing from the federal government, borrowed heavily from foreign capitalists (particularly the English) to finance public works. Due to the financial crisis of 1837, many repudiated their bonds and thus weakened American credit abroad.

Some Americans thought this remark was just another example of the contempt for the United States the Englishman Dickens had been expressing in *American Notes* (1842) and *Martin Chuzzlewit* (1844). "Was there ever more misplaced malevolence and absurd ignorance embraced in as few words?" demanded an observer in *The Spirit of the Times* (February 24, 1844). "He has here aspersed a whole nation, from whose people he had received almost unexampled, and certainly very unmerited, hos-

days after sight of this First of Exchange pay to Mr. Ebenezer Scrooge or his order,"[5] and so forth, would have become a mere United States' security[6] if there were no days to count by.

Scrooge went to bed again, and thought, and thought, and thought it over and over and over, and could make nothing of it. The more he thought, the more perplexed he was; and the more he endeavoured not to think, the more he thought. Marley's Ghost bothered him exceedingly. Every time he resolved within himself, after mature inquiry, that it was all a dream, his mind flew back again, like a strong spring released, to its first position, and presented the same problem to be worked all through, "Was it a dream or not?"

Scrooge lay in this state until the chimes had gone three quarters more, when he remembered, on a sudden, that the Ghost had warned him of a visitation when the bell tolled one. He resolved to lie awake until the hour was past; and, considering that he could no more go to sleep than go to Heaven, this was perhaps the wisest resolution in his power.

The quarter was so long, that he was more than once convinced he must have sunk into a doze unconsciously, and missed the clock. At length it broke upon his listening ear.

"Ding, dong!"

"A quarter past," said Scrooge, counting.

"Ding, dong!"

"Half past!" said Scrooge.

"Ding, dong!"

"A quarter to it," said Scrooge.

"Ding, dong!"

"The hour itself," said Scrooge, triumphantly, "and nothing else!"

He spoke before the hour bell sounded, which it now did with a deep, dull, hollow, melancholy ONE. Light flashed up in the room upon the instant, and the curtains of his bed were drawn.

The curtains of his bed were drawn aside, I tell you, by a hand. Not the curtains at his feet, nor the curtains at his back, but those to which his face was addressed. The curtains of his bed were drawn aside; and Scrooge, starting up into a half-recumbent attitude, found himself face to face with the unearthly visitor who drew them: as close to it as I am now to you, and I am standing in the spirit at your elbow.

It was a strange figure[7]—like a child: yet not so like a child as like an old man, viewed through some supernatural medium, which gave him the appearance of having receded from the view, and being diminished to a child's proportions. Its hair, which hung about its neck and down its back, was white as if with age; and yet the face had not a wrinkle in it, and the tenderest bloom was on the skin. The arms were very long and muscular; the hands the same, as if its hold were of uncommon strength. Its legs and feet, most delicately formed, were, like those upper members, bare. It wore a tunic of the purest white; and round its waist was bound a lustrous belt, the sheen of which was beautiful. It held a branch of fresh green holly in its hand; and, in singular contradiction of that wintry emblem, had its dress trimmed with summer flowers. But the strangest thing about it was, that from the crown of its head there sprung a bright clear jet of light, by which all this was visible; and which was doubtless the occasion of its using, in its duller moments, a great extinguisher for a cap, which it now held under its arm.

Even this, though, when Scrooge looked at it with increasing steadiness, was *not* its strangest quality. For as its belt sparkled and glittered now in one part and now in another, and what was light one instant, at another time was dark, so the figure itself fluctuated in its distinctness: being now a thing with one arm, now with one leg, now with twenty legs, now a pair of legs without a head, now a head without a body: of which dissolving parts, no outline would be visible in the dense gloom wherein they melted away. And in the very

pitality. So far from his insinuation having the least foundation, during the very last week, United States Six per cent Stock sold in the city of New York at a premium of 14 per cent above par. It must have a corresponding value in London. It is perhaps held there, at this moment, at a higher rate than English securities. The U. S. Government, it is well known to those informed upon the subject, has always, with punctuality, paid its debts, as they became due, and has never even been suspected of dreaming of repudiation" (p. 613). Dickens wisely dropped the line in his 1867–68 American Public Reading tour, but not everyone in the United States was willing to forget it. "The people are getting tired of Dickens," insisted the New York *Evening Telegram* (January 4, 1868). "Before his readings are over here his ticket of admission, like Ebenezer Scrooge's First of Exchange, will 'have become a mere United States' security.'"

7. *It was a strange figure.* The ambiguity of the Ghost's age suggests that it is not only more than two thousand years old but as young and fresh as spring flowers, "for it is good to be children sometimes, and never better than at Christmas, when its mighty Founder was a child himself." This duality is symbolic of memory itself, which shifts from one age to another as uncontrollably as the Ghost; memory embraces one's entire life, from infancy through old age.

This illusion of youth suggests the *Christkindl*, the German Christ child who, during the Reformation, replaced the Roman Saint Nicholas; this spirit, generally depicted as a girl, was said to be the messenger who announced the coming birth of Christ. This *Christkindl* combined with Father Christmas (see Stave 3, note 12) to form Kriss Kringle, the prototype for the American Santa Claus. The *Christkindl* is traditionally dressed in a white gown and veil, wearing a wreath of candles on its head. But Dickens seems to be describing an actual candle, a perfect metaphor for memory. The strange alterations in the Ghost's form reflect the constant transmutations of the candle's flame and the dripping tallow. That Scrooge is actually staring at his "dip" is evident from the extinguisher the Ghost carries under its arm.

Again Dickens refers to a phantom only as "it"; the Ghost of Christmas Past is neither male nor female. It therefore has posed a problem for dramatists from the very beginning. Not surprisingly, it has been portrayed over the last century as both male and female, old and young. Mr. Lewis took the role at the Royal Surrey Theatre in 1844, while over at the Adelphi Miss E. Chaplin had the same part. In the 1951 Alastair Sim film, it was portrayed by an old man; in the 1962 Mr. Magoo television cartoon, as a child; and Dame Edith Evans played it in the 1970 movie musical *Scrooge*. John Leech, perhaps baffled as to how to draw the spirit, did not even attempt drawing it.

8. *The voice was soft and gentle. Singularly low.* Malcolm Andrews noted in *Dickens and the Grown-up Child* (London: Macmillan, 1994) the similarity between this description and Lear's observation on the death of his beloved daughter Cordelia: "Her voice was ever soft, / Gentle, and low, an excellent thing in woman" (*King Lear*, 5.3.271–72). "But the echo is quite appropriate," Andrews argued. "Lear's effort to revive the child he had renounced is analogous to Scrooge's confrontation with the childhood memories he has long repressed" (p. 104).

9. *Your past.* "The things you will see with me," explains the Ghost in the 1867 Ticknor and Fields Public Reading edition, "are shadows of the things that have been; they will have no consciousness of us." Dreams, according to Macnish in *The Philosophy of Sleep* (1838), "have the power of brightening

wonder of this, it would be itself again; distinct and clear as ever.

"Are you the Spirit, sir, whose coming was foretold to me?" asked Scrooge.

"I am!"

The voice was soft and gentle. Singularly low,[8] as if instead of being so close beside him, it were at a distance.

"Who, and what are you?" Scrooge demanded.

"I am the Ghost of Christmas Past."

"Long past?" inquired Scrooge: observant of its dwarfish stature.

"No. Your past."[9]

Perhaps, Scrooge could not have told anybody why, if anybody could have asked him; but he had a special desire to see the Spirit in his cap; and begged him to be covered.

"What!" exclaimed the Ghost, "would you so soon put out, with worldly hands, the light I give? Is it not enough that you are one of those whose passions made this cap, and force me through whole trains of years to wear it low upon my brow!"

Scrooge reverently disclaimed all intention to offend, or any knowledge of having wilfully "bonneted"[10] the Spirit at any period of his life. He then made bold to inquire what business brought him there.

"Your welfare!" said the Ghost.

Scrooge expressed himself much obliged, but could not help thinking that a night of unbroken rest would have been more conducive to that end.[11] The Spirit must have heard him thinking, for it said immediately:

"Your reclamation, then. Take heed!"

It put out its strong hand as it spoke, and clasped him gently by the arm.

"Rise! and walk with me!"

It would have been in vain for Scrooge to plead that the weather and the hour were not adapted to pedestrian purposes; that bed was warm, and the thermometer a long way below freezing; that he was clad but

up the dim regions of the past, and presenting them with a force which the mere effects of unassisted remembrance could never have accomplished in our waking hours. This property of reviving past images, is one of the most remarkable possessed by sleep. It even goes the length, of recalling circumstances which had been entirely forgotten, and presenting them to the mind with more than the force of their original impression" (p. 82).

10. *"bonneted."* A pun on the slang word for crushing a man's hat over his eyes with one blow, as one might snuff out a candle with its "bonnet," or extinguishing cap. It was a favorite expression used by Dickens: Sam Weller in Chapter 44 of *The Pickwick Papers* (1837) mistakenly "bonnets" his own father after the man steps on his toes.

11. *Scrooge . . . could not help thinking that a night of unbroken rest would have been more conducive to that end.* Scrooge still cannot avoid being facetious: despite the Ghost's appearance for his welfare, the old miser remains the perfect utilitarian.

"It was a strange figure—like a child." Wood engraving after Gustave Doré, *Journal pour tous,* June 29, 1861.
Courtesy Library of Congress.

12. *a thousand odours . . . connected with a thousand thoughts, and hopes, and joys, and cares long, long, forgotten!* Memory as revived by one's senses, here that of smell, recalls Marcel Proust and his madeleine, in summoning "the remembrance of things past."

13. *a pimple.* It is, of course, a tear, the first indication that Scrooge may still possess a heart.

14. *a little market-town . . . with its bridge, its church, and winding river.* Frank S. Johnson in "About *A Christmas Carol*" (*The Dickensian*, winter 1931–32, p. 8) identified this as Strood, Rochester, by the river Medway, where Dickens spent some of the happiest days of his own childhood, from 1817 to 1822. Johnson also pointed out that Dickens erased the word "castle" in the manuscript, an obvious reference to Rochester Castle there. Dickens described this area again as the market town in *Great Expectations* (1861) and as "Cloisterham" in Chapter 3 of his unfinished *The Mystery of Edwin Drood* (1870).

"Country Church—Christmas Morning." Etching by Robert Seymour, *The Book of Christmas* by Thomas K. Hervey, 1836. *Private collection.*

lightly in his slippers, dressing-gown, and nightcap; and that he had a cold upon him at that time. The grasp, though gentle as a woman's hand, was not to be resisted. He rose: but finding that the Spirit made towards the window, clasped its robe in supplication.

"I am a mortal," Scrooge remonstrated, "and liable to fall."

"Bear but a touch of my hand *there*," said the Spirit, laying it upon his heart, "and you shall be upheld in more than this!"

As the words were spoken, they passed through the wall, and stood upon an open country road, with fields on either hand. The city had entirely vanished. Not a vestige of it was to be seen. The darkness and the mist had vanished with it, for it was a clear, cold, winter day, with snow upon the ground.

"Good Heaven!" said Scrooge, clasping his hands together, as he looked about him. "I was bred in this place. I was a boy here!"

The Spirit gazed upon him mildly. Its gentle touch, though it had been light and instantaneous, appeared still present to the old man's sense of feeling. He was conscious of a thousand odours floating in the air, each one connected with a thousand thoughts, and hopes, and joys, and cares long, long, forgotten![12]

"Your lip is trembling," said the Ghost. "And what is that upon your cheek?"

Scrooge muttered, with an unusual catching in his voice, that it was a pimple;[13] and begged the Ghost to lead him where he would.

"You recollect the way?" inquired the Spirit.

"Remember it!" cried Scrooge with fervour; "I could walk it blindfold."

"Strange to have forgotten it for so many years!" observed the Ghost. "Let us go on."

They walked along the road; Scrooge recognising every gate, and post, and tree; until a little market-town appeared in the distance, with its bridge, its church, and winding river.[14] Some shaggy ponies now were seen trotting towards them with boys upon their backs, who called to other boys in country gigs[15] and carts, driven by farmers. All these boys were in great spirits,[16] and shouted to each other, until the broad fields were so full of merry music, that the crisp air laughed to hear it.

"These are but shadows of the things that have been," said the Ghost. "They have no consciousness of us."

The jocund travellers came on; and as they came, Scrooge knew and named them every one. Why was he rejoiced beyond all bounds to see them! Why did his cold eye glisten, and his heart leap up as they went past! Why was he filled with gladness when he heard them give each other Merry Christmas, as they parted at cross-roads and bye-ways, for their several homes! What was merry Christmas to Scrooge? Out upon merry Christmas![17] What good had it ever done to him?

"The school is not quite deserted," said the Ghost. "A solitary child, neglected by his friends, is left there still."

Scrooge said he knew it. And he sobbed.

They left the high-road, by a well remembered lane, and soon approached a mansion of dull red brick,[18] with a little weathercock-surmounted cupola, on the roof, and a bell hanging in it. It was a large house, but one of broken fortunes; for the spacious offices were little used, their walls were damp and mossy, their windows broken, and their gates decayed. Fowls clucked and strutted in the stables; and the coach-houses and sheds were overrun with grass. Nor was it more retentive of its ancient state, within; for entering the dreary hall, and glancing through the open doors of many rooms, they found them poorly furnished, cold, and vast. There was an earthy savour in the air, a chilly bareness in the place, which associated itself somehow with too much getting up by candle-light, and not too much to eat.

They went, the Ghost and Scrooge, across the hall,

15. *gigs.* Light two-wheeled, one-horse carriages.

16. *All these boys were in great spirits.* The 1867 Ticknor and Fields Public Reading edition explained exactly why: "at the breaking up of their school." See also note 32 below.

"Coming Home." Etching by Robert Seymour, *The Book of Christmas* by Thomas K. Hervey, 1836.
Private collection.

17. *Out upon merry Christmas!* Scrooge's own cruel words come back to haunt him again and again throughout the story.

18. *a mansion of dull red brick.* Compare this description of Scrooge's schoolhouse with that of another schoolhouse, in Chapter 5 of *David Copperfield* (1850):

Salem House was a square brick building with wings; of a bare and unfurnished appearance. All about it was so very quiet, that I said . . . I supposed the boys were out; but he seemed surprised at my not knowing that it was holiday-time. . . . I gazed upon the schoolroom into which he took me, as the most forlorn and desolate place I had ever seen. . . . A long room with three long rows of desks, and six of forms, and bristling all round with pegs for hats and slates. . . . There is a strange unwholesome smell about the place, like mildewed corduroys, sweet apples wanting air, and rotten books.

This was Wellington House Academy, Hampstead Road, in north London, where Dickens received a brief formal education (a year and a half) before leaving at fifteen to accept an apprenticeship in a law office. He also described the place in "Our School" (*Household Words*, October 11, 1851).

19. *plain deal forms.* Long, unpainted and unvarnished school benches made of deal wood, or pine.

20. *a lonely boy was reading.* This child was the boy Charles Dickens. "He was a very little and very sickly boy," Forster described him in vol. 1 of *The Life of Charles Dickens* (London: Chapman and Hall, 1872), "subject to attacks of violent spasm which disabled him from any active exertion. He was never a good little cricket-player. He was never a first-rate hand at marbles. . . . But he had great pleasure in watching the other boys . . . at these games,

Wood engraving after George Cruikshank,
Our Own Times, 1846.
Courtesy Prints Division, New York Public Library, Astor, Lenox and Tilden Foundations.

to a door at the back of the house. It opened before them, and disclosed a long, bare, melancholy room, made barer still by lines of plain deal forms[19] and desks. At one of these a lonely boy was reading[20] near a feeble fire; and Scrooge sat down upon a form, and wept to see his poor forgotten self as he had used to be.

Not a latent echo in the house, not a squeak and scuffle from the mice behind the panneling, not a drip from the half-thawed water-spout in the dull yard behind, not a sigh among the leafless boughs of one despondent poplar, not the idle swinging of an empty store-house door, no, not a clicking in the fire, but fell upon the heart of Scrooge with softening influence, and gave a freer passage to his tears.[21]

The Spirit touched him on the arm, and pointed to his younger self, intent upon his reading.[22] Suddenly a man,[23] in foreign garments: wonderfully real and distinct to look at: stood outside the window, with an axe stuck in his belt, and leading an ass laden with wood by the bridle.

"Why, it's Ali Baba!"[24] Scrooge exclaimed in ecstacy. "It's dear old honest Ali Baba! Yes, yes, I know! One Christmas time, when yonder solitary child was left here all alone, he *did* come, for the first time, just like that. Poor boy! And Valentine," said Scrooge, "and his wild brother, Orson;[25] there they go! And what's his name,[26] who was put down in his drawers, asleep, at the Gate of Damascus; don't you see him! And the Sultan's Groom[27] turned upside-down by the Genii; there he is upon his head! Serve him right. I'm glad of it. What business had *he* to be married to the Princess!"[28]

To hear Scrooge expending all the earnestness of his nature on such subjects, in a most extraordinary voice between laughing and crying; and to see his heightened and excited face; would have been a surprise to his business friends in the city, indeed.

"There's the Parrot!"[29] cried Scrooge. "Green body and yellow tail, with a thing like a lettuce growing out

reading while they played; and he had always the belief that this early sickness had brought to himself one inestimable advantage, in the circumstance of his weak health having strongly inclined him to reading" (pp. 5–6). Others recalled him as being more robust. See note 35 below.

"The whole passage [in *A Christmas Carol*] is in the spirit of [Charles] Lamb's 'New Year's Eve,' a favourite essay with Dickens," observed Kathleen Tillotson in "The Middle Years from *Carol* to *Copperfield*" (*Dickens Memorial Lectures 1970* [London: Dickens Fellowship, 1970]); "Elia looks back upon 'the "other me" there, in the background' in tender love and pity, and regret–'From what have I fallen!'–and suggests that 'over the intervention of forty years, a man may have leave to love himself without the intervention of self-love'" (p. 12).

21. *Not a latent echo in the house . . . but fell upon the heart of Scrooge with softening influence, and gave a freer passage to his tears.* Tillotson in her lecture (cited above, in note 20) said, of this passage, "The whole impression, and half the details, come from Tennyson's 'Mariana' (first published in *Poems, Chiefly Lyrical,* 1830)" (p. 13).

Following "his tears," Dickens originally went on a bit too much about Scrooge's tears in the manuscript but crossed out "that dropped down through his fingers as he spread his hands before his face" before the book went to press.

22. *his younger self, intent upon his reading.* In the autobiographical fragment that Dickens slightly revised as part of Chapter 4 in *David Copperfield* (1850), he described in detail his introduction to the world of literature, similar to that of Master Scrooge: "My father had left in a little room upstairs, to which I had access . . . a small col-lection of books which nobody else in our house ever troubled. From that blessed little room, Roderick Random, Peregrine Pickle, Humphrey Clinker, Tom Jones, The Vicar of Wakefield, Don Quixote, Gil Blas, and Robinson Crusoe, came out, a glorious host, to keep me company. They kept alive my fancy, and my hope of something beyond that place and time,—they, and the Arabian Nights, and the Tales of the Genii,—and did me no harm; for whatever harm was in some of them was not there for me; *I* knew nothing of it." They provided him with one solace and refuge from the harsh world outside. So dear was this little library to young Charles that it must have been tragic for the boy to have to pawn, among the first of his father's belongings when he fell into debt, these precious volumes.

Dickens loved giving and receiving books at Christmas. In "A Christmas Tree" (*Household Words*, September 21, 1850), he reveled in describing "how thick the books begin to hang . . . many of them, and with deliciously smooth covers of bright red or green." They contained the favorite tales of his and Scrooge's childhoods. The effect of these early books on Charles Dickens the man and the writer is inestimable.

The young Scrooge and David Copperfield are among the fortunate children in Dickens' work who find the rare treasures hidden in fanciful literature. Not all boys and girls are so blessed. For example, the young and appropriately named Smallweeds of Chapter 21 of *Bleak House* (1853), who have been denied this pleasure, are "complete little men and women" who "bear a likeness to old monkeys with something depressing on their minds." Their practical education "discarded all amusements, dis-countenanced all story-books, fairy tales, fictions, and fables, and banished all levities whatsoever." Judy has "never heard of Cinderella," Bart "knows no more of Jack the Giant Killer, or of Sinbad the Sailor, than he knows of the people in the stars."

23. *a man.* "A kind of a picture of a man" in the Berg prompt copy.

24. *Ali Baba!* The Berg prompt copy explained that "he has come out of the Arabian Nights." "Ali Baba and the Forty Thieves" was one of Dickens' favorite stories from one of his favorite books, one he always associated with Christmas. He first encountered the stories Scheherazade told when a boy himself, perhaps in Jonathan Scott's translation of 1811. "Oh, now all things become uncommon and enchanted to me," he wrote of the pleasures of *The Arabian Nights* in "A Christmas Tree" (*Household Words*, September 21, 1850). "All lamps are wonderful; all rings are talismans. Common flower-pots are full of treasure, with a little earth scattered on top; trees are for Ali Baba to hide in. . . . Yes, on every object that I recognize among those upper branches of my Christmas Tree, I see this fairy light! When I awake in bed, at day-

break, on the cold dark winter mornings, the white snow dimly beheld, outside, through the frost on the window-pane, I hear Dinarzade."

Next to Shakespeare and the New Testament, *The Arabian Nights* is the book most frequently alluded to in Dickens' writings; and among the tales most often cited is "Ali Baba and the Forty Thieves." For example, he mentions the cutting up of Casim Baba into quarters and the hanging of the pieces in the thieves' den in Chapter 5 of *Martin Chuzzlewit* (1844), the opening pages of *The Haunted Man* (1848), and Chapter 3 of *Little Dorrit* (1857), as well as in "A Christmas Tree"; in Chapter 2 of *Hard Times* (1854), he facetiously compares the teaching methods of M'Choakumchild to the slave girl Morgiana's search for thieves in jars. Passing references were not all: Dickens borrowed the device of Scheherazade's stringing together a series of stories for the structure of his magazine *Master Humphrey's Clock* (April 4, 1840–December 4, 1841) and for David Copperfield's dormitory sketches in *David Copperfield* (1850). "We'll make some

"'Why, it's Ali Baba!'" Wood engraving after Gustave Doré,
Journal pour tous, June 16, 1861.
Courtesy Library of Congress.

regular Arabian Nights of it," says his friend Steerforth in Chapter 7. Among the few worthy wares in the children's bookshop ("not quite so bad at first, but still a trying shop") that Tom Pinch visits in Chapter 5 of *Martin Chuzzlewit* are *The Arabian Nights* and *Robinson Crusoe*. See notes 26 and 27.

25. *Valentine . . . and his wild brother, Orson.* The heroes of a popular French medieval prose romance, first published in Lyons in 1489. It was translated into English about 1505 by Henry Watson and published by Wynken de Worde; the second edition, *The Hystory of Two Valyaunte Brethren, Valentyne and Orson, Sonnes of the Emperor of Grece*, was issued by William Copland about 1530. Valentine and Orson are the twin sons of Bellisant, the sister of King Pepin and wife of the emperor of Constantinople. They are separated at birth: Orson, one of the most famous feral children in Western literature, is carried off by a she-wolf and raised as a wild man; Valentine is groomed as a knight of the French court. They are eventually reunited, and Orson is restored to his proper birthright. Dickens makes other references to this story in his books, as in "The Boarding House," in *Sketches by Boz* (1839); Chapter 5 of *Barnaby Rudge* (1841); and Chapter 22 of *Martin Chuzzlewit* (1844).

This book, like *Robinson Crusoe* and *The Arabian Nights*, was originally written for adults, then abridged as a chapbook, and became a favorite with children as *The History of Valentine and Orson*. The complicated story had much to recommend it to young readers, as stated in a 1688 edition: "the battles of martial champions . . . courtly tournaments and combats of princes . . . travels of knightly adventures . . . sorrows of distressed ladies . . . of strange births and savage education . . . of friends long lost and their joyful meeting

again . . . of charmes and enchantments . . . of rewards of traytors and treasons . . . of long captivities and imprisonments." Elizabeth MacRae suggested in her afterward to *Valentine and Orson, or The Surprising Adventures of Two Sons of the Emperor of Greece* (Toronto: Toronto Public Library, 1971) that Dickens may have known the story through an 1822 toy book, published by John Harris and Son as part of the Cabinet of Amusement and Instruction. Dickens mentioned in "To Rome by Pisa and Siena," in *Pictures from Italy* (1846), his youthful acquaintance with the wares of Mr. Harris, Bookseller, at the corner of St. Paul's Churchyard, London. The story was also well known through dramatizations; for example, the pantomime *Harlequin and King Pepin, or Valentine and Orson* played the Drury Lane Theatre the year *A Christmas Carol* came out, and another *Valentine and Orson* was on the same bill as Edward Stirling's *The Chimes* at the Lyceum in January 1845.

26. *what's his name.* Bedreddin Hassan, who, like Ali Baba, was, as the Berg prompt copy explained, "out of the Arabian Nights, too." See next note.

27. *the Sultan's Groom.* A character in "Noureddin Ali of Cairo and His Son Bedreddin Hassan" (see Nights 20–23, *The Portable Arabian Nights*, edited by Joseph Campbell [New York: Random House, 1952]): A genie tells Bedreddin Hassan of a woman equal to him in beauty. But the vizier's daughter is already promised to another, a sultan's hunchbacked dwarf. The genie transports Bedreddin to the palace, displaces the hideous husband-to-be with the handsome young man, and has spirits hang the dwarf upside down during the wedding night. The genie must return before morning with Bedreddin still in his bedclothes, but as they are passing over Damascus, dawn breaks and Bedreddin is left at the city gates. He finds employment as a cook, and after a dozen years, he is finally reunited with his wife and their son, born while he was away. Dickens recalls this story again in "A Christmas Tree" (*Household Words*, September 21, 1850), as another example of how *The Arabian Nights* turned the commonplace into the marvelous: "Tarts are made, according to the recipe of the Vizier's son of Bussorah, who turned pastrycook after he was set down in his drawers at the gate of Damascus."

28. *What business had* he to *be married to the Princess!* Dickens added "d[am]n him" in the manuscript, but he removed the curse before the book went to press for being inappropriate for a Christmas tale.

29. *"There's the Parrot!"* The Berg prompt copy identified him as "Robinson Crusoe's." Although written for adults, *The Life and Adventures of Robinson Crusoe* (1719) by Daniel Defoe (1660–1731) had become by the time Dickens was a boy a standard Christmas gift book. "No doubt," suggested *Fraser's Magazine* (January 1851), "numerous cousins, uncles, and aunts, presented the same little boy with the same little books; so that repeated editions of the identical *Crusoe* . . . must have accumulated in the Juvenile Library, to the infinite vexation of its proprietor. How very tired that little boy must have grown of his man Friday, towards whom he was so cordially disposed at the beginning of their acquaintance; and how he must have hated that print in the sand, which he was expected to be as much surprised at every time he looked at it, as he was at first, when a great thrilling mystery lay behind it!" (p. 37).

Not so the young Charles Dickens. *Robinson Crusoe* was one of the favorite books of his childhood; references to it can be found in almost all of his books, even *American Notes* (1842) and *Pictures from Italy* (1846). One of the most famous events in the book

occurs after six years of isolation, when Crusoe returns to his hut weary after sailing all around the island. On lying down, this sole survivor of a shipwreck clearly hears someone calling, *"Robin, Robin, Robin Crusoe,* poor *Robin Crusoe,* where are you *Robin Crusoe?* Where are you? Where have you been?"* It turns out to be his par-

Wood engraving after George Cruikshank, *The Life and Adventures of Robinson Crusoe* by Daniel Defoe, 1831. *Courtesy Library of Congress.*

rot, speaking "in such bemoaning language I had used to talk to him, and teach him; and he had learn'd it so perfectly, that he would sit upon my finger, and lay his bill close to my face, and cry, *Poor* Robin Crusoe, *Where are you? Where have you been? How come you here?* and other things I had taught him."

Dickens warmly recalled this incident in "Where We Stopped Growing" (*Household Words*, January 1, 1853): "We have never grown the thousandth part of an inch out of Robinson Crusoe. He fits us just as well, and in exactly the same way as when we were among the smallest of the small. . . . Never sail we, idle, in a little boat . . . but we know

of the top of his head; there he is! Poor Robin Crusoe, he called him, when he came home again after sailing round the island. 'Poor Robin Crusoe, where have you been, Robin Crusoe?' The man thought he was dreaming, but he wasn't. It was the Parrot, you know. There goes Friday, running for his life[30] to the little creek! Halloa! Hoop! Halloo!"

Then, with a rapidity of transition very foreign to his usual character, he said, in pity for his former self, "Poor boy!" and cried again.

"I wish," Scrooge muttered, putting his hand in his pocket, and looking about him, after drying his eyes with his cuff: "but it's too late now."

"What is the matter?" asked the Spirit.

"Nothing," said Scrooge. "Nothing. There was a boy singing a Christmas Carol at my door last night. I should like to have given him something: that's all."

The Ghost smiled thoughtfully, and waved its hand: saying as it did so, "Let us see another Christmas!"

Scrooge's former self grew larger at the words, and the room became a little darker and more dirty. The pannels shrunk, the windows cracked;[31] fragments of plaster fell out of the ceiling, and the naked laths were shown instead; but how all this was brought about, Scrooge knew no more than you do. He only knew that it was quite correct; that everything had happened so; that there he was, alone again, when all the other boys had gone home for the jolly holidays.[32]

He was not reading now, but walking up and down despairingly. Scrooge looked at the Ghost, and with a mournful shaking of his head, glanced anxiously towards the door.

It opened; and a little girl, much younger than the boy, came darting in, and putting her arms about his neck, and often kissing him, addressed him as her "Dear, dear brother."

"I have come to bring you home, dear brother!" said the child, clapping her tiny hands, and bending down to laugh. "To bring you home, home, home!"

"Home, little Fan?"[33] returned the boy.

that our boat-growth stopped for ever, when Robinson Crusoe sailed round the Island, and, having been nearly lost, was so affectionately awakened out of his sleep at home again by that immortal parrot, great progenitor of all the parrots we have ever known."

30. *Friday, running for his life.* Another episode in *Robinson Crusoe*. In his twenty-fourth year of seclusion, Crusoe spies some cannibals on the shore on his side of the island. They drag "two miserable wretches" from their boats; and while they are slaughtering one, the other man makes his escape toward the creek and swims across with two men still in pursuit. Crusoe decides that he could use a servant, and "clapp'd myself in the way, between the pursuers, and the pursu'd; hollowing loud to him that fled." He knocks down one of the cannibals and shoots the other. "I hollow'd again to him," he reports, "and made signs to come forward, which he easily understood." The "poor savage" then takes Crusoe's sword and beheads the fallen man. Crusoe calls his new companion Friday, because he rescued him on that day of the week.

Dickens referred to this encounter again in "Nurse's Stories" (*All the Year Round*, September 8, 1860, noting that "no face is ever reflected in the waters of the little creek which Friday swam across when pursued by his two brother cannibals with sharpened stomachs"; and in jest, in his speech given at a dinner of the Printer's Pension Society, April 6, 1864, Dickens suggested that "from the savages enjoying their feast upon the beach [in *Robinson Crusoe*], I believe I might trace my first impression of a public dinner!" (*The Speeches of Charles Dickens*, edited by Kenneth J. Fielding [Oxford: Clarendon Press, 1960], p. 324).

31. *The panels shrunk, the windows cracked.* Dickens remarkably anticipates the magical effect of the time-accelerated motion picture camera. This swift alteration of the world about them as the spirit and Scrooge proceed through the memory of his childhood is also reminiscent of a similar phenomenon in Chapter 3 of H. G. Wells' *The Time Machine* (1895). "I am afraid I cannot convey the peculiar sensations of time traveling," confesses the Time Traveler. "As I put on pace, night followed day like the flapping of a black wing. The dim suggestion of the laboratory seemed presently to fall away from me, and I saw the sun hopping swiftly across the sky, leaping it every minute, and every minute marking a day. I supposed the laboratory had been destroyed and I had come into the open air. I had a dim impression of scaffolding, but I was already going too fast to be conscious of any moving things. . . . I saw trees growing and changing like puffs of vapour, now brown, now green; they grew, spread, shivered, and passed away. I saw huge buildings rise up faint and fair, and pass like dreams. The whole surface of the earth seemed changed—melting and flowing under my eyes." (See also Henry E. Vittum's comparison of *A Christmas Carol* with *The Time Machine* in the 1966 Bantam edition of the Dickens classic, pp. 109–12.)

32. *alone again, when all the other boys had gone home for the jolly holidays.* Dickens indicated in "A Christmas Tree" (*Household Words*, September 21, 1850) how heartbreaking it must have been for Scrooge to be left alone while all the others departed: "School-books shut up; Ovid and Virgil silenced; the Rule of Three, with its cool impertinent inquiries, long disposed of; Terence and Plautus acted no more, in an arena of huddled desks and forms, all chipped, and notched, and inked; cricket-bats, stumps, and balls, left higher up, with the smell of trodden grass and the softened noise of shouts in the evening air. . . . If I do no more come home at Christmas-time, there will be boys and girls (thank Heaven!) while the World lasts; and they do! . . . And I *do* come home at Christmas. We all do, or we all should. We all come home, or ought to come home, for a short holiday— the longer, the better—from the great boarding-school, where we are for ever working at our arithmetical slates, to take, and give a rest."

33. *Fan?* "Fanny" was the name of his favorite (but older) sister, Frances Elizabeth Dickens (1810–1848); she, like Scrooge's sister (as revealed in Stave 3), was gifted in music, both as a singer and a musician. Although traditionally in English homes boys had far more advantages than girls did, Scrooge's father treated his sister far better than him; Dickens thought the same of his own family. He always resented that his parents sent Fanny Dickens to the Royal Academy of Music, while he had to drudge in Warren's Blacking warehouse. See Stave 3, note 60.

"Yes!" said the child, brimful of glee. "Home, for good and all. Home, for ever and ever. Father is so much kinder than he used to be, that home's like Heaven! He spoke so gently to me one dear night when I was going to bed, that I was not afraid to ask him once more if you might come home; and he said Yes, you should; and sent me in a coach to bring you. And you're to be a man!" said the child, opening her eyes, "and are never to come back here; but first, we're to be together all the Christmas long, and have the merriest time in all the world."

"You are quite a woman, little Fan!" exclaimed the boy.

She clapped her hands and laughed, and tried to touch his head; but being too little, laughed again, and stood on tiptoe to embrace him. Then she began to drag him, in her childish eagerness, towards the door; and he, nothing loth to go, accompanied her.

A terrible voice in the hall cried, "Bring down Master[34] Scrooge's box, there!" and in the hall appeared the schoolmaster[35] himself, who glared on Master Scrooge with a ferocious condescension, and threw him into a dreadful state of mind by shaking hands with him. He then conveyed him and his sister into the veriest old well of a shivering best-parlour that ever was seen, where the maps upon the wall, and the celestial and terrestrial globes[36] in the windows, were waxy with cold. Here he produced a decanter of curiously light wine, and a block of curiously heavy cake,[37] and administered instalments of those dainties to the young people: at the same time, sending out a meagre servant to offer a glass of "something" to the postboy,[38] who answered that he thanked the gentleman, but if it was the same tap as he had tasted before, he had rather not. Master Scrooge's trunk being by this time tied on to the top of the chaise,[39] the children bade the schoolmaster good-bye right willingly; and getting into it, drove gaily down the garden-sweep:[40] the quick wheels dashing the hoar-frost and snow from off the dark leaves of the evergreens like spray.

34. *Master.* "Master was formerly a compellation of respect," explained Dr. L. Riechelmann in the 1864 B. G. Teubner edition of *A Christmas Carol*, "but is now generally applied to inferiors, to a young gentleman in his minority, or to a boy up to the age of fifteen or sixteen" (p. 31). Here obviously the schoolmaster says it with extreme condescension.

35. *the schoolmaster.* Another of the many unsympathetic educators in Dickens' work, who include Squeers in *Nicholas Nickleby* (1839), Mrs. Pipchin and Dr. Blimber in *Dombey and Son* (1848), Mr. Creakle in *David Copperfield* (1850), Bradley Headstone in *Our Mutual Friend* (1865), and Thomas Gradgrind in *Hard Times* (1854). Dickens considered schoolmasters, in general to be either fools or frauds. In the preface to the 1848 Cheap Edition of *Nicholas Nickleby*, Dickens protested against "the monstrous neglect of education in England, and the disregard of it by the State as a means of forming good or bad citizens." The worst were the Yorkshire schoolmasters, like Squeers of Dotheboys Hall, "traders in the avarice, indifference, or imbecility of parents, and the helplessness of children; ignorant, sordid brutal men, to whom few considerate persons would have entrusted the board and lodging of a horse or a dog." Dickens was outraged that "any man who had proved his unfitness for any other occupation in life, was free, without examination or qualification, to open a school anywhere." Among them is "a superannuated old Grinder of savage disposition, who had been appointed schoolmaster because he didn't know anything, and wasn't fit for anything, and for whose cruel cane all chubby little boys had a perfect fascination" (*Dombey and Son*, Chapter 6). Dickens' mother opened a school at 4 Gower Street North in 1823, with a big brass plate on the door reading "Mrs. Dickens's Establishment"; nobody came.

When his father was once asked about the famous novelist's schooling, John Dickens proudly replied that Charles must have educated himself! He did briefly attend the Reverend William Giles' school in Chatham, as well as Wellington House Academy in London (See note 18 above). Mr. Jones, the principal of the second school, was the model for Mr. Creakle, the tyrant in *David Copperfield*. One of his pupils said in "Recollections of Charles Dickens" (*The Dickensian*, September 1911) that Mr. Jones "was what might be termed 'a thrasher,' and without much discrimination in the distribution of chastisement; he was a Welshman of irascible temper and very excitable. . . . Sometimes he would charge down the schoolroom, striking right and left with his cane" (p. 230). The same gentleman remembered Dickens as "a rather short, stout, jolly-looking youth, very fresh coloured, and full of fun, and given to laugh immoderately without any apparent sufficient reason. He was not particularly studious, nor did he show any special signs of ability, although as a boy he would at times indite short tales" (p. 229). Although he was rarely the recipient of Mr. Jones' wrath, Dickens recalled him in an address given at the Warehousemen and Clerks' Schools, November 5, 1857, as "by far the most ignorant man I have ever had the pleasure to know . . . one of the worst-tempered men perhaps that ever lived" (*The Speeches of Charles Dickens*, edited by Kenneth J. Fielding [Oxford: Clarendon Press, 1960], p. 240. Subsequent references to Dickens' speeches are also from this book and are given by page only).

Perhaps the worst of Dickens' pedagogical ogres is "Thomas Gradgrind, sir. A man of realities. A man of facts and calculations." He offers his dreary theory of education in Chapter 1 of *Hard Times*: "Now, what I want is, Facts. Teach these boys and girls nothing but Facts. Facts alone are wanted in life. Plant nothing else, and root out everything else. You can only form the minds of reasoning animals upon Facts; nothing else will ever be of service to them." The consequences of such education is misery for his children and their classmates. Mr. Gradgrind belonged to the same school as did Mr. Barlow of Thomas Day's *The History of Sandford and Merton* (1783–89), one of the most famous teachers in juvenile literature, whom Dickens called "childhood's experience of a bore!" "He knew everything," Dickens complained in *The Uncommercial Traveller* (1861), "and didactically improved all sorts of occasions, from the consumption of a plate of cherries to the contemplation of a starlight night. . . . What right had he to bore his way into my *Arabian Nights*? . . . He was always hinting doubts of the veracity of Sinbad the Sailor. If he could have got hold of the Wonderful Lamp, I knew he would have trimmed it and lighted it, and delivered a lecture over it on the qualities of sperm-oil, with a glance at the whale fisheries." Dickens would have none of that. Instead, he said, "I took refuge in the caves of ignorance, wherein I have resided ever since, and which are still my private address."

36. *the celestial and terrestrial globes.* These were common apparatuses found in English classrooms of the period; celestial globes were decorated with the constellations, so that schoolmasters could instruct their charges in the geography of both Heaven and Earth. Wackford Squeers advertises in Chapter 3 of *Nicholas Nickleby* (1839) that among the instruction offered at the notorious Dotheboy's Hall in Yorkshire is "the use of the globes."

37. *a decanter of curiously light wine, and a block of curiously heavy cake.* As disclosed in *Punch's Snap-dragons for Christmas* (London: Punch Office, 1845), it was customary at English boarding schools before the students departed for the masters to pass around "half-baked cake and home-made wine" (p. 21).

38. *the postboy.* Or postilion, the driver of the vehicle.

39. *the chaise.* According to Samuel Johnson in *A Dictionary of the English Language* (1755), "a carriage of pleasure drawn by one horse."

40. *the garden-sweep.* The curve of the driveway through the grounds.

41. *Welch wig.* A woolen or worsted cap, originally made chiefly in Montgomery, Wales. In the Charles Dickens Edition of 1868, Dickens changed this spelling to the more common "Welsh wig."

42. *the hour of seven.* Fezziwig has chosen to close his shop early; the usual hour for closing a place of business was nine o'clock.

43. *his capacious waistcoat.* Compare Fezziwig's figure with that of the Ghost of Christmas Present, in Stave 3. See note 15 there. Dickens' jolly characters have trouble containing their abundant emotion.

44. *his organ of benevolence.* According to phrenology, the area above the forehead was said to be the center of one's "desire to see and make sentient beings happy; willingness to sacrifice for this end; kindness; sympathy for distress." Dickens explained in

"A 'Page' of Phrenology." Wood engraving after John Leech, *The Illuminated Magazine*, November 1844. *Courtesy Library of Congress.*

"Always a delicate creature, whom a breath might have withered," said the Ghost. "But she had a large heart!"

"So she had," cried Scrooge. "You're right. I will not gainsay it, Spirit. God forbid!"

"She died a woman," said the Ghost, "and had, as I think, children."

"One child," Scrooge returned.

"True," said the Ghost. "Your nephew!"

Scrooge seemed uneasy in his mind; and answered briefly, "Yes."

Although they had but that moment left the school behind them, they were now in the busy thoroughfares of a city, where shadowy passengers passed and repassed; where shadowy carts and coaches battled for the way, and all the strife and tumult of a real city were. It was made plain enough, by the dressing of the shops, that here too it was Christmas time again; but it was evening, and the streets were lighted up.

The Ghost stopped at a certain warehouse door, and asked Scrooge if he knew it.

"Know it!" said Scrooge. "Was I apprenticed here!"

They went in. At sight of an old gentleman in a Welch wig,[41] sitting behind such a high desk, that if he had been two inches taller he must have knocked his head against the ceiling, Scrooge cried in great excitement:

"Why, it's old Fezziwig! Bless his heart; it's Fezziwig alive again!"

Old Fezziwig laid down his pen, and looked up at the clock, which pointed to the hour of seven.[42] He rubbed his hands; adjusted his capacious waistcoat;[43] laughed all over himself, from his shoes to his organ of benevolence;[44] and called out in a comfortable, oily, rich, fat, jovial, voice:

"Yo ho, there! Ebenezer! Dick!"

Scrooge's former self,[45] now grown a young man, came briskly in, accompanied by his fellow-'prentice.

"Dick Wilkins, to be sure!" said Scrooge to the

"Our Next-door Neighbour," in *Sketches by Boz* (1839), "Some phrenologists affirm, that the agitation of a man's brain by different passions, produces corresponding developments in the form of his skull." Phrenology was a popular nineteenth-century pseudoscience invented by Franz Joseph Gall (1758–1828) and Johann Kaspar Spurzheim (1766–1832), who argued that one's moral and intellectual character was indicated by the contours of the skull. They divided the head into forty sections, or "organs," each corresponding to an individual mental or emotional faculty. Phrenological heads that provided maps of the cranium were common to Victorian parlors.

Dickens may have been recalling his own recent phrenological examination, which occurred on February 5, 1842, in Worcester, Massachusetts. Lorenzo N. Fowler, one of America's leading practitioners, stated in his report (now in the American Antiquarian Society, Worcester) that Dickens possessed a large organ of benevolence, indicating that the writer "is kind, obliging, glad to serve others even to his injury; feels lively sympathy for distress; does good to all." (By contrast, his smallest organ was a moderate one of veneration, suggesting that Dickens "disregards religious creeds, forms of worship, etc.; places religion in other things; is not serious nor respectful"

[p. 13].) "His brain was comparatively full in all its parts, but more prominently developed in the superior part of the front lobe, and in Benevolence than in any other part," Fowler explained in "Phrenological Description of Charles Dickens and Mark Lemon" (*Human Nature*, August 1870). "Benevolence was very large, as seen in the fulness and height of the front portion of the top head. This quality of mind mellowed his whole character and threw 'the milk of human kindness' into all his writings. His most bitter and sarcastic things amused while they stung. He lived and laboured for the good and the happiness and improvement of the race. If angry, it was in a just cause. If he wounded, it was to remove a tumour" (p. 367).

Oddly, George Eliot differed from Fowler in her evaluation of Dickens and his "bump": "His appearance is certainly disappointing—no benevolence in the face and I think little in the head—the anterior lobe not by any means remarkable" (*The George Eliot Letters*, edited by Gordon S. Haight, vol. 2 [Oxford: Oxford University Press; New Haven: Yale University Press, 1954], p. 23).

45. *Scrooge's former self.* "A living and moving picture of Scrooge's former self" in the 1867 Ticknor and Fields Public Reading edition.

46. *"before a man can say, Jack Robinson!"* "The words of this very popular saying [current in the late seventeenth century]," explained Albert F. Blaisdell in his 1899 edition of *A Christmas Carol*, "originated from a famous comic song. The last line is 'And he was off before he could say Jack Robinson.' The words were sung to the tune of the 'Sailor's Horn-pipe'" (p. 29). The story goes that Robinson was an old man in the habit of calling on his friends and leaving unexpectedly before his name was even announced. "Jack Robinson" was eventually added to the cast of Twelfth Night characters (see Stave 3, note 10).

Ghost. "Bless me, yes. There he is. He was very much attached to me, was Dick. Poor Dick! Dear, dear!"

"Yo ho, my boys!" said Fezziwig. "No more work tonight. Christmas Eve, Dick. Christmas, Ebenezer! Let's have the shutters up," cried old Fezziwig, with a sharp clap of his hands, "before a man can say, Jack Robinson!"[46]

You wouldn't believe how those two fellows went at it! They charged into the street with the shutters—one, two, three—had 'em up in their places—four, five, six—barred 'em and pinned 'em—seven, eight, nine—and came back before you could have got to twelve, panting like race-horses.

"Hilli-ho!" cried old Fezziwig, skipping down from the high desk, with wonderful agility. "Clear away, my lads, and let's have lots of room here! Hilli-ho, Dick! Chirrup, Ebenezer!"

Clear away! There was nothing they wouldn't have cleared away, or couldn't have cleared away, with old Fezziwig looking on. It was done in a minute. Every movable was packed off, as if it were dismissed from public life for evermore; the floor was swept and watered, the lamps were trimmed, fuel was heaped upon the fire; and the warehouse was as snug, and warm, and dry, and bright a ball-room, as you would desire to see upon a winter's night.

In came a fiddler with a music-book, and went up to the lofty desk, and made an orchestra of it, and tuned like fifty stomach-aches. In came Mrs. Fizziwig, one vast substantial smile. In came the three Miss Fezziwigs, beaming and loveable. In came the six young followers whose hearts they broke. In came all the young men and women employed in the business. In came the housemaid, with her cousin, the baker. In came the cook, with her brother's particular friend, the milkman. In came the boy from over the way, who was suspected of not having board enough from his master; trying to hide himself behind the girl from next door but one, who was proved to have had her ears pulled by her Mistress. In they all came, one after another; some shyly, some boldly, some gracefully, some awkwardly, some pushing, some pulling; in they all came, anyhow and everyhow. Away they all went, twenty couple at once, hands half round and back again the other way; down the middle and up again; round and round in various stages of affectionate grouping; old top couple always turning up in the wrong place; new top couple starting off again, as soon as they got there; all top couples at last, and not a bottom one to help them. When this result was brought about, old Fezziwig, clapping his hands to stop the dance, cried out, "Well done!" and the fiddler plunged his hot face into a pot of porter,[47] especially provided for that purpose. But scorning rest upon his reappearance, he instantly began again, though there were no dancers yet, as if the other fiddler had been carried home, exhausted, on a shutter; and he were a bran-new man resolved to beat him out of sight, or perish.

There were more dances, and there were forfeits,[48] and more dances, and there was cake, and there was negus,[49] and there was a great piece of Cold Roast, and there was a great piece of Cold Boiled,[50] and there were mince-pies,[51] and plenty of beer. But the great effect of the evening came after the Roast and Boiled, when the fiddler (an artful dog, mind! The sort of man who knew his business better than you or I could have told it him!) struck up "Sir Roger de Coverley."[52] Then old Fezziwig stood out to dance with Mrs. Fezziwig. Top couple too; with a good stiff piece of work cut out for them; three or four and twenty pair of partners, people who were not to be trifled with; people who *would* dance, and had no notion of walking.

But if they had been twice as many: ah, four times: old Fezziwig would have been a match for them, and so would Mrs. Fezziwig. As to *her*, she was worthy to be his partner in every sense of the term. If that's not high praise, tell me higher, and I'll use it. A positive light appeared to issue from Fezziwig's calves. They shone in

47. *porter.* Or "porter's beer," a heavy dark brown bitter beverage brewed from browned or charred malt; it was particularly popular with porters and other manual laborers. Dickens often mentions it in his novels: Sam Weller is introduced in Chapter 10 of *The Pickwick Papers* (1837) burnishing the painted tops of a farmer who is refreshing himself at lunch with a pot or two of porter; Nancy serves it to Bill Sikes in Chapter 20 of *Oliver Twist* (1838); Dick Swiveller buys a pint of mild porter in Chapter 34 of *The Old Curiosity Shop* (1841).

48. *forfeits.* Any one of many popular parlor games played at Christmas in which a fixed penalty is demanded of the player who misses his or her turn. According to the chapbook *Round About Our Coal-Fire* (1740), forfeits were "generally fixed at some certain Price, as a Shilling, Half a Crown, etc., so everyone knowing what to do if they be too stubborn to submit, making themselves easy at discretion"; by the early nineteenth century, payment in coin was universally replaced by that of a kiss. But such games had fallen out of favor with fashionable households by the time *A Christmas Carol* came out in 1843. "The Game of Forfeits is now, we believe, very rare in London," Thomas Miller insisted in *A Holiday Book for Christmas and the New Year* (1852); "it is too romping and noisy an amusement for the chilling atmosphere and somewhat too stately decorum of our modern drawing rooms" (p. 20). These games remained popular in the country, however; and neither Scrooge's nephew nor Dickens thought them too boisterous for their London holiday revels. Fred and his guests play some of the more popular forms of forfeits in Stave 3.

49. *negus.* A popular mixture of fortified wine (particularly port or sherry) and hot water, sweetened with sugar and flavored with lemon juice, nutmeg, and other spices; it was first concocted in the eighteenth century by Colonel Francis Negus (d. 1732). In Chapter 45 of *The Pickwick Papers* (1837), Dickens speaks of negus as "port wine, warmed with a little water, spice, and sugar as being grateful to the stomach, and savouring less of vanity than many other compounds." It is also enjoyed in Chapters 14 and 59 of *Dombey and Son* (1848) and Chapter 31 of *Bleak House* (1853).

50. *Cold Roast . . . Cold Boiled.* Roasted or boiled beef, served cold.

51. *mince-pies.* A staple of the medieval English Christmas table, which survives to the present. Yet the Protestants once objected to this Christmas pie as a superstitious remnant of the Roman Catholic Church; the ingredients (as late as the eighteenth century being neat's tongues, chicken, eggs, sugar, currants, lemon and orange peel, and various spices) were said to correspond to the gifts of the Magi, and the pastry was generally oblong in shape in imitation of the crèche. Fortunately, the custom was preserved in the countryside, notably in Cornwall. William Sandys included an ancient Cornish recipe in the introduction to *Christmas Carols, Ancient and Modern* (1833): "A pound of beef-suet chopped fine; a pound of raisins do. stoned. A pound of currants cleaned dry. A pound of apples chopped fine. Two or three eggs. Allspice beat very fine; and sugar to your taste. A little salt, and as much brandy and wine as you like." Sandys suggested that it was best to use little or no meat, as the pie would be lighter and stay fresher longer; he also advised that a piece of citron would improve the flavor. Sandys mentioned another Cornish Christmas custom: "in as many different houses as you can eat mince-pies during Christmas, so many happy months will you have in the ensuing year" (p. lxii).

52. *"Sir Roger de Coverley."* Also known as "slip or Sir Roger," a dance similar to the Virginia reel. Sir Richard Steele (1672–1729) took the name for a member of the fictitious club of *The Spectator* (March 2, 1711); his great-grandfather supposedly invented the dance. It was first described in John Playford's *Dancing Master* (1692): the first man goes below the second woman, then round her, and so below the second man into his own place; then the first woman goes below the second man, then round him, and so below the second woman into her own place; then the first couple cross over below the second couple, and take hands and turn round twice, then leap up through and cast off into the second couple's place. Dickens describes a more complex pattern, with steps borrowed from other dances. Sir Roger de Coverley was the most raucous and best known of country-dances in the nineteenth century and traditionally the last one performed on a night of merrymaking. It was a bit out of fashion at the time of the story, however. "Country-dances being

"Mr. Fezziwig's Ball." Preliminary pencil and wash drawing by John Leech, 1843.
Courtesy Houghton Library, Harvard University.

low, were utterly proscribed," Dickens notes in Chapter 8 of *The Old Curiosity Shop* (1841). The quadrille was considered far more chic at the time. *A Christmas Carol* and its dramatizations may well have done much to revive Sir Roger de Coverley in the cities.

Richard Henry Horne reported in *The New Spirit of the Age* (1844) that Charles Dickens was "very much given to dancing Sir Roger de Coverley" (p. 75). Dickens himself confessed in "Where We Stopped Growing" (*Household Words*, January 1, 1853)

Music of "Sir Roger de Coverley."
Courtesy Library of Congress.

"Mr. Fezziwig's Ball." Frontispiece by John Leech, *Christmas Books*, "Cheap Edition of the Works of Charles Dickens," 1852.
Courtesy Library of Congress.

that "we have not outgrown Sir Roger de Coverley, or any country dance in the music-book." He was by no means a gifted

dancer, but what he lacked in technique, he made up for in enthusiasm. "His dancing was at his best, I think, in the 'Sir Roger de Coverley'—and in what are known as country dances," wrote his daughter Mamie in *My Father As I Recall Him* (1896). "In the former, while the end couples are dancing, and the side couples are supposed to be still, my father would insist upon the sides keeping up a kind of jig step, and clapping his hands to add to the fun, and dancing at the backs of those whose enthusiasm he thought needed rousing, was himself never still for a moment until the dance was over" (p. 31). Her brother Henry confirmed in *My Father As I Knew Him* (London: William Heinemann, 1934) how Dickens, like old Fezziwig, would dance "down the middle and up again! There was no stopping him! His energy, his light-heartedness, his buoyancy, were simply immense" (p. 44).

53. *hold hands with.* Apparently Dickens felt uncomfortable with this phrase. Technically, it is a dance movement in which partners join inside hands. This seems not to have been Dickens' meaning, for he changed it to "seize" in the Berg prompt copy. This too bothered him: it appears as merely "turn" in the 1867 Ticknor and Fields Public Reading edition, in accordance with Playford's *Dancing Master*.

54. *corkscrew.* A movement borrowed from a Swedish dance, in which all join hands outstretched, face to face. The lead couple then threads their way in and out of the other couples, the lady backing and taking the lead, and then the gentleman. All hands are raised when they reach the bottom, and passing under the archway, they go to the end of the line, ready for the next and new top couple.

55. *thread-the-needle.* With the partners' hands joined, the lady passes under the man's arm. This dance term comes from an old English game "thread the taylor's needle," described in Book 4, Chapter 4, of Joseph Strutt's *The Sports and Past-times of the People of England* (1801): "In this sport the youth of both sexes frequently join. As many as chose to play lay hold of hands, and the last in the row runs to the top, where passing under the arms of the two first, the rest follow: the first then becoming the last, repeats the operation, and so on alternately as long as the game continues."

56. *"cut."* A fancy dance step, in which the dancer, on springing in the air, quickly alternates the feet, one in front of the other, before touching the ground again.

57. *their beds . . . were under a counter in the back-shop.* Apprentices at the time often slept on mattresses under the counters in their places of employment. Oliver learns

every part the dance like moons. You couldn't have predicted, at any given time, what would become of 'em next. And when old Fezziwig and Mrs. Fezziwig had gone all through the dance; advance and retire, hold hands with[53] your partner; bow and curtsey; corkscrew;[54] thread-the-needle,[55] and back again to your place; Fezziwig "cut"[56]—cut so deftly, that he appeared to wink with his legs, and came upon his feet again without a stagger.

When the clock struck eleven, this domestic ball broke up. Mr. and Mrs. Fezziwig took their stations, one on either side the door, and shaking hands with every person individually as he or she went out, wished him or her a Merry Christmas. When everybody had retired but the two 'prentices, they did the same to them; and thus the cheerful voices died away, and the lads were left to their beds; which were under a counter in the back-shop.[57]

During the whole of this time, Scrooge had acted like a man out of his wits. His heart and soul were in the scene, and with his former self. He corroborated everything, remembered everything, enjoyed everything, and underwent the strangest agitation. It was not until now, when the bright faces of his former self and Dick were turned from them, that he remembered the Ghost, and became conscious that it was looking full upon him, while the light upon its head burnt very clear.

"A small matter," said the Ghost, "to make these silly folks so full of gratitude."

"Small!" echoed Scrooge.

The Spirit signed to him to listen to the two apprentices, who were pouring out their hearts in praise of Fezziwig: and when he had done so, said,

"Why! Is it not? He has spent but a few pounds of your mortal money: three or four, perhaps. Is that so much that he deserves this praise?"

"It isn't that," said Scrooge, heated by the remark, and speaking unconsciously like his former, not his latter, self. "It isn't that, Spirit. He has the power to render us happy or unhappy; to make our service light or burdensome; a pleasure or a toil. Say that his power lies in words and looks; in things so slight and insignificant that it is impossible to add and count 'em up: what then? The happiness he gives, is quite as great as if it cost a fortune."

He felt the Spirit's glance, and stopped.

"What is the matter?" asked the Ghost.

"Nothing particular," said Scrooge.

"Something, I think?" the Ghost insisted.

"No," said Scrooge, "No. I should like to be able to say a word or two to my clerk just now! That's all."

His former self turned down the lamps as he gave utterance to the wish; and Scrooge and the Ghost again stood side by side in the open air.

"My time grows short," observed the Spirit. "Quick!"

This was not addressed to Scrooge, or to any one whom he could see, but it produced an immediate effect. For again Scrooge saw himself. He was older now; a man in the prime of life. His face had not the harsh and rigid lines of later years; but it had begun to wear the signs of care and avarice. There was an eager, greedy, restless motion in the eye, which showed the passion that had taken root, and where the shadow of the growing tree would fall.

He was not alone, but sat by the side of a fair young girl in a mourning-dress:**58** in whose eyes there were tears, which sparkled in the light that shone out of the Ghost of Christmas Past.

"It matters little," she said, softly.**59** "To you, very little. Another idol has displaced me; and if it can cheer and comfort you in time to come, as I would have tried to do, I have no just cause to grieve."

"What Idol has displaced you?" he rejoined.

"A golden one."**60**

"This is the even-handed dealing of the world!" he said. "There is nothing on which it is so hard as

when apprenticed to Mr. Sowerberry, the parochial undertaker, in Chapter 4 of *Oliver Twist* (1838), that "your bed's under the counter."

58. *mourning-dress.* "Black dress" in the 1867 Ticknor and Fields Public Reading edition. See also note 62.

59. *she said, softly.* "To Scrooge's former self" added in the 1867 Ticknor and Fields Public Reading edition.

60. *"A golden one."* A play on the biblical story of the golden calf (Exodus 32): When Moses was on Mount Sinai, receiving the holy covenant, the Israelites melted down their gold and made a false idol in the form of a calf; it was forbidden by the Lord to make false gods. This woman, in effect, is accusing Scrooge of cashing in his sacred love for a profane one.

"The Stolen Shoulders."
Wood engraving after John Leech,
The Illuminated Magazine,
October 1843.
Courtesy Library of Congress.

poverty; and there is nothing it professes to condemn with such severity as the pursuit of wealth!"

"You fear the world too much," she answered, gently. "All your other hopes have merged into the hope of being beyond the chance of its sordid reproach. I have seen your nobler aspirations fall off one by one, until the master-passion, Gain, engrosses you. Have I not?"

"What then?" he retorted. "Even if I have grown so much wiser, what then? I am not changed towards you."

She shook her head.

"Am I?"

"Our contract is an old one. It was made when we were both poor and content to be so, until, in good season, we could improve our worldly fortune by our patient industry. You *are* changed. When it was made, you were another man."

"I was a boy," he said impatiently.

"Your own feeling tells you that you were not what you are," she returned. "I am. That which promised happiness when we were one in heart, is fraught with misery now that we are two. How often and how keenly I have thought of this, I will not say. It is enough that I *have* thought of it, and can release you."[61]

"Have I ever sought release?"

"In words. No. Never."

"In what, then?"

"In a changed nature; in an altered spirit; in another atmosphere of life; another Hope as its great end. In everything that made my love of any worth or value in your sight. If this had never been between us," said the girl, looking mildly, but with steadiness, upon him; "tell me, would you seek me out and try to win me now? Ah, no!"

He seemed to yield to the justice of this supposition, in spite of himself. But he said, with a struggle, "You think not."

"I would gladly think otherwise if I could," she answered, "Heaven knows! When *I* have learned a Truth like this, I know how strong and irresistible it must be. But if you were free to-day, to-morrow, yesterday, can even I believe that you would choose a dowerless girl[62]—you who, in your very confidence with her, weigh everything by Gain: or, choosing her, if for a moment you were false enough to your one guiding principle to do so, do I not know that your repentance and regret would surely follow? I do; and I release you. With a full heart, for the love of him you once were."

He was about to speak; but with her head turned from him, she resumed.

"You may—the memory of what is past half makes me hope you will—have pain in this. A very, very brief time, and you will dismiss the recollection of it, gladly, as an unprofitable dream, from which it happened well that you awoke. May you be happy in the life you have chosen!"

She left him; and they parted.

"Spirit!" said Scrooge, "show me no more! Conduct me home. Why do you delight to torture me?"

"One shadow more!" exclaimed the Ghost.

"No more!" cried Scrooge. "No more. I don't wish to see it. Show me no more!"[63]

But the relentless Ghost pinioned him in both his arms, and forced him to observe what happened next.

They were in another scene and place: a room, not very large or handsome, but full of comfort. Near to the winter fire sat a beautiful young girl, so like the last that Scrooge believed it was the same, until he saw *her*, now a comely matron, sitting opposite her daughter. The noise in this room was perfectly tumultuous, for there were more children there, than Scrooge in his agitated state of mind could count; and, unlike the celebrated herd in the poem,[64] they were not forty children conducting themselves like one, but every child was conducting itself like forty. The consequences were uproarious beyond belief; but no one seemed to care; on the contrary, the mother and daughter laughed heartily, and enjoyed it very much; and the latter, soon beginning to mingle in the sports, got pillaged

62. *a dowerless girl.* Dickens deleted the word "orphan" before "girl" in the galley stage; apparently, the woman is mourning the death of one or both of her parents, who have left her penniless.

63. *"No more. . . . Show me no more!"* Scrooge was far more demonstrative in the manuscript, which continued: " . . . And as he spoke he pressed his hands against his head, and stamped upon the ground." This embarrassing display did not make it to the printers.

64. *the poem.* William Wordsworth's "Written in March" (1802):

> The oldest and the youngest
> Are at work with the strongest;
> The cattle are grazing,
> Their heads never raising;
> There are forty feeding like one!

65. *time to greet the father, who.* In the galley stage, Dickens wisely deleted a lengthy, gratuitous phrase at this point ("in observance of a custom annually maintained in the family on Christmas Eve") from what is already an extraordinary run-on sentence. The custom in the Dickens family was quite different from this gentleman's holiday shopping. "In our childish days," his daughter Mamie revealed in *My Father As I Recall Him* (1896), "my father used to take us, every twenty-fourth day of December, to a toy shop in Holborn, where we were allowed to select our Christmas presents, and also any that we wished to give to our little companions. Although I believe we were often an hour or more in the shop before our several tastes were satisfied, he never showed the least impatience, was always interested, and as desirous as we, that we should choose exactly what we liked best" (p. 26). Dickens had introduced a similar scene of domestic bliss earlier in "The Story of the Goblins Who Stole a Sexton," Chapter 29 of *The Pickwick Papers* (1837).

"Christmas Presents." Wood engraving after Robert Seymour, *The Book of Christmas* by Thomas K. Hervey, 1836. *Private collection.*

by the young brigands most ruthlessly. What would I not have given to be one of them! Though I never could have been so rude, no, no! I wouldn't for the wealth of all the world have crushed that braided hair, and torn it down; and for the precious little shoe, I wouldn't have plucked it off, God bless my soul! to save my life. As to measuring her waist in sport, as they did, bold young brood, I couldn't have done it; I should have expected my arm to have grown round it for a punishment, and never come straight again. And yet I should have dearly liked, I own, to have touched her lips; to have questioned her, that she might have opened them; to have looked upon the lashes of her downcast eyes, and never raised a blush; to have let loose waves of hair, an inch of which would be a keepsake beyond price: in short, I should have liked, I do confess, to have had the lightest licence of a child, and yet been man enough to know its value.

But now a knocking at the door was heard, and such a rush immediately ensued that she with laughing face and plundered dress was borne towards it the centre of a flushed and boisterous group, just in time to greet the father, who,**65** came home attended by a man laden with Christmas toys and presents. Then the shouting and the struggling, and the onslaught that was made on the defenceless porter! The scaling him, with chairs for ladders, to dive into his pockets, despoil him of brown-paper parcels, hold on tight by his cravat, hug him round the neck, pommel his back, and kick his legs in irrepressible affection! The shouts of wonder and delight with which the development of every package was received! The terrible announcement that the baby had been taken in the act of putting a doll's frying-pan into his mouth, and was more than suspected of having swallowed a fictitious turkey, glued on a wooden platter! The immense relief of finding this a false alarm! The joy, and gratitude, and ecstacy! They are all indescribable alike. It is enough that by degrees the children and their emotions got out of the parlour and by one stair at a time, up to the top of the house; where they went to bed, and so subsided.

And now Scrooge looked on more attentively than ever, when the master of the house, having his daughter leaning fondly on him, sat down with her and her mother at his own fireside; and when he thought that such another creature, quite as graceful and as full of promise, might have called him father, and been a spring-time in the haggard winter of his life, his sight grew dim indeed.

"Belle,"[66] said the husband, turning to his wife with a smile, "I saw an old friend of yours this afternoon."

"Who was it?"

"Guess!"

"How can I? Tut, don't I know," she added in the same breath, laughing as he laughed. "Mr. Scrooge."

"Mr. Scrooge it was. I passed his office window; and as it was not shut up, and he had a candle inside, I could scarcely help seeing him. His partner lies upon the point of death, I hear; and there he sat alone. Quite alone in the world, I do believe."

"Spirit!" said Scrooge in a broken voice, "remove me from this place."

"I told you these were shadows of the things that have been," said the Ghost. "That they are what they are, do not blame me!"

"Remove me!" Scrooge exclaimed. "I cannot bear it!"

He turned upon the Ghost, and seeing that it looked upon him with a face, in which in some strange way there were fragments of all the faces it had shown him, wrestled with it.

"Leave me! Take me back. Haunt me no longer!"

In the struggle, if that can be called a struggle in which the Ghost with no visible resistance on its own part was undisturbed by any effort of its adversary, Scrooge observed that its light was burning high and bright; and dimly connecting that with its influence

66. *"Belle."* Could this name be an abbreviation of Beadnell, the surname of the girl young Dickens loved and lost? Scrooge's sentiments toward Belle, like those David Copperfield harbors for Dora Spenlow, reflect how Dickens felt for Maria Beadnell (1819–1886). But this banker's daughter was far from being dowerless; her family forbade the union because of the writer's low economic prospects as a husband. She eventually married Henry Winter, a merchant; Dickens wed Catherine Hogarth, the daughter of a music critic and editor of the London *Evening Chronicle*, to which young Dickens contributed. "Why is it," Dickens asked Forster in a letter in early February 1855, "that as with poor David [Copperfield], a sense comes always crushing on me now, when I fall into low spirits, as of one happiness I have missed in life, and one friend and companion I have never made?" (p. 523).

This vision of Belle's domestic bliss was completely the author's fabrication. Mrs. Winter had no further contact with her old flame until 1855, when she wrote him out of the blue. They arranged a meeting, and Dickens was shocked by the plump matron his former love had become. He mercilessly caricatured her as Flora Finching in *Little Dorrit* (1857). "Flora, always tall, had grown to be very broad too, and short of breath; but that was not much," he wrote in Book 1, Chapter 13. "Flora, whom he had left as a lily, had become a peony; but that was too much. Flora, who had seemed enchanting in all she said and thought, was diffuse and silly. That was much. Flora, who had been spoiled and artless long ago, was determined to be spoiled and artless now. That was a fatal blow."

Contemporary playwrights evidently did not think much of the name "Belle." Edward Stirling renamed her Bella Morton in *A Christmas Carol; or, Past, Present, and Future*, first staged in February 1844, C. Z. Barnett called her Ellen in *A Christmas*

Carol, or The Miser's Warning. Charles Webb discounted the girl's fate in the original story; instead, he conveniently reconciled Scrooge and Ellen Williams in the last scene of his drama *A Christmas Carol; or, The Past, Present, and Future*.

Dickens compromises the probability of his story in this visit to Belle's household at holiday time. The Ghost of Christmas Past may represent the miser's long repressed memory, but Scrooge never witnessed this scene of domestic bliss. "I believe," argued Macnish in *The Philosophy of Sleep* (1838), "that dreams are uniformly the resuscitation or re-embodiment of thoughts which have formerly, in some shape or other, occupied the mind. They are old ideas revived either in an entire state, or heterogeneously mingled together. I doubt if it be possible for a person to have, in a dream, any idea whose elements did not, in some form, strike him at a previous period" (p. 48). And it seems quite unlikely that Scrooge ever thought of what might have happened to his former fiancée.

67. *Scrooge . . . could not hide the light.* Dickens suggests that the light of memory is not so easily snuffed out; Scrooge, despite his struggle with the Ghost, cannot forget the lesson it has taught him.

"The End of the First Spirit."
Preliminary pencil and wash drawing
by John Leech, 1843.
Courtesy Houghton Library, Harvard University.

over him, he seized the extinguisher-cap, and by a sudden action pressed it down upon its head.

The Spirit dropped beneath it, so that the extinguisher covered its whole form; but though Scrooge pressed it down with all his force, he could not hide the light:**67** which streamed from under it, in an unbroken flood upon the ground.

He was conscious of being exhausted, and overcome by an irresistible drowsiness; and, further, of being in his own bedroom. He gave the cap a parting squeeze, in which his hand relaxed; and had barely time to reel to bed, before he sank into a heavy sleep.

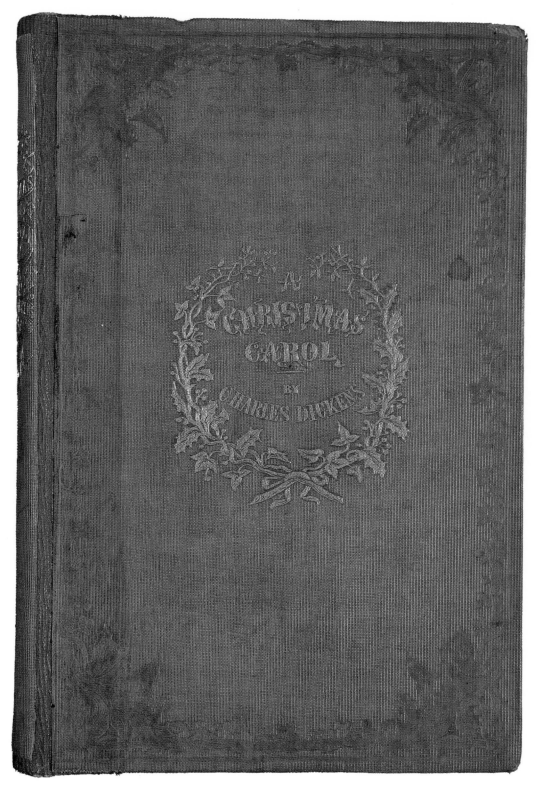

Front cover of *A Christmas Carol*, 1843.
Private collection.

Mr. Fezziwig's Ball.

"Mr. Fezziwig's Ball" and the title page of *A Christmas Carol in Prose*, 1843.
Private collection.

A CHRISTMAS CAROL.

IN PROSE.

BEING

A Ghost Story of Christmas.

BY

CHARLES DICKENS.

WITH ILLUSTRATIONS BY JOHN LEECH.

LONDON:
CHAPMAN & HALL, 186, STRAND.

MDCCCXLIII.

Marley's Ghost.

"Marley's Ghost." Hand-colored etching. *A Christmas Carol in Prose*, 1843.
Private collection.

"Scrooge's Third Visitor." Preliminary watercolor by John Leech, 1843.
Courtesy Pierpont Morgan Library.

"Scrooge's Third Visitor." Hand-colored etching. *A Christmas Carol in Prose*, 1843.
Private collection.

The Last of the Spirits.

"The Last of the Spirits." Hand-colored etching. *A Christmas Carol in Prose*, 1843.
Private collection.

"The Christmas Bowl." Preliminary watercolor by John Leech for *A Christmas Carol*, 1843.
Courtesy Pierpont Morgan Library.

STAVE THREE.

THE SECOND OF THE THREE SPIRITS.

Awaking in the middle of a prodigiously tough snore, and sitting up in bed to get his thoughts together, Scrooge had no occasion to be told that the bell was again upon the stroke of One. He felt that he was restored to consciousness in the right nick of time, for the especial purpose of holding a conference with the second messenger despatched to him through Jacob Marley's intervention. But finding that he turned uncomfortably cold when he began to wonder which of his curtains this new spectre would draw back, he put them every one aside with his own hands; and lying down again, established a sharp look-out all round the bed. For he wished to challenge the Spirit on the moment of its appearance, and did not wish to be taken by surprise and made nervous.

Gentlemen of the free-and-easy sort,[1] who plume themselves[2] on being acquainted with a move or two,[3] and being usually equal to the time-of-day,[4] express the wide range of their capacity for adventure by observing that they are good for anything from pitch-and-toss[5] to manslaughter; between which opposite extremes, no doubt, there lies a tolerably wide and comprehensive range of subjects. Without venturing for Scrooge quite as hardily as this, I don't mind calling on you to believe that he was ready for a good broad field of strange appearances, and that nothing between a baby and a rhinoceros would have astonished him very much.

Now, being prepared for almost anything, he was not by any means prepared for nothing; and, conse-

1. *Gentlemen of the free-and-easy sort.* Sporting types; a "free-and-easy" was a gathering place, catering to smoking, drinking, singing, and gambling.

2. *who plume themselves.* Who pride themselves, usually over an insignificant point, to which they have no true claim.

3. *acquainted with a move or two.* Wordly.

4. *equal to the time-of-day.* Ready for whatever might happen.

5. *pitch-and-toss.* A form of "heads-or-tails"; as F. H. Ahn explained in his 1871 edition of *A Christmas Carol,* "a street gambling game in which pence are pitched, or thrown, at a certain mark, and then tossed in the air, the player who pitches his coin nearest the mark having the privilege of tossing up the remaining pence and of claiming all those that fall with their faces upward" (p. 157).

6. *spontaneous combustion.* A popular myth of the early nineteenth century that insisted a person's body chemicals could be (as Dickens argued in Chapter 32 of *Bleak House*, 1853) "so inborn, inbred, engendered in the corrupted humours of the vicious body itself" that the individual could be destroyed suddenly in a self-generated conflagration. Dickens was widely criticized for killing off Mr. Krook in *Bleak House* by this absurd means. It was illustrated with an

"The Appointed Time." Etching by
"Phiz" (Hablôt Knight Browne),
Bleak House, 1853.
Courtesy Library of Congress.

equally alarming picture by "Phiz" (Hablôt Knight Browne), "The Appointed Time." George H. Lewes, the critic and companion of George Eliot, protested in *The Leader* (December 11, 1852) that there was no shred of evidence that such a thing could occur. "It is allowable to introduce the Supernatural in Art," he said, "but not the Improbable." Dickens responded to his critics with heavy irony in Chapter 33 of *Bleak House* by attacking those "men of science" who believed that "the deceased had no business to die in the alleged manner." Lewes found

quently, when the Bell struck One, and no shape appeared, he was taken with a violent fit of trembling. Five minutes, ten minutes, a quarter of an hour went by, yet nothing came. All this time, he lay upon his bed, the very core and centre of a blaze of ruddy light, which streamed upon it when the clock proclaimed the hour; and which being only light, was more alarming than a dozen ghosts, as he was powerless to make out what it meant, or would be at; and was sometimes apprehensive that he might be at that very moment an interesting case of spontaneous combustion,[6] without having the consolation of knowing it. At last, however, he began to think—as you or I would have thought at first; for it is always the person not in the predicament who knows what ought to have been done in it, and would unquestionably have done it too—at last, I say, he began to think that the source and secret of this ghostly light might be in the adjoining room: from whence, on further tracing it, it seemed to shine. This idea taking full possession of his mind, he got up softly and shuffled in his slippers to the door.

The moment Scrooge's hand was on the lock, a strange voice called him by his name, and bade him enter. He obeyed.

It was his own room. There was no doubt about that. But it had undergone a surprising transformation. The walls and ceiling were so hung with living green,[7] that it looked a perfect grove, from every part of which, bright gleaming berries glistened. The crisp leaves of holly, mistletoe, and ivy reflected back the light, as if so many little mirrors had been scattered there; and such a mighty blaze went roaring up the chimney, as that dull petrifaction of a hearth had never known in Scrooge's time, or Marley's, or for many and many a winter season gone. Heaped up upon the floor, to form a kind of throne, were turkeys, geese, game, poultry, brawn,[8] great joints of meat, sucking-pigs,[9] long wreaths of sausages, mince-pies, plum-puddings, barrels of oysters, red-hot chestnuts, cherry-cheeked

the reply "humourous but not convincing," and concluded that "the evidence in favour of the notion is worthless; that the theories in the explanation are absurd; and, that, according to all known chemical and physiological laws, Spontaneous Combustion is an *impossibility*."

But Dickens was not ready to concede. "I have no need to observe that I do not willfully or negligently mislead my readers, and that, before I wrote that description I took pains to investigate the subject," he persisted in the preface to *Bleak House*, when it was published in book form. He said that he knew of thirty cases, the most famous being that of Countess Cornelia di Bandi Cesenate of Verona. "I do not think it necessary to add to these notable facts," he continued, "the recorded opinions and experiences of distinguished medical professors . . . in more modern days; contenting myself with observing, that I shall not abandon the facts until there shall have been considerable a Spontaneous Combustion of the testimony on which human occurrences usually received."

7. *living green.* Evergreens appropriate to the season. There are no Christmas trees in *A Christmas Carol*, perhaps because they were a German tradition and not an English one at the time.

8. *brawn.* Dr. Johnson in his *Dictionary of the English Language* (1755) identified this traditional Christmas dish as "the flesh of a boar." This cooked meat is made of pork muscle and cheap parts of the pig and is of a gelatinous pink color. Sandys noted in his introduction to *Christmas Carols, Ancient and Modern* (1833) that brawn was "a dish of great antiquity, and may be found in most of the old bills of fare, for coronation, and other great feasts" (p. lx).

9. *sucking-pigs.* Young (generally no older than four weeks), milk-fed pigs, often roasted whole as shown in John Leech's picture "Scrooge's Third Visitor."

" 'I am the Ghost of Christmas Present.' " Wood engraving after Gustave Doré, *Journal pour tous*, June 29, 1861. *Courtesy Library of Congress.*

10. *twelfth-cakes.* Also known as twelfth-night, or twelfth-tide, cakes; large pastries served on Twelfth Night, the last official celebration of the English Christmas, falling on the eve before Epiphany, January 6, the day the Three Magi visited the Christ child. Generally made of flour, honey, ginger, and pepper, they were often quite elaborately decorated confections. *Punch's Snap-dragons for Christmas* (1845) described one "with its iced sugar walls, and roof decorated gaily—with its quaint figures painted and gilded—with wondrous twisted love-knots in green and crimson-coloured apple jelly—with bunches of candied angelica, and other devices most tastefully and healthfully frosted with flaked *glass!*" Once it was cut into, the cake exuded "a blackish brown hue of burnt sugar and brandy, currants baked into hard pellets, and bitter almonds" (p. 91).

According to a custom dating back to the thirteenth century, a bean or coin is baked inside the cake, and whoever receives the slice with this prize becomes King or Queen of the feast. Other objects have been baked in these cakes to determine other Twelfth Night characters: pea for the Queen, forked stick for the Cuckold, rag for the Slut, etc. By the early nineteenth century, these "types" (originally representatives of the English court, later comic figures) were sold as prints during holidays; they were then colored and cut out and placed in a bowl to be drawn by the guests. Perhaps the most famous Twelfth Night party in literary history was celebrated by William Makepeace Thackeray and his family in Rome. As there were no ready-made Twelfth Night characters to be found where they were staying, Thackeray drew and colored his own assortment of these silly figures to entertain the children; and from the stories he told about them, he wrote the charming fairy tale *The Rose and the Ring* (1855), the best known Christmas Book after *A Christ-*

apples, juicy oranges, luscious pears, immense twelfth-cakes,[10] and seething bowls of punch,[11] that made the chamber dim with their delicious steam. In easy state upon this couch, there sat a jolly Giant,[12] glorious to see; who bore a glowing torch,[13] in shape not unlike Plenty's horn,[14] and held it up, high up, to shed its light on Scrooge, as he came peeping round the door.

Scrooge's third Visitor.

"Come in!" exclaimed the Ghost. "Come in! and know me better, man!"

Scrooge entered timidly, and hung his head before this Spirit. He was not the dogged Scrooge he had been; and though its eyes were clear and kind, he did not like to meet them.

"I am the Ghost of Christmas Present," said the Spirit. "Look upon me!"

mas Carol. The manuscripts of both books are now in the Pierpont Morgan Library.

11. *bowls of punch.* Although Dickens mentions numerous kinds of holiday spirits throughout the story, the drink here is most likely wassail, or Lamb's Wool, the traditional drink of Father Christmas. Washington Irving in "The Christmas Dinner," in his *Sketch-Book* (1819–20), described this nut-brown beverage as "composed of the richest and raciest wines, highly spiced and sweetened, with roasted apples bobbing about the surface . . . sometimes ale instead of wine, with nutmeg, sugar, toast, ginger, and roasted crabs [apples]." The revelers at Dingley Dell in Chapter 28 of *The Pickwick Papers* are served "a mighty bowl of wassail, something smaller than an ordinary wash-house copper, in which the hot apples were hissing and bubbling with a rich look, and a jolly sound, that were perfectly irresistible." The name "wassail" (or "wassel") comes from the early fifth century: Rowena, daughter of the Saxon Hengist, presented a bowl of punch to the English king Vortigern, and greeted him with "Louerd king, wass-heil"—"be of good health" (see Chapter 2, *A Child's History of England,* 1852–54,). The term "keep wassail" (as in *Hamlet* 1.4.10) is also synonymous with carousing or revelry. "Lamb's Wool" is a corruption of "La Mas Ubhal" (pronounced "Lammas ool"), an ancient pagan harvest celebration venerating the apple.

12. *a jolly Giant.* The Ghost is no more than Father Christmas, the ancient patriarch of the English holiday, traditionally a pagan giant dressed in a fur-lined green robe and a crown of holly, bearing mistletoe, the yule log, and a bowl of Christmas punch. The legendary Santa Claus, immortalized in America by Clement C. Moore in his poem "A Visit from Saint Nicholas" (1822), better known as "The Night Before Christmas," owes much of

"Scrooge's Third Visitor." Preliminary pencil and wash drawing by John Leech, 1843.
Courtesy Houghton Library, Harvard University.

its origins to both this English giant and the gift-giving Saint Nicholas of Myra, the patron saint of children; but the Ghost of Christmas Present should not be confused with the Yankee elf, whom Scrooge would not have known. Father Christmas derives from the Roman Saturnalia, from Saturn himself; while that ancient god devoured his children, Dickens' giant protects the demon girl and boy, Ignorance and Want. See note 94.

13. *a glowing torch.* Similar to the Ghost of Christmas Past, from whose head "there sprung a bright clear jet of light." The two earlier spirits differ from their fellow phantom, the Ghost of Christmas Yet to Come, "draped and hooded, coming, like a mist along the ground."

14. *Plenty's horn.* An obvious allusion to the pagan origins of this spirit; the cornucopia (filled with fruits and flowers) often appears in the left hand of the goddess Ceres, in whose honor the Saturnalia rites were celebrated.

"Old Christmas." Etching by Robert Seymour, *The Book of Christmas* by Thomas K. Hervey, 1836.
Private collection.

Scrooge reverently did so. It was clothed in one simple deep green robe, or mantle, bordered with white fur. This garment hung so loosely on the figure, that its capacious breast[15] was bare, as if disdaining to be warded or concealed by any artifice. Its feet, observable beneath the ample folds of the garment, were also bare; and on its head it wore no other covering than a holly wreath set here and there with shining icicles. Its dark brown curls were long and free: free as its genial face, its sparkling eye, its open hand, its cheery voice, its unconstrained demeanour, and its joyful air. Girded round its middle was an antique scabbard; but no sword was in it,[16] and the ancient sheath was eaten up with rust.

"You have never seen the like of me before!" exclaimed the Spirit.

"Never," Scrooge made answer to it.

"Have never walked forth with the younger members of my family; meaning (for I am very young) my elder brothers born in these later years?" pursued the Phantom.

"I don't think I have," said Scrooge. "I am afraid I have not. Have you had many brothers, Spirit?"

"More than eighteen hundred,"[17] said the Ghost.

"A tremendous family to provide for!" muttered Scrooge.

The Ghost of Christmas Present rose.[18]

"Spirit," said Scrooge submissively, "conduct me where you will. I went forth last night on compulsion, and I learnt a lesson which is working now. To-night, if you have aught to teach me, let me profit by it."

"Touch my robe!"[19]

Scrooge did as he was told, and held it fast.

Holly, mistletoe, red berries, ivy, turkeys, geese, game, poultry, brawn, meat, pigs, sausages, oysters, pies, puddings, fruit, and punch, all vanished instantly. So did the room, the fire, the ruddy glow, the hour of night, and they stood in the city streets on Christmas morning,[20] where (for the weather was severe) the peo-

15. *its capacious breast.* The breast, where lies the heart, is traditionally the center of warm emotion; the Ghost of Christmas Present is overflowing with generous good feeling, just like the season itself.

16. *no sword was in it.* Dickens suggests the ultimate conquest of military tyranny through the Prince of Peace, as pagan warlords embraced the civilizing agency of the Christian good fellowship of the season. *A Holiday Book for Christmas and the New Year* (1852) described the carved screen of an old baronial hall that was decorated with the symbols of physical triumph, a helmet, a sword, and a surcoat, and encircled with the traditional signs of Christmas, holly and evergreens, as an expression of "the victory gained over the powers of darkness by the coming of Christ" (p. 17).

17. *"More than eighteen hundred."* Eighteen hundred and forty-two, to be exact.

18. *The Ghost of Christmas Present rose.* The manuscript contains the following passage:

> . . . and as it did so Scrooge observed that at its skirts it seemed to have some object which it sought to hide. He fancied that he saw either the claw of a great bird or a foot much smaller than the Spirit's own protruding for a moment from its robes; and being curious in everything concerning these unearthly visitors, he asked the Spirit what it meant.
>
> "They are not so many as they might be," replied the Ghost, "who care to know or ask. No matter what it is, just now. Are you ready to go forth with me?"

This foreshadowing of the emergence of the specter children Ignorance and Want from within the Ghost's robes is merely a tease and weakens their appearance at the end of the stave, so Dickens wisely deleted this passage before the book went to press. See note 94.

19. *"Touch my robe!"* Scrooge's journey with the Ghost of Christmas Present reminded *The Atlas* (December 23, 1843) and *The Gentleman's Magazine* (February 1844) of the satiric novel *Le Diable Boiteux* (1707), by the French novelist and dramatist Alain-René Lesage (1668–1747), best known for *Gil Blas* (1715–35). Asmodeus, the lame demon of voluptuousness, comes to the wastrel student Don Cleophas Leandro Perez Zambullo to expose "the follies and the vices of mankind." "Hold fast to the end of my mantle," commands the Devil; and it takes the young man to the tower of San Salvador in Madrid, where it makes the roofs disappear and reveals "the interiors of the surrounding dwellings as plainly as if the noon-day sun shone over them."

This book was first translated into English in 1790, and many stage versions followed. Dickens owned the 1841 French edition with pictures by Tony Johannot, and he more than once evoked *The Devil on Two Sticks* in his own work. "The historian takes the friendly reader by the hand," he wrote in Chapter 33 of *The Old Curiosity Shop* (1841), "and springing with him into the air, and cleaving the same at a greater rate than ever Don Cleophas Leandro Perez Zambullo and his familiar travelled through that pleasant region in company, alights him upon the pavement of Bevis Market." In Chapter 6 of the first volume of *American Notes* (1842), he accuses the New York press of "pimping and pandering for all degrees of vicious taste" like "pulling off the roofs of private houses, as the Halting Devil did in Spain." He referred to this book again in one of his most fervent pleas for social reform, in Chapter 47 of *Dombey and Son* (1848):

> Oh for a good spirit who would take the house-tops off, with a more potent and benignant hand than the lame demon in the tale, and show a Christian people what dark shapes issue from amidst their homes, to swell the retinue of the Destroying Angel as he moves forth among them! For only one night's view of the pale phantoms rising from the scenes of our too-long neglect; and from the thick and sullen air where Vice and Fever propagate together, raining the tremendous social retributions which are ever pouring down, and ever coming thicker! Bright and blest the morning that should rise on such a night: for men, delayed no more by stumbling-blocks of their own making, which are but specks of dust upon the path between them and eternity, would then apply themselves, like creatures of one common origin, owing one duty to the Father of one family, and tending to one common end, to make the world a brighter place!
>
> Not the less bright and blest would that day be for rousing some who never have looked out upon the world of human life around them, to a knowledge of their own relation to it, and for making them acquainted with a perversion of nature in their own contracted sympathies and estimates; as great, and yet as natural in its development when once begun, as the lowest degradation known.

And Dickens created just such a good spirit in the Ghost of Christmas Present. This passage from *Dombey and Son* neatly summarizes the major themes of *A Christmas Carol.*

20. *they stood in the city streets on Christmas morning.* Beginning here, *The Mirror of Literature, Amusement, and Instruction* (January 6, 1844) reprinted the next four paragraphs as a little self-contained essay, "Christmas Morning" (pp. 6–7). Notice how carefully Dickens employed all five senses in constructing this vivid description of London at holiday time. Dickens summarized this entire section in the 1867 Ticknor and Fields Public Reading version as "upon a snowy Christmas morning."

Ironically, England was unusually warm the winter of 1843–44, when *A Christmas Carol* was published. The London *Times* reported on December 25 that just the day before, Christmas Eve, the high was 62 degrees. "The mildness of the weather has given rise to hundreds of newspaper paragraphs," a London correspondent wrote the New York *Evening Post* (February 9) on January 12. "All worth the name of winter, so far, has been a twenty-four hour's frost, and a fall of snow, which speedily disappeared. As far north as Northumberland, the boys were bathing in the river Aln, on Christmas day! and there is no end to the accounts of violets, primroses, etc., in full bloom, birds nests with eggs, and other signs of the mildness of the season. I myself saw a wild strawberry, which had been gathered by the roadside at the close of December!"

This greeting card picture of Christmas has often been attributed to Dickens, but it was being popularized also in engravings in *The Illustrated London News* and other English publications at the time *A Christmas Carol* came out. "Did Charles Dickens conjure up a Christmas tradition, or had it a basis in fact?" wondered English meteorologist Kenneth Ullyett in *Country Fair* (December 1954). "As in much else he wrote, Dickens dwelt in the past." Ullyett suggested that "the weather portrayed by Dickens was also a throwback to his boyhood days. From 1782 to 1821 there was a long period of snowy Christmases, and Dickens would have known six of them in his youth" (p. 1).

21. *The poulterers' shops.* Dickens never specifies exactly which London market is described here. However, Edward Stirling's *A Christmas Carol; or, Past, Present, and Future* at the Adelphi in February 1844 recreated Christmas Eve at Clare Market by gaslight. "Any one in the least acquainted with the aspect, the incessant noise, confusion, and crowd of this busy mart, where every necessary of life may be purchased on such a night, cannot fail to approve the truth of the picture," said the London *Era* (February 18, 1844).

"The Goose Club." Wood engraving after "Phiz" (Hablôt Knight Browne), *The Illustrated London News*, December 24, 1853. *Courtesy Library of Congress.*

22. *There were great, round, pot-bellied baskets of chestnuts.* Ernest Bolt suggested in "Charles Dickens and Washington Irving" (*Modern Language Quarterly*, December 1944, p. 459) that the animism Dickens employs so prevalently in *A Christmas Carol* was likely learned from Washington Irving. As an example, he compared this exuberant view of wares in the Christmas shops with another particularly Dickensian passage, from "The Legend of Sleepy Hollow," in Irving's *The Sketch-Book of Geoffrey Crayon* (1819–20):

The pedagogue's mouth watered, as he looked upon this sumptuous promise of

ple made a rough, but brisk and not unpleasant kind of music, in scraping the snow from the pavement in front of their dwellings, and from the tops of their houses: whence it was mad delight to the boys to see it come plumping down into the road below, and splitting into artificial little snowstorms.

The house fronts looked black enough, and the windows blacker, contrasting with the smooth white sheet of snow upon the roofs, and with the dirtier snow upon the ground; which last deposit had been ploughed up in deep furrows by the heavy wheels of carts and waggons; furrows that crossed and recrossed each other hundreds of times where the great streets branched off; and made intricate channels, hard to trace, in the thick yellow mud and icy water. The sky was gloomy, and the shortest streets were choked up with a dingy mist, half thawed half frozen, whose heavier particles descended in a shower of sooty atoms, as if all the chimneys in Great Britain had, by one consent, caught fire, and were blazing away to their dear hearts' content. There was nothing very cheerful in the climate or the town, and yet was there an air of cheerfulness abroad that the clearest summer air and brightest summer sun might have endeavoured to diffuse in vain.

For the people who were shovelling away on the house-tops were jovial and full of glee; calling out to one another from the parapets, and now and then exchanging a facetious snowball—better-natured missile far than many a wordy jest—laughing heartily if it went right, and not less heartily if it went wrong. The poulterers' shops[21] were still half open, and the fruiterers' were radiant in their glory. There were great, round, pot-bellied baskets of chestnuts,[22] shaped like the waistcoats of jolly old gentlemen, lolling at the doors, and tumbling out into the street in their apoplectic opulence. There were ruddy, brown-faced, broad-girthed Spanish Onions, shining in the fatness of their growth like Spanish Friars; and winking from their shelves in wanton slyness at the girls as they went by, and glanced demurely at the hung-up mistletoe.[23] There were pears and apples, clustered high in blooming pyramids; there were bunches of grapes, made, in the shopkeepers' benevolence, to dangle from conspicuous hooks, that people's mouths might water gratis as they passed; there were piles of filberts, mossy and brown, recalling, in their fragrance, ancient walks among the woods, and pleasant shufflings ankle deep through withered leaves; there were Norfolk Biffins,[24] squab and swarthy, setting off the yellow of the oranges and lemons, and, in the great compactness of their juicy persons, urgently entreating and beseeching to be carried home in paper bags and eaten after dinner. The very gold and silver fish,[25] set forth among these choice fruits in a bowl, though members of a dull and stagnant-blooded race, appeared to know that there was something going on; and, to a fish, went gasping round and round their little world in slow and passionless excitement.

The Grocers'! oh the Grocers'! nearly closed, with perhaps two shutters down, or one; but through those gaps such glimpses! It was not alone that the scales descending on the counter made a merry sound, or that the twine and roller, parted company so briskly, or that the canisters were rattled up and down like juggling tricks, or even that the blended scents of tea and coffee were so grateful to the nose, or even that the raisins were so plentiful and rare, the almonds so extremely white, the sticks of cinnamon so long and straight, the other spices so delicious, the candied fruits so caked and spotted with molten sugar as to make the coldest lookers-on feel faint and subsequently bilious. Nor was it that the figs were moist and pulpy, or that the French plums[26] blushed in modest tartness from their highly-decorated boxes, or that everything was good to eat and in its Christmas dress: but the customers were all so hurried and so eager in the hopeful promise of the day, that they tumbled up against each other at the door, crashing their wicker baskets wildly, and left their pur-

luxurious winter fare. In his devouring mind's eye he pictured to himself every roasting-pig running about with a pudding in his belly, and an apple in his mouth; the pigeons were snuggly put to bed in a comfortable pie, and tucked in with a coverlet of crust; the geese were swimming in their own gravy; and the ducks pairing cosily in dishes, like snug married couples, with a decent competency of onion-sauce. In the porkers he saw carved out the future sleek side of bacon, and juicy relishing ham; not a turkey but he beheld daintily trussed up, with its gizzard under its wing, and, peradventure, a necklace of savory sausages; and even bright chanticleer himself lay sprawling on his back, in a side-dish, with up-lifted claws, as if craving that quarter which his chivalrous spirit disdained to ask while living.

23. *glanced demurely at the hung-up mistletoe.* "The mistletoe is still hung up in

"The Funny Young Gentlemen." Etching by "Phiz" (Hablôt Knight Browne), *Sketches of Young Gentlemen*, 1838. *Courtesy British Library Board.*

farmhouses and kitchens at Christmas," noted Irving in "Christmas Eve" (*The Sketch-Book*, 1819–20); "and the young men have the privilege of kissing the girls under it, plucking each time a berry from the bush. When the berries are all plucked, the privilege ceases." One of the highlights of the Christmas festivities at Dingley Dell in Chapter 28 of *The Pickwick Papers* (1837) is all the kissing beneath the mistletoe in the kitchen.

24. *Norfolk Biffins.* A variety of cooking apple, grown particularly in the county of Norfolk in eastern England; the name comes from "beefing," referring to the deep red-rust color of the fruit. They were baked slowly in coal ovens, crushed between iron plates, into round, flat cakes and packed in straw for sale in London and elsewhere. Dickens was fond of this fruit and referred to it again in Chapter 60 of *Dombey and Son* (1848) and in "The Holly-Tree" (*Household Words*, December 15, 1855).

25. *gold and silver fish.* Members of the carp family, commonly hawked at the time in glass bowls on London streets. These natives of China were introduced to England as house pets from Portugal about 1690; eventually they were both imported and native grown. According to vol. 2 of Henry Mayhew's *London Labour and London Poor* (London: George Woodfall and Son, 1851, p. 78), there were at that time at least seventy sellers of gold and silver fish in London alone.

26. *French plums.* This preserved fruit, grown primarily in the Loire Valley in France, was a highly prized delicacy of the English Christmas. Their fancy packaging was nearly as famous as their flavor. "It is worth while," suggested *The Illustrated London News* in its 1848 Christmas Supplement, "to spend a few hours in the shop of a large importer of these elegant articles—not merely for the sake of the fruits themselves, crystalised and uncrystalised, but for a sight of the boxes in which they are packed. The French prints used for the purpose have long been celebrated for their beauty and fancy; and the boxes in which plums . . . are packed, are worth preserving for their own sakes, after the fruit has been consumed. Some of the larger receptacles are fit to convert into work-boxes, after they have served their original intention; and many are prepared with a view to such a purpose" (p. 407).

"Market—Christmas Eve." Etching by Robert Seymour,
The Book of Christmas by Thomas K. Hervey, 1836.
Private collection.

chases upon the counter, and came running back to fetch them, and committed hundreds of the like mistakes in the best humour possible; while the Grocer and his people were so frank and fresh that the polished hearts with which they fastened their aprons behind might have been their own, worn outside for general inspection, and for Christmas daws to peck at[27] if they chose.

But soon the steeples called good people all, to church and chapel, and away they came, flocking through the streets in their best clothes, and with their gayest faces, And at the same time there emerged from scores of bye streets, lanes, and nameless turnings, innumerable people, carrying their dinners to the bakers' shops.[28] The sight of these poor revellers appeared to interest the Spirit very much, for he stood with Scrooge beside him in a baker's doorway, and taking off the covers as their bearers passed, sprinkled incense[29] on their dinners from his torch. And it was a very uncommon kind of torch, for once or twice when there were angry words between some dinner-carriers who had jostled with each other, he shed a few drops of water on them from it, and their good humour was restored directly. For they said, it was a shame to quarrel upon Christmas Day. And so it was! God love it, so it was!

In time the bells ceased, and the bakers' were shut up; and yet there was a genial shadowing forth of all these dinners and the progress of their cooking, in the thawed blotch of wet above each baker's oven; where the pavement smoked as if its stones were cooking too.

"Is there a peculiar flavour in what you sprinkle from your torch?" asked Scrooge.

"There is. My own."

"Would it apply to any kind of dinner on this day?" asked Scrooge.

"To any kindly given. To a poor one most."

"Why to a poor one most?" asked Scrooge.

"Because it needs it most."[30]

27. *the polished hearts . . . worn . . . for Christmas daws to peck at.* F. H. Ahn identified this last phrase in his 1871 edition as a common figurative expression, meaning "for folks to find fault with" (p. 158). Dickens likely knew it from *Othello* (1.1.61–65):

> From when my outward action doth
>   demonstrate
> The native act and figure of my heart
> In compliment extern, 'tis not long after
> But I will wear my heart upon my sleeve
> For daws to peck at.

Ladies in the Middle Ages accepted the favors of their suitors by having an emblem of their affection sewn on their sleeves. Iago in *Othello* has in mind the opposite purpose of Dickens': the external symbol is only a mask of his villainy.

28. *carrying their dinners to the bakers' shops.* "As poor houses at that time . . . were very poorly equipped for cooking, and all the cookery had to be done over an open fire," explained London *Notes and Queries* (January 27, 1940), "it was an excellent custom then to send large dishes to the baker's, where they were cooked in the professional

"Fetching Home the Christmas Dinner."
Wood engraving after John Leech,
The Illustrated London News,
Christmas Number 1848.
Courtesy Library of Congress.

oven for a small charge" (p. 68). As it was illegal for bakers to bake on Sunday and Christmas Day, they instead opened their shops to the poor, who then had at least one hot meal a week.

29. *incense.* One of the gifts of the Three Magi, offered as a blessing to Jesus, born in poverty, and here bestowed in the same spirit. Dickens originally wrote "fire," but changed it to the Christian symbol when going over the galleys.

30. *"Because it needs it most."* Dickens originally wrote, "Because my eldest brother took them especially under his protection." But he dropped this reference to Jesus Christ to remove even the hint of irreverence.

"Spirit," said Scrooge, after a moment's thought, "I wonder you, of all the beings in the many worlds about us, should desire to cramp these people's opportunities of innocent enjoyment."

"I!" cried the Spirit.

"You would deprive them of their means of dining every seventh day, often the only day on which they can be said to dine at all," said Scrooge. "Wouldn't you?"

"I!" cried the Spirit.

"You seek to close these places on the Seventh Day?"[31] said Scrooge. "And it comes to the same thing."

"*I* seek!" exclaimed the Spirit.

"Forgive me if I am wrong. It has been done in your name, or at least in that of your family," said Scrooge.

"There are some upon this earth of yours," returned the Spirit, "who lay claim to know us, and who do their deeds of passion, pride, ill-will, hatred, envy, bigotry, and selfishness in our name; who are as strange to us and all our kith and kin, as if they had never lived. Remember that, and charge their doings on themselves, not us."

Scrooge promised that he would; and they went on, invisible, as they had been before, into the suburbs of the town. It was a remarkable quality of the Ghost (which Scrooge had observed at the baker's) that notwithstanding his gigantic size, he could accommodate himself to any place with ease; and that he stood beneath a low roof quite as gracefully and like a supernatural creature, as it was possible he could have done in any lofty hall.

And perhaps it was the pleasure the good Spirit had in showing off this power of his, or else it was his own kind, generous, hearty nature, and his sympathy with all poor men, that led him straight to Scrooge's clerk's; for there he went, and took Scrooge with him, holding to his robe; and on the threshold of the door the Spirit smiled, and stopped to Bless Bob Cratchit's[32] dwelling with the sprinklings of his torch. Think of that! Bob had but fifteen "Bob" a-week[33] himself; he pocketed on

31. *to close these places on the Seventh Day?* Dickens described a typical "dismal, close and stale" Sunday in London in Chapter 3 of *Little Dorrit* (1857):

> Melancholy streets in a penitential garb of soot, steeped the souls of the people who were condemned to look at them out of windows, in dire despondency. . . . Everything was bolted and barred that could possibly furnish relief to an overworked people. No pictures, no unfamiliar animals, no rare plants or flowers, no natural or artificial wonders of the ancient world—all *taboo* with the enlightened strictness, that the ugly South sea gods in the British Museum might have supposed themselves at home again. Nothing to see but streets, streets, streets. Nothing to breathe but streets, streets, streets. Nothing to change the brooding mind, or raise it up. Nothing for the spent toiler to do, but to compare the monotony of his seventh day with the monotony of his six days, think what a weary life he led, and make the best of it—or the worst, according to the probabilities.

On behalf of pious individuals who believed that the Sabbath should remain holy, Sir Andrew Agnew introduced in the House of Commons a Sunday observance bill several times between 1832 and 1837; it was designed not only to close the bakeries but also to limit the other "innocent enjoyments" of the poor, while not affecting the amusements of the rich. In response to the bill's recent defeat in Parliament, Dickens published the pamphlet *Sunday under Three Heads* (1836) under the name "Timothy Sparks"; he later supported the National Sunday League, which lobbied for the relaxation of Sunday restrictions. He said in Chapter 1 of that booklet that the working man emerging from a bakery on

Sunday, "with the reeking dish, in which a diminutive joint of mutton simmers above a vast heap of half-browned potatoes . . . would fill Sir Andrew Agnew with astonishment; as well it might seeing that Baronets, generally speaking, eat pretty comfortable dinners all the week through, and cannot be expected to understand what people feel, who only have a meat dinner on one day out of every seven." He insisted, "The Sabbath was made for man, not man to serve the Sabbath." The Ghost of Christmas Present, likewise, attacks such falsely pious people as Sir Andrew Agnew.

32. *Cratchit's.* Likely from "cratch," an archaic English word for crèche, the manger in which the infant Jesus was laid. Christmas pies were often cratch-shaped. The name also suggests the scratching of the clerk's pen in the countinghouse of Scrooge and Marley.

33. *fifteen "Bob" a-week.* Fifteen shillings, "bob" being Cockney slang for a shilling (worth twelve pence, or pennies), from "baubee," a debased copper coin of Scotland, worth an English halfpenny when issued during the reign of King James VI of Scotland. C. Z. Barnett revealed in his dramatization *A Christmas Carol, or The Miser's Warning*, staged at the Royal Theatre Surrey in 1844, that it cost Bob Cratchit a full week's wages to buy the ingredients for the Christmas feast: the goose seven shillings; the pudding five; the oranges, sage, onions, potatoes, and gin three more. It must have been a prodigious bird, for the London *Times* (December 23, 1843) reported in "Christmas Preparations" that geese were then moderately priced in London and running from four to eight shillings, according to weight. But when Bob's pocket is picked, in Barnett's version of the story, Scrooge's nephew, Fred, loans him a sovereign, worth one pound, or twelve shillings, with which he can buy his holiday meal.

Charles Webb apparently thought it unlikely that a man as poor as Bob Cratchit would have spent every cent of his pay on this one meal. In his 1844 play *A Christmas Carol; or, The Past, Present, and Future*, the clerk is all set to enjoy a meal of "a beautiful cushion of bacon and some potatoes" when Fred comes through again and surprises him with the gift of a Christmas goose. According to "Christmas Preparations," bacon cost only five to eight pence at the time.

Saturdays but fifteen copies of his Christian name; and yet the Ghost of Christmas Present blessed his four-roomed house![34]

Then up rose Mrs. Cratchit,[35] Cratchit's wife, dressed out but poorly in a twice-turned gown, but brave[36] in ribbons, which are cheap and make a goodly show for sixpence; and she laid the cloth,[37] assisted by Belinda Cratchit, second of her daughters,[38] also brave in ribbons; while Master Peter Cratchit plunged a fork into the saucepan of potatoes, and getting the corners of his monstrous shirt-collar (Bob's private property, conferred upon his son and heir in honour of the day) into his mouth, rejoiced to find himself so gallantly attired, and yearned to show his linen in the fashionable Parks.[39] And now two smaller Cratchits, boy and girl, came tearing in, screaming that outside the baker's they had smelt the goose, and known it for their own; and basking in luxurious thoughts of sage-and-onion, these young Cratchits danced about the table, and exalted Master Peter Cratchit to the skies, while he (not proud, although his collars nearly choked him) blew the fire, until the slow potatoes bubbling up, knocked loudly at the saucepan-lid to be let out and peeled.

"What has ever got your precious father then," said Mrs. Cratchit. "And your brother, Tiny Tim![40] and Martha warn't as late last Christmas Day by half-an-hour!"

"Here's Martha, mother!" said a girl, appearing as she spoke.

"Here's Martha, mother!" cried the two young Cratchits. "Hurrah! There's *such* a goose, Martha!"

"Why, bless your heart alive, my dear, how late you are!" said Mrs. Cratchit, kissing her a dozen times, and taking off her shawl and bonnet for her, with officious zeal.

"We'd a deal of work to finish up last night," replied the girl, "and had to clear away this morning,[41] mother!"

34. *his four-roomed house!* Willoughby Matchett in "Dickens in Bayham Street" (*The Dickensian*, July 1909, p. 183) argued that the home of the Cratchits (as well as that of the Micawbers, where Traddles was a lodger in *David Copperfield*, 1850) was also the first one in London occupied by the Dickenses when Charles was a boy. His father moved the family to 16 Bayham Street, when the Navy Pay Office relocated him from Chatham to the capital in June 1822; they moved once again on the day after Christmas 1823. "Bayham Street was about

16 Bayham Street, Camden Town.
Courtesy The Charles Dickens Museum, London.

the poorest part of the London suburbs then," wrote Forster in vol. 1 of his biography of Dickens, "and the house was a mean small tenement, with a wretched little back-garden abutting on a squalid court. Here was no place for new acquaintances to him: not a boy was near with whom he might hope to become in any way familiar." He said that living here gave Dickens "his first impression of that struggling poverty which is nowhere more vividly shown than in the commoner streets of the ordinary London suburb" (pp. 16–17). Forster's opinion was no doubt colored by Dickens' bitter memories of the place. Dickens said in "An Unsettled Neighbourhood" (*Household Words*, November 11, 1854) that "the neighbourhood was as quiet and dismal as any neighbourhood about London." In Chapter 27 of *David Copperfield*, he wrote of a row of houses of "faded gentility" on his street, "all built on one monotonous pattern, and looked like the early copies of a blundering boy who was learning to make houses, and had not yet got out of his cramped brick and mortar pothooks."

When Forster's book came out in 1872, some former residents of the area protested his description of the place. It was not so bad as he said, and there were other boys there. "To my childish apprehension it was a country village," said one. "It seemed a green and pleasant spot." "The district has perhaps somewhat degenerated since Dickens's boyhood," admitted Matchett in the June 1909 *Dickensian,* "but Bayham Street remains in essentials what it was then—a broad, quietish, respectable street, not in the least slummy; grass, however, no longer growing in it as it did then" (p. 150). The Bayham Street house was demolished in 1910 and replaced by a hospital.

35. *Then up rose Mrs. Cratchit.* The following scene of domestic bliss in a poor man's home derived from a similar incident in "The Story of the Goblins Who Stole a Sexton," Chapter 29 of *The Pickwick Papers* (1837), in which a family eagerly awaits the coming of the father, and the children gather around him on his arrival, just as the Cratchits do around Bob, where "all seemed happiness and comfort." See Stave 4, note 31.

36. *brave.* Wonderful, splendid; as in *The Tempest* 5.1.186–87: "O brave new world / That has such people in't!"

37. *laid the cloth.* Meaning set the table, which always commences with spreading out the tablecloth.

38. *Belinda Cratchit, second of her daughters.* The six Cratchit children correspond to the six Dickenses of 16 Bayham Street, Camden Town: the eldest, Martha, is Frances "Fanny" Elizabeth (1810–1848); Peter is Charles John Huffam (1812–1870); Belinda is Laetitia Mary (1816–1893); the unnamed boy and girl are Frederick (1820–1868) and Harriet (1819–?); and the youngest, Tiny Tim, is Alfred Allen (1813–1814). Two more children, Alfred Lamert (1822–1860) and Augustus (1827–1866), were born after the family left Camden Town. See also note 40 below.

39. *to show his linen in the fashionable Parks.* To show off his fine clothes in St. James Park, one of the Royal Parks of London, south of the Mall, near Buckingham Palace, or in other such areas, principally St. James's Park, Green Park, and Hyde Park, where fashionable young men were expected to show off their finery; it was necessary to be "seen in the Parks" to maintain one's high position in English society.

40. *Tiny Tim!* According to Frank S. Johnson's "About *A Christmas Carol*" (*The Dickensian*, winter 1931–32, p. 9), Tiny Tim was originally called "Little Fred" in the manuscript. In age, he would have corresponded to Dickens' younger brother Frederick, but he may also represent another sibling, Alfred, who like Tiny Tim in Stave 4 died in childhood. Dickens evidently found inspiration for the crippled little boy during his historic visit to Manchester in October 1843, when he visited his sister Fanny and

Harry Burnett, Charles Dickens' nephew.
Courtesy Berg Collection, New York Public Library, Astor, Lenox and Tilden Foundations.

her invalid son Harry Burnett Jr. When his nephew finally died of tuberculosis at the age of nine in 1849, he became the model for another lost boy, Paul Dombey.

"It is one of my rules in life," Dickens declared in a speech at the Hospital for Sick Children on Great Ormand Street, February 9, 1858, "not to believe a man who may happen to tell me that he feels no interest in children." The great novelist feared "that any heart which could really toughen its affections and sympathies against those dear little people must be wanting in so many humanizing experiences of innocence and tenderness, as to be quite an unsafe monstrosity among men" (p. 248). Perhaps no other writer before or since has shown such enormous compassion for the young as

did Charles Dickens. "Certainly there is nothing more touching than the suffering of a child," he once told his friend and publisher James T. Fields, "nothing more overwhelming" (quoted in Fields, *Biographical Notes and Personal Sketches* [Boston: Houghton Mifflin, 1891], p. 174). He knew personally what it was to suffer when a boy, and he never forgot the deep pain he felt then. Dickens was the first important English novelist to write from the child's point of view and to take the child's side. He grew up in an age of high infant mortality and horrendous child labor practices. (It was once estimated that one third of all deaths in a year in London were those of children.) And Dickens did his utmost to change society's treatment of young people. Not everyone was moved by his particular form of pathos. The child mortality rate may well be higher in Dickens' novels than in any by any other Victorian novelist. Tiny Tim belongs to what Henry James in *The Nation* (November 21, 1865) contemptuously called "the troop of hunchbacks, imbeciles, and precocious children who have carried on the sentimental business in all Mr. Dickens's novels." He is just another "little monster . . . deformed, unhealthy, unnatural" (p. 787).

As H. Philip Bolton reported in *Dickens Dramatized* (Boston: G. K. Hall, 1987, p. 235), actresses usually played Tiny Tim on the nineteenth-century stage, such as Miss Maynard at the Adelphi and Miss Ranoe at the Strand, both in February 1844. When the Edward Stirling version was revived at the Adelphi, on December 24, 1859, the daughter of one of the sceneshifters, Miss Hamilton, took the role. A real goose and a real pudding were served hot onstage to the actors playing the Cratchits; and John Lawrence Toole, who played her father, was astonished at how much a little thing like her could eat. "That child's appetite appalled me," he told Joseph Hatton in *Rem-*

iniscences of J. L. Toole (vol. 1, London: Hurst and Blackett, 1889). "I could not help noticing the extraordinary rapidity with which she consumed what I gave her, and she looked so wan and thin, and so pitiful, that her face used positively to haunt me" (p. 64). And yet he piled up her plate every night; one time she took nearly half the goose along with plenty of potatoes and apple sauce. He found out later that the child passed the food on to her little sister waiting on the other side of the stage fireplace, so that their family could have a hearty supper every night on Bob Cratchit. When Toole told Dickens the story, the novelist smiled a little sadly and shook the actor's hand, saying, "Ah, you ought to have given her the whole goose" (p. 67).

41. *We'd a deal of work to finish up last night . . . and had to clear away this morning.* Like her father, Martha Cratchit is dependant upon the whim of her employer to get the holiday off. Her boss must be even worse than Scrooge, making the girls work on Christmas morning!

"Well! Never mind so long as you are come," said Mrs. Cratchit. "Sit ye down before the fire, my dear, and have a warm,[42] Lord bless ye!"

"No no! There's father coming," cried the two young Cratchits, who were everywhere at once. "Hide Martha, hide!"

So Martha hid herself, and in came little Bob, the father, with at least three feet of comforter exclusive of the fringe, hanging down before him; and his thread-bare clothes darned up and brushed, to look season-able; and Tiny Tim upon his shoulder. Alas for Tiny Tim, he bore a little crutch, and had his limbs sup-ported by an iron frame![43]

"Why, where's our Martha?" cried Bob Cratchit looking round.

"Not coming," said Mrs. Cratchit.

"Not coming!" said Bob, with a sudden declension in his high spirits; for he had been Tim's blood horse[44] all the way from church, and had come home rampant. "Not coming upon Christmas Day!"

Martha didn't like to see him disappointed, if it were only in joke; so she came out prematurely from behind the closet door, and ran into his arms, while the two young Cratchits hustled Tiny Tim, and bore him off into the wash-house, that he might hear the pudding singing in the copper.[45]

"And how did little Tim behave?" asked Mrs. Cratchit, when she had rallied Bob on his credulity and Bob had hugged his daughter to his heart's content.

"As good as gold," said Bob, "and better. Somehow he gets thoughtful, sitting by himself so much, and thinks the strangest things you ever heard. He told me coming home that he hoped the people saw him[46] in the church,[47] because he was a cripple, and it might be pleasant to them to remember upon Christmas Day, who made lame beggars walk and blind men see."[48]

Bob's voice was tremulous when he told them this, and trembled more when he said that Tiny Tim was growing strong and hearty.[49]

42. *have a warm.* Colloquialism, warm yourself; in Chapter 1 of *Oliver Twist* (1838), the surgeon gives "the palms of his hands a warm, and a rub alternatively"; in Chapter 7 of *Nicholas Nickleby* (1839), Smike admits to going to the kitchen "for a warm."

43. *his limbs supported by an iron frame!* Playwright Edward Stirling recalled in his memoir, *Old Drury Lane* (London: Chatto and Windus, 1881), that he wanted to add a little more realism to this scene in his dramatization *A Christmas Carol; or, Past, Present, and Future*, at the Adelphi The-atre, by dressing the youngster playing Tiny Tim in bandages and a set of irons. But Dickens objected. "No, Stirling, no," he protested; "this won't do! remember how painful it would be to many of the audience having crippled children" (p. 187).

But what exactly was Tiny Tim's disease? Colonel Charles Callahan, chief of the Department of Pediatrics and Pediatric Pulmonology at Tripler Army Medical Cen-ter in Honolulu told Roxanne Nelson in "The Case of Tiny Tim" (*The Washington Post,* December 24, 2002) that the boy possi-bly suffered from Pott's disease, also called tuberculosis spondylitis, or spinal tubercu-losis, which commonly strikes children under ten years old. Tuberculosis infected half the population in nineteenth-century England and was then the chief cause of death in the Western world. While primarily a respiratory illness, Pott's disease can spread to other parts of the body, such as the bones and joints. It is a crippling condi-tion that deteriorates the vertebrae. Dr. Callahan explained that although antitu-bercular drugs were not then available, Scrooge could have had Tiny Tim fitted with a back brace and sent to a sanitarium in the country. Fresh air, good nutrition, and rest might have arrested his disease. It might even have gone into remission.

But tuberculosis was not curable at the

time. Dr. Donald W. Lewis, an associate professor at Eastern Virginia Medical School in Norfolk, suggested in "What Was Wrong with Tiny Tim?" (*American Journal of Diseases of Children,* December 1992) that the boy had a kidney disease, renal tubular acidosis. Symptoms include muscle weakness, retarded growth, and softening of the bones; untreated it can be fatal. Dr. Lewis believed that Tiny Tim might have been saved at the time through "fresh air and sunshine, a balanced diet with starchy meat dishes, halibut or cod liver oils, and mineral waters or tonics emphasizing alkaline solutions with bitters" (p. 1407).

44. *blood horse.* A thoroughbred, particularly a racehorse.

45. *the copper.* A boiler; it is kept in the washhouse because the rest of the year

"The Christmas Pudding." Etching by Robert Seymour, *The Book of Christmas* by Thomas K. Hervey, 1836.
Private collection.

Mrs. Cratchit uses it to boil her laundry. These often large vessels were originally made of copper; the name remained even after they were constructed of other metals, such as cast iron.

46. *he hoped the people saw him.* Some people did notice. "Tiny Tim," observed the reviewer in *The Gentleman's Magazine* (February 1844), "will serve as an illustration of the great affection shewn by the poorer classes to a diseased or deformed child. Indeed it is impossible to visit the gardens of Hampton Court on a Monday in the summer without seeing numerous proofs of this. Often have we watched a mechanic carrying in his arms a little cripple, eying it with affection, and occasionally pointing out some object of interest to it. Sometimes he will gently seat it on the grass, watching it while it plucks a daisy, or crawls over the verdant turf." This strong and tender bond between father and son, between Bob Cratchit and Tiny Tim, was neither unusual nor a surprise at the time. "The children of the poor," the reviewer explained, "are partakers with their parents of the same dish, the same room, and frequently of the same bed. They are the sharers of their poverty as well as of their more smiling hours, and are their constant companions, the objects of their love, whether in weal or woe; and to the credit of the poor it may be added, that when sickness and old age arrive, the tie of affection is still unbroken, and they continue to share in the hard earnings of their offspring" (pp. 170–71).

47. *the church.* Matchett in "Dickens in Bayham Street" (*The Dickensian,* July 1909, p. 184) suggested that this place might be St. Stephan's Church in Camden Town, not far from where the Dickenses once lived.

48. *lame beggars walk and blind men see.* According to John 5.1–9: "And a certain man was there, which had an infirmity thirty and eight years. . . . Jesus saith unto him, Rise, take up thy bed, and walk. And immediately the man was made whole, and took up his bed and walked." And Mark 8.22–25: ". . . . and they bring a blind man unto him, and besought him to touch him. . . . and when he had spit on his eyes, and put his hands upon him, he asked if he saw ought. And he looked up, and said, I see men as trees, walking. After that he put *his* hands again upon his eyes, and made him look up: and he was restored, and saw every man clearly."

49. *Tiny Tim was growing strong and hearty.* Dickens originally added the following passage:

"Is that so, Spirit?" Scrooge demanded, with an interest he never felt before. "I hope it is?"

"I see a vacant seat beside the chimney corner," said the Ghost. "The child will die!"

He wisely deleted this exchange when he found a more effective use for it toward the end of the visit to the Cratchit home.

50. *a black swan.* Juvenal, Book 2, Satire 6, line 165: "As rare a bird in the world as a black swan." It was a phrase familiar to almost anyone with even a rudimentary knowledge of Latin. Paul Dombey's tutor, Cordelia Blimber, "working in the graves of deceased languages" in Chapter 11 of *Dombey and Son* (1848), makes sure her pupil knows *simillima cygno* ("like a swan") in Chapter 14.

51. *grace was said.* The family was originally more formal in the manuscript: "all stood up while Bob said grace."

His active little crutch was heard upon the floor, and back came Tiny Tim before another word was spoken, escorted by his brother and sister to his stool beside the fire; and while Bob, turning up his cuffs—as if, poor fellow, they were capable of being made more shabby—compounded some hot mixture in a jug with gin and lemons, and stirred it round and round and put it on the hob to simmer; Master Peter and the two ubiquitous young Cratchits went to fetch the goose, with which they soon returned in high procession.

Such a hustle ensued that you might have thought a goose the rarest of all birds; a feathered phenomenon, to which a black swan[50] was a matter of course: and in truth it was something very like it in that house. Mrs. Cratchit made the gravy (ready beforehand in a little saucepan) hissing hot; Master Peter mashed the potatoes with incredible vigour; Miss Belinda sweetened up the apple-sauce; Martha dusted the hot plates; Bob took Tiny Tim beside him in a tiny corner at the table; the two young Cratchits set chairs for everybody, not forgetting themselves, and mounting guard upon their posts, crammed spoons into their mouths, lest they should shriek for goose before their turn came to be helped. At last the dishes were set on, and grace was said.[51] It was succeeded by a breathless pause, as Mrs. Cratchit, looking slowly all along the carving-knife, prepared to plunge it in the breast; but when she did, and when the long expected gush of stuffing issued forth, one murmur of delight arose all round the board, and even Tiny Tim, excited by the two young Cratchits, beat on the table with the handle of his knife, and feebly cried Hurrah!

There never was such a goose. Bob said he didn't believe there ever was such a goose cooked. Its tenderness and flavour, size and cheapness, were the themes of universal admiration. Eked out by the apple-sauce and mashed potatoes, it was a sufficient dinner for the whole family; indeed, as Mrs. Cratchit said with great delight (surveying one small atom of a bone upon the dish), they hadn't ate it all at last! Yet every one had had enough, and the youngest Cratchits in particular, were steeped in sage and onion to the eyebrows! But now, the plates being changed by Miss Belinda, Mrs. Cratchit left the room alone—too nervous to bear witnesses—to take the pudding up, and bring it in.

Suppose it should not be done enough! Suppose it should break in turning out! Suppose somebody should have got over the wall of the back-yard, and stolen it,[52] while they were merry with the goose; a supposition at which the two young Cratchits became livid! All sorts of horrors were supposed.

Hallo! A great deal of steam! The pudding was out of the copper. A smell like a washing-day![53] That was the cloth. A smell like an eating-house and a pastry cook's next door to each other, with a laundress's next door to that! That was the pudding. In half a minute Mrs. Cratchit entered: flushed, but smiling proudly: with the pudding, like a speckled cannon-ball, so hard and firm, blazing in half of half-a-quartern[54] of ignited brandy, and bedight[55] with Christmas holly stuck into the top.[56]

Oh, a wonderful pudding! Bob Cratchit said, and calmly too, that he regarded it as the greatest success achieved by Mrs. Cratchit since their marriage. Mrs. Cratchit said that now the weight was off her mind, she would confess she had had her doubts about the quantity of flour. Everybody had something to say about it, but nobody said or thought it was at all a small pudding for a large family. It would have been flat heresy to do so. Any Cratchit would have blushed to hint at such a thing.

At last the dinner was all done, the cloth was cleared, the hearth swept, and the fire made up. The compound in the jug being tasted and considered perfect, apples and oranges were put upon the table, and a shovel-full of chesnuts on the fire. Then all the Cratchit family drew round the hearth, in what Bob Cratchit called a circle, meaning half a one; and at Bob

52. *Suppose somebody should have got over the wall of the back-yard, and stolen it.* This suspicion is not so far-fetched as it sounds. Matchett reported in "Dickens in Bayham

The back of 16 Bayham Street,
Camden Town.
Courtesy The Charles Dickens Museum, London.

Street" (*The Dickensian,* July 1909) that "robbery from outhouses and back premises was the peculiar trouble of this otherwise quiet district. . . . The mere fact that the Dickens back-yard or garden gave on to a secluded public passage would make the likelihood of being robbed double that of ordinary houses" (p. 184).

53. *A smell like a washing-day!* The pudding was cooked in a cloth, here in a boiler generally used for laundry.

54. *half of a half-a-quartern.* A tiny bit of spirits as a quartern is only a gill, or one-fourth of a pint.

55. *bedight*. Adorned, dressed; according to Dr. Johnson's dictionary, "an old word, now only used in humorous writing."

56. *with Christmas holly stuck into the top*. Charles Dickens followed the same custom: His daughter Mamie revealed in *My Father As I Recall Him* (1896) that the family's Christmas pudding was always ornamented "with a sprig of real holly in the centre, lighted, and in this state placed in front of my father, its arrival being always the signal for applause" (p. 37).

Cratchit's elbow stood the family display of glass; two tumblers, and a custard-cup without a handle.

These held the hot stuff from the jug, however, as well as golden goblets would have done; and Bob served it out with beaming looks, while the chestnuts on the fire sputtered and crackled noisily. Then Bob proposed:

"A Merry Christmas to us all, my dears. God bless us!"

Which all the family re-echoed.

"God bless us every one!"[57] said Tiny Tim, the last of all.

He sat very close to his father's side, upon his little stool. Bob held his withered little hand in his, as if he loved the child, and wished to keep him by his side, and dreaded that he might be taken from him.

"Spirit," said Scrooge, with an interest he had never felt before, "tell me if Tiny Tim will live."

"I see a vacant seat,"[58] replied the Ghost, "in the poor chimney corner, and a crutch without an owner, carefully preserved. If these shadows remain unaltered by the Future,[59] the child will die."

"No, no," said Scrooge. "Oh no, kind Spirit! say he will be spared."

"If these shadows remain unaltered by the Future, none other of my race," returned the Ghost, "will find him here. What then? If he be like to die, he had better do it, and decrease the surplus population."

Scrooge hung his head to hear his own words quoted by the Spirit, and was overcome with penitence and grief.

"Man," said the Ghost, "if man you be in heart, not adamant, forbear that wicked cant until you have discovered What the surplus is, and Where it is. Will you decide what men shall live, what men shall die? It may be, that in the sight of Heaven, you are more worthless and less fit to live than millions like this poor man's child. Oh God! to hear the Insect on the leaf pronouncing on the too much life among his hungry brothers in the dust!"

57. *"God bless us every one!"* Johnson suggested in "About *A Christmas Carol*" (*The Dickensian,* winter 1931–32, p. 8) that this, the most famous phrase in the story, may have come from the carol about the Holy Well ("As it fell out one May morning") in Sandys' collection, *Christmas Carols, Ancient and Modern* (1833):

He said, God bless you every one
And your bodies Christ save and see.
    (p. 150)

As one was forbidden to say "god" on the London stage in 1844, the sentiment was changed to "Heaven bless us, every one!" at the Adelphi, the Strand, and elsewhere.

58. *"I see a vacant seat."* Dickens may have been recalling the deaths of children in his own family when he first made this observation in "A Christmas Dinner," in *Sketches by Boz* (1839): "Look on the merry faces of your children as they sit round the fire. One little seat may be empty; one slight form that gladdened the father's heart, and roused the mother's pride to look upon, may not be there."

59. *If these shadows remain unaltered by the Future.* This phrase here and repeated in the Ghost's next speech was an afterthought; it does not appear in either place in the manuscript in the Pierpont Morgan Library. Apparently, when reading the galleys, Dickens saw the necessity of giving the reader some hope that Tiny Tim would live. See also Stave 5, note 18.

60. *a situation . . . for Master Peter.* If Peter Cratchit is the boy Charles Dickens, the mention of early employment at so festive a time is bitterly ironic; it may be a private joke at the author's own expense. The situation twelve-year-old Charles was offered was pasting labels on bottles for six shillings a week at Warren's Blacking factory. There were actually two competing firms: Robert Warren's, 30 Strand, for whom George Cruikshank designed advertisements when a young man; and Jonathan Warren's, 30 Hungerford Stairs, where Dickens worked. Child labor was a hotly debated subject in nineteenth-century industrial

MOTHER GOOSE.

Ask for WARREN's BLACKING, made 30, STRAND—all others are inferior.

From Mother Goose a lesson take,
   Nor think the warning vain,
Ne'er thro' thy life's endeavours be
   Too eager after gain.
WARREN has found a golden egg,
   And won't his friends forget,
Then call at 30, in the STRAND,
   And try his brilliant Jet.

Advertisement for Warren's Blacking designed by George Cruikshank.
Private collection.

Scrooge bent before the Ghost's rebuke, and trembling cast his eyes upon the ground. But he raised them speedily, on hearing his own name.

"Mr. Scrooge!" said Bob; "I'll give you Mr. Scrooge, the Founder of the Feast!"

"The Founder of the Feast indeed!" cried Mrs. Cratchit, reddening. "I wish I had him here. I'd give him a piece of my mind to feast upon, and I hope he'd have a good appetite for it."

"My dear," said Bob, "the children; Christmas Day."

"It should be Christmas Day, I am sure," said she, "on which one drinks the health of such an odious, stingy, hard, unfeeling man as Mr. Scrooge. You know he is, Robert! Nobody knows it better than you do, poor fellow!"

"My dear," was Bob's mild answer, "Christmas Day."

"I'll drink his health for your sake and the Day's," said Mrs. Cratchit, "not for his. Long life to him! A merry Christmas and a happy new year! He'll be very merry and very happy, I have no doubt!"

The children drank the toast after her. It was the first of their proceedings which had no heartiness in it. Tiny Tim drank it last of all, but he didn't care twopence for it. Scrooge was the Ogre of the family. The mention of his name cast a dark shadow on the party, which was not dispelled for full five minutes.

After it had passed away, they were ten times merrier than before, from the mere relief of Scrooge the Baleful being done with. Bob Cratchit told them how he had a situation in his eye for Master Peter,[60] which would bring in, if obtained, full five-and-sixpence weekly.[61] The two young Cratchits laughed tremendously at the idea of Peter's being a man of business; and Peter himself looked thoughtfully at the fire from between his collars, as if he were deliberating what particular investments he should favour when he came into the receipt of that bewildering income. Martha, who was a poor apprentice at a milliner's,[62] then told

England. The Cotton Factories Regulation Act of 1819 restricted the minimum working age to nine years and the hours to twelve per day. Warren's was open from 8 A.M. to 8 P.M., with an hour for dinner and a half hour for tea. Dickens considered the few months he spent there the worst period of his childhood, describing it in painful detail in an autobiographical fragment he later worked into Chapter 11 of *David Copperfield* (1850): "No words can express the secret agony of my soul as I sank into this companionship; compared these henceforth everyday associates with those of my happier childhood; . . . and felt my early hopes of growing up to be a learned and distinguished man, crushed in my breast. The deep remembrance of the sense I had, of being utterly without hope now; of the shame I felt in my position; of the misery it was to my young heart to believe that day by day what I had learned, and thought and delighted in, and raised my fancy and my emulation up by, would pass away from me, little by little, never to be brought back any more; cannot be written." But Dickens dropped these concluding remarks that Forster did publish in vol. 1 of his biography in 1872: "My whole nature was penetrated with grief and humiliation of such considerations, that even now, famous and caressed and happy, I often forget in my dreams . . . that I am a man; and wander desolately back to that time in my life" (p. 33).

Within this passage lies the poor, neglected, helpless boy who grew into Charles Dickens the novelist, who defended those other children Want and Ignorance. He supplies no details of Peter Cratchit's work. Perhaps his memories of his own childhood employment were then too painful, so that he had to wait until he was writing *David Copperfield* to describe "at ten years old, a little labouring hind" who, as David Copperfield, drudges in the dismal Murdstone and Grinby warehouse. Dickens got his

revenge by mentioning Warren's often and unflatteringly in his books: "Seven Dials," in *Sketches by Boz* (1839); Chapter 10 of *The Pickwick Papers* (1837); Chapter 28 of *The Old Curiosity Shop* (1841); Book 2, Chapter 7, of *Hard Times* (1854); vol. 2, Chapter 8, of *Great Expectations* (1861); and elsewhere. See also notes 87 and 94.

61. *full five-and-sixpence weekly.* Five shillings and a sixpence was hardly a princely wage: office boys in "The Streets—Morning," in *Sketches by Boz* (1839), received "seven shillings a week, with the prospect of an early rise to eight." Dickens recalled six or seven shillings as his weekly salary at Warren's Blacking in 1824; he started at ten shillings and a sixpence when apprenticed to the firm of Ellis and Blackmore, solicitors, in 1827. See Carlton, "Mr. Blackmore Engages an Office Boy," *The Dickensian*, September 1952, p. 164.

62. *Martha . . . was a poor apprentice at a milliner's.* Dickens reported in "The Streets—Morning" (*Sketches by Boz*, 1839) that the milliner's apprentices were among "the hardest worked, the worst paid, and too often, the worst used class of the community." Ralph Nickleby secures a position for his niece Kate with the milliner Madame Mantalini in Chapter 18 of *Nicholas Nickleby* (1839). "I am afraid it is an unhealthy occupation," the miniaturist Miss La Creevy warns the girl. "I recollect getting three young milliners to sit to me when I first began to paint, and I remember that they were all very pale and sickly." Dickens, in referring to Kate's employment, refuses to detail "the very dullness, unhealthy confinement, and bodily fatigue, which made up its sum and substance." C. Z. Barnett commented on the current condition of English working women in his 1844 play *A Christmas Carol, or The Miser's Warning* by making Martha Cratchit a dressmaker; her father reports that she "can only come to see us once in about four months."

63. *a song, about a lost child travelling in the snow.* Apparently Dickens had no specific carol in mind; no such song has been found in any old collection of Christmas carols. G. K. Chesterton realized this omission, and included in his *Poems* (1926) "A Child of the Snows," which might stand for Tiny Tim's carol until another might be found.

64. *Peter might have known . . . the inside of a pawnbroker's.* Just like little Charles Dickens. As Forster revealed in vol. 1 of his *Life* (1872), the Dickenses had to sell or pawn their belongings, and little Charles was "the principal agent in those sorrowful transactions" (p. 25). "At the pawnbrokers's shop, too," Dickens admitted in Chapter 11 of *David Copperfield* (1850), "I began to be very well known."

"Going to the Pantomime." Wood engraving after John Leech, *The Illustrated London News*, December 24, 1854. *Courtesy Library of Congress.*

65. *wo.* Colloquial spelling for "woe."

them what kind of work she had to do, and how many hours she worked at a stretch, and how she meant to lie a-bed to-morrow morning for a good long rest; to-morrow being a holiday she passed at home. Also how she had seen a countess and a lord some days before, and how the lord "was much about as tall as Peter;" at which Peter pulled up his collars so high that you couldn't have seen his head if you had been there. All this time the chesnuts and the jug went round and round; and bye and bye they had a song, about a lost child travelling in the snow,[63] from Tiny Tim; who had a plaintive little voice, and sang it very well indeed.

There was nothing of high mark in this. They were not a handsome family; they were not well dressed; their shoes were far from being water-proof; their clothes were scanty; and Peter might have known, and very likely did, the inside of a pawnbroker's.[64] But they were happy, grateful, pleased with one another, and contented with the time; and when they faded, and looked happier yet in the bright sprinklings of the Spirit's torch at parting, Scrooge had his eye upon them, and especially on Tiny Tim, until the last.

By this time it was getting dark, and snowing pretty heavily; and as Scrooge and the Spirit went along the streets, the brightness of the roaring fires in kitchens, parlours, and all sorts of rooms, was wonderful. Here, the flickering of the blaze showed preparations for a cosy dinner, with hot plates baking through and through before the fire, and deep red curtains, ready to be drawn, to shut out cold and darkness. There, all the children of the house were running out into the snow to meet their married sisters, brothers, cousins, uncles, aunts, and be the first to greet them. Here, again, were shadows on the window-blind of guests assembling; and there a group of handsome girls, all hooded and fur-booted, and all chattering at once, tripped lightly off to some near neighbour's house; where, wo[65] upon the single man who saw them enter—artful witches: well they knew it—in a glow!

But if you had judged from the numbers of people on their way to friendly gatherings, you might have thought that no one was at home to give them welcome when they got there, instead of every house expecting company, and piling up its fires half-chimney high. Blessings on it, how the Ghost exulted! How it bared its breadth of breast, and opened its capacious palm, and floated on, outpouring, with a generous hand, its bright and harmless mirth on everything within its reach! The very lamplighter, who ran on before dotting the dusky street with specks of light, and who was dressed to spend the evening somewhere, laughed out loudly as the Spirit passed: though little kenned[66] the lamplighter that he had any company but Christmas!

And now, without a word of warning from the Ghost, they stood upon a bleak and desert moor,[67] where monstrous masses of rude stone were cast about, as though it were the burial-place of giants;[68] and water spread itself wheresoever it listed—or would have done so, but for the frost that held it prisoner; and nothing grew but moss and furze,[69] and coarse, rank grass. Down in the west the setting sun[70] had left a streak of fiery red, which glared upon the desolation for an instant, like a sullen eye, and frowning lower, lower, lower yet, was lost in the thick gloom of darkest night.

"What place is this?" asked Scrooge.

"A place where Miners live,[71] who labour in the bowels of the earth," returned the Spirit. "But they know me. See!"

A light shone from the window of a hut, and swiftly they advanced towards it. Passing through the wall of mud and stone, they found a cheerful company assembled round a glowing fire. An old, old man and woman, with their children and their children's children, and another generation beyond that, all decked out gaily in their holiday attire. The old man, in a voice that seldom rose above the howling of the wind upon the barren waste, was singing them a Christmas song;[72] it had

66. *kenned.* Knew.

67. *a bleak and desert moor.* In Cornwall, where Dickens, Forster, Daniel Maclise, and Clarkson Stanfield spent about ten days in late October and early November 1842. Dickens had been so moved by the Infant Labour Commission's recent report on child labor in the Cornish mines that he immediately made plans, as he wrote Dr. Southwood Smith (one of the commissioners) on October 22, "to see the very dreariest and most desolate portion of the sea-coast of Cornwall." He wanted to know "the next best bleak and barren part? And can you, furthermore, while I am in those regions, help me down a mine?" (p. 356). He was also eager to open his new novel, *Martin Chuzzlewit* (1844), as he wrote Forster on September 16, "on the Coast of Cornwall, in some dreary iron-bound spot" (p. 326).

They had a glorious time at Land's End. "Blessed star of the morning, such a trip as we had in Cornwall," he reported to his American friend C. C. Felton on December 31, 1842. "If you could have followed us into the earthy old Churches we visited, and into the strange caverns on the gloomy seashore, and down into the depths of Mines, and up the tops of giddy heights where the unspeakably green water was roaring I don't know how many hundred feet below! If you could have seen but one gleam of the bright fires by which we sat in the big rooms of ancient Inns at night, until long after the small hours had come and gone . . . I never laughed in my life as I did on this journey. . . . Seriously, I do believe there never was such a trip" (pp. 414–15). But he did not open *Martin Chuzzlewit* in a Cornish mine. Instead, he made use of this material in *A Christmas Carol*, with both laughter and affection for the miners.

68. *the burial-place of giants.* An obvious reference to Cornwall, the traditional home

"Jack the Giant Killer." Wood engraving after John Leech, *Jack the Giant Killer* by Percival Leigh, 1843.
Courtesy British Library Board.

of Dickens' boyhood hero Jack the Giant-Killer. In "A Christmas Tree" (*Household Words*, September 21, 1850), he fondly recalled this storybook: Suddenly the tree becomes "the marvellous bean-stalk up which Jack climbed to the Giant's house! And now, those dreadfully interesting double-headed giants, with their clubs over their shoulders, begin to stride along the boughs in a perfect throng, dragging knights and ladies home for dinner by the hair of their heads. And Jack—how noble, with his sword of sharpness, and his shoes of swiftness! Again those old meditations come upon me as I gaze up at him; and I debate within myself whether there was more than one Jack (which I am loath to believe possible), or only one genuine original admirable Jack, who achieved all the recorded exploits."

Not everyone at the time shared Dickens' love for this old nursery lore. Many pious pedagogues and religious leaders on both sides of the Atlantic tried to censor fairy tales and other fanciful literature for children. Dickens was outraged when George Cruikshank rewrote the old stories as temperance tracts in *George Cruikshank's Fairy Library* (1853). "In an utilitarian age, of all times," he wrote in "Frauds on the Fairies"

(*Household Words*, October 1, 1853), "it is a matter of grave importance that Fairy tales should be respected. . . . a nation without fancy, without some romance, never did, never can, never will hold, a great place under the sun. . . . To preserve them in their usefulness, they must be as much preserved in their simplicity, and purity, and innocent extravagance, as if they were actual fact. Whosoever alters them to suit his own opinions, whatever they are, is guilty, to our thinking, of an act of presumption, and appropriates to himself what does not belong to him." This essay remains a brilliant condemnation of politically correct juvenile literature. "Imagine a Total abstinence edition of *Robinson Crusoe*, with the rum left out," he wrote. "Imagine a Peace edition, with the gunpowder left out, and the rum left it. Imagine a Vegetarian edition, with the goat's flesh left out. Imagine a Kentucky edition, to introduce a flogging of that 'tarnation old nigger Friday, twice a week. Imagine the Aborigines Protection Society edition, to deny the cannibalism and make Robinson embrace the amiable savages whenever they landed. Robinson Crusoe would be 'edited' out of his island in a hundred years, and the island would be swallowed up in the editorial ocean."

69. *furze.* Or gorse; Samuel Johnson in his dictionary identified this evergreen as "a thick prickly shrub that bears yellow flowers in winter."

70. *the setting sun.* This sunset is likely the one Forster described in vol. 2 of his *Life of Charles Dickens* (1873). "Land and sea yielded each its marvels to us; but of all impressions brought away, of which some afterwards took forms as lasting as they could receive from the most delightful art, I doubt if any were the source of such deep emotion to us all as a sunset. . . . I was familiar from boyhood with border and Scottish scenery, and Dickens was fresh from Niagara; but there was something in the sinking of the sun behind the Atlantic that autumn afternoon, as we viewed it together from the top of the rock projecting farthest into the sea, which each in turn declared to have no parallel in memory" (pp. 19–20). This was just one of the many marvellous sights Dickens, Forster, Maclise, and Stanfield saw on their ten-day visit to Cornwall in the autumn of 1842.

"Botallick Mine, Cornwall." Landscape by Clarkson Stanfield, *Stanfield's Coast Scenery*, 1836.
Courtesy British Library Board.

71. *A place where Miners live.* Land's End, at St. Just, Cornwall, most likely the Botallick Mine. "The most celebrated tin mines in Cornwall are . . . close to the sea," Dickens wrote in Chapter 1 of *A Child's History of England* (1852–54). "One of them which I have seen, is so close to it that it is hollowed out underneath the ocean; and the miners say, that, in stormy weather, when they are at work down in the deep place, they can hear the noise of the waves, thundering about their heads."

72. *a Christmas song.* According to Sandys' *Christmas Carols, Ancient and*

Modern (1833), Cornwall was famous for its Christmas songs, several of which were said to be over three hundred years old.

"Land's End, Cornwall . . ." Landscape by Clarkson Stanfield, *Stanfield's Coast Scenery*, 1836.
Courtesy British Library Board.

"The Logan Rock, Cornwall, climbed by Charles Dickens, John Forster, Daniel Maclise, and the Artist." Watercolor by Clarkson Stanfield, 1842.
Courtesy Victoria and Albert Museum.

73. *a solitary lighthouse.* Dickens and his companions visited the Eddystone lighthouse in 1842; it was also the locale for Wilkie Collins' play *The Lighthouse* (1855), in which Dickens himself played the lighthouse keeper. Before they left for Cornwall, Dickens wrote Forster in early August 1842, "I have some notion of opening the new book in the lantern of a lighthouse!" (p. 303). The novel was *Martin Chuzzlewit* (1844), which begins not on the coast of Cornwall but in a Wiltshire village.

74. *grog.* Mixture of spirits (originally rum, later gin) and water, often served hot; from "Old Grog," the nickname of Admiral Vernon (d. 1745), who was known for his coat of grogram (a coarse fabric of silk, wool, and mohair) and who introduced the drink to the British navy about 1740. It was generally given to sailors as a substitute for straight rum.

been a very old song when he was a boy; and from time to time they all joined in the chorus. So surely as they raised their voices, the old man got quite blithe and loud; and so surely as they stopped, his vigour sank again.

The Spirit did not tarry here, but bade Scrooge hold his robe, and passing on above the moor, sped whither? Not to sea? To sea. To Scrooge's horror, looking back, he saw the last of the land, a frightful range of rocks, behind them; and his ears were deafened by the thundering of water, as it rolled, and roared, and raged among the dreadful caverns it had worn, and fiercely tried to undermine the earth.

Built upon a dismal reef of sunken rocks, some league or so from shore, on which the waters chafed and dashed, the wild year through, there stood a solitary lighthouse.[73] Great heaps of sea-weed clung to its base, and storm-birds—born of the wind one might suppose, as sea-weed of the water—rose and fell about it, like the waves they skimmed.

But even here, two men who watched the light had made a fire, that through the loophole in the thick stone wall shed out a ray of brightness on the awful sea. Joining their horny hands over the rough table at which they sat, they wished each other Merry Christmas in their can of grog;[74] and one of them: the elder, too, with his face all damaged and scarred with hard weather, as the figure-head of an old ship might be: struck up a sturdy song that was like a Gale in itself.

Again the Ghost sped on, above the black and heaving sea—on, on—until, being far away, as he told Scrooge, from any shore, they lighted on a ship. They stood beside the helmsman at the wheel, the look-out in the bow, the officers who had the watch; dark, ghostly figures in their several stations; but every man among them hummed a Christmas tune, or had a Christmas thought, or spoke below his breath to his companion of some bygone Christmas Day, with homeward hopes belonging to it. And every man on board, waking or sleeping, good or bad, had had a kinder word for another on that day than on any day in the year; and had shared to some extent in its festivities; and had remembered those he cared for at a distance, and had known that they delighted to remember him.

It was a great surprise to Scrooge, while listening to the moaning of the wind, and thinking what a solemn thing it was to move on through the lonely darkness over an unknown abyss, whose depths were secrets as profound as Death: it was a great surprise to Scrooge, while thus engaged, to hear a hearty laugh. It was a much greater surprise to Scrooge to recognise it as his own nephew's,[75] and to find himself in a bright, dry, gleaming room, with the Spirit standing smiling by his side, and looking at that same nephew with approving affability!

"Ha, ha!" laughed Scrooge's nephew. "Ha, ha, ha!"

If you should happen, by any unlikely chance, to know a man more blest in a laugh than Scrooge's nephew, all I can say is, I should like to know him too. Introduce him to me, and I'll cultivate his acquaintance.

It is a fair, even-handed, noble adjustment of things, that while there is infection in disease and sorrow, there is nothing in the world so irresistibly contagious as laughter and good-humour. When Scrooge's nephew laughed in this way: holding his sides, rolling his head, and twisting his face into the most extravagant contortions: Scrooge's niece, by marriage, laughed as heartily as he. And their assembled friends being not a bit behindhand,[76] roared out, lustily.

"Ha, ha! Ha, ha, ha, ha!"

"He said that Christmas was a humbug, as I live!" cried Scrooge's nephew. "He believed it too!"

"More shame for him, Fred!"[77] said Scrooge's niece, indignantly. Bless those women; they never do anything by halves. They are always in earnest.

She was very pretty: exceedingly pretty. With a dimpled, surprised-looking, capital face; a ripe little

75. *It was a much greater surprise to Scrooge to recognise it as his own nephew's.* Compare Fred's sudden appearance here to his equally startling arrival at Scrooge and Marley in Stave 1. But Scrooge gets the last laugh: he breaks this pattern by bursting in unexpectedly on his nephew's Christmas party in Stave 5.

76. *behindhand.* Tardy.

77. *Fred!* Dickens never discloses the young man's surname: it is definitely not Scrooge. C. Z. Barnett called him Frank Freeheart in his dramatization *A Christmas Carol, or The Miser's Warning*; he was Fred Pleasant in Charles Webb's *A Christmas Carol; or, The Past, Present, and Future.*

78. *He don't . . . He don't.* Cockney dialect (as in "the major don't know" in Chapter 31 of *Dombey and Son*, 1848). Dickens had difficulty with this slang: first he wrote "doesn't" in the manuscript and then changed it to "don't"; he altered "don't do any" to "does no" in the Berg prompt copy and then crossed it out. Some reprints of *A Christmas Carol* change "don't" to "doesn't."

Michael Slater explained in his introduction to the 1971 Penguin edition of *A Christmas Carol* that the author in the 1840s was playing with "a style more colloquial than that which Dickens usually adopted in his big novels." This experiment involved odd spellings and a more "rhetorical" use of punctuation, "based on speech rhythms rather than on grammatical sense . . . especially the lavish use of dashes, colons and semicolons." It was such peculiarities that so offended Samuel Rogers, who "said there was no wit in putting bad grammar into the mouths of all his characters, and showing their vulgar pronunciation by spelling 'are' 'air;' a horse without an h: none of our best writers do that" (quoted in P. W. Clayden, *Rogers and His Contemporaries*, vol. 2 [London: Smith Elder, 1889], p. 240).

mouth, that seemed made to be kissed—as no doubt it was; all kinds of good little dots about her chin, that melted into one another when she laughed; and the sunniest pair of eyes you ever saw in any little creature's head. Altogether she was what you would have called provoking, you know; but satisfactory, too. Oh, perfectly satisfactory!

"He's a comical old fellow," said Scrooge's nephew, "that's the truth; and not so pleasant as he might be. However, his offences carry their own punishment, and I have nothing to say against him."

"I'm sure he is very rich, Fred," hinted Scrooge's niece. "At least you always tell *me* so."

"What of that, my dear!" said Scrooge's nephew. "His wealth is of no use to him. He don't do any good with it. He don't[78] make himself comfortable with it. He hasn't the satisfaction of thinking—ha, ha, ha!—that he is ever going to benefit Us with it."

"I have no patience with him," observed Scrooge's niece. Scrooge's niece's sisters, and all the other ladies, expressed the same opinion.

"Oh, I have!" said Scrooge's nephew. "I am sorry for him; I couldn't be angry with him if I tried. Who suffers by his ill whims? Himself, always. Here, he takes it into his head to dislike us, and he won't come and dine with us. What's the consequence? He don't lose much of a dinner."

"Indeed, I think he loses a very good dinner," interrupted Scrooge's niece. Everybody else said the same, and they must be allowed to have been competent judges, because they had just had dinner; and, with the dessert upon the table, were clustered round the fire, by lamplight.

"Well! I am very glad to hear it," said Scrooge's nephew, "because I haven't any great faith in these young housekeepers. What do *you* say, Topper?"

Topper had clearly got his eye upon one of Scrooge's niece's sisters, for he answered that a bachelor was a wretched outcast, who had no right to express an opinion on the subject. Whereat Scrooge's niece's sister—the plump one with the lace tucker:[79] not the one with the roses—blushed.

"Do go on, Fred," said Scrooge's niece, clapping her hands. "He never finishes what he begins to say! He is such a ridiculous fellow!"

Scrooge's nephew revelled in another laugh, and as it was impossible to keep the infection off; though the plump sister tried hard to do it with aromatic vinegar;[80] his example was unanimously followed.

"I was only going to say," said Scrooge's nephew, "that the consequence of his taking a dislike to us, and not making merry with us, is, as I think, that he loses some pleasant moments, which could do him no harm. I am sure he loses pleasanter companions than he can find in his own thoughts, either in his mouldy old office, or his dusty chambers. I mean to give him the same chance every year, whether he likes it or not, for I pity him. He may rail at Christmas till he dies, but he can't help thinking better of it—I defy him—if he finds me going there, in good temper, year after year, and saying Uncle Scrooge, how are you? If it only puts him in the vein to leave his poor clerk fifty pounds, *that's* something; and I think I shook him, yesterday."

It was their turn to laugh now, at the notion of his shaking Scrooge. But being thoroughly good-natured, and not much caring what they laughed at, so that they laughed at any rate, he encouraged them in their merriment, and passed the bottle, joyously.

After tea, they had some music. For they were a musical family, and knew what they were about, when they sung a Glee[81] or Catch,[82] I can assure you: especially Topper, who could growl away in the bass like a good one, and never swell the large veins in his forehead, or get red in the face over it. Scrooge's niece played well upon the harp; and played among other tunes a simple little air (a mere nothing: you might learn to whistle it in two minutes), which had been familiar to the child who fetched Scrooge from the

79. *tucker.* Also called a "pinner," a piece of lace or other delicate fabric, worn in the neckline of a woman's dress and covering part of her bosom.

80. *aromatic vinegar.* A solution of acetic acid, strongly perfumed, used as a specific against headaches; not to be confused with later smelling salts, which use carbonate of ammonia as their base. T. W. Hill in his notes to *Little Dorrit* (*The Dickensian,* spring 1946) described its preparation: "A mixture of 1 oz. of camphor, 15 grs. of oil of cloves, 10 grs. of oil of cinnamon, 6 grs. of oil of English lavender, half a pint of acetic acid. It is usually poured over small pieces of sponge and kept in a tight-stoppered bottle" (p. 87). Delicate ladies of the period such as Lucretia Tox in *Dombey and Son* (1848) and Miss Mills and Misses Clarissa and Lavinia Spenlow of *David Copperfield* (1850), who were prone to swooning, revived themselves with a few quick whiffs of their smelling bottles. Edmund Sparkler recommends it to Fanny Dorrit in Chapter 24 of *Little Dorrit* (1857) as a cure for the fidgets. "I have often seen my mother try it," he assures her, "and it seemingly refreshed her." Some of these ladies may have used R. B. Ede's Highly-Concentrated Aromatic Spirits of Vinegar, as advertised in the monthly parts of *Nicholas Nickleby* (1839).

81. *Glee.* A musical composition for three or more voices with distinct parts for each, forming a series of interwoven melodies; usually of a light or secular nature.

82. *Catch.* A comic canon or round for three or more voices, in which, after the first singer has finished a line, the second begins, or "catches," the words just sung, and is then followed in the same manner by the third singer, and so on, so that each is singing a different line at the same time.

83. *it is good to be children sometimes, and never better than at Christmas, when its mighty Founder was a child himself.* Although this remark is now one of the most quoted passages of the story, it was surprisingly controversial in its day. The author's friend Laman Blanchard suggested in *Ainsworth's Magazine* (January 1844) that this one statement, spoken "with a seriousness touched with sacredness," "expresses the whole philosophy of the Ghost-story" (p. 88). "The whole volume is replete with touching allusions," observed the London *Sunday Times* (January 7, 1844) in its review, "but none of these is more exquisitely so than that which is made to Him who loved little children, and whose birth hallowed, and will forever hallow, the season of Christmas. The passage in which this thought occurs is brief, exceedingly brief, but it is quite sufficient, we are sure, to reconcile to Mr. Dickens and his manner to all those who may have required to be so reconciled."

But not everyone so readily embraced the sentiment when the book first came out. "We do not believe that Mr. Dickens is aware of the extreme irreverence of this way of speaking," protested the pious reviewer in *Christian Remembrancer* (January 1844); "but we are mistaken if numbers of his readers will not be pained by it; and we feel bold to assure him, that his expunging, or altering, the sentence in the next edition, will give general satisfaction" (p. 119). But they were not, and he did not.

Frederic G. Kitton recounted in "Some Famous Christmas Stories" (*The Library Review*, January 1893) an incident (perhaps apocryphal) at the Poet's Corner in Westminster Abbey: A ten-year-old boy one evening before prayers placed at the grave of Charles Dickens a little bunch of violets with a note, written in childish block letters: "For it is good to be children sometimes, and never better than at Christmas,

boarding-school, as he had been reminded by the Ghost of Christmas Past. When this strain of music sounded, all the things that Ghost had shown him, came upon his mind; he softened more and more; and thought that if he could have listened to it often, years ago, he might have cultivated the kindness of life for his own happiness with his own hands, without resorting to the sexton's spade that buried Jacob Marley.

But they didn't devote the whole evening to music. After a while they played at forfeits; for it is good to be children sometimes, and never better than at Christmas, when its mighty Founder was a child himself.[83] Stop! There was first a game at blindman's buff.[84] Of course there was. And I no more believe Topper was really blind than I believe he had eyes in his boots. My opinion is, that it was a done thing between him and Scrooge's nephew; and that the Ghost of Christmas Present knew it. The way he went after that plump sister in the lace tucker, was an outrage on the credulity of human nature. Knocking down the fire-irons, tumbling over the chairs, bumping up against the piano, smothering himself among the curtains, wherever she went, there went he. He always knew where the plump sister was. He wouldn't catch anybody else. If you had fallen up against him, as some of them did, and stood there; he would have made a feint of endeavouring to seize you, which would have been an affront to your understanding; and would instantly have sidled off in the direction of the plump sister. She often cried out that it wasn't fair; and it really was not. But when at last, he caught her; when, in spite of all her silken rustlings, and her rapid flutterings past him, he got her into a corner whence there was no escape; then his conduct was the most execrable. For his pretending not to know her; his pretending that it was necessary to touch her head-dress, and further to assure himself of her identity by pressing a certain ring upon her finger, and a certain chain about her neck; was vile, monstrous! No doubt she told him her opinion of it, when, another when the mighty Founder was a child Him-self" (p. 710).

84. *blindman's buff.* Compare Topper's boisterous performance with that of another riotous blindman, in "The Christmas Dinner," in Irving's *Sketch-Book* (1819–20):

> Master Simon . . . was blinded in the midst of the hall. The little beings were as busy about him as the mock fairies about Falstaff, pinching him, plucking at the skirts of his coat, and tickling him with straws. One fine blue-eyed girl of about thirteen, with her flaxen hair all a beautiful confusion, her frolic face in a glow, her frock half torn off her shoulders, a complete picture of a romp, was the chief tormentor; and, from the slyness with which Master Simon avoided the smaller game, and hemmed this wild little nymph in corners, and obliged her to jump shrieking over chairs, I suspected the rogue of not being one whit more blinded than was convenient.

85. *another blindman.* Dickens suggests not only the next player in the game, but Cupid, the blinded god of love.

"A Christmas Canticle." Wood engraving after John Leech, *The Illuminated Magazine*, December 1843.
Courtesy Library of Congress.

86. *loved her love to admiration with all the letters of the alphabet.* The old parlor game "I love my love with an A," once popular in both Great Britain and the United States; it was also used by mothers to teach children the alphabet. Each player in turn must complete a series of sentences using the next letter in each blank. The pattern is given in Book 2, Chapter 1, of *Our Mutual Friend* (1865): "I'll give you a clue to my trade, in a game of forfeits," says Jenny Wren. "I love my love with a B because she's Beautiful; I hate my love with a B because she is Brazen; I took her to the sign of the Blue Boar, and

blindman[85] being in office, they were so very confidential together, behind the curtains.

Scrooge's niece was not one of the blind-man's buff party, but was made comfortable with a large chair and a footstool, in a snug corner, where the Ghost and Scrooge were close behind her. But she joined in the forfeits, and loved her love to admiration with all the letters of the alphabet.[86] Likewise at the game of How, When, and Where,[87] she was very great, and to the secret joy of Scrooge's nephew, beat her sisters hollow: though they were sharp girls too, as Topper could have told you. There might have been twenty people there, young and old, but they all played, and so did Scrooge; for, wholly forgetting in the interest he had in what was going on, that his voice made no sound in their ears, he sometimes came out with his guess quite loud, and very often guessed right, too, for the sharpest needle, best Whitechapel,[88] warranted not to cut in the eye, was not sharper than Scrooge: blunt as he took it in his head to be.

The Ghost was greatly pleased to find him in this mood, and looked upon him with such favour that he begged like a boy to be allowed to stay until the guests departed. But this the Spirit said could not be done.

"Here's a new game," said Scrooge. "One half hour, Spirit, only one!"

It was a Game called Yes and No,[89] where Scrooge's nephew had to think of something, and the rest must find out what; he only answering to their questions yes or no as the case was. The brisk fire of questioning to which he was exposed, elicited from him that he was thinking of an animal, a live animal, rather a disagreeable animal, a savage animal, an animal that growled and grunted sometimes, and talked sometimes, and lived in London, and walked about the streets, and wasn't made a show of, and wasn't led by anybody, and didn't live in a menagerie, and was never killed in a market, and was not a horse, or an ass, or a cow, or a bull, or a tiger, or a dog, or a pig, or a cat, or a bear. At every fresh

I treated her with Bonnets; her name's Bouncer, and she lives in Bedlam.—Now, what do I make with my straw?" (The answer is "ladies' bonnets"; she is a doll's dressmaker.) Lewis Carroll also plays with this game in Chapter 7 of *Through the Looking-Glass* (1872): Alice, however, in loving her love, must commence with H, because her companions in Looking-Glass Land aspirate their As.

87. *How, When, and Where.* Another game of forfeits, in which each player in turn must ask, "How do you like it?" "When do you like it?" and "Where do you like it?"

The author's son Henry Fielding Dickens recalled in *My Father As I Knew Him* (1934) another parlor game, similar to the one at Fred's Christmas party but called "The Memory Game": "The players sitting in a circle, one of them starts by giving some name or object (not necessarily confined to one word) such as Beefsteak, the next person has to repeat Beefsteak and add something such as Caligula, and so on, each person having to repeat all the names in order which they were given. . . . The game had been proceeding for some time and the volume of words had grown to a fairly staggering length when it came once more to my father's turn. . . . After successfully repeating the string of words the time came for him to add his own contribution. There was a pause for a while, and then, with a strange twinkle in his eye and a curious modulation in his voice, he gave it as '*Warren's Blacking, 30 Strand.*' . . . It was only when Forster's *Life* appeared, with that terrible fragment of autobiography, that I understood; and then the memory of that scene at Christmas flashed across my mind" (pp. 44–45).

88. *Whitechapel.* Whitechapel was a poor, congested parish between Aldgate and Mile End Road, famous for its thieves, fences, and whores. "Not a wery nice neighbourhood, this, Sir," observes Sam Weller in Chapter 22 of *The Pickwick Papers* (1837). Fagin and the boys take Oliver to a house in Whitechapel in Chapter 19 of *Oliver Twist* (1838) to plan a burglary elsewhere in the city. It was the scene of the famous Whitechapel murders, committed by the most famous of serial killers, Jack the Ripper, in the late summer and early fall of 1888.

89. *Yes and No.* Also known as "Investigation," according to "On Christmas Games" (*The Magazine of Domestic Economy*, November 1838): "one of the party thinks of a thing, and the others endeavor, by questions, to ascertain what it is; the first person being allowed to answer yes and no only. First, it is necessary to ascertain the nature of the substance thought of, whether animal, vegetable, or mineral, or compounded of two or more of these divisions. Then the question should be asked, whether it be useful or ornamental; the produce or manufacture of our own country, or brought from abroad; whether used by the poor, as well as by the rich, or vice versa; and so on, through many questions, which will suggest themselves in the progress of the game, until the respondent having been led to give a full and complete account of the subject thought of, her questioners guess it. This game may also be applied to persons and places, and much anecdote may be introduced" (p. 138). "In this particular game," Percy Fitzgerald revealed in *The Life of Charles Dickens* (vol. 1, London: Chatto and Windus, 1905), "Boz himself excelled . . . however, he would reverse the process, going out of the room while we fixed on some subject. Then he came back and plied us with a shower of enquiries until he actually *forced* his way to the solution" (p. 214).

90. *vain man in his little brief authority.* In his notes to the 1971 Penguin edition of *Christmas Books*, Michael Slater identified the source for this phrase as *Measure for Measure* 2.2.120–25:

> But man, proud man,
> Dressed in a little brief authority,
> Most ignorant of what he's most
>   assured,
> His glassy essence, like an angry ape
> Plays such fantastic tricks before high
>   heaven
> As makes the angels weep . . .

question that was put to him, this nephew burst into a fresh roar of laughter; and was so inexpressibly tickled, that he was obliged to get up off the sofa and stamp. At last the plump sister, falling into a similar state, cried out:

"I have found it out! I know what it is, Fred! I know what it is!"

"What is it?" cried Fred.

"It's your Uncle Scro-o-o-o-oge!"

Which it certainly was. Admiration was the universal sentiment, though some objected that the reply to "Is it a bear?" ought to have been "Yes ;" inasmuch as an answer in the negative was sufficient to have diverted their thoughts from Mr. Scrooge, supposing they had ever had any tendency that way.

"He has given us plenty of merriment, I am sure," said Fred, "and it would be ungrateful not to drink his health. Here is a glass of mulled wine ready to our hand at the moment; and I say 'Uncle Scrooge!'"

"Well! Uncle Scrooge!" they cried.

"A Merry Christmas and a happy New Year to the old man, whatever he is!" said Scrooge's nephew. "He wouldn't take it from me, but may he have it, nevertheless. Uncle Scrooge!"

Uncle Scrooge had imperceptibly become so gay and light of heart, that he would have pledged the unconscious company in return, and thanked them in an inaudible speech, if the Ghost had given him time. But the whole scene passed off in the breath of the last word spoken by his nephew; and he and the Spirit were again upon their travels.

Much they saw, and far they went, and many homes they visited, but always with a happy end. The Spirit stood beside sick beds, and they were cheerful; on foreign lands, and they were close at home; by struggling men, and they were patient in their greater hope; by poverty, and it was rich. In almshouse, hospital, and jail, in misery's every refuge, where vain man in his little brief authority[90] had not made fast the door, and barred the Spirit out, he left his blessing, and taught Scrooge his precepts.

It was a long night, if it were only a night; but Scrooge had his doubts of this, because the Christmas Holidays[91] appeared to be condensed into the space of time they passed together. It was strange, too, that while Scrooge remained unaltered in his outward form, the Ghost grew older, clearly older. Scrooge had observed this change, but never spoke of it, until they left a children's Twelfth Night party,[92] when, looking at the Spirit as they stood together in an open place, he noticed that its hair was gray.

"Are spirits' lives so short?" asked Scrooge.

"My life upon this globe, is very brief," replied the Ghost. "It ends to-night."

"To-night!" cried Scrooge.

"Tonight at midnight. Hark! The time is drawing near."

The chimes were ringing the three quarters past eleven at that moment.

"Forgive me if I am not justified in what I ask," said Scrooge, looking intently at the Spirit's robe, "but I see something strange, and not belonging to yourself, protruding from your skirts. Is it a foot or a claw!"

"It might be a claw, for the flesh there is upon it," was the Spirit's sorrowful reply. "Look here."

From the foldings of its robe, it brought two children; wretched, abject, frightful, hideous, miserable. They knelt down at its feet, and clung upon the outside of its garment.

"Oh, Man! look here. Look, look, down here!" exclaimed the Ghost.

They were a boy and girl. Yellow, meagre, ragged, scowling, wolfish; but prostrate, too, in their humility. Where graceful youth should have filled their features out, and touched them with its freshest tints, a stale and shrivelled hand, like that of age, had pinched, and twisted them, and pulled them into shreds. Where angels might have sat enthroned, devils lurked, and

91. *the Christmas Holidays.* In Dickens' day, the season ran for twelve days, from Christmas Day until Epiphany, January 6.

92. *a children's Twelfth Night party.* The Dickenses celebrated Twelfth Night with great gusto and invention because it was also his son Charles Boz's birthday. The novelist often invited "children of a larger growth" from his wide circle of literary acquaintances to join in the festivities. He announced his ambitious plans for the party in a letter to his American friend C. C. Felton on December 31, 1842: "The actuary of the National Debt couldn't calculate the number of children who are coming here on Twelfth Night, in honour of Charley's birthday, for which occasion I have provided a Magic Lantern and divers other tremendous engines of that nature. But the best of it is that Forster and I have purchased between us the entire stock in trade of a conjuror. . . . And . . . if you could see me conjuring the company's watches into impossible tea caddies, and causing pieces of money to fly, and burning pocket handkerchiefs without hurting 'em . . . you would never forget it as long as you live" (p. 416).

The "entire stock of a conjuror" was pulled out for several Twelfth Nights to come. "One of these conjuring tricks," reported his daughter Mamie in *My Father As I Recall Him* (1896), "comprised the disappearance and reappearance of a tiny doll, which would announce most unexpected news and messages to the different children in the audience; this doll was a particular favorite, and its arrival eagerly awaited and welcomed" (p. 34). Dickens reveled in these slight-of-hand demonstrations and proudly wrote his friend William Macready (then in America) of a child's party where he performed on January 3, 1844: "Forster and I conjured bravely; that a plum-pudding was produced from an empty saucepan, held over a blazing fire kindled by Stanfield's hat without damage to the lining; that a box of bran was changed into a live guinea-pig, which ran between my Godchild's feet . . . and you might have heard it (and I daresay did) in America; that three half-crowns being taken . . . and put into a tumbler-glass . . . did then and there give jingling answers to the questions asked of them by me . . . to the unspeakable admiration of the whole assembly" (p. 10). Dickens was not exaggerating his ability as a holiday magician: Jane Carlyle, who attended the party, confessed that the Inimitable Boz was the greatest conjuror she had ever seen.

The evening was not limited to magic tricks; there was also dancing. Dickens once insisted that Mamie and her sister Katie teach John Leech and himself the polka. "My father was as much in earnest about learning to take that wonderful step correctly, as though there were nothing of greater importance in the world," Mamie recalled. "No one can imagine our excitement and nervousness when the evening came on which we were to dance with our pupils. Katie, who was a very little girl was to have Mr. Leech, who was over six feet tall, for her partner, while my father was to be mine. My heart beat so fast I could scarcely breathe. . . . But my fears were groundless, and we were greeted at the finish of our dance with hearty applause, which was more than compensation for the work which had been expended upon its learning" (p. 27–28).

"Twelfth Night in London Streets." Etching by Robert Seymour, *The Book of Christmas* by Thomas K. Hervey, 1836. *Private collection.*

"Twelfth Night." Etching by Robert Seymour, *The Book of Christmas* by Thomas K. Hervey, 1836. *Private collection.*

glared out menacing. No change, no degradation, no perversion of humanity, in any grade, through all the mysteries of wonderful creation, has monsters half so horrible and dread.

Scrooge started back, appalled. Having them shown to him in this way, he tried to say they were fine children, but the words choked themselves, rather than be parties to a lie of such enormous magnitude.

"Spirit! are they yours?" Scrooge could say no more.

"They are Man's," said the Spirit, looking down upon them. "And they cling to me, appealing from their fathers.[93] This boy is Ignorance. This girl is Want.[94] Beware them both, and all of their degree, but most of all beware this boy, for on his brow I see that written which is Doom, unless the writing be erased. Deny it!"

93. *their fathers.* "Mankind" in the Berg prompt copy.

94. *Ignorance. . . . Want.* Through these two demons, Dickens metaphorically makes his strongest plea in the story for the salvation of the children of the poor. He had been like these children himself once, when he was taken out of school to drudge in Warren's Blacking warehouse. "I know I do not exaggerate, consciously and unintentionally, the scantiness of my resources and the difficulties of my life," he wrote of this time in the autobiographical fragment Forster published in his book. "I know that if a shilling or so were given me by any one, I spent it on a dinner or a tea. I know that I worked, from morning to night, with common men and boys, a shabby child. . . . I know that I have lounged about the streets, insufficiently and unsatisfactorily fed. I know that, but for the mercy of God, I might easily have been, for any care that was taken of me, a little robber or a little

"Ignorance and Want." Preliminary pencil and wash drawing by John Leech, 1843. *Courtesy Houghton Library, Harvard University.*

vagabond" (*The Life of Charles Dickens*, vol. 1, 1872, p. 37). He was not only a companion of these demon children but one of them.

They returned to haunt him on a visit to the Ragged School of Field Lane, Holborn, a free institution located in the sordid part of London where Fagin lived. As he wrote his friend the philanthropist Angela Georgina Burdett-Coutts on September 16, 1843, these wretched students "know nothing of affection, care, love or kindness of any sort." He confessed, "I have very seldom seen, in all the strange and dreadful things I have seen in London and elsewhere, anything so shocking as the dire neglect of soul and body exhibited in these children. . . . in that prodigious misery and ignorance of the swarming masses of mankind in England, the seeds of its certain ruin are sown, I never saw that Truth so staring out in hopeless characters, as it does from the walls of this place. The children in the Jails are almost as common sights to me as my own; but these are worse, for they have not arrived there yet, but are as plainly and certainly travelling there, as are to their Graves" (p. 362).

Dickens repeated this warning in a speech delivered at the Polytechnic Institute in Birmingham on February 28, 1844, soon after *A Christmas Carol* was published. Taking his metaphor from "The Genii in the Bottle" of *The Arabian Nights*, he said, "Now, there is a spirit of great power, the Spirit of Ignorance, long shut up in a vessel of Obstinate Neglect, with a great deal of lead in its composition, and sealed with the seal of many, many Solomons, and which is exactly in the same position. Release it in time, and it will bless, restore, and reanimate society; but let it lie under the rolling waves of years, and its blind revenge at last will be destruction" (p. 61).

Dickens could not easily forget the boy Ignorance and the girl Want. In Chapter 1 of his last Christmas Book, *The Haunted Man* (1848), he introduced this theme in a child with no name: "a baby savage, a young monster, a child who had never been a child, a creature who might live to take the outward form of man, but who, within, would live and perish a mere beast."

cried the Spirit, stretching out its hand towards the city. "Slander those who tell it ye! Admit it for your factious purposes, and make it worse! And bide the end!"

"Have they no refuge or resource?" cried Scrooge.

"Are there no prisons?" said the Spirit, turning on him for the last time with his own words. "Are there no workhouses?"

The bell struck twelve.[95]

Scrooge looked about him for the Ghost and saw it not. As the last stroke ceased to vibrate, he remembered the prediction of old Jacob Marley, and lifting up his eyes, beheld a solemn Phantom, draped and hooded, coming, like a mist along the ground, towards him.

95. *twelve.* This hour, of course, corresponds to the twelfth, or last, day of Christmas when the Ghost of Christmas Present must depart; note also that while the first two spirits came at the stroke of one, or the start of the new day, the Ghost of Christmas Yet to Come, in its black shroud, appears at twelve, the traditional bewitching hour, the final hour of the day.

THE LAST OF THE SPIRITS.

1. *The Phantom*. The Ghost of Christmas Yet To Come, dressed in a "dusky shroud" and protecting Scrooge in the "shadow of its dress," is of course Death, "cold, cold, rigid, dreadful Death." This phantom may seem an odd choice for a Christmas ghost, but Dickens (like many other people) often reflected on the loss of loved ones during the holidays. Ghosts were once generally believed to have the power to foretell the future, including one's death.

No matter how festive the celebration, it could not remove from his fireside "the shadow that darkens the whole globe . . . the shadow of the City of Death." "Of all days in the year," he explained in "What Christmas Is, As We Grow Older" (*Household Words*, Christmas Number 1851), "we will turn our faces towards that City upon Christmas Day, and from its silent hosts bring those we loved, among us. City of the Dead, in the blessed name wherein we are gathered together at this time, and in the Presence that is here among us according to the promise, we will receive, and not dismiss, thy people who are dear to us!"

His most devastating depiction of this holiday specter lies in "A December Vision" (*Household Words*, December 14, 1850). In its slow, steady, unwavering persistence, in its ability to enter any place at will, in its shaded face and its ghostly eyes, this image of death could be the Ghost of Christmas Yet To Come. Coupling Death with Christ-

The Phantom[1] slowly, gravely, silently, approached. When it came near him, Scrooge bent down upon his knee; for in the very air through which this Spirit moved it seemed to scatter gloom and mystery.

It was shrouded in a deep black garment, which concealed its head, its face, its form, and left nothing of it visible save one outstretched hand. But for this it would have been difficult to detach its figure from the night, and separate it from the darkness by which it was surrounded.

He felt that it was tall and stately when it came beside him, and that its mysterious presence filled him with a solemn dread. He knew no more, for the Spirit neither spoke nor moved.

"I am in the presence of the Ghost of Christmas Yet To Come?" said Scrooge.

The Spirit answered not, but pointed onward[2] with its hand.

"You are about to show me shadows of the things that have not happened, but will happen in the time before us," Scrooge pursued. "Is that so, Spirit?"

The upper portion of the garment was contracted for an instant to its folds, as if the Spirit had inclined its head. That was the only answer he received.

Although well used to ghostly company by this time, Scrooge feared the silent shape so much that his legs trembled beneath him, and he found that he could hardly stand when he prepared to follow it. The Spirit paused a moment, as observing his condition, and giving him time to recover.

But Scrooge was all the worse for this. It thrilled him with a vague uncertain horror, to know that behind the dusky shroud there were ghostly eyes intently fixed upon him, while he, though he stretched his own to the utmost, could see nothing but a spectral hand and one great heap of black.

"Ghost of the Future!" he exclaimed, "I fear you more than any Spectre I have seen. But, as I know your purpose is to do me good, and as I hope to live to be another man from what I was, I am prepared to bear you company, and do it with a thankful heart. Will you not speak to me?"

It gave him no reply. The hand was pointed straight before them.

"Lead on!" said Scrooge. "Lead on! The night is waning fast, and it is precious time to me, I know. Lead on, Spirit!"

The Phantom moved away as it had come towards him. Scrooge followed in the shadow of its dress, which bore him up, he thought, and carried him along.

They scarcely seemed to enter the city; for the city rather seemed to spring up about them, and encompass them of its own act. But there they were, in the heart of it; on 'Change,[3] amongst the merchants; who hurried up and down, and chinked the money in their pockets, and conversed in groups, and looked at their watches, and trifled thoughtfully with their great gold seals; and so forth, as Scrooge had seen them often.

The Spirit stopped beside one little knot of business men. Observing that the hand was pointed to them, Scrooge advanced to listen to their talk.

"No," said a great fat man with a monstrous chin, "I don't know much about it, either way. I only know he's dead."

"When did he die?" inquired another.

"Last night, I believe."

"Why, what was the matter with him?" asked a

mas is not difficult to understand: the holidays come at the end of the year, a time of recollection and resolution. The birth of Christ is also a reminder of the Crucifixion; for example, the American folk song "I Wonder As I Wander" laments "how Jesus the Savior was born for to die."

2. *onward.* The first edition says "downward," but this printer's error was corrected in the second edition.

3. *'Change.* The Royal Exchange. See Stave 1, note 5.

"Scrooge followed in the shadow of its dress." Wood engraving after Gustave Doré, *Journal pour tous,* July 3, 1861. *Courtesy Library of Congress.*

4. *a pendulous excrescence.* A hanging wart.

5. *That's all I know.* "I wish he had," he added in the manuscript, but the remark did not make it to the printers.

"This pleasantry was received with a general laugh." Wood engraving by Gustave Doré, *Journal pour tous,* July 3, 1861. *Courtesy Library of Congress.*

6. *if a lunch is provided.* It was customary at the time that no matter how cheap the funeral some food should be provided for the mourners. Joe Gargery serves sandwiches, cut-up oranges, plum cake, biscuits, a decanter of port, and another of sherry at his wife's in *Great Expectations* (vol. 2, Chapter 16, 1861).

7. *black gloves.* "It is customary at most English funerals," explained F. H. Ahn in his 1871 edition of *A Christmas Carol,* "to present all who attend as mourners with a pair of black gloves, which of course likewise prove useful on other occasions" (p. 164). As everyone who attended received a pair, even those who were not at all close to the deceased had to wear them in paying their respects. This individual's reluctance to express even this small gesture for the deceased is a remarkable insult from one who then says he must have been the dead man's "most particular friend." He will not even take advantage of a free meal, for it

third, taking a vast quantity of snuff out of a very large snuff-box. "I thought he'd never die."

"God knows," said the first, with a yawn.

"What has he done with his money?" asked a red-faced gentleman with a pendulous excrescence[4] on the end of his nose, that shook like the gills of a turkey-cock.

"I haven't heard," said the man with the large chin, yawning again. "Left it to his Company, perhaps. He hasn't left it to *me.* That's all I know."[5]

This pleasantry was received with a general laugh.

"It's likely to be a very cheap funeral," said the same speaker; "for upon my life I don't know of anybody to go to it. Suppose we make up a party and volunteer?"

"I don't mind going if a lunch is provided,"[6] observed the gentleman with the excrescence on his nose. "But I must be fed, if I make one."

Another laugh.

"Well, I am the most disinterested among you, after all," said the first speaker, "for I never wear black gloves,[7] and I never eat lunch. But I'll offer to go, if anybody else will. When I come to think of it, I'm not at all sure that I wasn't his most particular friend; for we used to stop and speak whenever we met. Bye, bye!"

Speakers and listeners strolled away, and mixed with other groups. Scrooge knew the men, and looked towards the Spirit for an explanation.

The Phantom glided on into a street. Its finger pointed to two persons meeting. Scrooge listened again, thinking that the explanation might lie here.

He knew these men, also, perfectly. They were men of business; very wealthy, and of great importance. He had made a point always of standing well in their esteem: in a business point of view, that is; strictly in a business point of view.

"How are you?" said one.

"How are you?" returned the other.

"Well!" said the first, "Old Scratch[8] has got his own at last, hey?"

So I am told," returned the second. "Cold, isn't it?"

"Seasonable for Christmas time. You're not a skaiter,[9] I suppose?"

"No. No. Something else to think of. Good morning!"

Not another word. That was their meeting, their conversation, and their parting.

Scrooge was at first inclined to be surprised that the Spirit should attach importance to conversations apparently so trivial; but feeling assured that they must have some hidden purpose, he set himself to consider what it was likely to be. They could scarcely be supposed to have any bearing on the death of Jacob, his old partner, for that was Past, and this Ghost's province was the Future. Nor could he think of any one immediately connected with himself, to whom he could apply them. But nothing doubting that to whomsoever they applied they had some latent moral for his own improvement, he resolved to treasure up every word he heard, and everything he saw; and especially to observe the shadow of himself when it appeared. For he had an expectation that the conduct of his future self would give him the clue he missed, and would render the solution of these riddles easy.

He looked about to that very place for his own image; but another man stood in his accustomed corner, and though the clock pointed to his usual time of day for being there, he saw no likeness of himself among the multitudes that poured in through the Porch. It gave him little surprise, however; for he had been revolving in his mind a change of life, and thought and hoped he saw his new-born resolutions carried out in this.

Quiet and dark, beside him stood the Phantom, with its outstretched hand. When he roused himself from his thoughtful quest, he fancied from the turn of the hand, and its situation in reference to himself, that the Unseen Eyes were looking at him keenly. It made him shudder, and feel very cold.

goes against his habits. Personally finding no worldly use for these customs, this unsentimental businessman, like Scrooge, is the perfect utilitarian. The funeral must profit him somehow or he will not attend. Recall that the day of Marley's burial did not prove to be an entire waste of time for his partner, for Scrooge "solemnised it with an undoubted bargain."

8. *Old Scratch.* The Devil. "The English language abounds in ludicrous epithets of the Devil," observed Dr. L. Reichelmann in his notes to the 1864 B. G. Teubrer edition (p. 69). These include the Old Boy, the Old Enemy, the Old Fellow, the Old Gentleman, the Old One, the Old Davy, the Old Harry, the Old Nick, the Old Podger, the Old Sam, the Deuce, the Dickens. . . .

9. *skaiter.* Not until the 1868 Charles Dickens Edition of *Christmas Books* did the author change this word to the more common spelling, "skater."

10. *an obscure part of the town.* Charles Webb suggested in his 1844 play *A Christmas Carol; or, The Past, Present, and Future* that this area is Saffron Hill, the locale of Fagin's den of thieves in *Oliver Twist* (1838). It was a notorious criminal district between Holborn and Clerkenwell, in East London. It could be Field Lane, "a narrow and dismal alley leading to Saffron Hill," described in Chapter 26 of *Oliver Twist*: "In its filthy shops are exposed for sale huge bunches of second-hand silk handkerchiefs, of all sizes and patterns; for here reside the traders who purchase them from pickpockets. . . . It is a commercial colony of itself: the emporium of petty larceny: visited at early morning, and setting-in of dusk, by silent merchants, who traffic in dark back-parlours, and who go as strangely as they come. Here, the clothesman, the shoe-vamper, and the rag-merchant, display their goods, as sign-boards to the petty thief; here, stores of old iron and bones, and heaps of mildewy fragments of woollen-stuff and linen, rust and rot in the grimy cellars." Dickens had just been to Saffron Hill in September 1843, visiting the Field Lane Ragged School at 65 West Street.

11. *beetling.* Projecting, overhanging.

12. *shop.* C. Z. Barnett, Edward Stirling, and Charles Webb in their 1844 plays of *A Christmas Carol* all identified this place as a "marine-store shop," like Mr. Krook's establishment in Chapter 5 of *Bleak House* (1853): "BONES BOUGHT . . . KITCHEN-STUFF . . . OLD IRON BOUGHT . . . WASTE PAPER BOUGHT . . . LADIES' AND GENTLEMAN'S WARDROBES BOUGHT." There was one in the part of Camden Town where Dickens lived as a boy, and he first described another in "Brokers' and Marine-store Shops," in *Sketches by Boz* (1839): "a small dirty shop exposing for sale the most extraordinary and confused jumble of old, worn-out, wretched articles, that

They left the busy scene, and went into an obscure part of the town,[10] where Scrooge had never penetrated before, although he recognised its situation, and its bad repute. The ways were foul and narrow; the shops and houses wretched; the people half-naked, drunken, slipshod, ugly. Alleys and archways, like so many cesspools, disgorged their offences of smell, and dirt, and life, upon the straggling streets; and the whole quarter reeked with crime, with filth, and misery.

Far in this den of infamous resort, there was a low-browed, beetling[11] shop,[12] below a pent-house roof,[13] where iron, old rags, bottles, bones, and greasy offal, were bought. Upon the floor within, were piled up heaps of rusty keys, nails, chains, hinges, files, scales, weights, and refuse iron of all kinds. Secrets that few would like to scrutinise were bred and hidden in mountains of unseemly rags, masses of corrupted fat,[14] and sepulchres of bones. Sitting in among the wares he dealt in, by a charcoal-stove, made of old bricks, was a gray-haired rascal,[15] nearly seventy years of age;[16] who had screened himself from the cold air without, by a frousy curtaining of miscellaneous tatters, hung upon a line; and smoked his pipe in all the luxury of calm retirement.

Scrooge and the Phantom came into the presence of this man, just as a woman with a heavy bundle slunk into the shop.[17] But she had scarcely entered, when another woman, similarly laden, came in too; and she was closely followed by a man in faded black, who was no less startled by the sight of them, than they had been upon the recognition of each other. After a short period of blank astonishment, in which the old man with the pipe had joined them, they all three burst into a laugh.

"Let the charwoman[18] alone to be the first!" cried she who had entered first. "Let the laundress alone to be the second; and let the undertaker's man alone to be the third. Look here, old Joe, here's a chance! If we haven't all three met here without meaning it!"[19]

can well be imagined. Our wonder at their ever having been bought, is only to be equalled by our astonishment at the idea of their ever being sold again." They were pawnshops that dealt in all sorts of items, stolen or otherwise; they originally sold goods needed on shipboard. Instead of the traditional three gold balls out front of a pawnbroker's, a marine-store shop was recognizable by "a black doll in a white frock, with two faces—one looking up the street, and the other looking up the street, and the other looking down, swinging over the door."

Technically, what Dickens describes is a rag-and-bottle shop, because marine-store shops did not trade in grease and other "kitchen-stuff." Dickens, like many people

"The Lord Chancellor copies from memory." Etching by "Phiz" (Hablôt Knight Browne), *Bleak House*, 1853.
Courtesy Library of Congress.

"Tom's-all-alone's." Etching by "Phiz" (Hablôt Knight Browne), *Bleak House*, 1853.
Courtesy Library of Congress.

of his time, seems to have thought of them interchangeably: there are two signs in the store's door in Chapter 5 of *Bleak House* (1853), "KROOK, RAG AND BOTTLE WAREHOUSE" and "KROOK, DEALER IN MARINE STORES." "The stench in these shops is positively sickening," wrote Henry Mayhew in vol. 2 of *London Labour and the London Poor.* "Here in a small apartment may be a pile of rags, a sack-full of bones, the many varieties of grease and 'kitchen-stuff,' corrupting an atmosphere which, even without such accompaniments, would be too close. The windows are often crowded with bottles, which exclude the light; while the floor and shelves are thick with grease and dirt" (p. 372).

13. *a pent-house roof.* A roof sloping up from a wall.

14. *masses of corrupted fat.* Proprietors of the rag-and-bottle shops bought grease, drippings, and other "kitchen-stuff" for resale: the grease went to candle makers and soap boilers, the drippings to the poor as a substitute for butter.

15. *a gray-haired rascal.* Unhappy with what he gets for his loot in Charles Webb's 1844 drama *A Christmas Carol; or, The Past, Present, and Future*, the undertaker's man accuses old Joe of being "worse than any other Jew that ever lived!" Whether this remark was a result of Webb's own anti-Semitism or was implied by Dickens in his text is not known. Nevertheless, Dickens did create in another of old Joe's class, that other "receiver of stolen goods," Fagin in *Oliver Twist* (1838), the most notorious Jew in English literature since Shakespeare's Shylock. Even more through the countless dramatizations of the story than through the book itself, Fagin came to represent "the dirty Jew" in nineteenth-century England. Even as late as 1948, Alec Guinness' portrayal of Fagin in the famous David Lean film was challenged by censors before the picture could be released in the United States. However, Ron Moody's performance in the 1968 Academy Award–winning musical *Oliver* went largely unscathed.

Dickens did not understand how anyone could be offended by Fagin or believe that he bore any ill feeling toward his people. "I know of no reason that the Jews can have for regarding me as 'inimical' to them," he defended himself in a letter published in the *Jewish Chronicle* (April 12, 1854). "On the contrary, I believe I do my part, whenever I can, towards the assertion of civil and religious liberty; and in the *Child's History of England*, I have expressed a strong abhorrence of their persecution in old times. If they have any *un*-reasonable fancy on the subject, I regret it; but the fault is in them, not in me" (p. 237).

Dickens did not shy from describing the great wrongs done the Jews over the centuries in England. On the coronation of Richard the Lion-Hearted, described in Chapter 13 of *A Child's History of England*, Dickens mentions "a dreadful murdering of the Jews, which seems to have been given great delight to numbers of savage persons calling themselves Christians." He notes that the Jews "were generally hated, though they were the most useful merchants in England." The slaughter resulted from the king's decree forbidding Jews from attending the ceremony. "Thereupon the crowd rushed through the narrow streets of the city, slaughtering all the Jews they met; and when they could find no more out of doors . . . they ran madly about, breaking open all the houses where the Jews lived, rushing in and stabbing or spearing them, sometimes even flinging old people and children out of window into blazing fires they had lighted up below." It continued for twenty-four hours and resulted in only three arrests and executions, not for killing Jews but for burning houses of Christians.

In Chapter 14, Dickens describes how King John extorted an enormous sum of money from a wealthy Jew of Bristol by extracting one tooth a day until he gave in after a week. Chapter 16 dealt with the persecution of the Jews under Edward I:

> They were hanged in great numbers, on accusations of having clipped the King's coin—which all kinds of people had done. They were heavily taxed; they were disgracefully badged; they were, on one day, thirteen years after the coronation, taken up with their wives and children and thrown into beastly prisons, until they purchased their release by paying the King twelve thousand pounds. Finally, every kind of property belonging to them was seized by the King, except so little as would defray the charge of their taking themselves away into foreign countries. Many years elapsed before the hope of gain induced any of their race to return to England, where they had been

treated so heartlessly and had suffered so much.

In 1860, Dickens sold his home, Tavistock House, to James Phineas Davis, a Jewish banker, but he rudely referred to the purchaser in private as "the Jew Money Lender." "Of course I shall never believe in him until he has paid the money," Dickens wrote his lawyer Thomas Mitton on August 19 (p. 289). He was proved wrong: although Dickens had been informed that the man was "one of the greatest rascals in London," he admitted in a letter of February 1, 1861, that Davis "behaved much better than a Christian in that transaction" (p. 381). He liked those "Children of Israel," Davis and his wife Eliza. "Mrs. Davis appears to be a very kind and agreeable woman," he admitted to a friend on September 8, 1860. "And I have never had any money transaction with any one, more promptly, fairly, and considerately than the purchase of Tavistock House has been" (p. 307).

When Eliza Davis wrote Dickens on June 22, 1863, requesting a contribution to a Jewish memorial, she reminded him that in creating Fagin he had fueled "a vile prejudice against the despised Hebrew" (p. 269). He was taken aback and insisted on July 10, "I have no feeling towards the Jewish people but a friendly one. I always speak well of them, whether in public or in private, and bear my testimony (as I ought to do) to their perfect good faith in such transactions as I have ever had with them" (p. 270).

He was now determined to prove it. Dickens tried to correct a past wrong by creating the sympathetic "Aaron" Riah in *Our Mutual Friend* (1865). Dickens considers a long line of anti-Semitic remarks in Book 2, Chapter 5. "Your people," demands the non-Jewish moneylender Fascination Fledgely, "the meanest cur existing, with a single pair of legs," "need speak the truth sometimes,

for they lie enough." "Sir," Riah reminds his employer, "there is much untruth among all denominations of men." In recognition of his kind treatment of the Jews in this book, Mrs. Davis presented Dickens with a Hebrew and English Bible "in grateful and admiring recognition of his having exercised the noblest quality one can possess— that of atoning for an injury as soon as conscious of inflicting it" (p. 322). He assured her on March 1, 1867, on receiving the book, that "there is nothing but good will between me and a People for whom I have a real regard and to whom I would not willfully have given an offense or done an injustice for any worldly consideration" (p. 323). Dickens went further and revised *Oliver Twist* for the 1867 Charles Dickens Edition by toning down some of the offensive remarks, but the damage had been done. "With murderous Jews and their murdering agents we have probably but a distant acquaintance," admitted Anthony Trollope in *The St. Paul's Magazine* (July 1870), "but we fancy that they should be as are Fagin and Sikes" (p. 323).

16. *nearly seventy years of age.* He is "of great age" in the 1867 Ticknor and Fields Public Reading edition.

17. *a woman with a heavy bundle slunk into the shop.* The following grotesque scene may at first seem odd for a Christmas story, but the poor often visited these shops at holiday time to sell all sorts of odd items to help pay for their roast beef and plum pudding. Albert Smith in "The Legend of the Fairy Black-a-Dollar, or How to Turn Old Iron into Current Copper," his parody of the *Christmas Books*, in *The Man in the Moon* (vol. 1, 1847), described how men, women, and children turned in bundles of "useless iron and fusty rags, choking and stenchy, and blurred phials with unwholesome breath, and lumps of dripping, of an unctuous and oily nature," for "sixpenny pieces, and fourpenny pieces, and penny pieces, and halfpenny pieces" (pp. 13, 15).

18. *charwoman.* A servant hired by the day to do odd housework; she was obviously employed by whoever was settling the deceased's affairs. Scrooge would never have paid for one. Charwomen often sold drippings and other "kitchen-stuff" (as well as miscellaneous pilfered items) from the various households where they worked to the proprietors of rag-and-bottle and marine-store shops. See Mayhew, *London Labour and the London Poor* (vol. 2, London: George Woodfall, 1851, p. 111).

19. *If we haven't all three met here without meaning it!* "It reminds us of nothing so much as the midnight meetings of the demon Ghouls of the *Arabian Nights* feasting on the bodies of the dead," said *The Atlas* (December 23, 1843); "and yet, doubtless, it is drawn from the life." Kate Field noted in *Pen Photographs of Charles Dickens's Readings* (1871), "There is something positively and Shakespearianly weird in the laugh and tone of the charwoman. Unconsciously the three witches of *Macbeth* arise before the imagination, which perceived by Dickens's treatment of this short but graphic scene how fine a sketch he would make did fate ever cast him for one of the sisters three" (p. 35).

"You couldn't have met in a better place," said old Joe, removing his pipe from his mouth. "Come into the parlour. You were made free of it long ago, you know; and the other two an't strangers. Stop till I shut the door of the shop. Ah! How it skreeks![20] There an't such a rusty bit of metal in the place as its own hinges, I believe; and I'm sure there's no such old bones here, as mine. Ha, ha! We're all suitable to our calling, we're well matched. Come into the parlour. Come into the parlour."[21]

The parlour was the space behind the screen of rags. The old man raked the fire together with an old stair-rod,[22] and having trimmed his smoky lamp (for it was night), with the stem of his pipe, put it in his mouth again.

While he did this, the woman who had already spoken threw her bundle on the floor and sat down in a flaunting manner on a stool; crossing her elbows on her knees, and looking with a bold defiance at the other two.

"What odds then![23] What odds, Mrs. Dilber?" said the woman. "Every person has a right to take care of themselves. *He* always did!"

"That's true, indeed!" said the laundress. "No man more so."

"Why, then, don't stand staring as if you was afraid, woman; who's the wiser? We're not going to pick holes in each other's coats,[24] I suppose?"

"No, indeed!" said Mrs. Dilber[25] and the man together. "We should hope not."

"Very well, then!" cried the woman. "That's enough. Who's the worse for the loss of a few things like these? Not a dead man, I suppose."

"No, indeed," said Mrs. Dilber, laughing.

"If he wanted to keep 'em after he was dead, a wicked old screw,"[26] pursued the woman, "why wasn't he natural in his lifetime? If he had been, he'd have had somebody to look after him when he was struck with Death, instead of lying gasping out his last there, alone by himself."

20. *skreeks!* Colloquialism, usually spelled "screaks," to scream or creak, to screech or shriek.

21. *Come into the parlour. Come into the parlour.* He asks instead in the 1867 Ticknor and Fields Public Reading edition, "What have you got to sell? What have you got to sell?" "Half a minute's patience, Joe, and you shall see," replies Mrs. Dilber.

22. *stair-rod.* Brass rod that keeps a carpet down and in its place.

23. *What odds then!* What does it matter!

24. *pick holes in each other's coats.* Have a quarrel.

25. *Mrs. Dilber.* Dickens added in the 1867 Ticknor and Fields Public Reading edition that she was a woman "whose manner was remarkable for a general propitiation."

26. *old screw.* Slang for miser, apparent in the name Scrooge.

27. *mounting the breach.* Military term, taking the lead.

28. *A seal or two, a pencil-case, a pair of sleeve-buttons, and a brooch of no great value.* Being the undertaker's man, the gentleman in faded black must have found these miscellaneous items of little value either on or in the clothes in which he dressed the corpse.

"It's the truest word that ever was spoke," said Mrs. Dilber. "It's a judgment on him."

"I wish it was a little heavier one," replied the woman; "and it should have been, you may depend upon it, if I could have laid my hands on anything else. Open that bundle, old Joe and let me know the value of it. Speak out plain. I'm not afraid to be the first, nor afraid for them to see it. We knew pretty well that we were helping ourselves, before we met here, I believe. It's no sin. Open the bundle, Joe."

But the gallantry of her friends would not allow of this; and the man in faded black, mounting the breach[27] first, produced *his* plunder. It was not extensive. A seal or two, a pencil-case, a pair of sleeve-buttons, and a brooch of no great value,[28] were all. They were severally examined and appraised by old Joe, who chalked the sums he was disposed to give for each upon the wall, and added them up into a total when he found that there was nothing more to come.

"That's your account," said Joe, "and I wouldn't give another sixpence, if I was to be boiled for not doing it. Who's next?"

Mrs. Dilber was next. Sheets and towels, a little wearing apparel, two old-fashioned silver teaspoons, a pair of sugar-tongs, and a few boots. Her account was stated on the wall in the same manner.

"I always give too much to ladies. It's a weakness of mine, and that's the way I ruin myself," said old Joe. "That's your account. If you asked me for another penny, and made it an open question, I'd repent of being so liberal, and knock off half-a-crown."

"And now undo *my* bundle, Joe," said the first woman.

Joe went down on his knees for the greater convenience of opening it, and having unfastened a great many knots, dragged out a large and heavy roll of some dark stuff.

"What do you call this?" said Joe. "Bed-curtains!"

"Ah!" returned the woman, laughing and leaning forward on her crossed arms. "Bed-curtains!"

"You don't mean to say you took 'em down, rings and all, with him lying there?" said Joe.

"Yes I do," replied the woman. "Why not?"

"You were born to make your fortune," said Joe, "and you'll certainly do it."

"I certainly shan't hold my hand, when I can get anything in it by reaching it out, for the sake of such a man as He was, I promise you, Joe," returned the woman coolly. "Don't drop that oil upon the blankets, now."

"His blankets?" asked Joe.

"Whose else's do you think?" replied the woman. "He isn't likely to take cold without 'em, I dare say."

"I hope he didn't die of anything catching? Eh?" said old Joe, stopping in his work, and looking up.

"Don't you be afraid of that," returned the woman. "I an't so fond of his company that I'd loiter about him for such things, if he did. Ah! You may look through that shirt till your eyes ache; but you won't find a hole in it, nor a threadbare place. It's the best he had, and a fine one too. They'd have wasted it, if it hadn't been for me."

"What do you call wasting of it?" asked old Joe.

"Putting it on him to be buried in, to be sure," replied the woman with a laugh. "Somebody was fool enough to do it, but I took it off again. If calico an't good enough for such a purpose, it isn't good enough for anything. It's quite as becoming to the body. He can't look uglier than he did in that one."

Scrooge listened to this dialogue in horror. As they sat grouped about their spoil, in the scanty light afforded by the old man's lamp, he viewed them with a detestation and disgust, which could hardly have been greater, though they had been obscene demons, marketing the corpse itself.

"Ha, ha!" laughed the same woman, when old Joe,

29. *this man.* "This plundered unknown man" in the 1867 Ticknor and Fields Public Reading edition.

producing a flannel bag with money in it, told out their several gains upon the ground. "This is the end of it, you see! He frightened every one away from him when he was alive, to profit us when he was dead! Ha, ha, ha!"

"Spirit!" said Scrooge, shuddering from head to foot. "I see, I see. The case of this unhappy man might be my own. My life tends that way, now. Merciful Heaven, what is this!"

He recoiled in terror, for the scene had changed, and now he almost touched a bed: a bare, uncurtained bed: on which, beneath a ragged sheet, there lay a something covered up, which, though it was dumb, announced itself in awful language.

The room was very dark, too dark to be observed with any accuracy, though Scrooge glanced round it in obedience to a secret impulse, anxious to know what kind of room it was. A pale light, rising in the outer air, fell straight upon the bed; and on it, plundered and bereft, unwatched, unwept, uncared for, was the body of this man.[29]

Scrooge glanced towards the Phantom. Its steady hand was pointed to the head. The cover was so carelessly adjusted that the slightest raising of it, the motion of a finger upon Scrooge's part, would have disclosed the face. He thought of it, felt how easy it would be to do, and longed to do it; but had no more power to withdraw the veil than to dismiss the spectre at his side.

Oh cold, cold, rigid, dreadful Death, set up thine altar here, and dress it with such terrors as thou hast at thy command: for this is thy dominion! But of the loved, revered, and honoured head, thou canst not turn one hair to thy dread purposes, or make one feature odious. It is not that the hand is heavy and will fall down when released; it is not that the heart and pulse are still; but that the hand WAS open, generous, and true; the heart brave, warm, and tender; and the pulse a man's. Strike, Shadow, strike! And see his good deeds springing from the wound, to sow the world with life immortal!

No voice pronounced these words in Scrooge's ears, and yet he heard them when he looked upon the bed. He thought, if this man could be raised up now, what would be his foremost thoughts? Avarice, hard dealing, griping cares? They have brought him to a rich end, truly!

He lay, in the dark empty house, with not a man, a woman, or a child, to say he was kind to me in this or that, and for the memory of one kind word I will be kind to him.[30] A cat was tearing at the door, and there was a sound of gnawing rats beneath the hearth-stone. What *they* wanted in the room of death, and why they were so restless and disturbed, Scrooge did not dare to think.

"Spirit!" he said, "this is a fearful place. In leaving it, I shall not leave its lesson, trust me. Let us go!"

Still the Ghost pointed with an unmoved finger to the head.

"I understand you," Scrooge returned, "and I would do it, if I could. But I have not the power, Spirit. I have not the power."

Again it seemed to look upon him.

"If there is any person in the town, who feels emotion caused by this man's death," said Scrooge quite agonized, "show that person to me, Spirit, I beseech you!"

The phantom spread its dark robe before him for a moment, like a wing; and withdrawing it, revealed a room by daylight, where a mother and her children were.

She was expecting some one, and with anxious eagerness; for she walked up and down the room; started at every sound; looked out from the window; glanced at the clock; tried, but in vain, to work with her needle; and could hardly bear the voices of the children in their play.

30. *He lay . . . with not a man, a woman, or a child, to say he was kind to me in this or that, and for the memory of one kind word I will be kind to him.* This man's lonely death is not that different from that of William the Conqueror, as described by Dickens in Chapter 8 of *A Child's History of England* (1852–54): "The moment he was dead . . . the mercenary servants of the court began to rob and plunder; the body of the King, in the indecent strife, was rolled from the bed, and lay, alone, for hours, upon the ground. O Conqueror, of whom so many great names are praised now, of whom so many great names thought nothing then, it were better to have conquered one true heart, than England!"

31. *hoarding*. Here used in an unusual sense: saving for him and put by the fire to be kept warm.

At length the long-expected knock was heard. She hurried to the door, and met her husband; a man whose face was care-worn and depressed, though he was young. There was a remarkable expression in it now; a kind of serious delight of which he felt ashamed, and which he struggled to repress.

He sat down to the dinner that had been hoarding[31] for him by the fire; and when she asked him faintly what news (which was not until after a long silence), he appeared embarrassed how to answer.

"Is it good," she said, "or bad?"—to help him.

"Bad," he answered.

"We are quite ruined?"

"No. There is hope yet, Caroline."

"If *he* relents," she said, amazed, "there is! Nothing is past hope, if such a miracle has happened."

"He is past relenting," said her husband "He is dead."

She was a mild and patient creature if her face spoke truth; but she was thankful in her soul to hear it, and she said so, with clasped hands. She prayed forgiveness the next moment, and was sorry; but the first was the emotion of her heart.

"What the half-drunken woman whom I told you of last night, said to me, when I tried to see him and obtain a week's delay; and what I thought was a mere excuse to avoid me; turns out to have been quite true. He was not only very ill, but dying, then."

"To whom will our debt be transferred?"

"I don't know. But before that time we shall be ready with the money; and even though we were not, it would be bad fortune indeed to find so merciless a creditor in his successor. We may sleep to-night with light hearts, Caroline!"

Yes. Soften it as they would, their hearts were lighter. The children's faces hushed, and clustered round to hear what they so little understood, were brighter; and it was a happier house for this man's death! The only emotion that the Ghost could show him, caused by the event, was one of pleasure.

"Let me see some tenderness connected with a death," said Scrooge; "or that dark chamber, Spirit, which we left just now, will be for ever present to me."

The Ghost conducted him through several streets familiar to his feet; and as they went along, Scrooge looked here and there to find himself, but nowhere was he to be seen. They entered poor Bob Cratchit's house;[32] the dwelling he had visited before; and found the mother and the children seated round the fire.

Quiet. Very quiet. The noisy little Cratchits were as still as statues in one corner, and sat looking up at Peter, who had a book before him. The mother and her daughters were engaged in sewing.[33] But surely they were very quiet!

"'And He took a child, and set him in the midst of them.'"[34]

Where had Scrooge heard those words? He had not dreamed them. The boy must have read them out, as he and the Spirit crossed the threshold. Why did he not go on?

The mother laid her work upon the table, and put her hand up to her face.

"The colour hurts my eyes," she said.

The colour?[35] Ah, poor Tiny Tim!

"They're better now again," said Cratchit's wife. "It makes them weak by candle-light; and I wouldn't show weak eyes to your father when he comes home, for the world. It must be near his time."

"Past it rather," Peter answered, shutting up his book. "But I think he's walked a little slower than he used, these few last evenings, mother."

They were very quiet again. At last she said, and in a steady cheerful voice, that only faultered once:

"I have known him walk with—I have known him walk with Tiny Tim upon his shoulder, very fast indeed."

32. *They entered poor Bob Cratchit's house.* Again Dickens borrows an incident from "The Goblins Who Stole a Sexton" (Chapter 29 of *The Pickwick Papers*, 1837): Gabriel Grub visits a poor family's tragic Christmas, where "the fairest and youngest child lay dying." Here the sentimentality is spread a little thick: "His young brothers and sisters crowded round his little bed, and seized his tiny hand, so cold and heavy; but they shrunk back from its touch, and looked with awe on his infant face; for calm and tranquil as it was, and sleeping in rest and peace as the beautiful child seemed to be, they saw that he was dead, and they knew he was an angel looking down upon, and blessing them, from a bright and happy Heaven." Here is one of the earliest of the many examples of child death in Dickens' works. This vast necrology includes most famously Little Nell in *The Old Curiosity Shop* (1841) and Paul Dombey in *Dombey and Son* (1848). Dickens personally knew about the high infant mortality rate in England: he lost a brother and a sister when he was a boy.

33. *sewing.* "Needlework" in the 1867 Ticknor and Fields Public Reading edition.

34. *"'And He took a child, and set him in the midst of them.'"* One of Dickens' favorite passages from the Bible (Matthew 18.2 and Mark 9.36). Here Dickens may be recalling the epitaph he composed for Charles Irving Deane, son of Dr. Francis H. Deane of Richmond, Virginia, who died on March 12, 1842, aged thirteen months and nineteen days, which quoted, "And Jesus called a little child unto him, and set him in the midst of them" (*Letters*, p. 187). It is appropriate that the young Cratchits are reading this story at Christmastime, when "its mighty Founder was a child himself." It has no place in "the gloomy theology of the Murdstones," in Chapter 4 of *David Copperfield* (1850), which "made all children out to be a nest of vipers (though there *was* a child once set in the midst of the Disciples)." Those were pious times, when an actor could not speak Scripture on the London stage. In February 1844, Charles Webb replaced this line from the Bible in his play *A Christmas Carol; or, The Past, Present, and Future* with another quite different sentiment, "And in the midst of their comforts, the little child was taken from them."

Dickens retold this incident from the Gospels in *The Life of Our Lord* (1934), which he wrote for his own children in 1849:

> The Disciples asked him, "Master, who is the greatest in the Kingdom of Heaven?" Jesus called a little child to him, and took him in his arms, and stood him among them, and answered, "a child like this. I say unto you that none but those who are as humble as little children shall enter into Heaven. Whosoever shall receive one such little child in my name receiveth me. But whosoever hurts one of them, it was better for him that he had a millstone tied about his neck, and were drowned in the depths of the sea. The angels are all children." Our Saviour loved the child, and loved all children. Yes, and all the world. No one ever loved all people so well and so truly as He did.

This book was never intended for publication, but his descendants released it in 1934. Based largely on St. Luke's Gospel, *The Life of Our Lord* emphasized the good works of Jesus and his humble origins. Dickens told about the shepherds who paid homage to the Baby Jesus, but nothing about Three Wise Men. "No one ever lived, who was so good, so kind, so gentle, and so sorry for all people who did wrong, or were in anyway ill or miserable, as he was," Dickens began his new gospel. "And as he is now in Heaven, where we hope to go, and all to meet each

other after we are dead, and there be happy always together, you never can think what a good place Heaven is, without knowing who he was and what he did." Jesus Christ for Charles Dickens was, as he said in a speech at the Hospital for Sick Children on Great Ormand Street, February 9, 1858, "the universal embodiment of all mercy and compassion . . . Him who was once a child himself, and a poor one" (p. 251).

His parents were technically Church of England, but not particularly devout. Dickens turned to liberal Unitarianism after he returned from America in 1842, drawn to its emphasis on the moral teachings of the New Testament, especially the Sermon on the Mount, rather than on theology. He believed that one should, like Harriet in Chapter 58 of *Dombey and Son* (1848), "read the eternal book for all the weary, and the heavy-laden; for all the wretched, fallen, and neglected of this earth—read the blessed history, in which the blind lame palsied beggar, the criminal, the woman stained with shame, the shunned of all our dainty clay, has each a portion, that no human pride, indifference, or sophistry, through all the ages that this world shall last, can take away, or by the thousandth atom of a grain reduce—read the ministry of Him who, through the round of human life, and all its hopes and griefs, from birth to death, from infancy to age, had sweet compassion for, and interest in, its every scene and stage, its every suffering and sorrow." Dickens was interested in deeds, not dogma. Even in his last will and testament of June 2, 1870, he exhorted "my children humbly to try to guide themselves by the teaching of the New Testament in its broad spirit, and to put no faith in any man's narrow construction of its letter here or there" (*Letters*, p. 732). This was the gospel he preached in *A Christmas Carol*.

He was shocked when a pious reader took offense to a phrase "drawn from a passage of

Holy Writ which is greatly reverenced . . . as a prophetic description of the sufferings of our Saviour." He replied on June 8, 1870, in one of the last letters he ever wrote, "I have always striven in my writings to express the veneration for the life and lessons of our Savior; because I feel it. . . . But I have never made proclamation of this from the house tops" (p. 548).

35. *The colour?* Dickens crossed out "black" in the manuscript; Mrs. Cratchit and the girls are sewing their mourning clothes in memory of Tiny Tim.

36. *little Bob in his comforter—he had need of it, poor fellow.* An odd place for a pun. Here, Dickens, like Scrooge in the face of Marley's Ghost, "tried to be smart, as a means of distracting his own attention," in this case from the deep sadness of the scene.

37. *Sunday! You went to-day then.* Dickens may have been recalling December 1842; Christmas Day did not fall on Sunday again until 1853.

38. *on a Sunday.* Each Sunday, every Sunday.

39. *Christmas.* "Christmas holly" in the Berg prompt book.

"And so have I," cried Peter. "Often."

"And so have I!" exclaimed another. So had all.

"But he was very light to carry," she resumed, intent upon her work, "and his father loved him so, that it was no trouble—no trouble. And there is your father at the door!"

She hurried out to meet him; and little Bob in his comforter—he had need of it, poor fellow[36]—came in. His tea was ready for him on the hob, and they all tried who should help him to it most. Then the two young Cratchits got upon his knees and laid, each child a little cheek, against his face, as if they said, "Don't mind it, father. Don't be grieved!"

Bob was very cheerful with them, and spoke pleasantly to all the family. He looked at the work upon the table, and praised the industry and speed of Mrs. Cratchit and the girls. They would be done long before Sunday he said.

"Sunday! You went to-day then,[37] Robert?" said his wife.

"Yes, my dear," returned Bob. "I wish you could have gone. It would have done you good to see how green a place it is. But you'll see it often. I promised him that I would walk there on a Sunday.[38] My little, little child!" cried Bob. "My little child!"

He broke down all at once. He couldn't help it. If he could have helped it, he and his child would have been farther apart perhaps than they were.

He left the room, and went up stairs into the room above, which was lighted cheerfully, and hung with Christmas.[39] There was a chair set close beside the child, and there were signs of some one having been there, lately. Poor Bob sat down in it, and when he had thought a little and composed himself, he kissed the little face. He was reconciled to what had happened, and went down again quite happy.

They drew about the fire, and talked; the girls and mother working still. Bob told them of the extraordinary kindness of Mr. Scrooge's nephew, whom he had scarcely seen but once, and who, meeting him in the street that day, and seeing that he looked a little—"just a little down you know" said Bob, enquired what had happened to distress him. "On which," said Bob, "for he is the pleasantest-spoken gentleman you ever heard, I told him. 'I am heartily sorry for it, Mr. Cratchit,' he said, 'and heartily sorry for your good wife.' By the bye, how he ever knew *that*, I don't know."

"Knew what, my dear?"

"Why, that you were a good wife," replied Bob.

"Everybody knows that!" said Peter.

"Very well observed, my boy!" cried Bob. "I hope they do. 'Heartily sorry,' he said, 'for your good wife. If I can be of service to you in any way,' he said, giving me his card, 'that's where I live. Pray come to me.' Now, it wasn't," cried Bob, "for the sake of anything he might be able to do for us, so much as for his kind way, that this was quite delightful. It really seemed as if he had known our Tiny Tim, and felt with us."

"I'm sure he's a good soul!" said Mrs. Cratchit.

"You would be surer of it, my dear," returned Bob, "if you saw and spoke to him. I shouldn't be at all surprised, mark what I say, if he got Peter a better situation."

"Only hear that, Peter," said Mrs. Cratchit.

"And then," cried one of the girls, "Peter will be keeping company with some one, and setting up for himself."**40**

"Get along with you!" retorted Peter, grinning.

"It's just as likely as not," said Bob, "one of these days; though there's plenty of time for that, my dear. But however and whenever we part from one another, I am sure we shall none of us forget poor Tiny Tim—shall we—or this first parting that there was among us?"

"Never, father!" cried they all.

"And I know," said Bob, "I know, my dears, that when we recollect how patient and how mild he was; although he was a little, little child; we shall not quar-

40. *keeping company with some one, and setting up for himself.* He will soon be of marrying age and going into business for himself.

41. *what man that was.* "With the covered face" added in the 1867 Ticknor and Fields Public Reading edition.

42. *A churchyard.* "A dismal, wretched, ruinous churchyard" in the 1867 Ticknor and Fields Public Reading edition. Major in her article "Scrooge's Chambers" (*The Dickensian*, winter 1932–33, p. 14) identified this graveyard as that of All Hallows Staining, Star Alley, off Mark Lane in the Langborn Ward.

rel easily among ourselves, and forget poor Tiny Tim in doing it."

"No, never, father!" they all cried again.

"I am very happy," said little Bob, "I am very happy!"

Mrs. Cratchit kissed him, his daughters kissed him, the two young Cratchits kissed him, and Peter and himself shook hands. Spirit of Tiny Tim, thy childish essence was from God!

"Spectre," said Scrooge, "something informs me that our parting moment is at hand. I know it, but I know not how. Tell me what man that was[41] whom we saw lying dead?"

The Ghost of Christmas Yet To Come conveyed him, as before—though at a different time, he thought: indeed, there seemed no order in these latter visions, save that they were in the Future—into the resorts of business men, but showed him not himself. Indeed, the Spirit did not stay for anything, but went straight on, as to the end just now desired, until besought by Scrooge to tarry for a moment.

"This court," said Scrooge, "through which we hurry now, is where my place of occupation is, and has been for a length of time. I see the house. Let me behold what I shall be, in days to come."

The Spirit stopped; the hand was pointed elsewhere.

"The house is yonder," Scrooge exclaimed. "Why do you point away?"

The inexorable finger underwent no change.

Scrooge hastened to the window of his office, and looked in. It was an office still, but not his. The furniture was not the same, and the figure in the chair was not himself. The Phantom pointed as before.

He joined it once again, and wondering why and whither he had gone, accompanied it until they reached an iron gate. He paused to look round before entering.

A churchyard.[42] Here, then, the wretched man

whose name he had now to learn, lay underneath the ground. It was a worthy place. Walled in by houses; overrun by grass and weeds, the growth of vegetation's death,[43] not life; choked up with too much burying; fat with repleted appetite.[44] A worthy place!

The Spirit stood among the graves, and pointed down to One. He advanced towards it trembling. The Phantom was exactly as it had been, but he dreaded that he saw new meaning in its solemn shape.

"Before I draw nearer to that stone to which you point," said Scrooge, "answer me one question. Are these the shadows of the things that Will be, or are they shadows of the things that May be, only?"

Still the Ghost pointed downward to the grave by which it stood.

"Men's courses will foreshadow certain ends, to which, if persevered in, they must lead" said Scrooge. "But if the courses be departed from, the ends will change. Say it is thus with what you show me!"

The Spirit was immovable as ever.

Scrooge crept towards it, trembling as he went; and following the finger, read upon the stone of the neglected grave his own name, EBENEZER SCROOGE.

"Am *I* that man who lay upon the bed?" he cried, upon his knees.

The finger pointed from the grave to him, and back again.

"No, Spirit! Oh no, no!"

The finger still was there.

"Spirit!" he cried, tight clutching at its robe, "hear me! I am not the man I was. I will not be the man I must have been but for this intercourse. Why show me this, if I am past all hope?"

For the first time the hand appeared to shake.[45]

"Good Spirit," he pursued, as down upon the ground he fell before it: "Your nature intercedes for me, and pities me. Assure me that I yet may change these shadows you have shown me, by an altered life!"

The kind hand trembled.

43. *vegetation's death.* Weeds and rank grass kill other plants.

44. *choked up with too much burying; fat with repleted appetite.* Dickens is being ironic in describing a graveyard in terms of eating and abundance. Many of London's graveyards at the time were overcrowded or overgrown and neglected.

45. *For the first time the hand appeared to shake.* "For the first time the kind hand faltered" in the 1867 Ticknor and Fields Public Reading edition.

"The Last of the Spirits." Preliminary pencil and wash drawing by John Leech, 1843. *Courtesy Houghton Library, Harvard University.*

"I will honour Christmas in my heart, and try to keep it all the year. I will live in the Past, the Present, and the Future. The Spirits of all Three shall strive within me. I will not shut out the lessons that they teach. Oh, tell me I may sponge away the writing on this stone!"

In his agony, he caught the spectral hand. It sought to free itself, but he was strong in his entreaty, and detained it. The Spirit, stronger yet, repulsed him.

Holding up his hands in one last prayer to have his fate reversed, he saw an alteration in the Phantom's hood and dress. It shrunk, collapsed, and dwindled down into a bedpost.

The Last of the Spirits.

STAVE FIVE.

THE END OF IT.

es! and the bedpost was his own. The bed was his own, the room was his own. Best and happiest of all, the Time before him was his own, to make amends in!

"I will live in the Past, the Present, and the Future!" Scrooge repeated, as he scrambled out of bed. "The Spirits of all Three shall strive within me. Oh Jacob Marley! Heaven, and the Christmas Time be praised for this! I say it on my knees, old Jacob; on my knees!"

He was so fluttered and so glowing with his good intentions, that his broken voice would scarcely answer to his call. He had been sobbing violently in his conflict with the Spirit, and his face was wet with tears.

"They are not torn down," cried Scrooge, folding one of his bed-curtains in his arms, "they are not torn down, rings and all. They are here: I am here: the shadows of the things that would have been, may be dispelled. They will be. I know they will!"

His hands were busy with his garments all this time: turning them inside out, putting them on upside down, tearing them, mislaying them, making them parties to every kind of extravagance.

"I don't know what to do!" cried Scrooge, laughing and crying in the same breath; and making a perfect Laocoön of himself with his stockings.[1] "I am as light as a feather, I am as happy as an angel, I am as merry as a school-boy. I am as giddy as a drunken man. A merry

1. *and making a perfect Laocoön of himself with his stockings.* This fine metaphor was an afterthought, added in the galleys. Laocoôn was a Trojan priest, who according to Virgil (*The Aeneid*, Book 2, line 230), so offended the goddess Athena by warning his people against the giant wooden horse left by the Greeks at the city gates, that two great sea serpents strangled him and his two sons. Scrooge's struggle with his stockings no doubt reminded Dickens of the famous classical statue of the fifth century B.C. depicting Laocoön's struggle with the serpents (actually a Roman copy of a Greek original), unearthed in the baths of Titus in Rome in 1506 and now in the Vatican Museum. A copy of this copy is in the Ashmolean Museum in London.

"Old Scrooge." Ink sketch by John Leech, Albert Schloss
autograph album, January 22, 1844.
Courtesy Beinecke Rare Book and Manuscript Library, Yale University.

Christmas to everybody! A happy New Year to all the
world. Hallo here! Whoop! Hallo!"

He had frisked into the sitting-room, and was now
standing there: perfectly winded.

"There's the saucepan that the gruel was in!" cried
Scrooge, starting off again, and frisking round the fireplace. "There's the door, by which the Ghost of Jacob
Marley entered! There's the corner where the Ghost of
Christmas Present, sat! There's the window where I saw
the wandering Spirits! It's all right, it's all true, it all
happened. Ha ha ha!"

Really, for a man who had been out of practice for

so many years, it was a splendid laugh, a most illustrious laugh. The father of a long, long, line of brilliant laughs!

"I don't know what day of the month it is!" said Scrooge. "I don't know how long I've been among the Spirits. I don't know anything. I'm quite a baby. Never mind. I don't care. I'd rather be a baby. Hallo! Whoop! Hallo here!"

He was checked in his transports by the churches ringing out the lustiest peals he had ever heard. Clash, clang, hammer, ding, dong, bell. Bell, dong, ding, hammer, clang, clash! Oh, glorious, glorious!

Running to the window, he opened it, and put out his head. No fog, no mist;[2] clear, bright, jovial, stirring, cold; cold, piping for the blood to dance to; Golden sunlight; Heavenly sky; sweet fresh air; merry bells. Oh, glorious. Glorious!

"What's to-day?" cried Scrooge, calling downward to a boy in Sunday clothes, who perhaps had loitered in to look about him.

"EH?" returned the boy, with all his might of wonder.

"What's to-day, my fine fellow?" said Scrooge.

"To-day!" replied the boy. "Why, CHRISTMAS DAY."

"It's Christmas Day!" said Scrooge to himself. "I haven't missed it. The Spirits have done it all in one night.[3] They can do anything they like. Of course they can. Of course they can. Hallo, my fine fellow!"

"Hallo!" returned the boy.

"Do you know the Poulterer's, in the next street but one, at the corner?" Scrooge inquired.

"I should hope I did," replied the lad.

"An intelligent boy!" said Scrooge. "A remarkable boy! Do you know whether they've sold the prize Turkey that was hanging up there? Not the little prize Turkey: the big one?"

"What, the one as big as me?" returned the boy.

"What a delightful boy!" said Scrooge. "It's a pleasure to talk to him. Yes, my buck!"[4]

"It's hanging there now," replied the boy.

2. *No fog, no mist.* "No night" added in the 1867 Ticknor and Fields Public Reading edition.

3. *The Spirits have done it all in one night.* Dreams distort our sense of durations of time. "I sometimes seemed to have lived for seventy or one hundred years in one night," admitted Thomas De Quincey in *Confessions of an English Opium Eater* (1821); "nay, sometimes had feelings representative of a millennium, passed in that time, or, however, of a duration far beyond the limits of any human experience." Macnish explained in *The Philosophy of Sleep* (1838) that time in dreams "seems to be in a great measure annihilated. An extensive period of time is reduced, as it were, to a single point, or rather a single point is made to embrace an extensive period. In one instance, we pass through many adventures, see many strange sights, and hear many strange sounds" (p. 60). Freud in *The Interpretation of Dreams* (1900) argued that the distortion occurs during the recollection of a dream; one arouses the progression of events, however long, on awakening, and the seemingly conscious remembrance may not have been actually dreamed.

4. *buck!* A merry or fashionable young man, here used facetiously.

5. *"Walk-ER!"* A Cockney expression of surprise or incredulity, often used by Dickens; Sam Weller's father is particularly fond of the word in *The Pickwick Papers* (1837). As reported in *Notes and Queries* (November 29, 1851, pp. 424–25), an American lecturer was puzzled that whenever she mentioned a Professor Walker as an authority, her British audience burst out laughing. The correspondent wondered, "Why do people say 'Walker' when they wish to express ridicule or disbelief of a questionable statement?" There are actually several theories as to the origin of this expression. *Notes*

"Walk-ER!" Lithograph by John Leech, *Portraits of the Children of the Mobility* by Percival Leigh, 1841.
Private collection.

and Queries said that it referred to John "Hooky" Walker, an outdoor clerk in Cheapside with a crooked or hooked nose, whose responsibility was to keep an eye on his fellow employees. His reports were constantly being challenged by his colleagues as fabrications; he was eventually dis-

"Is it?" said Scrooge. "Go and buy it."

"Walk-ER!"[5] exclaimed the boy.

"No, no," said Scrooge, "I am in earnest. Go and buy it, and tell 'em to bring it here, that I may give them the direction where to take it. Come back with the man, and I'll give you a shilling. Come back with him in less than five minutes, and I'll give you half-a-crown!"

The boy was off like a shot. He must have had a steady hand at a trigger who could have got a shot off half so fast.

"I'll send it to Bob Cratchit's!"[6] whispered Scrooge, rubbing his hands, and splitting with a laugh. "He sha'n't know who sends it. It's twice the size of Tiny Tim. Joe Miller[7] never made such a joke as sending it to Bob's will be!"

The hand in which he wrote the address was not a steady one, but write it he did, somehow, and went down stairs to open the street door, ready for the coming of the poulterer's man. As he stood there, waiting his arrival, the knocker caught his eye.

"I shall love it, as long as I live!" cried Scrooge, patting it with his hand. "I scarcely ever looked at it before. What an honest expression it has in its face! It's a wonderful knocker!—Here's the Turkey. Hallo! Whoop! How are you! Merry Christmas!"

It *was* a Turkey![8] He never could have stood upon his legs, that bird. He would have snapped 'em short off in a minute, like sticks of sealing-wax.

"Why, it's impossible to carry that to Camden Town," said Scrooge. "You must have a cab."

The chuckle with which be said this, and the chuckle with which he paid for the Turkey, and the chuckle with which he paid for the cab, and the chuckle with which he recompensed the boy, were only to be exceeded by the chuckle with which he sat down breathless in his chair again, and chuckled till he cried.

Shaving was not an easy task, for his hand continued to shake very much; and shaving requires attention, even when you don't dance while you are at it. But

charged, but the sullied reputation of "Hooky Walker" remained behind. T. W. Hill mentioned two other possibilities in his notes to *The Pickwick Papers* in *The Dickensian* (summer 1948); "a London Magistrate with a hooked nose that gave the title of 'beak' to all magistrates"; and "an aquiline-nosed Jew named Walker who lectured on Astronomy and invited his pupils to 'take a sight' at the heavenly bodies; the doubting pupils imitated behind his back his actions in 'taking a sight' at his nose" (p. 145).

Dickens may well have known all of these theories, particularly that latter concerning "taking a sight." "Dickens as the boy," recalled Rowland Hill, a Dickensian who saw him read *A Christmas Carol* many times, "put his thumb to his nose, and spread out his fingers, with a jeer, at the syllable ER. This was a common way to call your pals 'Fools' without using the word" (*A Christmas Carol: The Public Reading Version*, edited by Philip Collins [New York: New York Public Library, 1971], p. 204).

6. *"I'll send it to Bob Cratchit's!"* Not everyone at the time approved of such generosity. "The processes whereby poor men are to be enabled to earn good wages, wherewith to buy turkeys for themselves, does not enter into the account," scolded Nassau Senior in the *Westminster Review* (June 1844); "indeed, it would quite spoil the *dénouement* and all the generosity. Who went without turkey and punch in order that Bob Cratchit might get them—for, unless there were turkey and punch in surplus, some one must go without—is a disagreeable reflector kept wholly out of sight" (p. 376).

Dickens had no patience for such Toryism: he wrote Forster in early November 1844 how annoyed he was "that the *Westminster Review* considered Scrooge's presentation of the turkey to Bob Cratchit as

"Merry Christmas to you!" Etching by Robert Seymour, *The Book of Christmas* by Thomas K. Hervey, 1836.
Private collection.

grossly incompatible with political economy" (p. 209). He then introduced Mr. Filer in the First Quarter of *The Chimes* (1844), "a real good old city Tory, in a blue coat and bright buttons and a white cravat, and with a tendency of blood to the head," someone "who recognizes no virtue in anything but the good old times, and talks of them, parrot-like, whatever the matter is."

7. *Joe Miller.* A popular but illiterate English comic (1684–1738), whose purported jokes and sayings were collected by the dramatist John Mottley in *Joe Miller's Jest-Book, or The Wit's Vade Mecum* (1739). The book itself may have been a joke: Miller reportedly never came up with any especially clever or original remark. Nonetheless, Mottley's book quickly became the best-known English collection of witticisms, and almost any stray joke was attributed to this apparently unfunny person.

Dickens mentions him or this book often in his writings; for example, he described the humorless Bill Bitherstone, in Chapter 12 of *Dombey and Son* (1848), with heavy irony as "a perfect Joe Miller or complete Jest Book." The name Joe Miller has also come to mean any stale joke.

8. *It* was *a Turkey!* "That top-heavy and monstrous bird," G. K. Chesterton suggested in *Appreciations and Criticisms of the Works of Charles Dickens* (London: J. M. Dent; New York: E. P. Dutton, 1911), "is a good symbol of the top-heavy happiness of the stories" (p. 112). Dickens' business associates Bradbury and Evans, his printers, had been for some time in the habit of presenting him and his family with a prize Christmas turkey ("your annual recollection of us, which we value very highly as one of the pleasant circumstances of a

pleasant season") much like that which Scrooge bestowed on the Cratchits. "I determined not to thank you for the Turkey until it was *quite gone*, in order that you might have a becoming idea of its astonishing capabilities," Dickens wrote them on January 2, 1840. "The last remnant of that blessed bird made its appearance at breakfast yesterday—I repeat it, yesterday—the other portions having furnished forth seven grills, one boil, and a cold lunch or two" (p. 1). Dickens and *A Christmas Carol* did much to make turkey the preferred bird of choice at Christmas; before that, goose was the standard English fare. "Dickens' *Christmas Carol* helps the poultry business amazingly," noted *Wilkes's Spirit of the Times* (December 21, 1867). "Everybody who reads it and who has money immediately rushes off and buys a turkey for the poor."

if he had cut the end of his nose off, he would have put a piece of sticking-plaister[9] over it, and been quite satisfied.

He dressed himself "all in his best," and at last got out into the streets. The people were by this time pouring forth, as he had seen them with the Ghost of Christmas Present; and walking with his hands behind him, Scrooge regarded every one with a delighted smile. He looked so irresistibly pleasant, in a word, that three or four good-humoured fellows said, "Good morning, sir! A merry Christmas to you!" And Scrooge said often afterwards, that of all the blithe sounds he had ever heard, those were the blithest in his ears.

He had not gone far, when coming on towards him he beheld the portly gentleman, who had walked into his counting-house the day before and said, "Scrooge and Marley's, I believe?" It sent a pang across his heart to think how this old gentleman would look upon him when they met; but he knew what path lay straight before him, and he took it.

"My dear sir," said Scrooge, quickening his pace, and taking the old gentleman by both his hands. "How do you do? I hope you succeeded yesterday. It was very kind of you. A merry Christmas to you, sir!"

"Mr. Scrooge?"

"Yes," said Scrooge, "That is my name, and I fear it may not be pleasant to you. Allow me to ask your pardon. And will you have the goodness"—here Scrooge whispered in his ear.

"Lord bless me!" cried the gentleman, as if his breath were gone. "My dear Mr. Scrooge, are you serious?"

"If you please," said Scrooge. "Not a farthing[10] less. A great many back-payments are included in it, I assure you. Will you do me that favour?"

"My dear sir," said the other, shaking hands with him. "I don't know what to say to such munifi—"

"Don't say anything, please," retorted Scrooge. "Come and see me. Will you come and see me?"

9. *sticking-plaister.* Or sticking plaster, a small swatch of linen, silk, or other textured cloth, spread with an adhesive and some medication to close superficial wounds such as shaving cuts.

"Christmas Dinner." Etching by Robert Seymour, *The Book of Christmas* by Thomas K. Hervey, 1836. *Private collection.*

10. *a farthing.* A small coin worth only one quarter of a penny, a tiny amount of money.

"December." Etching by George Cruikshank, *The Comic Almanac*, 1835. *Courtesy Library of Congress.*

11. *Your uncle Scrooge.* He is obviously recalling how the plump sister while playing Yes and No at Fred's Christmas party in Stave 3 blurted out, "It's your Uncle Scro-o-o-o-oge!"

"Heads of the Family." Etching by Robert Seymour, *The Book of Christmas* by Thomas K. Hervey, 1836.
Private collection.

"I will!" cried the old gentleman. And it was clear he meant to do it.

"Thank 'ee," said Scrooge. "I am much obliged to you. I thank you fifty times. Bless you!"

He went to church, and walked about the streets, and watched the people hurrying to and fro, and patted children on the head, and questioned beggars, and looked down into the kitchens of houses, and up to the windows; and found that everything could yield him pleasure. He had never dreamed that any walk—that anything—could give him so much happiness. In the afternoon, he turned his steps towards his nephew's house.

He passed the door a dozen times, before he had the courage to go up and knock. But he made a dash, and did it:

"Is your master at home, my dear?" said Scrooge to the girl. Nice girl! Very.

"Yes, sir."

"Where is he, my love?" said Scrooge.

"He's in the dining-room, sir, along with mistress. I'll show you up stairs, if you please."

"Thank'ee. He knows me," said Scrooge, with his hand already on the dining-room lock. "I'll go in here, my dear."

He turned it gently, and sidled his face in, round the door. They were looking at the table (which was spread out in great array); for these young housekeepers are always nervous on such points, and like to see that everything is right.

"Fred!" said Scrooge

Dear heart alive, how his niece by marriage started! Scrooge had forgotten, for the moment about her sitting in the corner with the footstool, or he wouldn't have done it, on any account.

"Why bless my soul!" cried Fred, "who's that?"

"It's I. Your uncle Scrooge.[11] I have come to dinner. Will you let me in, Fred?"

Let him in! It is a mercy he didn't shake his arm off. He was at home in five minutes. Nothing could be heartier. His niece looked just the same. So did Topper when *he* came. So did the plump sister, when *she* came. So did every one when *they* came. Wonderful party, wonderful games, wonderful unanimity, won-der-ful happiness!

But he was early at the office next morning.[12] Oh he was early there. If he could only be there first, and catch Bob Cratchit coming late! That was the thing he had set his heart upon.

And he did it; yes he did! The clock struck nine. No Bob. A quarter past. No Bob. He was full eighteen minutes and a half, behind his time. Scrooge sat with his door wide open, that he might see him come into the Tank.

His hat was off, before he opened the door; his comforter too. He was on his stool in a jiffy; driving away with his pen, as if he were trying to overtake nine o'clock.

"Hallo!" growled Scrooge, in his accustomed voice as near as he could feign it. "What do you mean by coming here at this time of day?"

"I'm very sorry, sir," said Bob. "I *am* behind my time."

"You are?" repeated Scrooge. "Yes. I think you are. Step this way, if you please."

"It's only once a year, sir," pleaded Bob, appearing from the Tank. "It shall not be repeated. I was making rather merry yesterday, sir."

"Now, I'll tell you what, my friend," said Scrooge, "I am not going to stand this sort of thing any longer. And therefore," he continued, leaping from his stool, and giving Bob such a dig in the waistcoat[13] that he staggered back into the Tank again: "and therefore I am about to raise your salary!"

Bob trembled, and got a little nearer to the ruler. He had a momentary idea of knocking Scrooge down

12. *next morning.* Saint Stephen's Day, commonly called in England Boxing Day; it did not become a bank holiday until 1871. It is not celebrated in the United States. "The day after Christmas is termed Boxing Day," noted the New York *Commercial Advertiser* (January 22, 1868), "not because on that day the populace indulge to an unusual extent in practising the 'art of box,' or for any other purely pugilistic reason, but because the day is celebrated by donating servants the seasonable gifts known as Christmas Boxes." Henry Wood explained in *Change for the American Notes in Letters from London to New York* (London: Wiley and Putnam, 1843), "people go round for their Christmas boxes (or gifts), and housekeepers are in evil humour. The day is injudiciously chosen, for the gentleman of the house may be bilious from his yesterday's carouse . . . but the men of police and scavengers, parish clerks, bell-ringers, beadles, and all their tribe are on the wing for Christmas-boxes; frequent were the knocks at our hall-door, and not very brief the colloquies in the hall" (p. 177). It seems especially appropriate that on the day when employers are expected to reward the help for a year's job well done that Scrooge should raise Bob's salary.

13. *in the waistcoat.* Meaning in the gut or ribs; Dickens must be speaking euphemistically, for Bob Cratchit could hardly have afforded a waistcoat, and John Leech does not show him in one. "Let's not forget that Victorians did not like to mention the parts of the body," noted Georges Hermet in his 1989 Presses Pocket edition (p. 212). Mr. Dombey strikes the Game Chicken, a prizefighter, in Chapter 31 of *Dombey and Son* (1848), as being "as stiff as a cove as ever he see, but that it is within the resources of Science to double him up, with one blow to the waistcoat."

14. *a strait-waistcoat.* A straitjacket, used in subduing violent prisoners and patients by binding their arms and bodies. "Ve thought ve should ha' been obliged to straightvesit him last night," Sam Weller refers to desperate Mr. Winkle in Chapter 39 of *The Pickwick Papers* (1837), "he's been a-ravin' all day." Likewise, when Bet "went off mad, screaming and raving and beating her head against the boards" after viewing her friend Nancy's body in Chapter 50 of *Oliver Twist* (1838), "they put a straight-weskit on her and took her away to the hospital."

15. *smoking bishop.* This Christmas punch, was a popular tavern drink in the eighteenth century. Dr. Johnson too was fond of it and defined it in his dictionary as "a cant word for a mixture of wine, oranges and sugar." E. Gordon Browne explained in his 1907 edition that this drink is "made by

"The Christmas Bowl." Preliminary pencil and wash drawing by John Leech, 1843. *Courtesy Houghton Library, Harvard University.*

with it; holding him; and calling to the people in the court for help and a strait-waistcoat.[14]

"A merry Christmas, Bob!" said Scrooge, with an earnestness that could not be mistaken, as he clapped him on the back. "A merrier Christmas, Bob, my good fellow, than I have given you, for many a year! I'll raise your salary, and endeavour to assist your struggling family, and we will discuss your affairs this very afternoon, over a Christmas bowl of smoking bishop,[15] Bob! Make up the fires, and buy another coal-scuttle[16] before you dot another i, Bob Cratchit!"

Scrooge was better than his word.[17] He did it all, and infinitely more; and to Tiny Tim, who did NOT die, he was a second father.[18] He became as good a friend, as good a master, and as good a man, as the good old city knew, or any other good old city, town, or borough, in the good old world. Some people laughed to see the alteration in him,[19] but he let them laugh, and little

pouring red wine [often port], either hot or cold, upon ripe bitter oranges. The liquor is heated or 'mulled' in a vessel with a long funnel, which could be pushed far down into the fire. Sugar and spice [chiefly cloves, star anise, and cinnamon] are added according to taste. It is sometimes called 'purple wine,' and received the name 'Bishop' from its colour." A one-eyed man and a landlord share a bowl of bishop in Chapter 49 of *The Pickwick Papers* (1837), as does Tim Linkinwater in Chapter 37 of *Nicholas Nickleby* (1839).

16. *another coal-scuttle.* Here, another shovelful of coal; "a second coal-scuttle" in the 1867 Ticknor and Fields Public Reading edition.

17. *Scrooge was better than his word.* Dickens hinted at the miser's change of heart in a letter to his friend W. H. Wills on September 16, 1855: "Scrooge is delighted to find that Bob Cratchit is enjoying his holiday in such a delightful situation; and he says (with that warmth of that nature which has distinguished him since his conversion) 'Make the most of it, Bob; make the most of it!' " (p. 704).

18. *and to Tiny Tim, who did NOT die, he was a second father.* This statement was an afterthought, for it does not appear in the manuscript. Dickens obviously realized when going over the galley proofs that he must reassure his readers that the shadow of the vacant seat mentioned by the Ghost of Christmas Present was now gone and that the reformed Scrooge was able to save at least one child from the fate of the demons Ignorance and Want.

19. *Some people laughed to see the alteration in him.* Among them James Manus McCaffery in "A Kind Word for Ebenezer"

(*Mensa Bulletin*, December 1981). He could not understand why Scrooge "provokes indignant anger by telling the truth, and corrosive envy by being rich" (p. 18). All he did was provide Bob Cratchit with "this good job with a respected man of business whose name was synonymous with financial integrity, and whose signature was 'good upon 'Change, for anything he chose to put his hand to." McCaffery mocked what he thought were the lessons of *A Christmas Carol*, "Spend your money now! Don't work hard! Don't save your money! Have a good time today and don't worry about tomorrow!" (p. 20). He offered an exaggerated vision of the consequences of Scrooge's indiscriminating beneficence:

Scrooge's frenzied orgy of spending ceased only when the crazed, old man was locked up in a dark, dank cell in debtor's prison—a cell he shared with Bob, who had given Scrooge all his savings, and all that he could borrow, to get his former employer out of gaol. Of course, Scrooge promptly lavished this money on the mob that swarmed around him, even in prison, as long as he had a penny left to squander. Bob could not pay off these loans, since nobody would now hire a man so closely connected with a notorious bankrupt. Therefore, Bob's sons, including Tiny Tim, were forced to become chimney sweeps, the only jobs they could get, and soon died painful deaths from various pulmonary diseases aggravated by malnutrition (no more roast goose for them from the bounteous wage paid by old Scrooge). Mrs. Cratchit and the girls, driven by hunger, ended their days as diseased streetwalkers of the London slums. On a larger scale, the collapse of Scrooge and Marley caused a minor financial panic resulting in the failure of dozens of other firms— throwing hundreds out of work and into penury and possible starvation. (p. 20)

20. *He had no further intercourse.* Dickens added "in that respect" in the 1867 Ticknor and Fields Public Reading edition.

21. *the Total Abstinence Principle.* Here Dickens is making a pun on alcoholic spirits and supernatural spirits. Teetotalers, in accordance with the Total Abstinence Principle, took a pledge to abstain from all intoxicating beverages. Gabriel Grub, the prototype for Scrooge, made such a vow himself on his conversion at the end of "The Story of the Goblins Who Stole a Sexton," in Chapter 29 of *The Pickwick Papers* (1837). Dickens received considerable criticism on both sides of the Atlantic for his frequent mention of the convivial consumption of alcohol in his novels. (It has been estimated that *The Pickwick Papers* alone contains 295 references to intoxicating beverages.) "All his people have a love of liquor," complained *The Northern Monthly Magazine* (January 1868) in "Some Plain Words Concerning Mr. Charles Dickens"; "his happy scenes, in the private home circle or in the tavern, are odorous with hot rum and sugar; and there was nothing in American inventions or institutions that elicited from his such high praise as the sherry cobblers" (p. 244).

A Christmas Carol too received its share of criticism for its numerous references to liquor. While acknowledging that some temperance advocates "have been productive of unspeakable good amongst Drunkards," Dickens assured one offended woman in a letter on March 25, 1847, "I have no doubt whatever that the warm stuff in the jug at Bob Cratchit's Christmas dinner, had a very pleasant effect on the simple party. I am certain that if I had been at Mr. Fezziwig's ball, I should have taken a little Negus—and possibly not a little beer—and been none the worst for it, in heart or head. I am very sure that working people of this country have not too many household enjoyments; and I

heeded them; for he was wise enough to know that nothing ever happened on this globe, for good, at which some people did not have their fill of laughter in the outset; and knowing that such as these would be blind anyway, he thought it quite as well that they should wrinkle up their eyes in grins, as have the malady in less attractive forms. His own heart laughed: and that was quite enough for him.

He had no further intercourse[20] with Spirits, but lived upon the Total Abstinence Principle,[21] ever afterwards; and it was always said of him, that he knew how to keep Christmas well, if any man alive possessed the knowledge. May that be truly said of us, and all of us! And so, as Tiny Tim observed, God Bless Us, Every One!

THE END.

"and so, as Tiny Tim observed, God Bless Us Every one!"

Charles Dickens

London
Fifteenth March 1844.

Autograph of Charles Dickens with quote from *A Christmas Carol*, March 15, 1844. *Courtesy Pierpont Morgan Library.*

could not, in my fancy, or in actual deed, deprive them of this one when it is innocently shared. Neither do I see why I should deny it to myself." He reminded this pious lady "of a certain Marriage in Galilee [John 2], and of a certain supper where a cup was filled with Wine and not with water [Mark 14]" (pp. 45–46).

Dickens "enjoyed all the attendant paraphernalia of Christmas, particularly the jovial drinks which attend the season!" reported Percy Fitzgerald in *The Life of Charles Dickens* (vol. 1, 1905). "To hear him talk of the steaming bowl of punch, with apples 'bobbing about' merrily, of the Garrick matchless gin-punch particularly, and the anticipating zest and relish with which he compounded these mixtures, one would fancy him quaffing many a tumbler. But alas! how often had it been noted to the general surprise, that his whole enjoyment was in the romantic association! Never was there a more abstemious bibber" (pp. 202–3). James T. Fields confirmed this observation in *Yesterdays with Authors* (Boston: James R. Osgood, 1872), noting that Dickens "liked to dilate in imagination over the brewing of a bowl of punch, but I always noticed that when the punch was ready, he drank less of it than any one who might be present. It was the sentiment of the thing, and not the thing itself, that engaged his attention" (p. 167).

Song sheet cover of "God Bless Us Every One."
Words by George Cooper and music by J. R. Thomas, 1868.
Courtesy Music Division, Free Library of Philadelphia.

INTRODUCTION TO

𝔄 Christmas Carol. In Four Staves.

(1 8 6 7)

Charles Dickens was not content with just being the greatest English novelist of his time. He craved adulation in other directions. From the age of seven, when he was taken into London to one of the Christmas pantomimes, Dickens was fascinated with the theater. His earliest literary effort, now lost, was a tragedy, *Misnar, the Sultan of India*, taken from the Reverend James Ridley's *Tales of the Genii* (1764) and written at age nine. A cousin made and painted a toy theater for him and he and his friends put on *The Dog of Montargis, Cherry and the Fair Star*, and best of all, *The Miller and His Men*. He was also clever at telling stories and singing comic songs and his proud father put his child phenomenon on tables and chairs to show off his histrionic and musical talents. In 1832, he found the courage to arrange an audition at the Lyceum Theatre. Had he not fallen ill with a bad cold that inflamed his face, England might have lost one of its greatest literary men to the stage. That same year, an uncle hired him to join the reporting staff of the London *True Sun*, and his literary career was on its way. The aspiring actor had written the stage manager at the Lyceum that "I believed I had a strong perception of character and oddity, and a natural power of reproducing in my own person what I observed in others."[1] These very qualities proved to be advantageous in his pursuit of fiction. The novelist harbored ambitions of being a playwright; but like Henry James, Dickens, despite his flair for melodramatic plot, memorable characters, and lively dialogue, never wrote a memorable play. He was at heart a storyteller, not a dramatist.

Charles Dickens was an incredibly energetic and ambitious individual, and he could not possibly devote all of his time to writing. "He was haunted at times," his son Henry said, "by a dread of failure, or of a sudden waning of his imaginative powers."[2] There seemed to be no evidence of the latter as he steadily published the masterpieces of his mature years, *David Copperfield* (1850), *Bleak House* (1853), *Hard Times* (1854), and *Little Dorrit* (1857). He also found time to issue three volumes of *A Child's History of England* (1852–54). He was editor of one of the most popular magazines of the day, *Household Words*. He kept up a voluminous correspondence and developed into a powerful and much sought after after-dinner speaker. He threw the weight of his vast reputation behind many charitable causes.

He also kept his interest in the stage alive through amateur productions. This was the era of family theatricals, when grown-ups and children enticed their friends and associates to join them in household entertainments. In addition to members of his family, Dickens over the years recruited friends from literature. Dickens learned his craft so well that the London *Times* (April 16, 1858) could declare that he was "an amateur actor of such proficiency that he is hardly to be termed an amateur at all."

In his youth he appeared in forgotten farces that he not only produced, directed, and stage-managed but for which he also designed the scenery and played accordion in the band. Somehow Dickens found time during his American visit to stage-manage and play in four farces in private theatricals to benefit a local charity in Montreal at the end of May 1842. After his return from a stay in Italy in 1845, he began in earnest on a private production of Ben Jonson's *Every Man in His Humour* set for

---

[1] Quoted in a letter to John Forster of late 1844 or early 1845 (*The Letters of Charles Dickens*, edited by Madeline House and others, 12 vols. [Oxford: Clarendon Press, 1965–2002], p. 244. Unless otherwise indicated, all subsequent citations of Dickens' and his family's correspondence are from this source and are given within the text by date and page number only).

[2] Henry Fielding Dickens, "A Chat about Charles Dickens," *Harper's Monthly Magazine*, July 1914, p. 187.

Charles Dickens as Bobadil and John Leech as Master Matthew in
Every Man in His Humour.
Wood engravings by Kenny Meadows,
The Illustrated London News, November 22, 1845.
Courtesy Library of Congress.

September 20. The company was flooded with invitations for another performance, including one from Prince Albert, so they agreed to give
another one for charity on November 15, with the prince; the dukes of
Wellington, Cambridge, and Devonshire; Baron de Rothschilde; and
Lord Melbourne all in attendance. "Professional performers . . . would do
well to take a lesson from these tyros," recommended *The Illustrated London News* (November 22). "The play could not have been so *intelligently*
performed by any dramatic company now in London." And "the best performance of the night" was Dickens as Captain Bobadil (p. 329).

Dickens revived *Every Man in His Humour* in 1848, to alternate with
The Merry Wives of Windsor, with himself as Shallow, in a series of charity performances to help (among other things) to purchase William
Shakespeare's house at Stratford-upon-Avon for the nation. The success
of these plays in London was immense; they even drew the queen and the

prince consort to *Every Man in His Humour* on May 17. Subsequent performances of this troupe funded "The Amateur Company Guild of Literature & Art," loosely organized by Dickens and Edward Bulwer-Lytton in 1850 to provide financial support to needy artists and writers. Bulwer-Lytton supplied a new five-act comedy, *Not So Bad As We Seem*, which was performed on the Queen's Night of May 16, 1851. Dickens and Mark Lemon provided a clever afterpiece, *Mr. Nightingale's Diary*, in which the writer showed off his versatility as an actor in taking six parts: lawyer, waiter, walker, hypochondriac, old woman, and old sexton.

When the family moved to Tavistock House in Bloomsbury in 1851, Dickens readily helped with the Twelfth Night plays his children put on with their friends. It was remarkable that Dickens was able to stage such marvels in so small a space as the schoolroom. "*Private* theatricals in one sense they were," admitted one of the players, the Reverend Canon Alfred Ainger, in *Macmillan's Magazine* (January 1872); "but the size and the character of the audiences which they brought together placed them in a different category from the entertainments which commonly bear that name." Ainger recalled William Makepeace Thackeray, "towering in bodily form above the crowd, even as he towered in genius above them all, save only one"; and John Leech, "with his frank and manly beauty" (p. 206). Dickens went at these amateur showcases with a fierceness he applied to all his work. It seemed to his son Charley (as he recalled in *The North American Review*, May 1895) that his father was "doing everybody's work, and more, in the course of preparation and rehearsal. He revised and adapted the plays, selected and arranged the music, chose and altered the costumes, wrote the new incidental songs, invented all the stage business, taught everybody his or her part, and was, in fact, everywhere and everything at once" (p. 531).

In 1855, Wilkie Collins wrote an original melodrama, *The Lighthouse*, for the Tavistock House players, and Dickens readily took the role of the old lighthouse keeper, Aaron Gurnock. He also composed the play's poetic prologue and supplied "The Song of the Wreck." After several private performances in Tavistock House in June, the play was moved for one charity engagement on July 10. "He was, indeed, a born actor," said his son Charley, "and no line of character that I ever saw him essay came amiss to him. . . . That he brought to his acting the same earnestness and energy that he gave to everything else is of course true, but no amount of work could have produced the same result if the power had not been there, strongly, unusually strongly, developed" (p. 530).

Scene from *The Frozen Deep*. Wood engraving,
The Illustrated London News, January 17, 1857.
Courtesy Library of Congress.

Dickens threw himself into these amateur productions very intensely, demanding, for example, that the fight in *The Lighthouse* be so realistically staged that he went at it like a prizefighter and left his thespian adversaries black and blue. He was so impressive in the part that a former actress gushed, "Oh, Mr. Dickens, what a pity it is you can do anything else!"[3]

Even more ambitious was his performance in a new Twelfth Night play for 1857, Collins' three-act melodrama *The Frozen Deep*. Dickens again worked closely with Collins, providing the prologue, suggesting elements of the plot, and rewriting dialogue. It was while playing Richard Wardour, a man who dies saving the life of the rival who stole his sweetheart, that the idea of *A Tale of Two Cities* (1859) came to him.

When his good friend Douglas Jerrold died in June, Dickens

[3.] Elizabeth Yates quoted in a letter to Angela Georgina Burdett-Coutts, June 19, 1855 (*Letters*, p. 650).

arranged to have *The Frozen Deep* performed in London and Manchester to benefit the widow and family. Her Majesty was eager to see it, and a command performance was arranged on July 4. She was so touched by his portrayal that she requested Dickens come to her during the interval so that she might express her appreciation for his histrionic talent. But he begged to be excused for he was already in his costume and makeup for the subsequent farce and did not wish to be presented to the queen in any dress but his own. It was not until thirteen years later that she could personally thank him for the entertainment.

"To say that his acting was amateurish is to depreciate it in view of a professional actor, but it is not necessarily to disparage it," explained Canon Ainger in *Macmillan's Magazine*; "it is only another way of saying that he was not of the stage, stagey" (pp. 209–10). A stage carpenter at the Haymarket Theatre was so impressed with his acting that he said, "Ah, Mr. Dickens, it was a sad loss to the public when you took to writing."[4] The writer cultivated the friendship of professional actors, including William Macready, perhaps the greatest Shakespearean actor of his day, as well as John Lawrence Toole, who played among other Dickens characters Bob Cratchit in the 1859 revival of *A Christmas Carol* at the Adelphi. "He once told me he had at one time almost made up his mind to be an actor," Toole recalled. "I said it was a good thing for some of us and a splendid thing for literature that he changed his mind."[5]

Although his amateur acting ended with *The Frozen Deep*, Dickens was soon engaged in a second career as a public reader. The first of his works to be read before an audience was *The Chimes*. He was so proud of what he had accomplished in that little book that he asked Forster to host a small party in his rooms in Lincoln's Inn Fields, London, so he might read it on the night of December 3, 1844. "I have tried to strike a blow upon that part of the brass countenance of Wicked Cant, where such a compliment is sorely needed at this time," he had warned Douglas Jerrold in a letter on November 16. "And I trust that the result of my training is at least the exhibition of a strong desire to make it a staggerer. If *you* should think at the end of the four rounds (there are no more) that the said Cant, in the language of *Bell's Life* [*in London*],

4. Quoted in Charles Dickens Jr., "Reminiscences of My Father," *Windsor Magazine*, Christmas Supplement 1934, p. 14.

5. *Reminiscences of J. L. Toole*, edited by Joseph Hatton, vol. 1 (London: Hurdst and Blackett, 1889), p. 63. Dickens also told Toole that he had him in mind to play Joe Gargery while he was writing *Great Expectations* (1861).

Charles Dickens reading *The Chimes* to his friends.
Drawing by Daniel Maclise, 1844.
Courtesy Library of Congress.

'comes up piping,' I shall be very much the better for it" (p. 218). He came out like a champion. "There was not a dry eye in the house," the artist Daniel Maclise reported to Catherine Dickens on December 8. "We should borrow the high language of the minor theater and even then not do the effect justice—shrieks of laughter—there were indeed—and floods of tears as a relief to them—I do not think that there ever was such a triumphant hour for Charles" (p. 317, note 2). Dickens repeated the performance to another audience on December 5 and proudly wrote his wife, "If you had seen Macready last night—undisguisedly sobbing, and crying on the sofa, as I read—you would have felt (as I did) what a thing it is to have Power" (p. 235).

The following summer, Dickens agreed to give another reading from his works at the British consulate in Genoa. Catherine Dickens informed the consul, Timothy Yeats-Brown, in a letter that her husband "has made up his mind to read the *Christmas Carol through*, instead of any detached pieces from his other works" (p. 317). Apparently, he was expecting only a small family group. He was alarmed, as he wrote Yeats-Brown on June 3, to learn that the consul had invited "guests whom I have never seen or heard of in my life. . . . I have an invincible repugnance to that kind of exhibition which an otherwise pleasant recreation becomes under such circumstances" (p. 317). So he reluctantly asked to be excused from the event. It eventually did come off, Dickens being so nervous he asked that no one sit behind him.[6]

He did read aloud the first part of *Dombey and Son* to a select audience prior to publication, in September 1846, and the second part on October 10. "I was thinking the other day," he wrote Forster on October 11, 1846, "that in these days of lecturings and readings, a great deal of money might possibly be made . . . by one's having Readings of one's own work. It would be an *odd* thing. I think it would take immensely" (p. 631). But Forster did not approve of the idea of a distinguished man of letters making a public spectacle of himself in this manner for money.

Instead, Dickens got practice by giving occasional Charity Readings. On January 6, 1853, the working men of Birmingham presented the famous and beloved novelist with a silver-gilt salver and a diamond ring, as a testimony of their great admiration and esteem for his good works. He was truly touched by their generous gesture. He explained in his acceptance speech, "I have tried to hold up to admiration their fortitude, patience, gentleness, the reasonableness of their nature, so accessible to persuasion, and their extraordinary goodness one towards another."[7] He promised to do something for the new Birmingham and Midland Institute and agreed to return at Christmastime to read *A Christmas Carol* on December 27 and 30. The committee wanted him to read *The Cricket on the Health* as well on December 29. He made one request in a letter of August 27, that on the final night, "I shall read the *Carol* to two thousand working people—stipulating that they shall have that night entirely to themselves" (p. 135).

A Christmas Carol was the perfect choice for the occasion. "The little book itself is well fitted for public reading," observed the London *Globe and Traveller* (April 16, 1858); "it is full of dramatic interest, and is very varied—from its sketches of city life to its pictures of the very poor—from the middle-class festivity at Scrooge's nephew's to the humble, yet delightful home of the poor clerk—from the incidental passages

[6.] See Francis Yeats-Brown, "Dickens in Genoa," *The Spectator*, September 22, 1928, p. 358.

[7.] *The Speeches of Charles Dickens*, edited by Kenneth J. Fielding (Oxford: Clarendon Press, 1960), p. 155. All subsequent quotations from Dickens' speeches are also from this book.

of pure fun and oddity to the few touching words with which Tiny Tim is occasionally introduced." The Manchester *Guardian* (October 25, 1858) added, "The *Carol* is a story which never fails to excite the sympathies and quicken the beneficent resolves of those who read it."

He cut up a copy of the 1849 twelfth edition of *A Christmas Carol* to use as a prompt book (now in the Berg Collection in the New York Public Library). He then mounted the pages on large white sheets of paper, providing wide margins suitable for voluminous interpolations and revisions, if need be. He had it rebound in three quarter red morocco and the title stamped in gold on the front cover. He followed the same pattern with other books he later read from the platform. Apparently, the story as read in Birmingham remained largely as written, with few deletions. Some changes in the text were no more than matters of punctuation and the removal of now gratuitous or redundant phrases such as "he said," "she said." He had promised it would last two hours, with a ten-minute intermission: it took a little over three hours. No one seemed bored for a second. "Everybody was charmed by the way in which the story was told," reported the *Birmingham Journal* (December 28, 1853). "How Mr. Dickens twirled his mustache, or played with his paper knife, or laid down his book, and leant forward confidently, or twinkled his eyes as if he enjoyed the whole affair immensely!"

He was not happy with the reading of *The Cricket on the Hearth*, but he was proud of the third night and its audience of laborers. They all rose up and cheered him when he appeared. The reading went off brilliantly. "They lost nothing," he wrote a friend on January 13, 1854, "misinterpreted nothing, followed everything closely, laughed and cried with most delightful earnestness, and animated me to that extent that I felt as if we were all bodily going up into the clouds together" (p. 244). His friend and colleague W. H. Wills predicted from Birmingham, "If Dickens does turn Reader he will make another fortune. He will never offer to do so of course. But if they *will* have him he will do it, he told me today."[8]

He repeated the experiment the following December in a series of provincial Charity Readings of *A Christmas Carol* in Reading, Sherborne, and Bradford. "It was a triumph of elocutionary power," reported the *Reading Mercury, Oxford Gazette, Newbury Herald, and Berks County Paper* on December 23, 1854; "it is, after all, the best tribute we can pay to the genius of Mr. Dickens, when we say that he was listened

---

[8.] Quoted in Eliza Priestley, *The Story of a Lifetime* (London: Kegan Paul, 1908), p. 215.

to with unabated attention, and with increasing admiration and delight for nearly three hours. Never was there a better story, better told, or one with a moral so sure of hearty response from every truly Christian heart." Dickens too was pleased. "Wonderful audiences," he bragged in a letter on January 3, 1855, after finishing up in Bradford; "the number at the last place, 3,700! And yet, but for the noise of their laughing and cheering, they 'went' like one man" (p. 495). He was especially touched, as he wrote a friend on December 23, 1855, when the audience in Sheffield responded to the phrase "And to Tiny Tim who did *not* die" "with a most prodigious shout and roll of thunder" (p. 771). "It was not a mere reading of the tale," said *The Sheffield Times* (December 29, 1855). "To a certain modified extent, all the characters in the story were *acted*; and in voice and gesture their peculiarities were admirably represented and sustained throughout."

All sorts of organizations now wanted him to read for them. He bragged to Forster on September 16, 1855, that within a fortnight he had had to turn down thirty requests from deserving institutions in England, Scotland, and Ireland. All of his Charity Readings between 1853 and 1858, except that one night of *The Cricket on the Hearth* in Birmingham, were of *A Christmas Carol* around Christmastime. "Readings by Mr. Charles Dickens are now looked for as a matter of course at this season of the year," declared the London *Daily News* on January 16, 1857, "and were they not forthcoming, there is no doubt that a large section of the public would be grievously disappointed."

In June 1857, Dickens helped organize other benefits for the Jerrold Fund besides *The Frozen Deep*. He got Thackeray to lecture the first night, and Dickens took the stage the second with *A Christmas Carol*, on June 30. It was also his London début as a public reader. Everyone wanted to hear him. *The Times* reported the day after that "at an early hour the hall was crammed with an audience anxious to become acquainted with the most popular of living authors in a new capacity. Indeed, so large was the number sent away from the doors, through want of room, that long before the assembly had dispersed placards were affixed in various parts of the building . . . announcing a repetition of the 'reading' at the same place on Friday, the 24th inst." It drew a crowd of over two thousand. "To many occupants in the shilling seats," said *The Times*, "Charles Dickens was familiar as a friendly name, and they were delighted to see him a visible reality."

He did not disappoint them. "Mr. Dickens," said the *Globe and Trav-*

eller on the same day, "is an admirable elocutionist, his utterance is perfectly clear and distinct, and his modulation adjusts itself to the character of the scene with happy flexibility and dramatic effect." That day's *Times* said the reader "held the sympathies of his hearers as firmly as one might grasp a tangible object. The very aspect of that crowd, composed of the most various classes, hanging on the utterance of one man, was in itself an imposing spectacle." The *Daily News* (also July 1) reported that "from first to last the audience hung upon the reader's every word; a more appreciative set of people we have never seen. Not a point was lost, not a joke fell flat; not one noble or touching idea (and how many there are of these in the *Carol* the world at large well knows) but received its due meed of applause and sympathy." This response was so loud and vigorous that Dickens was compelled to return to the platform more than once. "The St. Martin's Hall audience was, I must confess, a very extraordinary thing," he readily reported to Macready on July 13. "The two thousand and odd people were like one, and their enthusiasm was something awful" (p. 377).

On April 15, 1858, Dickens gave another Charity Reading of *A Christmas Carol*, this time for the benefit of the Hospital for Sick Children on Great Ormond Street, London. *The Times* reported the next day, "A 'reading' by Mr. Dickens is something altogether *sui generis*, a happy blending of the narrative and dramatic style, by which the author gives additional colouring to his already highly elaborated work, and astonishes the auditor by revelations of meaning that had escaped the solitary student." Then *The Times* mentioned "the announcement that the benevolent 'reader' is at last about to employ his elocutionary talents for his own advantage."

Dickens was being bombarded with lucrative requests to read all over the United Kingdom. Also, he had just purchased Gad's Hill and needed the money. He asked Forster in a letter on September 5, 1857, "What do you think of my paying for this place, by reviving that old idea of some Readings from my books? I am very strongly tempted" (p. 435). But Forster violently opposed the notion of any writer, especially the Inimitable Boz, doing something so vulgar as to read for cash. Most people thought he was being paid anyway. He said that "out of the twenty or five-and-twenty letters a week that I get about Readings, twenty will ask at what price, or on what terms, it can be done. The only exceptions, in truth, are when the correspondent is a clergyman, or a banker, or the member for the place in question" (p. 534).

Dickens needed some serious diversion. Touring through the countryside in amateur theatricals or giving Public Readings had provided a welcome escape from his domestic troubles. Life with Catherine in Tavistock House had become intolerable. She was clumsy and accident-prone, she neglected the children and the household, he thought. She annoyed him terribly. "My poor mother was afraid of my father," Kate Dickens insisted. "She was never allowed to express an opinion—never allowed to say what she felt."[9] She did object to his flirtations with other women, however innocent; more than once she threatened to leave him.

He explained to Baroness Burdett-Coutts in a letter of May 9, 1858, "that no two people were ever created, with such an impossibility of interest, sympathy, confidence, sentiment, tender union of any kind between them, as there is between my wife and me. It is an immense misfortune to her—it is an immense misfortune to me—but Nature has put an insurmountable barrier between us, which never in this world can be thrown down" (p. 558). He cruelly wrote to Burdett-Coutts on August 23, 1858, that his wife "does not—and she never did—care for the children; and the children do not—and they never did—care for her. . . . She has always disconcerted them; they have always disconcerted her; and she is glad to be rid of them, and they are glad to be rid of her" (p. 632). Kate Dickens insisted, however, "There was nothing wrong with my mother; she had her faults, of course, as we all have—but she was a sweet, kind, peace-loving woman, a lady—a lady born" (pp. 22–23). Dickens did admit to possessing "the many impulsive faults which often belong to my impulsive way of life and exercise of fancy; but I am very patient and considerate at heart, and would have beaten out a path to a better journey's end than we have come to, if I could" (p. 558).

Also, at forty-six, Charles Dickens had become infatuated with an eighteen-year-old actress, Ellen Lawless Ternan (1839–1914), who had performed with him in *The Frozen Deep*. What so attracted her to him may never be known. He did not specifically discuss her in his letters, and no correspondence between the two survive. Although he traveled with her and her mother and set her and her sister up in an apartment off Oxford Street, and later she and her family moved to a house off the Hampstead Road, Dickens suppressed all details of their relationship.

---

9. Quoted in Gladys Storey, *Dickens and Daughter* (London: Frederick Muller, 1939), p. 219. All subsequent quotations of Kate Dickens are also from this book.

He publicly mentioned Ellen Ternan only once, in his will, which left the actress £1,000, with no further explanation.

In 1857, Dickens instructed his servants that the marital bedroom must be cut in half with a partition put in between: husband and wife would no longer be sharing the same bed. While he showed infinite concern for the poor and neglected of the world, he was less than charitable to the woman who had stood by him for twenty-two years and had borne him ten children. "With such an imaginative disposition it is not to be wondered at that his nature was mercurial," admitted his son Henry Fielding Dickens. "He had strange fits of depression from time to time, but his vitality was extraordinary, and, except in those rare intervals, his animal spirits and the brightness of his nature were delightful to see."[10] By chance, a bracelet intended for Miss Ternan was sent to Mrs. Dickens, and she accused her husband of taking a mistress. Furious, he denied it and demanded that she call on the actress and her mother; no matter how humiliating this request was for her, Catherine went and then complained to her parents. Her mother told her to leave him at once and seek a separation.

Reconciliation was now impossible. "Quite dismiss from your mind any reference whatever to present circumstances at home," he instructed Forster on March 30, 1858. "Nothing can put *them* right, until we are dead and buried and risen. It is not, with me, a matter of will, or trial, or sufferance, or good humour, or making the best of it, or making the worst of it, any longer. It is all despairingly over" (p. 539). But divorce, of course, was out of the question for the famous editor of *Household Words*, which promoted the domestic virtues of the Victorian family. With Forster acting as his representative and Mark Lemon of *Punch* hers, Dickens agreed to provide his wife with a house of her own and an annual income of £600. Their oldest son, Charley, went to live with her, but her sister Georgina remained behind to look after his home. She had joined the household in 1842, at fifteen, to help her sister; and Dickens and the children had come to love and rely on her, rather than Catherine, to look after them. "When the separation took place," insisted their son Alfred Tennyson Dickens, also speaking for Charley, "it made no difference in our feelings toward them: we their children always loved them both equally, having free intercourse with both, as of old: while not one

10. Henry Fielding Dickens, "A Chat about Charles Dickens," p. 187.

word on the subject ever passed from the lips of either father or mother. Of the causes which led to this unfortunate event, we know no more than the rest of the world. Our dear mother has suffered very much."[11]

His in-laws began spreading vicious rumors that Ternan was his mistress, that she might even be bearing his child. Dickens responded to these "fabulous stories and unaccountable statements" by publishing a public statement in *Household Words* on June 2, 1858. "Some domestic trouble of mine, of long-standing, on which I will make no further remark than it claims to be respected, as being of a sacredly private nature," he clumsily tried to explain, "has lately been brought to an arrangement, which involves no anger or ill-will of any kind." He insisted that his children had a thorough knowledge of the matter and that it had been forgotten by all those it concerned. Nevertheless, the trouble caused "misrepresentations, most grossly false, most monstrous, and most cruel—involving, not only me, but innocent persons dear to my heart, and innocent persons of whom I have no knowledge, if, indeed, they have any existence." He then accused anyone daring to repeat "the lately whispered rumors" of lying "as willfully and as foully as it is possible for any false witness to lie, before Heaven and earth."

The statement failed to squelch the gossip. On the contrary, it merely baffled the public and made everyone more eager to know what the matter was all about. "Now really we should be very much obliged to anybody who will inform us—what is all this about?" wondered *The Critic* (June 12, 1858). "What are the 'misrepresentations'? What the 'slanders'? What the precise nature of the 'unwholesome air'?" *The Critic* questioned the wisdom in inscribing the rumors "upon the tablets of the press, upon the pages of *Household Words*; and, what is worse, he has done it so vaguely, and with such suggestiveness of indefinite vastness, that the imaginations of men will create phantoms ten times more horrible than any that have as yet been conjured up, and he will be compelled, for his own sake, to be more explicit" (p. 287). He would have done better for himself and all parties had he said nothing. G. W. Reynolds called this "Personal" in *Reynold's Weekly News* (June 20) "one of the most ill-advised things that we have ever known, . . . a palpable and, perhaps, irremedial blunder."

11. *Dickens: Interviews and Recollections*, edited by Philip Collins, vol. 1 (London: Macmillan, 1981), p. 156.

Rumors of all sorts spread everywhere. "All London, you must know," wrote a correspondent on June 8 to *The New York Times* (June 21, 1858), "had for some time been rife with legends concerning Dickens and an actress, with whom it was at last affirmed that the author . . . had eloped to Bologne." It also mentioned "a story that Mr. Dickens means to go on the stage," no doubt referring to his proposed Public Readings. *The Scotsman* (June 12) said that "the name of a young lady on the stage has been mixed up with the matter—most cruelly and untruly." Others said he was in love with Georgina, then tantamount to incest. Reynolds reported in his *Weekly News* (June 13), "The names of a female relative, and of a professional young lady, have both been, of late, so freely and intimately associated with that of Mr. Dickens, as to excite suspicion and surprise in the minds of those who had hitherto looked upon the popular novelist as a very Joseph in all that regards morality, chastity, and decorum."

Dickens called these charges libel and considered taking legal action. "The Charles Dickens *scandalum magnatum* rolls along the highways and byways of public conversation and gathers as it rolls," Reynolds persisted on June 20. "He has told too much, or else too little; and what with (wordy) incontinence on the one hand, and ill-considered reticence on the other, he is in danger of having divers most ugly interpretations put upon his explanation." He further accused Dickens in his "Personal" of having exposed Mrs. Dickens "to all sorts of evil surmises."

Dickens refused to keep still. He gave his business manager a letter with permission "to show, to any one who wishes to do me right, or to any one who may have been misled into doing me wrong." He protested any mention of "the name of a young lady for whom I have a great attachment and regard" in reference to his marital troubles. "I will not repeat her name—I honor it too much," he said. "Upon my soul and honor, there is not on this earth a more virtuous and spotless creature than that young lady. I know her to be innocent and pure as my own dear daughters." He reiterated that he and Catherine "are, in all respects, of character and temperament, wonderfully unsuited to each other. I suppose that no two people, not vicious in themselves, ever were joined together, who had a greater difficulty in understanding one another, or who had less in common." He said that it was her decision that they part, "that she felt herself unfit for the life she had to lead as my wife and that she would be far better away." He also alluded to some "mental disorder under which she sometimes labours." His kind words for Georgina ("who has a higher claim . . . upon my affection, respect and gratitude than anybody in the world") merely inflamed further speculation on their relation-ship.[12]

Somehow the letter got into Horace Greeley's hands, and he pub-lished it in his *New-York Daily Tribune* on August 16. Then papers everywhere reprinted it. "Mr. Dickens appears to us in the light of a gen-tleman badly in need of good advice," Greeley scolded. "In a case of mat-rimonial abrasion, the public sympathy instinctively takes the side of the weaker party—that is, the wife—unless she persists in proving herself a vulgar shrew and virago . . . but where the wife maintains perfect silence and the husband issues bulletin after bulletin, he is sure to lose ground with each succeeding hour. One more uncalled for letter from Mr. D. will finish him." It was the last he said publicly about the matter.

"My father was like a madman when my mother left home," Kate recalled; "this affair brought out all that was worst—all that was weak-est in him. He did not care a damn what happened to any of us. Nothing could surpass the misery and unhappiness of our home" (p. 94). He broke with Thackeray when he learned that Thackeray had corrected someone at the Garrick Club, their club, that the Dickens matter concerned "an actress" and not Miss Georgina Hogarth. He broke with his publishers Bradbury and Evans when they refused to published his "Personal" from *Household Words* in *Punch*. He left *Household Words* to found a new journal, *All the Year Round*, on June 5, 1859; and he began a new novel, *A Tale of Two Cities* (1859), in its pages. He finally sold Tavistock House and moved into Gad's Hill permanently. In a final act of defiance to his past, he burned all of his letters in a great bonfire in the garden behind the house.

While some journals gleefully spread gossip of the separation, others had the courage to defend the famous writer. "We regret to hear that the vile poisonous calumny is continued to be whispered in reference to his domestic affairs, notwithstanding his own manly explanation," com-mented *Chambers's Exeter Journal* on August 7; "the reptiles who bite at his heel he can well despise. That he is the greatest author of modern times, all must admit. His teachings work wonders in his own day, and his name will go down to posterity with Shakespeare and Scott." American feminist Elizabeth Cady Stanton too made a point of mentioning the sep-

12. Quoted in K. J. Fielding, "Dickens and the Hogarth Scandal," *Nineteenth-Century Fic-tion*, June 1955, pp. 64–74.

aration, as an example in "a long list of failures in marriage" in her lecture on a woman's right to divorce at Apollo Hall in New York City, on May 17, 1870.[13]

With all these rumors buzzing, Dickens boldly gave his first professional reading on April 29, 1858, in St. Martin's Hall. He chose for his début *The Cricket on the Hearth*, followed by *The Chimes* on May 6, and *A Christmas Carol* on May 13. He did not refer to the separation, but he did feel he had to defend his decision to desert charitable work to read for profit. "I have satisfied myself that it can involve no possible compromise of the credit and independence of literature," he explained. "I have long held the opinion, and have long acted on the opinion that in these times whatever brings a public man and his public face to face, on terms of mutual confidence and respect, is a good thing."[14] He need not have worried: the first series of Public Readings was a resounding success. His public had not deserted him; and he returned for a series of six Thursday evening readings in May and June.

Undeterred by the scandal, Dickens proceeded on his first professional provincial tour through England, Scotland, and Ireland. He added "The Trial from *Pickwick*" (also billed as "Bardel and Pickwick") to his repertoire as well as "The Story of Little Dombey" from *Dombey and Son*, "Mrs. Gamp" from *Martin Chuzzlewit*, and "The Poor Traveller" and "Boots at the Holly-Tree Inn," both Christmas Stories from *Household Words*. Even bad publicity is good publicity. Likely many people who bought tickets were as interested in getting a glimpse of the notorious Mr. Dickens as they were in hearing the Inimitable Boz read from his works. Those used to Maclise's youthful portrait of the famous author of *The Pickwick Papers* and *Oliver Twist* were startled by his radical change in appearance. "His passionate love of fresh air and sunshine had changed his once pale skin to a florid complexion," said his daughter Kate; "his hair, formerly chestnut brown and flowing, became almost daily darker and was worn shorter; the beard and moustache he had allowed to grow, which was a mistake for not only did it cover his very mobile sensitive mouth but it seemed in a curious way to detract from the beauty of the upper part of his face and make his features look often grave, though never self-conscious" (p. 93). He may have been getting on in years, but he remained a dandy. A female acquaintance recalled Dick-

[13.] See "'Woman's Right' to Divorce," *The New York Times*, May 18, 1870.

[14.] Quoted in "Mr. Charles Dickens' Readings," London *Globe and Traveller*, April 30, 1858.

ens as "a gaily dressed gentleman; his bright green waistcoat, vivid scarlet tie, and pale lavender trousers would have been noticed by any one, but the size of the nosegay in his buttonhole riveted my attention, for it was a regular flower garden."[15]

He had radically trimmed *A Christmas Carol* to an hour and a half, retaining those episodes which worked best with his audiences. Gone were the long descriptive passages along with most of the sociopolitical content. Instead, he retained the famous holiday set pieces, the Fezziwig ball, the Cratchit Christmas, and Fred's party. These scenes of jolly celebration contrasted beautifully with the horrors of old Joe's rag-and-bottle shop, the Cratchits in mourning, and the dénouement in the graveyard. He concentrated on character rather than setting. He merged Stave 4 with Stave 5. All that was left of Scrooge's conversion was the purchase of the prize turkey and Scrooge's unprecedented appearance at Fred's door on Christmas Day. He confessed to his son Henry in a letter on February 11, 1868, "from ten years ago to last night, I have never read to an audience but I have watched for an opportunity of striking out something better somewhere." The prompt copy that survives attests to the great care that went into its preparation, to "the patient hours devoted year after year to single lines" (p. 47). The only episode from the book that remained almost intact was Bob Cratchit's Christmas dinner. Apparently, he never read directly from the page. He carried a paper cutter not to separate the pages, but merely for effect. He was always trying out new ideas from the platform, slightly altering lines here and there whenever he thought appropriate.

His reading desk too evolved through trial and error. The earliest one was tall like a Punch and Judy booth and ridiculously concealed too much of his body. He finally settled on a specially constructed reading desk, now in the Dickens House, in London. It had two levels: the lower a shelf for a glass of water and a paper cutter; the upper for his books and the elbow rest upon which he leaned his left arm. The platform was covered with a red and black carpet, the desk with an embroidered red velvet cloth. A maroon screen was set up behind him, and overhead carefully adjusted gas lights illuminated the speaker. He always appeared punctually at 8:00 P.M., in evening dress, a red geranium in his buttonhole and a pair of white gloves draped over the edge of his reading table. He

15. Laura Hain Friswell, *In the Sixties and Seventies* (London: Hutchinson, 1905), p. 164.

held his prompt copy in his hand, but it was really no more than a prop. He memorized his stories; he turned the pages for effect, only occasionally glancing at the text, perhaps as much for dramatic emphasis as for need. He refreshed himself during the intermissions with little more than sherry and ice water.

Just as Forster predicted, not everyone approved of his putting himself on public display in this manner. It was a radical departure for a famous writer to read his work publicly and for profit. The provincial press was especially shrill in its criticism of what it considered a grave offense against the art of literature. "A great change this in the habits of authors from the days when it was their pleasure and privilege to entrench themselves in a halo of eminent obscurity," observed the *Liverpool Post* on August 17, 1858. "The risk Mr. Dickens ran was loss of caste—the loss implied in the phrase 'too cheap.' . . . a curious experiment to ascertain what advantages a great author lost in coming out of the dim and awful distance, and shaking hands with a public unaccustomed to personal associations when reading books." The Derby *Mercury* scolded on October 27, "we regret that their author should have been induced thus to make merchandise of himself, and to pander to one of the lowest tastes of the time, viz., the hunting after notabilities. . . . Who will esteem his future words, however burning, however eloquent, to be real words, when he has seen the writer framed for effect on a public platform, stooping to the most artificial conventionalities, even to the display of a monster pen-knife. . . . We could wish that the prince of social photographers had not thus bowed himself down in the house of Mammon." How dare a writer lower himself to the level of an actor and for the money? they gasped.

No matter: the crowds still loved him. "Half-neglected corners of his works, rich in humour and character, are lighted up with all an author's enthusiasm, speaking through an actor's talent," wrote John Hollingshead in *The Critic* (September 4, 1858); "and groups of perfect, well-defined beings are revealed, like insects in a microscope, to the wondering gaze of hundreds, who before this were probably scarcely aware of their existence" (p. 537). Each audience seemed better than the last. "It was a prodigious cram," he wrote Georgina from Exeter on August 5, "and we turned away no end of people. But not only that. I think they were the finest Audience I have ever read to; I don't think I ever read, in some respects so well; and I never beheld anything like the personal affection which they poured out upon me at the end. It was really a very remarkable sight, and I shall always look back upon it with pleasure" (p. 617). He reported to Forster from Liverpool on August 20, "They turned hundreds away, sold all the books, rolled on the ground of my room knee-deep in checks, and made a perfect pantomime of the whole thing" (p. 628).

The Irish, too, warmly received the Englishman and *A Christmas Carol*. The Dublin *Evening Freeman* said, "His appearance is eminently prepossessing. His figure slight, and graceful—his features regular and sharply chiselled, and his shaven cheeks, mustache, and pointed beard, in the American fashion, render still more striking and peculiar a face remarkable for character, energy, and expression. He has a broad and high forehead, underneath which flash eyes so deep and lustrous that lighted up by them even the plainest countenance would seem beautiful." In Ireland as in England, as *The Belfast News-Letter* reported on August 28, "Everyone knows the story, or ought to know it. It is redolent of Christmas; Christmas substantial, and Christmas ghostly; Christmas past, and Christmas future; Christmas expected, and Christmas present." Ladies begged his servant for the flower from his coat, and women swarmed for the petals that fell from his geranium during a reading. He was astonished at how unashamedly the men sometimes wept more than the ladies did.

He was away from home from August 2 to November 13, 1858, on a grueling series of eighty-seven readings in over forty cities and towns that required overnight trips by rail before the days of sleeper cars. He confessed to his Irish friend Percy Fitzgerald on August 9, "my tour is of such a very fatiguing nature that I know it to be impossible to unite any social enjoyments with its business. I have therefore forsworn all pleasure engagements whatsoever, during its progress. I accept no invitations, see no one, and am perfectly heroic against my nature and my will" (p. 619). Georgina Hogarth scrawled on her copy of the itinerary under the last entry, "The End.—Thank God!"[16] But it was worth it, realizing 3,500 guineas, a princely sum at the time.

It was all worth it, especially after the agony he had undergone earlier in the year. He wrote Burdett-Coutts on October 27, 1858, "The manner in which the people have everywhere delighted to express that they have a personal affection for me and the interest of tender friends in me,

[16.] Quoted in John D. Gordon, *Reading for Profit: The Other Career of Charles Dickens* (New York: New York Public Library, 1958), p. 12.

is (especially at this time) high and above all other considerations. I consider it a remarkable instance of good fortune that it should have fallen out that I should, in this autumn, of all others, have come face to face with so many multitudes" (p. 689). It paid off handsomely: he cleared over one thousand guineas a month. He gave another 125 readings between April 29 and October 27, 1859.

The queen expressed interest in hearing Mr. Dickens read *A Christmas Carol*. Unfortunately, it could not be arranged to everyone's convenience and satisfaction. Perhaps Dickens was less accommodating because of the awkward situation Her Majesty had created after *The Frozen Deep*. The Prince of Wales, however, brought his entourage to hear him read in Oxford on October 24, 1859. Apparently, Leo Tolstoy heard *A Christmas Carol* on March 14, 1861, on a trip to London. Ivan Turgenev thought, "his way of reading is dramatic, almost theatrical, and in his one person several first-class actors force you now to laugh and now to cry."[17] Even dour Thomas Carlyle was talked into attending a performance. "It didn't have a very attractive look at first," he admitted, "this of hearing a man read his works; but I pretty soon found that 'reading' was a very insufficient description of the thing provided for us. The man's face and voice were made into a kind of stage, and he called up his people upon it so that we might see them act their parts. His characters seemed, indeed, to be related to his physiognomy, the further projections of him, to be mastered at will like his tongue and eyes. Such alterations of drollery and pathos, such ingenious grotesque sidelings into all the corners and crannies of human eccentricity and sentiment, one would have imagined quite impossible to any one man."[18] He thought Dickens had missed his true calling, that of a comic actor. "He would have made a successful one if he had taken that sort of life," said the Scottish philosopher. "His public readings, which were a pitiful pursuit after all, were in fact acting, and very good acting too."[19]

[17.] See A. V. Knowles, "Some Aspects of L. N. Tolstoy's Visit to London in 1861: An Examination of the Evidence," *Slavonic and East European Review*, January 1978, p. 112; and Turgenev quoted in Patrick Waddington, "Dickens, Pauline Viardot and Turgenev," *New Zealand Slavonic Journal*, no. 1, 1974, p. 66.

[18.] Quoted in Moncure D. Conway, "Footprints of Charles Dickens," *Harper's New Monthly Magazine*, September 1870, p. 615.

[19.] Quoted in Sir George Gavan Duffy, *Conversations with Carlyle* (New York: Charles Scribner's Sons, 1892), p. 77.

Charles Dickens in Paris.
Caricature by André Gill,
L'Éclipse, June 14, 1868.
Courtesy Library of Congress.

He had to put them aside while he was busy establishing *All the Year Round* and writing *A Tale of Two Cities*, the series of sketches that became *The Uncommercial Traveller* (1861), and another novel, *Great Expectations* (1861). He resumed these professional readings with six readings at St. James's Hall, Piccadilly, March 14 to April 18, 1861. St. Martin's Hall had recently burned down, along with all the paraphernalia of the performances, everything from tickets and cash boxes to baggage and gas fittings. Once he finished *Great Expectations*, he gave forty-nine readings in twenty-four towns in England and Scotland, from October 28, 1861, to January 11, 1862. He had long wanted to read from "my favorite," *David Copperfield*. He also prepared the excerpt "Nicholas Nickleby at the Yorkshire School" from *Nicholas Nickleby* as well as "Bob Sawyer's Party" from *The Pickwick Papers*.

Other countries were eager to hear him, too. An impresario in Australia invited him to come there for an eight months' tour for £10,000; he thought £12,000 for six months more reasonable. He did spend the fall and winter of 1862–63 in Paris, where he gave three readings at the British embassy for the benefit of the British Charitable Fund on January 17, 29, and 30. He admitted in a letter to Wills on February 4 how it amazed him that "people who don't understand English, positively understood the Readings! . . . You have no idea what they made of me. I got things out of the old *Carol*—effects I mean—so entirely new and so very strong, that I quite amazed myself and wondered where I was going next" (pp. 210–11). On his return to London, he gave twelve or thirteen readings in the Hanover Square Rooms from March 6 to June 12, 1863.

He put aside his readings while he concentrated on the monthly parts of *Our Mutual Friend* from May 1864 to November 1865. In February 1865, he suffered a severe attack of lameness in his left foot, which his physician at first thought was gout. He completed only one more novel, *Our Mutual Friend* (1865). His health was failing, and he refused to accept it. Dickens was hardly an old man, but he suffered from chest and stomach pains and recurrent bouts of lameness. His eyes were affected as well. These were all signs of a degenerating heart. He suffered a serious jolt to his system on June 9, 1865: while he was returning to London by way of Folkstone from a trip with Ellen Ternan and her mother in France, their train came upon some unexpected rail work and jumped the tracks into the river near Staplehurst. They were all rescued, along with the manuscript of his latest installment of *Our Mutual Friend*, and no one breathed a word to the press about their traveling arrangements. But his nerves were shot, and he never fully recovered from the shock.

He finally returned to the road after a three years' absence, between April 10 and June 12, 1866. He had a new reading, "Doctor Marigold," from "Doctor Marigold's Prescriptions" in the 1865 Christmas Number of *All the Year Round*. There were two new selections, "Barbox Brothers" and "The Boy at Mugby," from the recent Christmas issue of *All the Year Round*, for the January 15 to May 13, 1867, tour. He traveled through England, Scotland, and Ireland. He even risked confronting Fenian activities in Dublin and Belfast. But he had his eye on a richer prize: America.

Dickens first considered reading in America as early as 1858, after his first successful professional tour in the British Isles and at the height of his domestic problems. "More unlikely things have happened since the world began," he informed an American friend in late May 1858. "I have been making an extraordinary sensation in diverse places by reading my Christmas Books, and sometimes I have thought, dreaming with my eyes open, 'Lord! I should not wonder if they would be very glad to hear me in America, after all!' " (p. 556). He was then offered £10,000 to come to the United States for eighty readings in 1859, but the Civil War intervened. His American publisher James T. Fields of Ticknor and Fields had been urging him to try the United States again. Now his booking agent pressed him to go abroad. He sent his business manager, George Dolby, to the United States in July 1867 to check on the demand and potential profit from an American tour. Forster feared that Dickens was foolhardy in his determination to make as much money in the shortest amount of time regardless of the physical labor it required. But Dickens would not listen to his objections. He had made up his mind. With the presidential election approaching, he decided to depart in November 9 to begins his four-month American tour in Boston on December 2, 1867.

"Au Revoir." Cartoon by Fred Barnard,
Judy, October 30, 1867.
Courtesy New York Public Library, Astor, Lenox and Tilden Foundations.

The anticipation was unprecedented, far greater than for his last visit to America, in 1842. "The position . . . of Charles Dickens in regard to America is wholly exceptional," declared *Every Saturday* (November 2) on its front page. "He is the most famous living writer of the English tongue. He is the brightest and most genial humorist extant. His literary popularity is as great in the States as in his own country." Dickens was visible all over the city on his arrival. "Every bookseller's window was stacked up with copies of Ticknor and Fields' new edition of 'Dickens,' to the temporary displacement of Longfellow's *Dante* and Dr. Holmes's *Guardian Angel*," reported Clarence Cook in the New York *Tribune* (December 3); "the cigar-shops came out as one man with their brands all new-christened, and nothing is smoked, chewed, or taken in snuff to-day but 'Little Nell Cigars,' Mr. Squeers's Fine Cut, the Mantalini Plug and the 'Genuine Pickwick Snuff'; while at every turn, in the illustrated newspapers, in the hotel office, and in all the shop windows the new portrait of Mr. Dickens is to be seen." J. M. Whittemore and Company,

"And as Tiny Tim observed, God Bless us every one!"
Lithograph by Sol Eytinge Jr., 1867.
Courtesy Library of Congress.

Boston, issued a new card game called "Dickens," "made up of names and characters from the stories of that author."[20] Ticknor and Fields was hardly the only publishing house that sought to reap a fine profit from all the free publicity. Hurd and Houghton of New York had "The Globe Dickens," "The Riverside Dickens," and the "Household Edition of Dickens' Works"; T. B. Peterson and Brothers of Philadelphia advertised "Peterson's Cheap Edition for the Million"; D. Appleton and Company of New York offered its own "Cheap Edition of Dickens" and "The People's

[20]. "The 'Dickens' Game," *Brooklyn Daily Union*, December 22, 1867.

CHARLES DICKENS.
Entered according to Act of Congress, in the year 1867, by J. GURNEY & SON, in the Clerk's Office of the District Court of the United States, for the Southern District of New York.
J. Gurney & Son   707 Broadway N.Y.

Charles Dickens. Photograph by
J. Gurney and Son, 1867.
Courtesy Colin Axon.

Edition of Dickens." The only collected series in America that Dickens personally authorized were the "Library Edition," the "Diamond Edition," and "The Charles Dickens Edition," all published by Ticknor and Fields.

Dolby thought the photographs displayed in the shop windows were "so wonderfully *unlike* him," that he induced Dickens to sit for the photographers J. Gurney and Son when they got to New York. Although Dickens suppressed some of the shots, Dolby thought the results included "the only good photograph of him in existence."[21] J. Gurney and Son thought they had exclusive rights to his photograph in America. But Dickens did stop by the studio of Mathew Brady, the famous Civil War photographer. His unflattering portrait revealed a glum, bloated, and aging Dickens, visibly wearied by his recent travels. Brady had permission to exhibit the photograph at his gallery, while Gurney sold several poses of the noble, handsome Boz in a variety of sizes—carte-de-visite (25¢), cabinet (50¢), and imperial ($3), even in stereoscopic form.

Theater managers too exploited his visit to America all along the route. "Wherever I go," Dickens complained to Wilkie Collins in a letter on January 31, 1868, "they play my books, with my name in big letters. *Oliver Twist* was at Baltimore when I left it last Wednesday. *Pickwick* is here [in Philadelphia], and *Bob* [*Sawyer's Party*] and the *Carrier* [*Dot, or The Cricket on the Hearth*] are here. *Pickwick* was in New York too, when I last passed that way; so was *Our Mutual Friend*; so was *No Thorough-*

21. George Dolby, *Charles Dickens As I Knew Him* (London: R. Fisher Unwin, 1885), p. 172. All subsequent quotations of Dolby are also from this book, unless otherwise indicated.

fare" (p. 31). A "new Burlesque," *The Arrival of Dickens*, incorporating scenes from *The Pickwick Papers* and other works, was playing in Philadelphia during his stay there; Dickens was even the subject of a minstrel troupe. Several elocutionists were touring the country simultaneously with Dickens, reading from the Englishman's books. Some papers even had the gall to call Dickens inferior to them!

Weeks before the readings began, Dolby heard rumors that American "pirates" were planning to send shorthand experts to transcribe the texts of the Public Readings, so he arranged with Ticknor and Fields (with the author's blessing) to print a cheap edition taken directly from the prompt copies. It was issued as both a series of paper-wrapped pamphlets and a hard-

Charles Dickens. Photograph by
Mathew Brady, 1867.
Courtesy Brady Collection, National Archives.

cover collection of all ten readings.[22] Dickens also approved the publication of *Child-Pictures from Dickens* (1867), a selection of self-contained excerpts "especially associated with children" from his novels. "Although they necessarily lose interest and purpose when detached from their context and removed from their niches in the works of fiction to which they respectively belong," he apologized in a prefatory note, "this compilation is made for American children with my free consent." Included was "Tiny Tim," which strung together only the Bob Cratchit episodes from the novel, concluding pathetically with the boy's death.

It was pointless to buy these cheap books and try to follow along with Dickens. "In reading these texts," reported the New York *Commercial*

[22.] These had not been available in England. "There are no printed abridgements of the *Carol, Dombey*, etc. as I read them, or nearly as I read them," he admitted in a letter of May 6, 1861. "Nor is there any such abridgement in existence, save in my own copies; and there it is made, in part physically, and in part mentally, and no human being but myself could hope to follow it" (p. 408). The "Readings Edition" of *A Christmas Carol* that Bradbury and Evans issued in 1858 was no more than a cheap paperbound reprint of the unabridged text.

Charles Dickens. Photograph by J. Gurney and Son, 1867.
Private collection.

Advertiser on December 3, "Mr. Dickens neither follows the original text, nor adheres closely by any means to the text of the pretty and convenient hand-books which he has himself condensed and prepared. He leaves out a good deal, changes words, mistakes words sometimes, and really much of it seems impromptu. I thought, now and then, that he was thinking of his present audience, and putting in what he fancied would suit better here than in London." *The Nation* (December 12) agreed, saying, "he went on, not following perfectly closely the text of that edition of his reading which Ticknor and Fields have just published, but varying from it in two ways—by omissions that included some of his finest bits of humor . . . and not only by omissions, but by interpolations" (p. 481). It annoyed Dickens to watch people with their noses in the books instead of paying full attention to his voice and gestures.

Dickens and Dolby feared there might be some retaliation for what he had said earlier about the United States in *American Notes* and *Martin Chuzzlewit*. "The Americans bear him no grudge for his somewhat scathing satire in both these books, because they fully recognize that there was much truth in what he wrote," insisted his son Henry; "but whatever feeling there might have been on the subject disappeared completely upon the occasion of his second visit in 1867–1868."[23] Not com-

[23] Henry Fielding Dickens, *My Father As I Knew Him* (London: William Heinemann, 1934), p. 66.

pletely, however. Charles Dickens had not been to the United States for twenty-five years, but some editors, such as James Gordon Bennett of the *New York Herald*, could not forgive *American Notes* and *Martin Chuzzlewit*. Bennett warned his readers on September 6 that Dickens was returning to write another scathing book on the country. Just in case anyone had forgotten, he published "Choice Excerpts" from *American Notes* in the next Sunday edition. He was not the only one. "Nothing that Mr. Dickens can say, or that his admirers can offer by way of excuse," sniffed *Putnam's Magazine* (June 1868), "will ever make the American chapters in *Martin Chuzzlewit* appear other than what they are,—a gross, one-sided, and spiteful caricature of a whole people" (p. 774). *The Northern Monthly Magazine* published a vicious attack on the "vulgar snob" in its January issue, mentioning everything from his criticism of America to his domestic infidelity and accusing him of writing about Christmas only because it paid. "We regret Mr. Dickens's presence in this country," said the anonymous writer in "Some Plain Words Concerning Mr. Dickens," "because he has vilified our countrymen and our flag, our press and our institutions; because he repaid munificent hospitality by unmerited abuse" (p. 251). He was nothing more than a hypocrite. "With all his apparent sympathy, he has shown himself the coldest and most ungrateful of men," the critic insisted. "While seeming as an author to possess generous emotions and impulses in the highest degree, his conduct in life has been a history of petty meannesses, petty revenges, petty vanities, and unbounded avarice" (p. 246).

All the press, good and bad, made Americans all the more eager to see the famous English writer. When tickets went on sale at Ticknor and Fields' bookstore in Boston, Dolby worked thirteen hours straight and sold $12,000 worth of tickets. Henry James did not bother even to try. "Dickens has arrived for his readings," he wrote his brother William. "It is impossible to get tickets. At 7 o'clock a.m. on the first day of the sale there were two or three hundred at the office, and at 9, when I strolled up, nearly a thousand. So I don't expect to hear him."[24] But he was

24. Henry James, *Letters*, edited by Leon Edel, vol. 1 (Cambridge, Mass.: Harvard University Press, 1974), p. 81. "Mr. Dickens is here, and everybody is running after him," William Cullen Bryant wrote a friend, "but I cannot muster up curiosity enough to go. Those of my household, and many of my friends, have been disappointed, but the newspapers praise him without a stint. They—I do not mean the newspapers—say that his voice is not good, neither strong nor musical, and, while, they admit his comic power as an actor, they call his reading of parts, doleful." (Quoted in Parke Godwin, *A Biography of William Cullen Bryant*, vol. 2 [New York: Russell and Russell, 1883], p. 399.)

delighted to meet the famous writer at a mutual friend's home. "What a charming impression of Dickens the other night at the Nortons' dinner!" he wrote a friend. "How innocent and honest and sweet he is maugre his fame!" James dared not speak to "the master." He was "so ineffably agitated, so mystically moved, in the presence of any exhibited idol of the mind who should be that character at all conceivably 'like' the author of *Pickwick* and *Copperfield*."[25]

One annoying problem Dickens and Dolby could not control were the scalpers who got the best spots in line; and after securing the prime two-dollar seats, they sold them for as much as $25, according to the classified ads in the papers. Men and boys who showed up early sold their places in line for as much as $30 in gold to anyone willing to buy a better position for getting tickets. Angry customers wrote the newspapers, and editorials attacked Dolby's way of doing business. Nothing he tried could appease them. There were also labor problems: when Dolby reprimanded an usher in New York for leaving during a performance, the man took his hat and walked out, as did every other usher in the house. When it was discovered along the route that one of their staff was speculating in tickets, Dolby dismissed him. Only at Dickens' insistence was the man reinstated. Tax collectors too pursued them, so Dolby met with the Commissioner of Internal Revenue in Washington, D.C., and secured an order exempting Dickens' occasional lectures from any taxation.

The usually reserved Bostonians greeted Dickens with cheers and waving handkerchiefs when he took the platform at Tremont Temple at 8:00 P.M. on December 2, to read *A Christmas Carol*. It was an eminent crowd, including Henry Wadsworth Longfellow, James Russell Lowell, Oliver Wendell Holmes, James T. Fields, Charles Eliot Norton, and Richard Henry Dana, Jr. "To say that his audience followed him with delight hardly expresses the interest with which they hung upon every word that fell from his lips," reported the *Boston Journal* the next morning, "and eyed every gesture with which his prolific genius clothed every idea embodied in the wonderful characters of his *Christmas Carol*." Dolby recalled that with the final sentence, "And so, as Tiny Tim observed, God Bless Us, Every One!" "a dead silence seemed to prevail— a sort of public sigh as it were—only to be broken by cheers and calls, the most enthusiastic and uproarious, causing Mr. Dickens to break his rule,

25. Henry James, *Autobiography*, edited by Frederick W. Dupee (Princeton, N.J.: Princeton University Press, 1983), p. 388.

"Charles Dickens as He Appears When Reading."
Wood engraving by C. A. Barry, *Harper's Weekly*, December 7, 1867.
Courtesy Library of Congress.

and again presenting himself before his audience, to bow his acknowl-
edgements" (p. 174). James T. Fields agreed, "The audience seemed one
vast ear and eye; the people sat fixed and speechless. Every one seemed
drawn to that great sympathetic nature, and as if they longed in some
peculiar way to give him their confidence!"[26] The *Boston Journal*
declared it "one of the greatest intellectual treats which the citizens of
Boston ever enjoyed."

It was the rule that only Dolby and the valet were allowed in the
dressing room at the break, but Fields was invited to join his friend back-
stage. "You have given me a new lease on life," the publisher gushed, "for
I have been so looking forward to this occasion that I have had an idea
all day that I should die at five minutes to eight to-night, and be deprived
of a longing desire I have had to hear you read in my country for the last

[26] James T. Fields, *Biographical Notes and Personal Sketches* (Boston: Houghton Mifflin,
1891), p. 153. Here and elsewhere he was apparently paraphrasing his wife's reaction. See
Annie Fields, *Memories of a Hostess: A Chronicle of Eminent Friendships*, edited by Mark
Antony De Wolf Howe (Boston: Atlantic Monthly Press, 1922), p. 144.

nineteen years."[27] Dickens proudly admitted to Fields that "he thought he had greatly improved his presentation of *A Christmas Carol* in this country."[28] Then Dickens was back on stage in ten minutes to do "Bardell and Pickwick." The next day, he wired W. H. Wills at the *All the Year Round* office simply, "Tremendous success greatest enthusiasm all well" (p. 503).

New York was next. Although suffering from a severe cold, he opened with *A Christmas Carol* at Steinway Hall on December 9. "The night Mr. Dickens chose for his first reading in New York turned out to be bitterly cold," reported the *Brooklyn Daily Union* the next morning. "The mercury shrunk ten degrees below the freezing point, and then did not get so low as the shrinking, shivering blood of mortals. The sky was faultlessly and hopelessly clear. Every vestige of vapor had been driven from it by the fierce wind. . . . The streets were almost impassable on foot save to the sturdiest." The Brooklyn Bridge had not yet been built, and those who ventured to Manhattan by ferry were met "by cruel blasts, which rushed out of the Northwest and made way down the avenues of the great city with an apparently insatiable rage that such corners should vex them in their turnings."

Nevertheless, it was a full and enthusiastic house. Dickens greeted the deafening applause with a respectful bow and had to repeat the gesture before they would let him begin. Fields, in *Biographical Notes*, thought this reading of *A Christmas Carol* "far better given than in Boston, because the applause was more ready and stimulated the reader. Indeed the enthusiasm was rapturous" (p. 154). Dickens agreed. "It is absolutely impossible that we could have made a more brilliant success than we made here last night," he gleefully reported to Wills on December 10. "The reception was splendid, the audience bright and perceptive. I believe that I never read so well since I began, and the general delight was most enthusiastic" (p. 507).

Even when questioning his elocutionary skills, the New York reviews were remarkably favorable. "To say [the readings] were a tremendous success is simply to enunciate a puerility," said *Wilkes's Spirit of the Times* on December 14. "They were what every body expected they would be—worthy of the greatest novelist the world has yet known" (p. 316). The

[27] Quoted in Dolby, *Charles Dickens As I Knew Him*, p. 174.

[28] Quoted in "Some Memories of Charles Dickens," *The Atlantic Monthly*, August 1870, p. 241.

"Buying Tickets for the Dickens Readings at Steinway Hall."
Wood engraving, *Harper's Weekly,* December 28, 1867.
Courtesy Library of Congress.

New York Herald declared on December 10, "The *Christmas Carol* becomes doubly enchanting when one hears it read by Dickens." "If the dialogue was invested with new life," observed the New York *Evening Post* (December 10), "the descriptive passages assumed a new richness, reality and significance." *The New York Times* concluded on the same day that "we have never had, and we venture to say we never shall have, any entertainments more charming in themselves, or more full of genuine, legitimate and elevating pleasure than these readings from Mr. Dickens."

The rush for tickets in New York was even wilder than in Boston. When it was announced that the sale for the second course of readings would begin at 9 A.M. at Steinway Hall on December 11, people began assembling at 10 the night before, and at least 150 stayed in line all night. By the time the ticket office opened, there were five hundred people (including two women) waiting in a queue that stretched east to Irving Place, then to Fifteenth Street and Fourth Avenue and back to Fourteenth Street. Police were called in to preserve order, and all seats were gone by 2. Demand in New York was so great that he had to repeat the original series of four readings twice.

Dickens also agreed to four performances in Brooklyn. He and his entourage of five men (Dolby and his assistant, the gas man, his valet, and his publisher James P. Osgood) had to travel by carriage each night on the ferry in inclement weather. "The sale of tickets there was an amazing scene," he wrote Georgina on January 12. "The noble army of speculators are now furnished (this is literally true, and I am quite serious), each man with a straw mattress, a little bag of bread and meat, two blankets, and a bottle of whiskey. With this outfit *they lie down on the pavement* the whole night before the tickets are sold, generally taking up their position at about ten" (p. 10). It was so cold that they built a bonfire, and a fight broke out when the police came to put it out.

The only place available in Brooklyn was Henry Ward Beecher's Plymouth Church, which, as Dickens wrote Georgina on January 21, was "a most wonderful place to speak in" (p. 20). It was big enough for two thousand people, and the pulpit was removed for the readings. Dickens admitted to his daughter Mamie in a letter on January 18, "it was very odd to see the pews crammed full of people, all in a broad roar at the *Carol* and 'Trial'" (p. 19). But here he also witnessed Northern racism in action: people refused to sit in the area of the church marked "Colored Gallery," and one man made quite a row when he realized he would be sitting next to two Black women. As he wrote Forster on January 30, "the Ghost of Slavery" haunted much of America and he held little hope for the nation's racial problems (p. 27). He wisely decided to go no further South than Washington, D.C. Resentment for what he wrote about slavery in *American Notes* was still high during Reconstruction.

Not all were favorably impressed with the Inimitable Boz onstage. The New York *Evening Telegram* on January 4 accused him of being "one of the prodigious humbugs of the day" with "a voice without force or modulation, and a constant, monotonous rising inflection." "The *Christmas Carol*, one of the most exquisite creations in English literature," complained the Baltimore *Gazette* (January 28), "is sadly marred by being rendered for the purpose of producing certain stage effects."

The Nation thought "that in the level passages he was not extraordinarily good; that his voice is not a particularly fine one; that many of his inflections and the spirit in which he reads many passages are not all what we should have expected or what we liked, but that wherever his admirable histrionic abilities could supplement or almost take the place of his abilities as a reader merely—then all things were done at least well, many things excellently well, and some things done so well that we have not as yet conceived of their being done better" (p. 481). The *New York Herald* (December 17) thought Dickens "descended to a little clap-trap for stage effect, as some of our Irish comedians or minstrels are apt to do before less cultivated audiences than the one at Steinway Hall." The New York *Commercial Advertiser*, on December 10, 1867, mentioned some peculiarities of the Englishman's pronunciation: "clark" for clerk, "wynde" for wind, and "ojus" for odious. They complained that he used the rising inflection too much, and some detected the trace of a lisp. "Away with such fawning, boot-licking spirit!" demanded *Frank Leslie's Illustrated Newspaper* on December 14. "Charles Dickens is a man like unto other men; his books are powerfully written and very interesting; but do not warrant the erection of a demi-god from the simple author in a country composed of sovereigns. Granting beforehand all that can be said in favor of this Englishman, does it become 'free and enlightened citizens' to act as though they believed him to be superhuman?" (p. 145).

Dickens could not possibly live up to everyone's expectations. "At the first glance I received a shock," Louisa May Alcott, who saw him in England, wrote in *The Commonwealth* (September 21, 1867), "and my idol tumbled off the pedestal whereon I placed him long ago, when I wove his hair in a locket, and thought Shakespeare was an idiot beside him." Of course, he was hardly "the handsome, foppish man who once paid us a visit, and caricatured us so capitally afterward"; but she still hoped that "some sign of genius would be visible—some glimpse of the genial creator of Little Nell, Tom Pinch and the Cheeryble Brothers." She was disappointed that "his youth and comeliness were gone, but the foppishness remained, and the red-faced man, with false teeth, and the voice of a worn-out actor, had his scanty grey hair curled; a posy in his button-hole; diamond-ring, pin, and studs; a ruffled front, and wristbands."

Mark Twain reported on a reading in New York for the San Francisco *Alta California* (February 3, 1868). Like Alcott, he was unimpressed with the Englishman. Dickens was "a tall, 'spry' (if I may say it), thin-legged old gentleman, gotten up regardless of expense, especially as to

Charles Dickens. Photograph by
J. Gurney and Son, 1867.
Courtesy Library of Congress.

shirt-front and diamonds, with a bright red flower in his button-hole, gray beard and mustache, bald head, and with side hair brushed fiercely and tempestuously forward, as if its owner were sweeping down before a gale of wind."

The performance was another matter. "I was a good deal disappointed in Mr. Dickens' reading—I will go further and say, a great deal disappointed," he said. Dickens did not enunciate properly, so that many of the words were lost in the back of the hall, where Twain was sitting. He thought it was "rather monotonous, as a general thing; his voice is husky; his pathos is only the beautiful pathos of the language—there is no heart, no feeling in it—it is glittering frostwork; his rich humor cannot fail to tickle an audience into ecstasies save when he reads himself." He thought Dickens should have "made them laugh, or cry, or shout, at his own good will or pleasure—but he did not. They were very much tamer than they should have been." Twain was far from tame himself when he took to the platform, under the management of the same George Dolby sometime later. Twain may have been a little distracted that evening. He happened to be on his first date with Miss Olivia L. Langdon, the future Mrs. Samuel L. Clemens.

One of the most aggressive purchasers of the precious tickets was Kate Field, a young American journalist, playwright, and lecturer, who published her report of "twenty-five of the most delightful and most instructive evenings of my life" as *Pen Photographs of Dickens's Readings* (1868); it was so popular that she expanded it in 1871. She later made a career of lecturing about Dickens' readings. The author's friend Charles Kent, assisted by Dickens himself, issued *Charles Dickens as a Reader* (1872). Dolby followed with his account of their association, *Charles Dickens As I Knew Him: The Story of the Reading Tours, 1866–1870* (1885). They vainly tried to recapture the magic of these performances, to somehow describe the remarkable power Dickens had over his audiences.

Dickens earned a fortune under extreme difficulties. What possessed him to tour America during winter? He was already weak and weary when he landed in Boston. He then proceeded to travel thousands of miles by rail to give dozens of readings in the worst weather. He had to battle snowstorms and then flooding from the thaw. He read in all seventy six times between December 2, 1867, and April 10, 1868, with an average of four readings a week. The pace was exhausting. He was forced to take only one week off during President Johnson's impeachment, when ticket sales fell off. On top of it all, he caught a cold in mid-December that developed into chronic influenza. He became so lame that he had to walk with a cane. He had no idea how seriously ill he was. The only time he was not depressed was when he was performing.

"Mr. C——S D——S and the Honest Little Boy."
Cartoon by Thomas Nast, *The Illustrated Chicago News,* April 24, 1868.
Courtesy Library of Congress.

He could not sleep, he lost his appetite. His diet was as strict as that of a prizefighter's in training. "I rarely take any breakfast but an egg and a cup of tea, not even toast or bread-and-butter," he explained his routine to Georgina on January 21. "My dinner at three, and a little quail or some such light thing when I come home at night, is my daily fare. At the Hall I have established the custom of taking an egg beaten up in sherry before going in, and another between the parts. I think this pulls me up; at all events, I have since no return of faintness"(p. 20). He later drank strong hot beef tea during the interval and ate some soup before he went to bed. He never consumed more than half a pound of solid food a day.

He was forced to cut social engagements to a minimum to save what little strength he had left. He insisted in a letter on January 28 that his

"Mr. Charles Dickens and His Former American Acquaintances—'Not at Home.'"
Cartoon by C. G. Bush, *Harper's Weekly*, December 21, 1867.
Courtesy Library of Congress.

"'true American Catarrh,' is infallibly brought back by every railway car I enter. It is so oppressive, and would, but for occasional rest and silence, be so incompatible with my Readings, that my only safe course is to hold to the principle I established when I left Boston, and gloomily deny myself all social relationships" (p. 24). The press, predictably, interpreted his seclusion differently. Unaware of the severity of his condition, Americans took offense at what they thought was British snobbery of the worst sort. But Dickens put up with the insults and the injury. "The work is hard, the climate is hard, the life is hard," he wrote Georgina around December 6; "but—so far—the gain is *enormous*" (p. 504).

He was especially depressed by the holidays. He read *A Christmas Carol* in Boston on Christmas Eve and promised to be back at Steinway Hall on December 26. James T. and Annie Fields gave him a lovely Christmas dinner complete with a plum pudding direct from England. "How beautiful it was!" wrote Fields of the reading in *Biographical Notes*.

"The whole house rose and cheered! The people looked at him with gratitude as to one who held a candle in a dark way" (p. 155). The next morning the Fieldses, Longfellow, Holmes, and others saw him off. But the train trip was gloomy; Dickens hardly said a word. Yet when they were crossing a river by ferry, a United States man-of-war struck up "God Save the Queen" as it unfurled the British flag and hoisted a wreath of holly and other evergreens in honor of Charles Dickens.

Dickens was front-page news everywhere he went, and his celebrity resulted in much bizarre and yet amusing newspaper copy. "Every night I read," he wrote to a friend back in London on March 8, "I am described (mostly by people who have not the faintest notion of observing) from the sole of my boot to where the topmost hair of my head ought to be, but is not. Sometimes I am described as being 'evidently nervous'; sometimes it is rather taken ill that 'Mr. Dickens is so extraordinarily composed.' My eyes are blue, red, grey, white, green, brown, black, hazel, violet, and rainbow-coloured." He was said to resemble everyone from the emperor of France to the emperor of China. "I say all sorts of things I never said," he wrote, "go to all sorts of places that I never saw or heard of, and have done all manner of things (in some previous state of existence I suppose) that have quite escaped my memory" (p. 68). Perhaps the most bizarre of all was the rumor in *Harper's Bazaar* (November 30) that Dickens "eats 'hasheesh,' and that some of his finest compositions have been formed under its influences" (p. 67).

Everyone had an opinion, even the provincial press. "Some were disappointed, some pleased, and others delighted," said the *Oneida Dispatch* on March 13. "Mr. Dickens' voice is neither pleasing nor displeasing. It is not loud or distinct, or flexible. He has a very keen perception of the manner in which a rendition of the several characters should be given, but lacks the vocal qualifications to render them as he would like to. Still, he does not fail in riveting the attention of the hearer, or somewhat fatiguing him by the apparent effort." College students too would not keep silent. "We fully agree with most of the critics, that Mr. Dickens has an utter disregard for all established rules of elocution," sniffed the editor of *Hamilton Literary Magazine* (January 1868), published by Hamilton College in Clinton, New York. "He has a peculiar method of his own, which, in descriptive passages, often strikes the hearer as monotonous; but in dialogue, or passages allowing variety of tone, has an indescribable charm. The only fault the most severe critic could find would be in the too great frequency of the rising inflection."

The young man added, "It is a misnomer to call these entertainments Readings, where there is no, or very little, reference to a book. Mr. Dickens is teaching us a new elocution, the more attractive on account of its simplicity" (pp. 154–55).

He went on to Philadelphia and Baltimore to packed houses, but Horace Greeley warned Dickens about going to Washington, D.C. It was still a Southern city and was especially full of rabble at the time, for Congress was considering the impeachment of President Andrew Johnson. The Washington, D.C., *Commercial Union* (February 4) thought that Dickens appeared "somewhat nervous, as the audience was, to some extent, Southern, and who received him with but faint applause, but as the readings progressed the enthusiasm of the audience was steadily on the increase, until it finally reached a point that must have been inspiring to the reader, if he was at all nervous, as we believed he was." It was another triumph. "The audience was a superior one, composed of the foremost public men and their families," he proudly wrote Mamie on February 4. "At the end of the *Carol* they gave a great break out, and applauded, I really believe, for five minutes. You would suppose them to be Manchester shillings instead of Washington half-sovereigns. Immense enthusiasm" (pp. 34–35).

It had been an unusual reading for another reason. "In the *Carol*, a most ridiculous incident occurred all of a sudden," he reported to Mamie. "I saw a dog look out from among the seats into centre aisle, and look very intently at me. . . . He was a very comic dog, and it was well for me that I was reading a very comic part of the book." Sure that he might show up again and start barking, Dickens kept an eye out for him as he continued to read. "But when he bounced out into the centre aisle again, in an entirely new place (still looking intently at me) and tried the effect of a bark upon my proceedings," he wrote to Mamie, "I was seized with such a paroxysm of laughter, that it communicated itself to the audience, and we roared at one another loud and long" (p. 35).

But that was not the last of the literary mutt. "Next night," he reported to Georgina on February 7, "I thought I heard . . . a suddenly suppressed bark. . . . Osgood, standing just within the doors felt his leg touched and looking down beheld the dog, staring intently at me, and evidently just about to bark. In a transport of presence of mind and fury, he instantly caught him up in both hands, and threw him, over his own head, out into the entry, where the check takers received him like a game at ball." But having heard *A Christmas Carol* and passages from *David*

Copperfield, the persistent cur could not miss "Doctor Marigold." "Last night he came again, *with another dog,*" Dickens wrote Georgina, "but our people were so sharply on the lookout for him that he didn't get in. He had evidently promised to pass the other dog, free" (pp. 40–41). He added in a letter to Annie Fields on February 9, "On the imposition being unmasked, the other dog apologised, cut him dead, and withdrew. His intentions were of the best, but he afterwards 'rose to explain,' outside, with inconvenient eloquence" (p. 44).

All of Washington society wanted to entertain the famous novelist, but Dickens had to respectfully decline all requests to reserve his strength for the readings. It was rumored that he might attend General and Mrs. Grant's last grand reception of the season on February 5. "Dickens did not appear, as was anticipated," the *Evening Express* reported the next day. "Much merriment, however, was occasioned during the evening by the wags continually pointing out some one gentleman or other as the identical C.D."

He did break his rule to dine with Senator Charles Summer from Massachusetts, an old friend from his first trip to America. They were joined by Edwin M. Stanton, secretary of war. It may have been a bit injudicious of Dickens to accept the invitation, for Secretary Stanton was at the center of the current impeachment proceedings. The House of Representatives charged President Johnson with "high crimes and misdemeanors" when he violated the Tenure of Office Act by dismissing Stanton without consent of the Senate. Dickens was pleasantly impressed with Stanton's wide knowledge of his work.

He also agreed to call on the president at the executive mansion on February 7, accompanied by Dolby and Osgood. "Tobacco spit this time did not soil the carpet," noted the *Evening Express* (February 7), "but the spittoons, both big and little, scattered around, attest that our people have been insensible to the fierce *spitting* to which the great satirist subjected them." The president regretted that he could not attend the evening's performance, Dickens' last in the city. He admitted it was not his best reading, but the president said writers are never the best judges of their own work. They exchanged a few pleasantries about responsibilities and the weather; then Dickens withdrew out of respect for the president's pressing duties.

All the papers mentioned that it was also Dickens' birthday; and, as he wrote Annie Fields on February 9, "my room was on that day a blooming garden. Nor were flowers alone represented there. The silversmith, the goldsmith, the landscape painter, all sent in their contributions. After the Reading was done at night the whole Audience rose; and it was spontaneous, hearty, and affecting" (p. 43). As he wrote Mamie on February 11, he was so ill later in the day that he almost did not go on. "Surely, Mr. Dolby," said Summer when he found Dickens at five o'clock, covered with a mustard poultice, "it is impossible that he can read to-night." "Sir," said Dolby, "I have told the dear Chief so four times to-day, and I have been very anxious. But you have no idea how he will change when he gets to the little table." In addition to thus describing this exchange, Dickens proudly reported back to Mamie how "the whole audience rose and remained (Secretaries of State, President's family, Judges of the Supreme Court, and so forth) standing and cheering until I went back to the table and made them a little speech" (p. 48). The nation's capital was not at all as he expected it to be. "This is considered the dullest and most apathetic place in America," he wrote Georgina on February 7. "*My* audiences have been superb" (p. 40). He was so touched by their reaction that he broke his silence and said a few words on the final night: "In all probability I shall never see your faces again; but I can assure you that yours have yielded me as much pleasure as I have given you."[29]

The trip through central and northern New York and back into New England was long and rough. Ill and exhausted, Dickens was homesick and wished it were all over. "An amusing incident occurred when Mr. Dickens was returning to Boston from his visit to Portland," reported the Boston *Herald* on April 5. "A little girl about eleven years old, whose parents reside in Hollis, Maine, was on board the train." The child was Kate Douglas Smith, the future Kate Douglas Wiggin, author of *Rebecca of Sunnybrook Farm* (1903). One of her favorite authors was Charles Dickens, and she could not believe her good fortune to be traveling on the same train with him. Her mother and aunt had just heard him read, but she had had to stay home. When Osgood got up to go to the smoking car, she took his seat. He was delighted to learn that so little a girl had read his big novels. When he asked her if she had wanted to hear him read, she replied with lips trembling, "Yes, I did, more than tongue can tell!" She wondered if he cried when he read out loud. She told him that in her house they never read about Tiny Tim on Saturday nights, "for fear our

[29]. Quoted in "Mr. Dickens' Last Reading," Washington, D.C., *National Republican*, February 8, 1868.

eyes will be too swollen to go to Sunday School." Yes, he did cry sometimes when he read from his works.[30]

It had been announced that there would be a series of western
engagements, in Chicago, Cincinatti, Detroit, and Cleveland, and up into
Canada, but his poor health made it impossible for him to do that much
traveling. Chicago in particular was furious that he canceled his trip
there. The Chicago *Tribune* began a smear campaign on March 21, accusing Dickens of being "A Hypocrite of Literature" for neglecting his
brother's widow and family, then living in the city. "You cannot imagine,"
he wrote Georgina on March 8, "the frenzy of Chicago at being left out
of the Readings—as I am heartily glad they are!" He added, "Of course
my lips are sealed." He also instructed Dolby and Osgood to say nothing,
"and they really writhe under it," he told Georgina (p. 70). He did not
respond to these accusations until *The New York Times* published an
obituary for "Mrs. Augustus Dickens" on December 28, 1869. "The widow
of my late brother in that paragraph referred to was never at Chicago,"
he wrote the London *Daily News* on January 14, 1869; "she is a lady now
living, and resident in London; she is a frequent guest at my house, and I
am one of the trustees under her marriage settlement" (p. 274). The truth
was his brother had abandoned his wife in England to elope to America
with another woman; and Dickens contributed to the support of both
ladies.

On his triumphant return to New York for his final appearances, the
press planned a magnificent farewell dinner hosted by Horace Greeley at
Delmonico's for April 18. The pain that day was excruciating, but Dickens went anyway. He had to leave early, but not before delivering a heartfelt speech to over two hundred guests. He said that this time he had
"been received with unsurpassable politeness, delicacy, sweet temper,
hospitality, consideration, and with unsurpassable respect for the privacy daily enforced upon me by the nature of my avocation here, and the
state of my health" (p. 381). He spoke of "the amazing changes that I have
seen around me on every side,—changes moral, changes physical,
changes in the amount of land subdued and peopled, changes in the rise
of vast new cities, changes in the growth of older cities almost out of
recognition, changes in the graces and amenities of life, changes in the

[30]. Kate Douglas Wiggin, *My Garden of Memory* (Boston and New York: Houghton Mifflin,
1923), p. 41.

"The Press Dinner to Mr. Dickens at Delmonico's, New York."
Wood engraving after Thomas Nast and Mr. Warren,
The Illustrated Chicago News, May 1, 1868.
Courtesy Library of Congress.

Press, without whose advancement no advancement can take place any-where" (p. 380). He then instructed his publishers to print this speech as a postscript in all subsequent editions of both *American Notes* and *Martin Chuzzlewit.*

He finally departed America on April 22, 1868. By chance, Anthony Trollope was entering New York Harbor just as Dickens was leaving, and the two met on board the *Russia* before it set off. "I found him with one of his feet bound up," Trollope recalled in *The St. Paul's Magazine* (July 1870), "and he told me, with that pleasant smile that was so common to him, that he had lectured himself off his legs; otherwise he was quite well. When I heard afterwards of his labours in the States, and of the condition in which those labours had been continued, it seemed to be marvellous that any constitution should have stood it" (p. 371).

Back in London, he had hardly caught his breath when he announced his "Farewell Series of Readings," an ambitious one hundred performances through England, Scotland, and Ireland. He had some-thing new in mind for his repertoire. He wrote Forster in November 1868, "I wanted to leave behind me the recollection of something very passionate and dramatic, done with simple means, if the art would justify the theme" (p. 220). He settled on "Sikes and Nancy," the famous murder from *Oliver Twist*. His son Charley recalled in *The North American Review* (June 1895) overhearing him rehearsing it at Gad's Hill one afternoon; at first he thought there was a terrible fight outside. When he mentioned this to his father, Dickens offered to read it again for his opinion. "The finest thing I have ever heard," the son confessed, "but don't do it." He did not listen and tested it in a private trial performance at St. James' Hall on November 14; it met all his grand expectations. Exhausted and exhilarated at the same time, he asked his son Charley afterward what he thought of it now. "It is finer even than I expected," the young man replied, "but I still say, don't do it" (p. 681).

He loved watching the effects of "Sikes and Nancy" on his audiences. Women often fainted and had to be taken out. It wore him out too. Dolby urged him to drop it from his repertoire. His lameness returned; his doctor forbade him to travel. All Dickens worried about was the money that would be lost. Feeling better, he went off to Edinburgh anyway and collapsed again. He had to cancel. He began suffering from internal bleeding and poor circulation that left him lame. "With too short a rest after the heavy American experience," he wrote a friend on May 6, "I undoubtedly overdid the work of the Readings and the jar of continual Express Trains; the latter, incessant and extending over great distances; the former, greatly enhanced by the Murder from *Oliver Twist*, continually done with great passion and fury. All of a sudden (as it seemed) I became exhausted,—giddy, faint, and oddly uncertain of touch and tread." As he reported in this letter, he turned to his doctor and asked, "What is this?" "It is a serious warning," was the reply. "I know it well. Leave off instantly, and come away with me" (p. 350). He was forbidden to read that night, and the rest of the tour was canceled. "I dare say I *should* have been very ill," he admitted in a letter on May 18, 1869, "if I had not suddenly stopped 'Farewell Readings,' when there were yet five and twenty remaining to be given. I was quite exhausted, and was warned by the doctors to stop (for the time) instantly" (p. 355). Remarkably, he had completed seventy-four of the projected hundred readings.

Despite his family's fears of another breakdown, Dickens resumed his Final Readings with twelve performances at St. James's Hall from January 11 to March 15, 1870. His physician instructed Charley to run up and catch his father if he faltered in the slightest bit and bring him to him immediately. Otherwise, Dickens might die right then and there in front of the public. "Sikes and Nancy" agitated him most. "My ordinary pulse is 72," he explained to Macready in a letter of January 23, 1870, "and it runs up under this effort to 112. Besides which, it takes me ten or twelve minutes to get my wind back at all: I being in the meantime like the man who lost the fight:—in fact, his express image" (p. 470). The only thing he took to invigorate himself during the intermission was weak brandy and water. One night he could not say "Pickwick": it came out "Pickswick" . . . "Picnic" . . . "Peckwicks" . . . and other inanities.

On Tuesday, March 15, Charles Dickens read *A Christmas Carol* and "The Trial from *Pickwick*" for the last time. It was the biggest crowd the hall had ever seen, and hundreds more could not get in.[31] Charley recalled in *The North American Review* (June 1895) that he had never heard his father read "so well and with so little effort, and almost felt inclined to hope against hope that things had not been really so serious as the doctors had supposed" (p. 683). *The Illustrated London News* reported on March 18 that *A Christmas Carol* "is the most delightful of little stories, and always commands the most profound attention. Mr. Dickens reads it with marvellous pathos, and in the reading discriminates the characters with wonderful tact and evidently well-practised ability" (p. 301).

Perhaps no one else in the audience was more profoundly affected by the final reading than was the writer's eldest grandchild, nine-year-old Mary Angela Dickens. She admitted almost thirty years later that this very last memory she had of her beloved grandfather was "the most vivid of all. . . . The awe and excitement of the occasion make my heart beat a little faster even now as I recall it." Her parents chose to take her to hear *A Christmas Carol*, perhaps thinking a child would have no trouble appreciating the famous tale about Tiny Tim. "But I regret to say that the reading itself went completely over my head," she confessed, "and I only recollect being very frightened and uncomfortable." She found that the

---

31. Sir William P. Treloar and his new wife were among those who were profoundly moved by the way he read *A Christmas Carol*. "We spent many happy times together hearing Dickens read at St. James's Hall," he wrote in his introduction to a 1907 charity edition of *A Christmas Carol*. "We used to go early and get good seats: the doors were opened an hour or two before the reading began, and I would take a book, and she her knitting, and so while away the time before the performance began." He was so moved by Tiny Tim's fate that when he became Lord Mayor of London in 1907, one of his first acts was to issue a general appeal on behalf of the Crippled Children of the Nation. Known as "the Children's Lord Mayor," he founded the Lord Mayor Treloar's Hospital and College (now Lord Mayor Treloar's Orthopedic Hospital).

"Mr. Charles Dickens's Last Reading." Wood engraving,
The Illustrated London News, March 19, 1870.
Courtesy Library of Congress.

man "on the platform was quite a stranger to me, and his proceedings were so eccentric to be most alarming. He took no notice of me, or of my mother; and yet it seemed to me that he never took his eyes off me." The way he expressed Bob Cratchit's grief at Tiny Tim's deathbed was "my one intensely painful and distressing memory of my grandfather." She had never before seen a grown person cry. It troubled her that he, "of all people in the world, should cry with all those people looking on, and that no one should dare . . . express sympathy, or offer consolation, was nothing short of an upheaval of my universe."[32]

The audience called him back with tremendous applause that lasted

[32] Mary Angela Dickens, "A Child's Recollections at Gad's Hill," *The Strand Magazine,* January 1897, p. 74.

for minutes. With tears streaming down his face, he addressed them on the closing of his fifteen-year career as a professional reader. "In this task," he said in his brief speech, "and in every other which I have ever undertaken, as a faithful servant of the public, always imbued with a sense of duty to them, and always striving to do his best, I have been uniformly cheered by the readiest response, the most generous sympathy, and the most stimulating report." Now he would devote his time "exclusively to that art which first brought us together." He concluded, "from these garish lights I vanish now forever more, with a heartfelt, grateful, respectful, and affectionate farewell" (p. 413). But they would be not be done with him, and brought him back with tremendous clapping and the waving of handkerchiefs. With his eyes still moist with tears, he respectfully kissed his hand and then retired for good. He had read *A Christmas Carol* 127 times between December 27, 1853, and March 15, 1870. Only "The Trial from *Pickwick*" he had read more times, at 164 performances. All in all, the Public Readings had brought in £45,000, nearly half of his considerable estate. They also did much to keep *A Christmas Carol* alive, and far beyond the holiday season. Through these performances, it became one of the books most closely associated with the great Charles Dickens.

"The Readings have been splendidly successful," he bragged to his American friend Charles Eliot Norton in a letter on March 8. "They have not prevented my writing hard at my book, and I am well ahead. Furthermore, I am well in all respects" (p. 487). But he was far from well. The London *Globe and Traveller* (June 10, 1870) mentioned how Dickens was now noticed "alone, treading the pavement with laborious steps, figure bent forward, and head a little raised." It was painful "to see in the whole man's attitude and bearing, even in his great overcoat thrown back as if too heavy for his shoulders, and his hat pushed off from his forehead, the well-known signs of breaking health."

And he did not rest for a moment. He had breakfast with Gladstone and dined with Disraeli; he visited the queen, who never did hear him read *A Christmas Carol*. He found time to direct some private theatricals for some friends, but he was too lame to take a role himself. He also was hard at work on the new serial, *The Mystery of Edwin Drood*, and *All the Year Round*. He had six of the projected twelve parts of the novel done when, on June 8, 1870, he suffered a massive paralytic stroke at dinner at Gad's Hill. He died the next day, never having regained consciousness. He was only fifty-eight years old. Everyone agreed later that the strain of the Public Readings, particularly "Sikes and Nancy," had contributed considerably to his untimely death.

It was the wish of the people of England that Charles Dickens be buried in the Poet's Corner of Westminster Abbey, on June 14. "His creations have become naturalized, so to speak, among all classes of the community, and are familiar to every man, high or low," said the London *Times* on June 11. He was the "great apostle of the people" who "touched their hearts and taught them that those inferior beings had hearts and souls of their own, and could be objects of sympathy as well as victims of neglect." *The New York Times* predicted the same day that the name of Charles Dickens "will be spoken with gratitude and affection as long as our language endures." "As *Pickwick* is his most amusing work, so the *Christmas Carol*, although so short, is his most touching," said the London *Globe and Traveller* on June 10; "and there are few men who have not felt better and more kindly disposed towards humanity at large than they ever felt before, when they had read, or still better listened to, Charles Dickens reading the exquisite pathos of Tiny Tim's contented but suffering life." Thomas Carlyle recalled his friend as "the good, the gentle, high-gifted, ever-friendly, noble Dickens; every inch of him an honest man." The day after he died, a laborer in Birmingham went into a tobacco shop and said, as he put his money on the counter, "Charles Dickens is dead. We have lost our best friend."[33]

[33.] Carlyle and laborer quoted in Henry Fielding Dickens, "A Chat about Charles Dickens," pp. 189, 188.

Scrooge's Christmas Visitors.

𝔄 𝔠𝔥𝔯𝔦𝔰𝔱𝔪𝔞𝔰 𝔠𝔞𝔯𝔬𝔩.
𝔍𝔫 𝔣𝔬𝔲𝔯 𝔖𝔱𝔞𝔳𝔢𝔰.[1]

ILLUSTRATED BY SOL EYTINGE, JR. (1868)

STAVE ONE.

MARLEY'S GHOST.

Marley was dead, to begin with.[2] There is no doubt whatever about that. The register of his burial was signed by the clergyman, the clerk, the undertaker, and the chief mourner. Scrooge signed it. And Scrooge's name was good upon 'Change for anything he chose to put his hand to.

Old Marley was as dead as door-nail.[3]

Scrooge[4] knew he was dead? Of course he did. How could it be otherwise? Scrooge and he were partners for I don't know how many years. Scrooge was his sole executor, his sole administrator, his sole assign, his sole residuary legatee, his sole friend, his sole mourner.

Scrooge never painted out old Marley's name, however. There it yet stood, years afterwards, above the warehouse door,—Scrooge and Marley. The firm was known as Scrooge and Marley. Sometimes people new to the business called Scrooge Scrooge, and sometimes Marley. He answered to both names. It was all the same to him.

Oh! But he was a tight-fisted hand at the grindstone, was Scrooge! a squeezing, wrenching, grasping, scraping, clutching, covetous old sinner! External heat and cold had little influence on him. No warmth could warm, no cold could chill him. No wind that blew was bitterer than he, no falling snow was more intent upon

1. *A CHRISTMAS CAROL. IN FOUR STAVES.* At one of his earliest Public Readings, Dickens gave the following introduction:

Allow me . . . before I commence, to express two wishes. The first is that you will have the kindness, by a great stretch of the imagination, to imagine this a small social party assembled to hear a tale told round the Christmas fire; and secondly, that if you feel disposed as we go along to give expression to any emotion, whether grave or gay, you will do so with perfect freedom from restraint, and without the least apprehension of disturbing me. Nothing can be so delightful to me on such occasions as the assurance that my hearers accompany me with something of the pleasure and interest I shall have in conducting them; and, believe me, I cannot desire anything so much as the establishment amongst us, from the very beginning, of a perfectly unfettered, cordial, friendly sentiment. (*Bradford Observer* January 4, 1855).

He slightly changed his remarks when he began his readings for profit in 1858:

Ladies and gentleman, the little book I am to have the honour of presenting to you is divided into four parts; I shall pause about five minutes at the end of the second. Before I begin, allow me to express a hope that you will be as easy and as natural with me as I shall try with all my heart to be with you; that you will give to any little emotion which the story may be so fortunate as to awaken within you the freest expression, and not be under any misapprehension of disturbing me thereby, as nothing can be more agreeable to me than to receive any assurance that you are interested. (*The Liverpool Mail*, August 21, 1858)

But by the time Dickens read in America in December 1867, his opening remarks were as brief as possible: "Ladies and gentlemen, —I am to have the pleasure of reading to you first, to-night, *A Christmas Carol in Four Staves*. Stave One. Marley's Ghost . . ." (Kate Field, *Pen Photographs of Dickens's Readings* [Boston: James R. Osgood, 1871], p. 28).

2. *Marley was dead, to begin with. There is no doubt whatever about that.* "His first words sounded like a trumpet blast of assured victory," the writer's friend John Hollingshead recalled Dickens' reading in *My Lifetime* (vol. 1, London: Sampson Low, Marston, 1895). "It was the great author breathing the breath of life into his great creations" (p. 187). Charles Kent confirmed in *Charles Dickens as a Reader* (London: Chapman and Hall, 1872), "The opening sentences were always given in those cheery, comfortable tones, indicative of a double relish on the part of the narrator— to wit, his own enjoyment of the tale he is

going to relate, and his anticipation of the enjoyment of it by those who are giving him their attention" (p. 96). But Kate Field was not impressed at first. "Dickens's voice is limited in power, husky, and naturally monotonous," she quoted a critic sitting next to her in *Pen Photographs of Dickens's Readings*. "If he succeeds in overcoming these defects, it will be by dramatic genius." She too began "to take a gloomy view of the situation, and wonder why Dickens constantly employs the rising inflection, and never comes to a full stop; but we are so pleasantly and naturally introduced to Scrooge that my spirits revive" (p. 28).

3. *dead as a door-nail.* "When he pronounced the sentence," reported the *Philadelphia Inquirer* on January 14, 1868, "his success that night at least was rendered certain. The dropping of a pin could have been heard in the room. The audience . . . had become as still as the grave."

4. *Scrooge.* Walter Pine reported in "The Return of the Native: Dickens's Readings at Portsmouth" (*The Dickensian*, summer 1939) that one of the most vivid memories his own father had of Dickens' reading of *A Christmas Carol* at Portsmouth on November 11, 1858, was "the blood-curdling and yet almost loving way in which the name of 'Scr-ooge' was pronounced—long-drawn-out and with tremendous emphasis" (p. 206). "His 'Scrooge,'" said the New York *Evening Express* (December 10, 1867) of the first reading at Steinway Hall, "is the perfect embodiment of the stony-hearted old screw we have pictured to us in the *Carol*."

its purpose, no pelting rain less open to entreaty. Foul weather didn't know where to have him. The heaviest rain and snow and hail and sleet could boast of the advantage over him in only one respect,—they often "came down" handsomely, and Scrooge never did.

Nobody ever stopped him in the street to say, with gladsome looks, "My dear Scrooge, how are you? When will you come to see me?" No beggars implored him to bestow a trifle, no children asked him what it was o'clock, no man or woman ever once in all his life inquired the way to such and such a place, of Scrooge. Even the blindmen's dogs appeared to know him; and when they saw him coming on, would tug their owners into doorways and up courts; and then would wag their tails as though they said, "No eye at all is better than an evil eye, dark master!"

But what did Scrooge care! It was the very thing he liked. To edge his way along the crowded paths of life, warning all human sympathy to keep its distance, was what the knowing ones call "nuts" to Scrooge.

Once upon a time—of all the good days in the year, upon a Christmas eve—old Scrooge sat busy in his counting-house.[5] It was cold, bleak, biting, foggy weather; and the city clocks had only just gone three, but it was quite dark already.

The door of Scrooge's counting-house was open, that he might keep his eye upon his clerk, who, in a dismal little cell beyond, a sort of tank, was copying letters. Scrooge had a very small fire, but the clerk's fire was so very much smaller that it looked like one coal. But he couldn't replenish it, for Scrooge kept the coal-box in his own room; and so surely as the clerk came in with the shovel the master predicted that it would be necessary for them to part. Wherefore the clerk put on his white comforter, and tried to warm himself at the candle; in which effort, not being a man of a strong imagination, he failed.

"A merry Christmas, uncle! God save you!" cried a cheerful voice. It was the voice of Scrooge's nephew,

5. *old Scrooge sat busy in his counting-house.* Henry M. Fields, who attended a public reading in London, on June 17, 1858, thought Dickens as Scrooge was worthy of comparison with Edmund Kean's Shylock in *The Merchant of Venice.* Dickens "drew down his face into his collar, like a great turtle drawing in his head, put on a surly look, and spoke in a gruff voice. . . . We see him there, crouching like a wolf in his den, snarling at any intruder, and keeping a sharp eye on a poor clerk . . . who trembles under that evil eye" (*Summer Pictures from Copenhagen to Venice* [New York: Sheldon, 1859], p. 32).

6. *He should!* Philip Collins in his 1971 edition of the Berg prompt copy quoted Rowland Hill, who attended several readings between 1868 and 1870, as reporting that Dickens here spoke "most emphatically, finishing the paragraph with a good bang on his reading table" (p. 179).

who came upon him so quickly that this was the first intimation Scrooge had of his approach.

"Bah!" said Scrooge; "humbug!"

"Christmas a humbug, uncle! You don't mean that, I am sure?"

"I do. Out upon merry Christmas! What's Christmas time to you but a time for paying bills without money; a time for finding yourself a year older, and not an hour richer; a time for balancing your books and having every item in 'em through a round dozen of months presented dead against you? If I had my will, every idiot who goes about with 'Merry Christmas' on his lips should be boiled with his own pudding, and buried with a stake of holly through his heart. He should!"[6]

"Uncle!"

"Nephew, keep Christmas in your own way, and let me keep it in mine."

"Keep it! But you don't keep it."

"Let me leave it alone, then. Much good may it do you! Much good it has ever done you!"

"There are many things from which I might have derived good, by which I have not profited, I dare say, Christmas among the rest. But I am sure I have always thought of Christmas time, when it has come round,— apart from the veneration due to its sacred origin, if anything belonging to it *can* be apart from that,—as a good time; a kind, forgiving, charitable, pleasant time; the only time I know of, in the long calendar of the year, when men and women seem by one consent to open their shut-up hearts freely, and to think of people below them as if they really were fellow-travellers to the grave, and not another race of creatures bound on other journeys. And therefore, uncle, though it has never put a scrap of gold or silver in my pocket, I believe that it *has* done me good, and *will* do me good; and I say, God bless it!"

The clerk in the tank involuntarily applauded.

"Let me hear another sound from *you*," said Scrooge, "and you'll keep your Christmas by losing your situation! You're quite a powerful speaker, sir," he added, turning to his nephew. "I wonder you don't go into Parliament."

"Don't be angry, uncle. Come! Dine with us to-morrow."

Scrooge said that he would see him—yes, indeed he did. He went the whole length of the expression, and said that he would see him in that extremity first.

"But why?" cried Scrooge's nephew. "Why?"

"Why did you get married?"

"Because I fell in love."

"Because you fell in love!" growled Scrooge, as if that were the only one thing in the world more ridiculous than a merry Christmas. "Good afternoon!"

"Nay, uncle, but you never came to see me before that happened. Why give it as a reason for not coming now?"

"Good afternoon."

"I want nothing from you; I ask nothing of you; why cannot we be friends?"

"Good afternoon."

"I am sorry, with all my heart, to find you so resolute. We have never had any quarrel, to which I have been a party. But I have made the trial in homage to Christmas, and I'll keep my Christmas humor to the last. So A Merry Christmas, uncle!"

"Good afternoon!"

"And A Happy New-Year!"

"Good afternoon!"[7]

His nephew left the room without an angry word, notwithstanding. The clerk, in letting Scrooge's nephew out, had let two other people in. They were portly gentlemen,[8] pleasant to behold, and now stood, with their hats off, in Scrooge's office. They had books and papers in their hands, and bowed to him.

"Scrooge and Marley's, I believe," said one of the gentlemen, referring to his list. "Have I the pleasure of addressing Mr. Scrooge, or Mr. Marley?"

"Mr. Marley has been dead these seven years. He died seven years ago, this very night."

7. *"Good afternoon!"* Charles Kent recalled in *Charles Dickens as a Reader* that this exclamation was "delivered with irresistibly ludicrous iteration" (p. 101).

8. *They were portly gentlemen.* "Here," noted Henry M. Fields in *Summer Pictures from Copenhagen to Venice*, "Dickens drew himself up with a dignified air, such as would become a portly and benevolent gentleman, and spoke in his blandest tones" (p. 32).

9. *"If quite convenient, sir."* "A few words," Kate Field observed in *Pen Photographs*, "but they denote Bob Cratchit in three feet of comforter exclusive of fringe, in well-darned, thread-bare clothes, with a mild, frightened, lisping voice, so thin you can see through it!" (p. 30). John Hollingshead reported in *The Critic* (September 4, 1858) that "Mr. Dickens throws himself into Bob Cratchit, leaning over the elbow-rest upon the reading-table, with a meek, subdued voice, and a mild timid expression of countenance," casting "an instantaneous impression of the poor, feeble, struggling clerk, which lights up the whole history of his past life" (p. 537). Charles Kent confirmed in *Charles Dickens as a Reader* that the clerk had "the thinnest and meekest of frightened voices" (p. 101). *The New York Times* (December 10, 1867) reported that with this line, "the audience caught sight at once of the little, round-faced, deferential, simple-hearted clerk as if he had entered bodily; and they greeted him with a hearty round of applause,—the first in which they had interrupted his reading." Dickens gave *The Scotsman* (December 21, 1868) the vivid picture of Bob Cratchit "with his teeth missing from his lower jaw and his upper lip drawn in, and a whistle in his speech and a cheery look about his wizened face, and a scared look in the eye."

"At this festive season of the year, Mr. Scrooge," said the gentleman, taking up a pen, "it is more than usually desirable that we should make some slight provision for the poor and destitute, who suffer greatly at the present time. Many thousands are in want of common necessaries; hundreds of thousands are in want of common comforts, sir."

"Are there no prisons?"

"Plenty of prisons. But under the impression that they scarcely furnish Christian cheer of mind or body to the unoffending multitude, a few of us are endeavoring to raise a fund to buy the poor some meat and drink, and means of warmth. We choose this time, because it is a time, of all others, when Want is keenly felt, and Abundance rejoices. What shall I put you down for?"

"Nothing!"

"You wish to be anonymous?"

"I wish to be left alone. Since you ask me what I wish, gentlemen, that is my answer. I don't make merry myself at Christmas, and I can't afford to make idle people merry. I help to support the prisons and the workhouses—they cost enough,—and those who are badly off must go there."

"Many can't go there; and many would rather die."

"If they would rather die, they had better do it, and decrease the surplus population."

At length the hour of shutting up the counting house arrived. With an ill-will Scrooge, dismounting from his stool, tacitly admitted the fact to the expectant clerk in the Tank, who instantly snuffed his candle out, and put on his hat.

"You'll want all day to-morrow, I suppose?"

"If quite convenient, sir."[9]

"It's not convenient, and it's not fair. If I was to stop half a crown for it, you'd think yourself mightily ill-used, I'll be bound?"

"Yes, sir."

"And yet you don't think *me* ill-used, when I pay a day's wages for no work."

"It's only once a year, sir."

"A poor excuse for picking a man's pocket every twenty-fifth of December! But I suppose you must have the whole day. Be here all the earlier *next* morning."

The clerk promised that he would; and Scrooge walked out with a growl. The office was closed in a twinkling, and the clerk, with the long ends of his white comforter dangling below his waist (for he boasted no great-coat), went down a slide, at the end of a lane of boys, twenty times, in honor of its being Christmas eve, and then ran home as hard as he could pelt, to play at blindman's-buff.

Scrooge took his melancholy dinner in his usual melancholy tavern; and having read all the newspapers, and beguiled the rest of the evening with his banker's book, went home to bed. He lived in chambers which had once belonged to his deceased partner. They were a gloomy suite of rooms, in a lowering pile of building up a yard. The building was old enough now, and dreary enough; for nobody lived in it but Scrooge, the other rooms being all let out as offices.

Now it is a fact, that there was nothing at all particular about the knocker on the door of this house, except that it was very large; also, that Scrooge had seen it, night and morning, during his whole residence in that place; also, that Scrooge had as little of what is called fancy about him as any man in the city of London. And yet Scrooge, having his key in the lock of the door, saw in the knocker, without its undergoing any intermediate process of change, not a knocker, but Marley's face.

Marley's face, with a dismal light about it, like a bad lobster in a dark cellar. It was not angry or ferocious, but it looked at Scrooge as Marley used to look,—with ghostly spectacles turned up upon its ghostly forehead.

As Scrooge looked fixedly at this phenomenon, it was a knocker again. He said, "Pooh, pooh!" and closed the door with a bang.

Marley's Face.

The sound resounded through the house like thunder. Every room above, and every cask in the wine-merchant's cellars below, appeared to have a separate peal of echoes of its own. Scrooge was not a man to be frightened by echoes. He fastened the door, and walked across the hall, and up the stairs. Slowly too, trimming his candle as he went.

Up Scrooge went, not caring a button for its being very dark. Darkness is cheap, and Scrooge liked it. But before he shut his heavy door, he walked through his rooms to see that all was right. He had just enough recollection of the face to desire to do that.

Sitting-room, bedroom, lumber-room, all as they

should be. Nobody under the table, nobody under the sofa; a small fire in the grate; spoon and basin ready; and the little saucepan of gruel (Scrooge had a cold in his head) upon the hob. Nobody under the bed; nobody in the closet; nobody in his dressing-gown, which was hanging up in a suspicious attitude against the wall. Lumber-room as usual. Old fire-guard, old shoes, two fish-baskets, washing-stand on three legs, and a poker.

Quite satisfied, he closed his door, and locked himself in; double-locked himself in, which was not his custom. Thus secured against surprise, he took off his cravat, put on his dressing-gown and slippers and his nightcap, and sat down before the very low fire to take his gruel.

As he threw his head back in the chair, his glance happened to rest upon a bell, a disused bell, that hung in the room, and communicated, for some purpose now forgotten, with a chamber in the highest story of the building. It was with great astonishment, and with a strange, inexplicable dread,[10] that, as he looked, he saw this bell begin to swing. Soon it rang out loudly, and so did every bell in the house.

This was succeeded by a clanking noise, deep down below, as if some person were dragging a heavy chain over the casks in the wine-merchant's cellar.

Then he heard the noise much louder, on the floors below; then coming up the stairs; then coming straight towards his door.

It came on through the heavy door, and a spectre passed into the room before his eyes. And upon its coming in, the dying flame leaped up, as though it cried, "I know him! Marley's Ghost!"[11]

The same face, the very same. Marley in his pigtail, usual waistcoat, tights, and boots. His body was transparent; so that Scrooge, observing him, and looking through his waistcoat, could see the two buttons on his coat behind.[12]

Scrooge had often heard it said that Marley had no bowels, but he had never believed it until now.[13]

10. *a strange, inexplicable dread.* "Dickens' voice grows husky with terror," Henry M. Fields noted in *Summer Pictures from Copenhagen to Venice*, "as if we were sitting in Scrooge's place, and felt his heart die within us" (p. 33).

11. *Marley's ghost!* "The apparition, although the description of which was nearly stenographically abbreviated in the Reading, appeared to be, in a very few words, no less startlingly realised," noticed Charles Kent in *Charles Dickens as a Reader* (p. 102). Kate Field reported in *Pen Photographs* that "Scrooge bites his fingers nervously as he peers at the ghost" (p. 30).

12. *could see the two buttons on his coat behind. The Aberdeen Journal* (October 6, 1858) said that this description "became a veritable realisation of all that table-rapping had ever dreamt of. The dismal facetiousness of Scrooge and his unearthly visitor, made an abundance of mirth without interrupting the spectral illusion."

13. *but he had never believed it until now.* "Here, if a man be great in the humorous line, Dickens *was* great," said the *Philadelphia Inquirer* (January 14, 1868). "The manner in which he uttered the two last sentences . . . and the grotesque countenance of horror which he exhibited, were laughable in the extreme. . . . The last sentence, as given by Dickens, brought down the house."

No, nor did he believe it even now. Though he looked the phantom through and through, and saw it standing before him,—though he felt the chilling influence of its death-cold eyes, and noticed the very texture of the folded kerchief bound about its head and chin,— he was still incredulous.

"How now!" said Scrooge, caustic and cold as ever. "What do you want with me?"

"Much!"—Marley's voice, no doubt about it.

"Who are you?"

"Ask me who I *was*."

"Who *were* you then?"

"In life I was your partner, Jacob Marley."

"Can you—can you sit down?"

"I can."

"Do it, then."

Scrooge asked the question, because he didn't know whether a ghost so transparent might find himself in a condition to take a chair; and felt that, in the event of its being impossible, it might involve the necessity of an embarrassing explanation. But the ghost sat down on the opposite side of the fireplace, as if he were quite used to it.

"You don't believe in me."

"I don't."

"What evidence would you have of my reality beyond that of your senses?"

"I don't know."

"Why do you doubt your senses?"

"Because a little thing affects them. A slight disorder of the stomach makes them cheats. You may be an undigested bit of beef, a blot of mustard, a crumb of cheese, a fragment of an underdone potato. There's more of gravy than of grave about you, whatever you are!"

Scrooge was not much in the habit of cracking jokes, nor did he feel in his heart by any means waggish then. The truth is, that he tried to be smart, as a means

Marley's Ghost.

of distracting his own attention, and keeping down his horror.

But how much greater was his horror when, the phantom taking off the bandage round its head, as if it were too warm to wear in-doors, its lower jaw dropped down upon its breast!

"Mercy! Dreadful apparition, why do you trouble me? Why do spirits walk the earth, and why do they come to me?"

"It is required of every man, that the spirit within him should walk abroad among his fellowmen, and travel far and wide; and if that spirit goes not forth in life, it is condemned to do so after death. I cannot tell you all I would. A very little more is permitted to me. I cannot rest, I cannot stay, I cannot linger anywhere. My spirit never walked beyond our counting-house—mark me!—in life my spirit never roved beyond the narrow limits of our money-changing hole; and weary journeys lie before me!"

"Seven years dead. And travelling all the time? You travel fast?"

"On the wings of the wind."

"You might have got over a great quantity of ground in seven years."

"O blind man, blind man! not to know that ages of incessant labor by immortal creatures for this earth must pass into eternity before the good of which it is susceptible is all developed. Not to know that any Christian spirit working kindly in its little sphere, whatever it may be, will find its mortal life too short for its vast means of usefulness. Not to know that no space of regret can make amends for one life's opportunities misused! Yet I was like this man; I once was like this man!"

"But you were always a good man of business, Jacob," faltered Scrooge, who now began to apply this to himself.

"Business!" cried the Ghost, wringing its hands again. "Mankind was my business. The common welfare was my business; charity, mercy, forbearance, benevolence, were all my business. The dealings of my trade were but a drop of water in the comprehensive ocean of my business!"

Scrooge was very much dismayed to hear the spectre going on at this rate, and began to quake exceedingly.

"Hear me! My time is nearly gone."

"I will. But don't be hard upon me! Don't be flowery, Jacob! Pray!"

"I am here to-night to warn you that you have yet a

chance and hope of escaping my fate. A chance and hope of my procuring, Ebenezer."

"You were always a good friend to me. Thank'ee!"

"You will be haunted by Three Spirits."

"Is that the chance and hope you mentioned, Jacob? I—I think I'd rather not."

"Without their visits, you cannot hope to shun the path I tread. Expect the first to-morrow night, when the bell tolls One. Expect the second on the next night at the same hour. The third, upon the next night, when the last stroke of Twelve has ceased to vibrate. Look to see me no more; and look that, for your own sake, you remember what has passed between us!"

It walked backward from him; and at every step it took, the window raised itself a little, so that, when the apparition reached it, it was wide open.[14]

Scrooge closed the window, and examined the door by which the Ghost had entered. It was double-locked, as he had locked it with his own hands, and the bolts were undisturbed. Scrooge tried to say, "Humbug!" but stopped at the first syllable. And being, from the emotion he had undergone, or the fatigues of the day, or his glimpse of the invisible world, or the dull conversation of the Ghost, or the lateness of the hour, much in need of repose, he went straight to bed, without undressing, and fell asleep on the instant.

14. *it was wide open.* Ticknor and Fields' printers failed to catch a line in the Berg prompt copy: "and [it] floated out through the self-opened window into the bleak dark night."

STAVE TWO.

THE FIRST OF THE THREE SPIRITS.

When Scrooge awoke, it was so dark, that, looking out of bed, he could scarcely distinguish the transparent window from the opaque walls of his chamber, until suddenly the church clock tolled a deep, dull, hollow, melancholy ONE.

Light flashed up in the room upon the instant, and the curtains of his bed were drawn aside by a strange figure,—like a child: yet not so like a child as like an old man, viewed through some supernatural medium, which gave him the appearance of having receded from the view, and being diminished to a child's proportions. Its hair, which hung about its neck and down its back, was white as if with age; and yet the face had not a wrinkle in it, and the tenderest bloom was on the skin. It held a branch of fresh green holly in its hand; and, in singular contradiction of that wintry emblem, had its dress trimmed with summer flowers. But the strangest thing about it was, that from the crown of its head there sprung a bright clear jet of light, by which all this was visible; and which was doubtless the occasion of its using, in its duller moments, a great extinguisher for a cap, which it now held under its arm.

"Are you the Spirit, sir, whose coming was foretold to me?"

"I am!"

"Who and what are you?"

"I am the Ghost of Christmas Past."

"Long past?"

The Spirit of Christmas Past.

"No. Your past. The things that you will see with me are shadows of the things that have been; they will have no consciousness of us."

Scrooge then made bold to inquire·what business brought him there.

"Your welfare. Rise, and walk with me!"

It would have been in vain for Scrooge·to plead that the weather and the hour were not adapted to pedestrian purposes; that bed was warm, and the thermometer a long way below freezing; that he was clad but lightly in his slippers, dressing-gown, and nightcap; and that he had a cold upon him at that time. The grasp, though gentle as a woman's hand, was not to be resisted. He rose; but finding that the Spirit made towards the window, clasped its robe in supplication.

"I am a mortal, and liable to fall."

"Bear but a touch of my hand *there,*" said the Spirit, laying it upon his heart, "and you shall be upheld in more than this!"

As the words were spoken, they passed through the wall, and stood in the busy thoroughfares of a city. It was made plain enough by the dressing of the shops that here, too, it was Christmas time.

The Ghost stopped at a certain warehouse door, and asked Scrooge if he knew it.

"Know it! Was I apprenticed here!"

They went in. At sight of an old gentleman in a Welsh wig, sitting behind such a high desk that, if he had been two inches taller, he must have knocked his head against the ceiling, Scrooge cried in great excitement: "Why, it's old Fezziwig! Bless his heart, it's Fezziwig, alive again!"

Old Fezziwig laid down his pen, and looked up at the clock, which pointed to the hour of seven. He rubbed his hands; adjusted his capacious waistcoat; laughed all over himself, from his shoes to his organ of benevolence; and called out in a comfortable, oily, rich, fat, jovial voice: "Yo ho, there! Ebenezer! Dick!"

A living and moving picture of Scrooge's former self, a young man, came briskly in, accompanied by his fellow-prentice.

"Dick Wilkins, to be sure!" said Scrooge to the Ghost. "My old fellow-prentice, bless me, yes. There he is. He was very much attached to me, was Dick. Poor Dick! Dear, dear!"

"Yo ho, my boys!" said Fezziwig. "No more work to-night. Christmas eve, Dick. Christmas, Ebenezer! Let's have the shutters up, before a man can say Jack Robinson! Clear away, my lads, and let's have lots of room here!"

Clear away! There was nothing they wouldn't have

cleared away, or couldn't have cleared away, with old Fezziwig looking on. It was done in a minute. Every movable was packed off, as if were dismissed from public life forevermore; the floor was swept and watered, the lamps were trimmed, fuel was heaped upon the fire; and the warehouse was as snug and warm and dry and bright a ball-room as you would desire to see upon a winter's night.

In came a fiddler with a music-book, and went up to the lofty desk, and made an orchestra of it, and tuned like fifty stomach-aches. In came Mrs. Fezziwig, one vast substantial smile. In came the three Miss Fezziwigs, beaming and lovable. In came the six young followers whose hearts they broke. In came all the young men and women employed in the business. In came the housemaid, with her cousin the baker. In came the cook, with her brother's particular friend the milkman. In they all came one after another; some shyly, some boldly, some gracefully, some awkwardly, some pushing, some pulling; in they all came, anyhow and everyhow. Away they all went,[1] twenty couple at once; hands half round and back again the other way; down the middle and up again; round and round in various stages of affectionate grouping; old top couple always turning up in the wrong place; new top couple starting off again, as soon as they got there; all top couples at last, and not a bottom one to help them. When this result was brought about, old Fezziwig, clapping his hands to stop the dance, cried out, "Well done!" and the fiddler plunged his hot face into a pot of porter especially provided for that purpose.

There were more dances, and there were forfeits, and more dances, and there was cake, and there was negus, and there was a great piece of Cold Roast, and there was a great piece of Cold Boiled, and there were mince-pies, and plenty of beer. But the great effect of the evening came after the Roast and Boiled, when the fiddler struck up "Sir Roger de Coverley." Then old Fezziwig stood out to dance with Mrs. Fezziwig. Top

1. *Away they all went.* Kate Field explained that the delightfully comic rendering of this dance was "owing to the inimitable action of his hands," which "actually perform upon the table, as if they were the floor of Fezziwig's room, and every finger were a leg belonging to one of the Fezziwig family. That *feat* is only surpassed by Dickens's illustration of Sir Roger de Coverley, as interpreted by Mr. and Mrs. Fezziwig" (*Pen Photographs*, p. 31).

couple, too; with a good stiff piece of work cut out for them; three or four and twenty pair of partners; people who were not to be trifled with; people who *would* dance, and had no notion of walking.

But if they had been twice as many,—four times,—old Fezziwig would have been a match for them and so would Mrs. Fezziwig. As to *her*, she was worthy to be his partner in every sense of the term. A positive light appeared to issue from Fezziwig's calves. They shone in every part of the dance. You couldn't have predicted, at any given time, what would become of 'em next. And when old Fezziwig and Mrs. Fezziwig had gone all through the dance,—advance and retire, turn your

The Fezziwig Ball.

partner, bow and courtesy, corkscrew, thread the needle, and back again to your place,—Fezziwig "cut,"—cut so deftly, that he appeared to wink with his legs.[2]

When the clock struck eleven this domestic ball broke up. Mr. and Mrs. Fezziwig took their stations, one on either side the door, and, shaking hands with every person individually as he or she went out, wished him or her a Merry Christmas. When everybody had retired but the two 'prentices, they did the same to them; and thus the cheerful voices died away, and the lads were left to their beds, which were under a counter in the back shop.

"A small matter," said the Ghost, "to make these silly folks so full of gratitude. He has spent but a few pounds of your mortal money,—three or four perhaps. Is that so much that he deserves this praise?"

"It isn't that," said Scrooge, heated by the remark, and speaking unconsciously like his former, not his latter self,—"it isn't that, Spirit. He has the power to render us happy or unhappy; to make our service light or burdensome; a pleasure or a toil. Say that his power lies in words and looks; in things so slight and insignificant that it is impossible to add and count 'em up: what then? The happiness he gives is quite as great as if it cost a fortune."

He felt the Spirit's glance, and stopped.

"What is the matter?"

"Nothing particular."

"Something, I think?"

"No, no. I should like to be able to say a word or two to my clerk just now. That's all."

"My time grows short," observed the Spirit. "Quick!"

This was not addressed to Scrooge, or to any one whom he could see, but it produced an immediate effect. For again he saw himself. He was older now; a man in the prime of life.

He was not alone, but sat by the side of a fair young girl in a black dress, in whose eyes there were tears.

2. *he appeared to wink with his legs.* Originally, according to John Hollingshead in his review in *The Critic* (September 4, 1858), Dickens spoke this phrase "with a spasmodic shake of the head and a twist of the paper knife" (p. 537). By the time he came to America in 1867, he found a more effective way of doing it. "Mr. Dickens, for the purpose of enforcing the fact, actually did wink with his eyes," reported *The New York Times* on December 10, 1867. The New York *Commercial Advertiser* (December 3, 1867) said that this incident proved to be "the greatest hit of the evening" on his American debut at Tremont Temple in Boston. "The contagion of the audience's laughter reached Mr. Dickens himself, who with difficulty brought out the inimitable drollery," wrote the Boston correspondent. "This was too much for Boston, and I thought the roof would go off." In New York, according to the *Commercial Advertiser* (December 10), it was received with loud "clapping, followed with peals of laughter." It seems to have had much the same effect throughout America. "As the last sentence was uttered," reported *The Providence Press* (February 21, 1868), "the audience was convulsed with laughter."

"It matters little," she said softly to Scrooge's former self. "To you, very little. Another idol has displaced me; and if it can comfort you in time to come, as I would have tried to do, I have no just cause to grieve."

"What Idol has displaced you?"

"A golden one. You fear the world too much. I have seen your nobler aspirations fall off one by one, until the master-passion, Gain, engrosses you. Have I not?"

"What then? Even if I have grown so much wiser, what then? I am not changed towards you. Have I ever sought release from our engagement?"

"In words, no. Never."

"In what, then?"

"In a changed nature; in an altered spirit; in another atmosphere of life; another Hope as its great end. If you were free to-day, to-morrow, yesterday, can even I believe that you would choose a dowerless girl; or, choosing her, do I not know that your repentance and regret would surely follow? I do; and I release you. With a full heart, for the love of him you once were."

"Spirit! remove me from this place."

"I told you these were shadows of the things that have been," said the Ghost. "That they are what they are, do not blame me!"

"Remove me!" Scrooge exclaimed. "I cannot bear it! Leave me! Take me back. Haunt me no longer!"

As he struggled with the Spirit he was conscious of being exhausted, and overcome by an irresistible drowsiness; and, further, of being in his own bedroom. He had barely time to reel to bed before he sank into a heavy sleep.

STAVE THREE.

THE SECOND OF THE THREE SPIRITS.

Scrooge awoke in his own bedroom. There was no doubt about that. But it and his own adjoining sitting-room, into which he shuffled in his slippers, attracted by a great light there, had undergone a surprising transformation. The walls and ceiling were so hung with living green, that it looked a perfect grove. The leaves of holly, mistletoe, and ivy reflected back the light, as if so many little mirrors had been scattered there; and such a mighty blaze went roaring up the chimney, as that petrifaction of a hearth had never known in Scrooge's time, or Marley's, or for many and many a winter season gone. Heaped upon the floor, to form a kind of throne, were turkeys, geese, game, brawn, great joints of meat, sucking pigs, long wreaths of sausages, mince-pies, plum-puddings, barrels of oysters, red-hot chestnuts, cherry-cheeked apples, juicy oranges, luscious pears, immense twelfth-cakes, and great bowls of punch. In easy state upon this couch there sat a Giant glorious to see; who bore a glowing torch, in shape not unlike Plenty's horn, and who raised it high to shed its light on Scrooge, as he came peeping round the door.

"Come in,—come in! and know me better, man! I am the Ghost of Christmas Present. Look upon me! You have never seen the like of me before!"

"Never."

"Have never walked forth with the younger members of my family; meaning (for I am very young) my

The Spirit of Christmas Present.

elder brothers born in these later years?" pursued the Phantom.

"I don't think I have, I am afraid I have not. Have you had many brothers, Spirit?"

"More than eighteen hundred."

"A tremendous family to provide for! Spirit, conduct me where you will. I went forth last night on compulsion, and I learnt a lesson which is working now. To-night, if you have aught to teach me, let me profit by it."

"Touch my robe!"

Scrooge did as he was told, and held it fast.

The room and its contents all vanished instantly, and they stood in the city streets upon a snowy Christmas morning.

Scrooge and the Ghost passed on, invisible, straight to Scrooge's clerk's; and on the threshold of the door the Spirit smiled, and stopped to bless Bob Cratchit's dwelling with the sprinklings of his torch. Think of that! Bob had but fifteen "Bob" a week himself; he pocketed on Saturdays but fifteen copies of his Christian name; and yet the Ghost of Christmas Present blessed his four-roomed house!

Then up rose Mrs. Cratchit, Cratchit's wife, dressed out but poorly in a twice-turned gown, but brave in ribbons, which are cheap and make a goodly show for sixpence; and she laid the cloth, assisted by Belinda Cratchit, second of her daughters, also brave in ribbons; while Master Peter Cratchit plunged a fork into the saucepan of potatoes, and, getting the corners of his monstrous shirt-collar (Bob's private property, conferred upon his son and heir in honor of the day) into his mouth, rejoiced to find himself so gallantly attired, and yearned to show his linen in the fashionable Parks. And now two smaller Cratchits, boy and girl, came tearing in, screaming that outside the baker's they had smelt the goose, and known it for their own; and, basking in luxurious thoughts of sage and onion, these young Cratchits danced about the table, and exalted Master Peter Cratchit to the skies, while he (not proud, although his collars nearly choked him) blew the fire, until the slow potatoes, bubbling up, knocked loudly at the saucepan-lid to be let out and peeled.

"What has ever got your precious father then?" said Mrs. Cratchit. "And your brother Tiny Tim! And Martha warn't as late last Christmas day by half an hour!"

"Here's Martha, mother!" said a girl, appearing as she spoke.

"Here's Martha, mother!" cried the two young Cratchits. "Hurrah! There's *such* a goose, Martha!"

1. *Alas for Tiny Tim.* Henry M. Fields reported in *Summer Pictures from Copenhagen to Venice* that here "Dickens' voice took a softer tone" (p. 36).

2. *the strangest things you ever heard.* "Gentler, gentler, was the speaker's voice," noted Fields in *Summer Pictures from Copenhagen to Venice* (pp. 36–37).

"Bob Cratchit and Tiny Tim."
Wood engraving after Sol Eytinge Jr.,
Every Saturday, December 31, 1870.
Courtesy Library of Congress.

"Why, bless your heart alive, my dear, how late you are!" said Mrs. Cratchit, kissing her a dozen times, and taking off her shawl and bonnet for her.

"We'd a deal of work to finish up last night," replied the girl, "and had to clear away this morning, mother!"

"Well! Never mind so long as you are come," said Mrs. Cratchit. "Sit ye down before the fire, my dear, and have a warm, Lord bless ye!"

"No, no! There's father coming," cried the two young Cratchits, who were everywhere at once. "Hide, Martha, hide!"

So Martha hid herself, and in came little Bob, the father, with at least three feet of comforter, exclusive of the fringe, hanging down before him; and his threadbare clothes darned up and brushed, to look seasonable; and Tiny Tim upon his shoulder. Alas for Tiny Tim,[1] he bore a little crutch, and had his limbs supported by an iron frame!

"Why, where's our Martha?" cried Bob Cratchit, looking round.

"Not coming," said Mrs. Cratchit.

"Not coming!" said Bob, with a sudden declension in his high spirits; for he had been Tim's blood-horse all the way from church, and had come home rampant,—"not coming upon Christmas day!"

Martha didn't like to see him disappointed, if it were only in joke; so she came out prematurely from behind the closet door, and ran into his arms, while the two young Cratchits hustled Tiny Tim, and bore him off into the wash-house, that he might hear the pudding singing in the copper.

"And how did little Tim behave?" asked Mrs. Cratchit, when she had rallied Bob on his credulity, and Bob had hugged his daughter to his heart's content.

"As good as gold," said Bob, "and better. Somehow he gets thoughtful, sitting by himself so much, and thinks the strangest things you ever heard.[2] He told me, coming home, that he hoped the people saw him in the church, because he was a cripple, and it might be pleasant to them to remember, upon Christmas day, who made lame beggars walk and blind men see."[3]

Bob's voice was tremulous when he told them this, and trembled more when he said that Tiny Tim was growing strong and hearty.

His active little crutch was heard upon the floor, and back came Tiny Tim before another word was spoken, escorted by his brother and sister to his stool beside the fire; and while Bob, turning up his cuffs,—as if, poor fellow, they were capable of being made more shabby,—compounded some hot mixture in a jug with gin and lemons, and stirred it round and round and put it on the hob to simmer, Master Peter and the two ubiquitous young Cratchits went to fetch the goose, with which they soon returned in high procession.

Mrs. Cratchit made the gravy[4] (ready beforehand in a little saucepan) hissing hot; Master Peter mashed the potatoes with incredible vigor; Miss Belinda sweetened up the apple-sauce; Martha dusted the hot plates; Bob took Tiny Tim beside him in a tiny corner at the table; the two young Cratchits set chairs for everybody, not forgetting themselves, and mounting guard upon their posts, crammed spoons into their mouths, lest they should shriek for goose before their turn came to be helped. At last the dishes were set on, and grace was said. It was succeeded by a breathless pause, as Mrs. Cratchit, looking slowly all along the carving-knife, prepared to plunge it in the breast; but when she did, and when the long-expected gush of stuffing issued forth, one murmur of delight arose all round the board, and even Tiny Tim, excited by the two young Cratchits, beat on the table with the handle of his knife; and feebly cried, Hurrah![5]

There never was such a goose. Bob said he didn't believe there ever was such a goose cooked. Its tenderness and flavor, size and cheapness, were the themes of universal admiration. Eked out by apple-sauce and mashed potatoes, it was a sufficient dinner for the

3. *made lame beggars walk and blind men see.* "The effect of these beautiful words, delivered in Mr. Dickens's indescribable manner, was profound," said the *Boston Journal* (December 3, 1867), "and more than one handkerchief was seen to wipe away tears that *would* rise as the vision of the poor little cripple reached sympathetic hearts." Kate Field said, "There is a volume of pathos in these words, which are the most delicate and artistic rendering of the whole reading" (*Pen Photographs*, p. 32).

4. *Mrs. Cratchit made the gravy.* Dickens used his whole body when reading how the Cratchit Christmas dinner was prepared. "He stirs the gravy, when telling how Mrs. Cratchit made it," reported *The New York Times* on December 10, 1867; "mashes the potatoes with something of Master Peter's 'incredible vigor';—dusts the hot plates as Martha did;—and makes a face of infinite wonderment and exultation when shouting, in the piping tones of the two young Cratchits, 'There's SUCH a goose, Martha!'" The New York *Evening Post* said on the same date, "The very odor of the feasts seemed to pervade the audience, as the reader smackingly and lovingly elaborated each detail."

5. *Hurrah!* "There was not much about Tiny Tim," said the Philadelphia *American and Gazette* (January 14, 1868), "but it was very, very quiet when the poor little fellow was speaking. We had expected more of this part, but perhaps the effect was impressive in the few powerful touches which brought him before us." While *The Belfast Morning News* (January 11, 1869) referred to "the delicate silvery shrillness of Tiny Tim," *The New York Times* (December 10, 1867) mentioned his "small, shrill pipe—which was little more than a sickly squeak." The New York *Commercial Advertiser*, also on December 10, spoke of Tiny Tim's "tremulous squeaking." Kate Field said he spoke "in such a still, small voice" (*Pen Photographs*, p. 33). The Philadelphia *Press* (February 14, 1868) reported, "Mr. Dickens has invented a sound something between a squeak and a wail, that is certainly unlike the sound of any other creature in the heavens above, or the earth beneath, or the waters under the earth; but it is unmistakably Tiny Tim's, and will be remembered forever as such by all who heard it." The Buffalo *Commercial Advertiser* (March 13, 1868) thought "the imitation of the voice of Tiny Tim being almost perfect."

Others found it annoying. "In 'Tiny Tim' . . . we miss the delicacy, the tenderness of the original picture," complained the New York *Evening Express* on December 10, 1867. "As read by him last evening it is like one of the crying babies or squeaking lambs that one sees in the toy windows." The New York *Evening Mail* (December 18) thought that "in the shrill voice of Tiny Tim there is too much of studied effort, too much exaggeration for the listener to feel the full sadness of the little fellow's childish tones, as he feels it when he *sees* it in print."

6. *The pudding was out of the copper.* The *New York Times* (December 10, 1867) reported in its review that at the arrival of the plum pudding, Dickens "*sniffs* and pronounces the smell 'like washing-day,'—sniffs again, and declares it like an eating-house,—again, and pronounces it a pastry cook's, with a laundress next door." Kate Field added, "Dickens's sniffing and smelling of that pudding would make a starving family believe that they had swallowed it, holly and all. It is infectious" (*Pen Photographs*, p. 33).

whole family; indeed, as Mrs. Cratchit said with great delight (surveying one small atom of a bone upon the dish), they hadn't ate it all at last! Yet every one had had enough, and the youngest Cratchits in particular were steeped in sage and onion to the eyebrows! But now, the "plates being changed by Miss Belinda, Mrs. Cratchit left the room alone,—too nervous to bear witnesses,—to take the pudding up, and bring it in.

Suppose it should not be done enough! Suppose it should break in turning out! Suppose somebody should have got over the wall of the back yard, and stolen it, while they were merry with the goose,—a supposition at which the two young Cratchits became livid! All sorts of horrors were supposed.

Hallo! A great deal of steam! The pudding was out of the copper.[6] A smell like a washing-day! That was the cloth. A smell like an eating-house and a pastrycook's next door to each other, with a laundress's next door to that! That was the pudding! In half a minute Mrs. Cratchit entered,—flushed but smiling proudly,—with the pudding, like a speckled cannon-ball, so hard and firm, blazing in half of half a quartern of ignited brandy, and bedight with Christmas holly stuck into the top.

O, a wonderful pudding! Bob Cratchit said, and calmly too, that he regarded it as the greatest success achieved by Mrs. Cratchit since their marriage. Mrs Cratchit said that now the weight was off her mind, she would confess she had had her doubts about the quantity of flour. Everybody had something to say about it, but nobody said or thought it was at all a small pudding for a large family. Any Cratchit would have blushed to hint at such a thing.

At last the dinner was all, done, the cloth was cleared, the hearth swept, and the fire made up. The compound in the jug being tasted, and considered perfect, apples and oranges were put upon the table, and a shovelful of chestnuts on the fire.

Then all the Cratchit family drew round the hearth,

The Wonderful Pudding.

in what Bob Cratchit called a circle, and at Bob Cratchit's elbow stood the family display of glass,—two tumblers, and a custard-cup without a handle.

These held the hot stuff from the jug, however, as well as golden goblets would have done; and Bob served it out with beaming looks, while the chestnuts on the fire sputtered and crackled noisily. Then Bob proposed:—

"A Merry Christmas to us all, my dears. God bless us!"

Which all the family re-echoed.

"God bless us every one!" said Tiny Tim, the last of all.

7. *Bob held his withered little hand in his.* "Nothing of its kind can be more touchingly beautiful than the manner in which Bob Cratchit . . . stoops down, with tears in his eyes, and places Tiny Tim's 'withered little hand in his,'" said Kate Field. "It is pantomime worthy of the finest actor" (*Pen Photographs*, p. 33). Clarence Cook in the New York *Tribune* (December 10, 1867) was duly impressed with the pantomime of "holding Tiny Tim's hand, then throwing him a kiss, and brushing a tear from his eyes, as he prepares to propose the health of Scrooge." The reviewer added, "Those only who have children and fear to lose them, or loving them *have* lost, can know how much it meant."

8. *"My dear . . . the children! Christmas Day!"* "Bob's picture ought to be taken at this moment," suggested Kate Field. "Indeed, now I think if it, I am astonished that artists who illustrate such of Dickens's books as are read by him do not make him their model. They can never approach his conception, they can never equal his execution, and to the virtue of truth would be added the charm of resembling the author" (*Pen Photographs*, p. 34).

He sat very close to his father's side, upon his little stool. Bob held his withered little hand in his,[7] as if he loved the child, and wished to keep him by his side, and dreaded that he might be taken from him.

Scrooge raised his head speedily, on hearing his own name.

"Mr. Scrooge!" said Bob; "I'll give you Mr. Scrooge, the Founder of the Feast!"

"The Founder of the Feast indeed!" cried Mrs. Cratchit, reddening. "I wish I had him here. I'd give him a piece of my mind to feast upon, and I hope he'd have a good appetite for it."

"My dear" said Bob "the children! Christmas day."[8]

"It should be Christmas day, I as sure," said she, "on which one drinks the health of such an odious, stingy, hard, unfeeling man as Mr. Scrooge. You know he is, Robert! Nobody knows it better than you do, poor fellow!"

"My dear," was Bob's mild answer, "Christmas day."

"I'll drink his health for your sake and the day's," said Mrs. Cratchit, "not for his. Long life to him! A merry Christmas and a happy New Year! He'll be very merry and very happy, I have no doubt!"

The children drank the toast after her. It was the first of their proceedings which had no heartiness in it. Tiny Tim drank it last of all, but he didn't care twopence for it. Scrooge was the Ogre of the family. The mention of his name cast a dark shadow on the party, which was not dispelled for full five minutes.

After it had passed away, they were ten times merrier than before; from the mere relief of Scrooge the Baleful being done with. Bob Cratchit told them how he had a situation in his eye for Master Peter, which would bring in, if obtained, full five and sixpence weekly. The two young Cratchits laughed tremendously at the idea of Peter's being a man of business; and Peter himself looked thoughtfully at the fire from between his collars, as if he were deliberating what particular investments he should favor when he came into the receipt of that bewildering income. Martha, who was a poor apprentice at a milliner's, then told them what kind of work she had to do, and how many hours she worked at a stretch, and how she meant to lie abed to-morrow morning for a good long rest; to-morrow being a holiday she passed at home. Also how she had seen a countess and a lord some days before, and how the lord "was much about as tall as Peter"; at which Peter pulled up his collars so high that you couldn't have seen his head if you had been there. All this time the chestnuts and the jug went round and round; and by and by they had a song, about a lost child travelling in the snow, from Tiny Tim, who had a plaintive little voice, and sang it very well indeed.

There was nothing of high mark in this. They were not a handsome family; they were not well dressed; their shoes were far from being waterproof; their clothes were scanty; and Peter might have known, and very likely did, the inside of a pawnbroker's. But they were happy, grateful, pleased with one another, and contented with the time; and when they faded, and looked happier yet in the bright sprinklings of the Spirit's torch at parting, Scrooge had his eye upon them, and especially on Tiny Tim, until the last.

It was a great surprise to Scrooge, as this scene vanished, to hear a hearty laugh. It was a much greater surprise to Scrooge to recognize it as his own nephew's, and to find himself in a bright, dry, gleaming room, with the Spirit standing smiling by his side, and looking at that same nephew.

It is a fair, even-handed, noble adjustment of things, that while there is infection in disease and sorrow, there is nothing in the world so irresistibly contagious as laughter and good-humor. When Scrooge's nephew laughed, Scrooge's niece by marriage laughed as heartily as he. And their assembled friends, being not a bit behindhand, laughed out lustily.

"He said that Christmas was a humbug, as I live!" cried Scrooge's nephew. "He believed it too!"

9. *O, perfectly satisfactory.* "The grave face and twinkling eyes with which this cordial acquiescence in the conclusion arrived at was expressed," said Charles Kent in *Charles Dickens as a Reader*, "were irresistibly exhilarating" (p. 106).

"More shame for him, Fred!" said Scrooge's niece, indignantly. Bless those women! they never do anything by halves. They are always in earnest.

She was very pretty; exceedingly pretty. With a dimpled, surprised-looking, capital face; a ripe little mouth that seemed made to be kissed,—as no doubt it was; all kinds of good little dots about her chin, that melted into one another when she laughed; and the sunniest pair of eyes you ever saw in any little creature's head. Altogether she was what you would have called provoking, but satisfactory, too. O, perfectly satisfactory.[9]

"He's a comical old-fellow," said Scrooge's nephew, "that's the truth; and not so pleasant as he might be. However, his offences carry their own punishment, and I have nothing to say against him. Who suffers by his ill whims? Himself, always. Here he takes it into his head to dislike us, and he won't come and dine with us. What's the consequence? He don't lose much of a dinner."

"Indeed, I think he loses a very good dinner," interrupted Scrooge's niece. Everybody else said the same, and they must be allowed to have been competent judges, because they had just had dinner; and, with the dessert upon the table, were clustered round the fire, by lamplight.

"Well, I am very glad to hear it," said Scrooge's nephew, "because I haven't any great faith in these young housekeepers. What do *you* say, Topper?"

Topper clearly had his eye on one of Scrooge's niece's sisters, for he answered that a bachelor was a wretched outcast, who had no right to express an opinion on the subject. Whereat Scrooge's niece's sister—the plump one with the lace tucker; not the one with the roses—blushed.

After tea they had some music. For they were a musical family, and knew what they were about, when they sung a Glee or Catch, I can assure you,—especially Topper, who could growl away in the bass like a good one, and never swell the large veins in his forehead, or get red in the face over it.

But they didn't devote the whole evening to music. After a while they played at forfeits; for it is good to be children sometimes, and never better than at Christmas, when its mighty Founder was a child himself. There was first a game at blind-man's-buff though. And I no more believe Topper was really blinded than I believe he had eyes in his boots.[10] Because the way in which he went after that plump sister in the lace tucker was an outrage on the credulity of human nature. Knocking down the fire-irons, tumbling over the chairs, bumping up against the piano, smothering himself among the curtains, wherever she went there went he! He always knew where the plump sister was. He wouldn't catch anybody else. If you had fallen up against him, as some of them did, and stood there, he would have made a feint of endeavoring to seize you, which would have been an affront to your understanding, and would instantly have sidled off in the direction of the plump sister.

"Here is a new game," said Scrooge. "One half-hour, Spirit, only one!"

It was a Game called Yes and No, where Scrooge's nephew had to think of something, and the rest must find out what; he only answering to their questions yes or no, as the case was. The fire of questioning to which he was exposed elicited from him that he was thinking of an animal, a live animal, rather a disagreeable animal, a savage animal, an animal that growled and grunted sometimes, and talked sometimes, and lived in London, and walked about the streets; and wasn't made a show of, and wasn't led by anybody, and didn't live in a menagerie, and was never killed in a market, and was not a horse, or an ass, or a cow, or a bull, or a tiger, or a dog, or a pig, or a cat, or a bear. At every new question put to him, this nephew burst into a fresh roar of laughter; and was so inexpressibly tickled, that he was obliged to get up off the sofa and stamp. At last the plump sister cried out:—

"I have found it out! I know what it is, Fred! I know what it is!"

10. *And I no more believe Topper was really blinded than I believe he had eyes in his boots.* Cook reported in the New York *Tribune* (December 3, 1867) that as Dickens read this passage in Boston, "his facial expression—indignant as of a man who is being put upon, and yet with a consciousness of the absurdity of the statement that makes him laugh in spite of his anger—was inimitable, and it was long before the audience would let him go on." Henry M. Fields said in *Summer Pictures from Copenhagen to Venice*, "the story-teller enters into a game of blind man's buff, like a romping boy. He enters into the very soul of Topper, and into his body too, when the young man, though his eyes are bandaged, and he has to grope in the dark, is always sure to catch 'the plump sister,' and nobody else!" (p. 38).

11. *"It's your uncle Scro-o-o-oge!"* "This capped the climax," *The Providence Press* reported on February 21, 1868. "The rising inflection of the voice being drawn out brought down the house with laughter." Kate Field reported in *Pen Photographs*, "I hear the plump sister's voice when she guesses the wonderful riddle. . . . Altogether, Mr. Dickens is better than any comedy" (p. 34).

"What is it?" cried Fred.

"It's your uncle Scro-o-o-oge!"[11]

Which it certainly was. Admiration was the universal sentiment, though some objected that the reply to "Is it a bear?" ought to have been "Yes."

Uncle Scrooge had imperceptibly become so gay and light of heart, that he would have drank to the unconscious company in an inaudible speech. But the whole scene passed off in the breath of the last word spoken by his nephew; and he and the Spirit were again upon their travels.

Much they saw, and far they went, and many homes they visited, but always with a happy end. The Spirit stood beside sick-beds, and they were cheerful; on foreign lands, and they were close at home; by struggling men, and they were patient in their greater hope; by poverty, and it was rich. In almshouse, hospital, and jail, in misery's every refuge, where vain man in his little brief authority had not made fast the door, and barred the Spirit out, he left his blessing, and taught Scrooge his precepts. Suddenly, as they stood together in an open place, the bell struck twelve.

Scrooge looked about him for the Ghost, and saw it no more. As the last stroke ceased to vibrate, he remembered the prediction of old Jacob Marley, and, lifting up his eyes, beheld a solemn Phantom, draped and hooded, coming like a mist along the ground towards him.

STAVE FOUR.

THE LAST OF THE SPIRITS.

The Phantom slowly, gravely, silently approached. When it came near him, Scrooge bent down upon his knee; for in the air through which this Spirit moved it seemed to scatter gloom and mystery.

It was shrouded in a deep black garment, which concealed its head, its face, its form, and left nothing of it visible save one outstretched hand. He knew no more, for the Spirit neither spoke nor moved.

"I am in the presence of the Ghost of Christmas Yet To Come? Ghost of the Future! I fear you more than any spectre I have seen. But as I know your purpose is to do me good, and as I hope to live to be another man from what I was, I am prepared to bear you company, and do it with a thankful heart. Will you not speak to me?"

It gave him no reply. The hand was pointed straight before them.

"Lead on! Lead on! The night is waning fast, and it is precious time to me, I know. Lead on, Spirit!"

They scarcely seemed to enter the city; for the city rather seemed to spring up about them. But there they were in the heart of it; on 'Change, amongst the merchants.

The Spirit stopped beside one little knot of business men. Observing that the hand was pointed to them, Scrooge advanced to listen to their talk.

"No," said a great fat man with a monstrous chin, "I

don't know much about it either way. I only know he's dead."

"When did he die?" inquired another.

"Last night, I believe."

"Why, what was the matter with him? I thought he'd never die."

"God knows," said the first, with a yawn.

"What has he done with his money?" asked a red-faced gentleman.

"I haven't heard," said the man with the large chin. "Company, perhaps. He hasn't left it to me. That's all I know. By, by!"

Scrooge was at first inclined to be surprised that the Spirit should attach importance to conversation apparently so trivial; but feeling assured that it must have some hidden purpose, he set himself to consider what it was likely to be. It could scarcely be supposed to have any bearing on the death of Jacob, his old partner, for that was Past, and this Ghost's province was the Future.

He looked about in that very place for his own image; but another man stood in his accustomed corner, and though the clock pointed to his usual time of day for being there, he saw no likeness of himself among the multitudes that poured in through the Porch. It gave him little surprise, however; for he had been revolving in his mind a change of life, and he thought and hoped he saw his new-born resolutions carried out in this.

They left this busy scene, and went into an obscure part of the town, to a low shop where iron, old rags, bottles, bones, and greasy offal were bought. A gray-haired rascal, of great age, sat ·smoking his pipe.

Scrooge and the Phantom came into the presence of this man, just as a woman with a heavy bundle slunk into the shop. But she had scarcely entered, when another woman, similarly laden, came in too; and she was closely followed by a man in faded black. After a short period of blank astonishment, in which the old man with the pipe had joined them, they all three burst into a laugh.

"Let the charwoman alone to be the first!" cried she who had entered first. "Let the laundress alone to be the second; and let the undertaker's man alone to be the third. Look here, old Joe, here's a chance! If we haven't all three met here without meaning it!"

"You couldn't have met in a better place. You were made free of it long ago, you know; and the other two ain't strangers. What have you got to sell? What have you got to sell?"

"Half a minute's patience, Joe, and you shall see."

"What odds then! What odds, Mrs. Dilber?" said the woman. "Every person has a right to take care of themselves. *He* always did! Who's the worse for the loss of a few things like these? Not a dead man, I suppose."

Mrs. Dilber, whose manner was remarkable for general propitiation, said, "No, indeed, ma'am."

"If he wanted to keep 'em after he was dead, a wicked old screw, why wasn't he natural in his lifetime? If he had been, he'd have had somebody to look after him when he was struck with Death, instead of lying gasping out his last there, alone by himself."

"It's the truest word that ever was spoke, it's a judgment on him."

"I wish it was a little heavier judgment, and it should have been, you may depend upon it, if I could have laid my hands on anything else. Open that bundle, old Joe, and let me know the value of it. Speak out plain. I'm not afraid to be the first, nor afraid for them to see it."

Joe went down on his knees for the greater convenience of opening the bundle, and dragged out a large and heavy roll of some dark stuff.

"What do you call this? Bed-curtains!"

"Ah! Bed-curtains! Don't drop that oil upon the blankets, now."

"*His* blankets?"

"Whose else's do you think? He isn't likely to take

1. *Ah, poor Tiny Tim!* Charles Kent was amazed, in looking over Dickens' prompt copy, how "only a very few indeed of the salient points were left in regard to the life and death of Tiny Tim. . . . Two utterances there *were*, however, the one breathing an exquisite tenderness, the other indicative of a long-suppressed but passionate outburst of grief, that thrilled to the hearts of all who heard them, and still, we doubt not, haunt their recollection" (*Charles Dickens as a Reader,* p. 104).

cold without 'em, I dare say. Ah! You may look through that shirt till your eyes ache; but you won't find a hole in it, nor a threadbare place. It's the best he had, and a fine one too. They'd have wasted it by dressing him up in it, if it hadn't been for me."

Scrooge listened to this dialogue in horror

"Spirit! I see, I see. The case of this unhappy man might be my own. My life tends that way, now. Merciful Heaven, what is this!"

The scene had changed, and now he almost touched a bare, uncurtained bed. A pale light, rising in the outer air, fell straight upon this bed; and on it, unwatched, unwept, uncared for, was the body of this plundered unknown man.

"Spirit, let me see some tenderness connected with a death, or this dark chamber, Spirit, will be forever present to me."

The Ghost conducted him to poor Bob Cratchit's house,—the dwelling he had visited before,—and found the mother and the children seated round the fire.

Quiet. Very quiet. The noisy little Cratchits were as still as statues in one corner, and sat looking up at Peter, who had a book before him. The mother and her daughters were engaged in needlework. But surely they were very quiet!

"'And he took a child, and set him in the midst of them.'"

Where had Scrooge heard those words? He had not dreamed them. The boy must have read them out, as he and the Spirit crossed the threshold. Why did he not go on?

The mother laid her work upon the table, and put her hand up to her face.

"The color hurts my eyes," she said.

The color? Ah, poor Tiny Tim![1]

"They're better now again. It makes them weak by candle-light; and I wouldn't show weak eyes to your father when he comes home, for the world. It must be near his time."

"Past it rather," Peter answered, shutting up his book. "But I think he has walked a little slower than he used, these few last evenings, mother."

"I have known him walk with—I have known him walk with Tiny Tim upon his shoulder, very fast indeed."

"And so have I," cried Peter. "Often."

"And so have I," exclaimed another. So had all.

"But he was very light to carry, and his father loved him so, that it was no trouble,—no trouble. And there is your father at the door!"

She huried out to meet him; and little Bob in his comforter—he had need of it, poor fellow—came in. His tea was ready for him on the hob, and they all tried who should help him to it most. Then the two young Cratchits got upon his knees and laid, each child, a little cheek against his face, as if they said, "Don't mind it, father. Don't be grieved!"

Bob was very cheerful with them, and spoke pleasantly to all the family. He looked at the work upon the table, and praised the industry and speed of Mrs. Cratchit and the girls. They would be done long before Sunday, he said.

"Sunday! You went to-day, then, Robert?"

"Yes, my dear," returned Bob. "I wish you could have gone. It would have done you good to see how green a place it is. But you'll see it often. I promised him that I would walk there on a Sunday. My little, little child! My little child!"[2]

He broke down all at once. He couldn't help it. If he could have helped it, he and his child would have been farther apart, perhaps, than they were.

"Spectre," said Scrooge, "something informs me that our parting moment is at hand. I know it, but I know not how. Tell me what man that was, with the covered face, whom we saw lying dead?"

The Ghost of Christmas Yet To Come conveyed him to a dismal, wretched, ruinous churchyard.

The Spirit stood among the graves, and pointed down to One.

2. *My little child!* "Perhaps the gem in all the *Christmas Carol* is the death of Tiny Tim," said Henry M. Fields in *Summer Pictures from Copenhagen to Venice*. "How he shared the household grief! You would have thought there had been a death in his family, that one of his own children had laid upon the bier" (p. 39). But Kate Field thought that the reader's lamentation should have been "a shade less dramatic. Here, and only here, Dickens forgets the nature of Bob's voice, and employs all the power of his own, carried away apparently by the situation. Bob would not thus give vent to his feelings" (*Pen Photographs*, p. 35). The Buffalo *Commercial Advertiser* (March 13, 1868) agreed, "It seemed a little overdone, and lacked the temperance which gives smoothness." Nevertheless, as Clarence Cook reported in the New York *Tribune* (December 3, 1867) of the Boston opening, Bob's speech "brought out so many pocket handkerchiefs that it looked as if a snow-storm had somehow got into the hall without tickets." George Dolby explained in *Charles Dickens As I Knew Him* (London: T. Fisher Unwin, 1885) that the scenes with Tiny Tim were "a special favourite with Dickens" and "affected him and the audience alike, and it not infrequently happened that he was interrupted by loud sobs from the female portion of his audience (and occasionally, too, from men) who, perhaps, had experienced the inexpressible grief of losing a child" (p. 26). Dickens was well aware of the enormous power this pathetic passage had over his audiences. "They took to it so tremendously last night that I was stopped every five minutes," he proudly reported to Georgina Hogarth from Boston on February 28, 1868. "One poor young girl in mourning burst into a passion of grief about Tiny Tim, and was taken out" (*The Letters of Charles Dickens*, edited by Madeline House and others, vol. 12 [Oxford: Clarendon Press, 2002], p. 63.)

"Poor Tiny Tim."

"Before I draw nearer to that stone to which you point, answer me one question. Are these the shadows of the things that Will be, or are they shadows of the things that May be only?"

Still the Ghost pointed downward to the grave by which it stood.

"Men's courses will foreshadow certain ends, to which, if persevered in, they must lead. But if the courses be departed from, the ends will change. Say it is thus with what you show me!"

The Spirit was immovable as ever.

Scrooge crept towards it, trembling as he went; and, following the finger, read upon the stone of the neglected grave his own name,—EBENEZER SCROOGE.

"Am *I* that man who lay upon the bed? No, Spirit! O no, no! Spirit! hear me! I am not the man I was. I will not be the man I must have been but for this intercourse. Why show me this, if I am past all hope? Assure me that I yet may change these shadows you have shown me by an altered life."

For the first time the kind hand faltered.

"I will honor Christmas in my heart, and try to keep it all the year. I will live in the Past, the Present, and the Future. The Spirits of all three shall strive within

In the Churchyard.

3. *"Walk-ER!"* "His little boy shouting up to Scrooge has a most painfully impuerile voice," complained the *Liverpool Post* (August 17, 1858). Nevertheless, according to John Hollingshead in *The Critic* (September 4, 1858), "every word in the conversation with the boy out of the window respecting the purchase of the goose, is watched for and listened to by the audiences like celebrated passages from a great standard play" (p. 537).

me. I will not shut out the lessons that they teach. O, tell me I may sponge away the writing on this stone!"

Holding up his hands in one last prayer to have his fate reversed, he saw an alteration in the Phantom's hood and dress. It shrunk, collapsed, and dwindled down into a bedpost.

Yes, and the bedpost was his own. The bed was his own, the room was his own. Best and happiest of all, the Time before him was his own, to make amends in!

He was checked in his transports by the churches ringing out the lustiest peals he had ever heard.

Running to the window, he opened it, and put out his head. No fog, no mist, no night; clear, bright, stirring, golden day.

"What's to-day?" cried Scrooge, calling downward to a boy in Sunday clothes, who perhaps had loitered in to look about him.

"EH?"

"What's to-day, my fine fellow?"

"To-day! Why, CHRISTMAS DAY."

"It's Christmas day! I haven't missed it. Hallo, my fine fellow!"

"Hallo!"

"Do you know the Poulterer's, in the next street but one, at the corner?"

"I should hope I did."

"An intelligent boy! A remarkable boy! Do you know whether they've sold the prize Turkey that was hanging up there? Not the little prize Turkey,—the big one?"

"What, the one as big as me?"

"What a delightful boy! It's a pleasure to talk to him. Yes, my buck!"

"It's hanging there now."

"Is it? Go and buy it."

"Walk-ER!"[3] exclaimed the boy.

"No, no, I am in earnest. Go and buy it, and tell 'em to bring it here, that I may give them the direction where to take it. Come back with the man, and I'll give you a shilling. Come back with him in less than five minutes, and I'll give you half a crown!"

The boy was off like a shot.

"I'll send it to Bob Cratchit's! He sha'n't know who sends it. It's twice the size of Tiny Tim. Joe Miller never made such a joke as sending it to Bob's will be!"

The hand in which he wrote the address was not a steady one; but write it he did, somehow, and went down stairs to open the street door, ready for the coming of the poulterer's man.

It *was* a Turkey! He never could have stood upon his legs, that bird. He would have snapped 'em short off in a minute, like sticks of sealing-wax.

The Prize Turkey.

4. *Nice girl! Very.* Charles Kent said that Dickens here gave "a sort of parenthetical smack of the lips" (*Charles Dickens as a Reader*, p. 107).

Scrooge dressed himself "all in his best," and at last got out into the streets. The people were by this time pouring forth, as he had seen them with the Ghost of Christmas Present; and, walking with his hands behind him, Scrooge regarded every one with a delighted smile. He looked so irresistibly pleasant, in a word, that three or four good-humored fellows said, "Good morning, sir! A merry Christmas to you!" And Scrooge said often afterwards, that, of all the blithe sounds he had ever heard, those were the blithest in his ears.

In the afternoon, he turned his steps towards his nephew's house.

He passed the door a dozen times, before he had the courage to go up and knock. But he made a dash, and did it.

"Is your master at home, my dear?" said Scrooge to the girl. Nice girl! Very.[4]

"Yes, sir."

"Where is he, my love?"

"He's in the dining-room, sir, along with mistress."

"He knows me," said Scrooge, with his hand already on the dining-room lock. "I'll go in here, my dear."

"Fred!"

"Why, bless my soul!" cried Fred, "who's that?"

"It's I. Your uncle Scrooge. I have come to dinner. Will you let me in, Fred?"

Let him in! It is a mercy he didn't shake his arm off. He was at home in five minutes. Nothing could be heartier. His niece looked just the same. So did Topper when *he* came. So did the plump sister, when *she* came. So did every one when *they* came. Wonderful party, wonderful games, wonderful unanimity, won-der-ful happiness!

But he was early at the office next morning. O, he was early there. If he could only be there first, and catch Bob Cratchit coming late! That was the thing he had set his heart upon.

And he did it. The clock struck nine. No Bob. A quarter past. No Bob. Bob was full eighteen minutes and a half behind his time. Scrooge sat with his door wide open, that he might see him come into the Tank.

Bob's hat was off, before he opened the door; his comforter too. He was on his stool in a jiffy; driving away with his pen, as if he were trying to overtake nine o'clock.

"Hallo!" growled Scrooge, in his accustomed voice, as near as he could feign it. "What do you mean by coming here at this time of day?"

"I am very sorry, sir. I *am* behind my time."

"You are? Yes. I think you are. Step this way, if you please."

"It's only once a year, sir. It shall not be repeated. I was making rather merry yesterday, sir."

"Now, I'll tell you what, my friend. I am not going to stand this sort of thing any longer. And therefore,"

"I'll Raise Your Salary."

Scrooge continued, leaping from his stool, and giving Bob such a dig in the waistcoat that he staggered back into the Tank again,—"and therefore I am about to raise your salary!"

Bob trembled, and got a little nearer to the ruler.

"A merry Christmas, Bob!" said Scrooge, with an earnestness that could not be mistaken, as he clapped him on the back. "A merrier Christmas, Bob, my good fellow, than I have given you for many a year! I'll raise your salary, and endeavor to assist your struggling family, and we will discuss your affairs this very afternoon, over a Christmas bowl of smoking bishop, Bob! Make up the fires, and buy a second coal-scuttle before you dot another i, Bob Cratchit!"

Scrooge was better than his word. He did it all, and infinitely more; and to Tiny Tim, who did NOT die, he was a second father. He became as good a friend, as good a master, and as good a man as the good old city knew, or any other good old city, town, or borough in the good old world. Some people laughed to see the alteration in him; but his own heart laughed, and that was quite enough for him.

He had no further intercourse with Spirits, but lived in that respect upon the Total-Abstinence Principle ever afterwards; and it was always said of him, that he knew how to keep Christmas well, if any man alive possessed the knowledge. May that be truly said of us, and all of us! And so, as Tiny Tim observed, God Bless Us, Every One!

BIBLIOGRAPHY

By Charles Dickens

Sunday under Three Heads. Illustrated by Hablôt Knight Browne. London: Chapman and Hall, 1836.

The Posthumous Papers of the Pickwick Club. Illustrated by Robert Seymour and Hablôt Knight Browne. London: Chapman and Hall, 1837.

Oliver Twist, or The Parish Boy's Progress. Illustrated by Hablôt Knight Browne. London: Chapman and Hall, 1838.

The Life and Adventures of Nicholas Nickleby. Illustrated by Hablôt Knight Browne. London: Chapman and Hall, 1839.

Sketches by Boz. Illustrated by George Cruikshank. London: John Macrone, 1839.

Master Humphrey's Clock. Illustrated by George Cattermole and Hablôt Knight Browne. London: Chapman and Hall, 1840–41.

Barnaby Rudge: A Tale of the Riots of 'Eighty. Illustrated by George Cattermole and Hablôt Knight Browne. London: Chapman and Hall, 1841.

The Old Curiosity Shop. Illustrated by George Cattermole and Hablôt Knight Browne. London: Chapman and Hall, 1841.

American Notes for General Circulation. 2 vols. London: Chapman and Hall, 1842.

A Christmas Carol. In Prose. Being a Ghost Story of Christmas. Illustrated by John Leech. London: Chapman and Hall, 1843.

The Chimes: A Goblin Story of Some Bells That Rang an Old Year Out and a New Year In. Illustrated by John Leech, Daniel Maclise, Richard Doyle, and Clarkson Stanfield. London: Chapman and Hall, 1844.

Martin Chuzzlewit. Illustrated by Hablôt Knight Browne. London: Chapman and Hall, 1844.

The Cricket on the Hearth, A Fairy Tale of Home. Illustrated by Daniel Maclise, John Leech, Richard Doyle, Edwin Landseer, and John Tenniel. London: Bradbury and Evans, 1845.

The Battle of Life, A Love Story. Illustrated by John Leech, Richard Doyle, Clarkson Stanfield, and Daniel Maclise. London: Bradbury and Evans, 1846.

Pictures from Italy. Wood engravings after Samuel Palmer. London: Bradbury and Evans, 1846.

Dealings with the Firm of Dombey and Son, Wholesale, Retail, and for Exportation. Illustrated by Hablôt Knight Browne. London: Bradbury and Evans, 1848.

"Fine Arts: *The Rising Generation* . . . by John Leech." London *Examiner*, December 30, 1848, p. 838.

The Haunted Man and the Ghost's Bargain, A Fancy for Christmas. Illustrated by John Leech, Clarkson Stanfield, John Tenniel, and Frank Stone. London: Bradbury and Evans, 1848.

"A December Vision." *Household Words*, December 14, 1850, pp. 265–67.

"A Christmas Tree." *Household Words*, Christmas Number 1850, pp. 289–95.

The Personal History of David Copperfield. Illustrated by Hablôt Knight Browne. London: Bradbury and Evans, 1850.

"What Christmas Is as We Get Older." *Household Words*, Christmas Number 1851, pp. 1–3.

Christmas Books. Frontispiece by John Leech. Cheap Edition of the Works of Charles Dickens. London: Chapman and Hall, 1852.

A Child's History of England. Frontispiece by F. W. Tropham. London: Bradbury and Evans, 1852–54.

Bleak House. Illustrated by Hablôt Knight Browne. London: Chapman and Hall, 1853.

"Where We Stopped Growing." *Household Words*, January 1, 1853, pp. 361–63.

"Frauds on the Fairies." *Household Words*, October 1, 1853, pp. 97–100.

Hard Times, for These Times. London: Bradbury and Evans, 1854.

Little Dorrit. Illustrated by Hablôt Knight Browne. London: Chapman and Hall, 1857.

Christmas Stories from the Household Words. London: Chapman and Hall, 1859.

A Tale of Two Cities. Illustrated by Hablôt Knight Browne. London: Chapman and Hall, 1859.

Great Expectations. London: Chapman and Hall, 1861.

The Uncommercial Traveller. London: Chapman and Hall, 1861.

Our Mutual Friend. Illustrated by Marcus Stone. London: Chapman and Hall, 1865.

Child-Pictures from Dickens. Illustrated by Sol Eytinge Jr. Boston: Ticknor and Fields, 1867.

Works. The Charles Dickens Edition. 21 vols. London: Chapman and Hall, 1867–75.

"A Holiday Romance." *All the Year Round,* January 25–April 4, 1868.

The Mystery of Edwin Drood. Illustrated by S. L. Fildes. London: Chapman and Hall, 1870.

Speeches, Letters, and Sayings of Charles Dickens. Biographical sketch by George Augustus Sala and sermon by Dean Stanley. New York: Harper and Bros., 1870.

The Life of Our Lord. London: Associated Newspapers, 1934.

The Nonesuch Dickens. Illustrated by George Cruikshank and others. Bloomsbury and London: Nonesuch Press, 1937–38.

The Speeches of Charles Dickens. Edited by Kenneth J. Fielding. Oxford: Clarendon Press, 1960.

The Letters of Charles Dickens. Edited by Madeline House and others. 12 vols. Oxford: Clarendon Press, 1965–2002.

Charles Dickens: The Public Readings. Edited by Philip Collins. Oxford: Clarendon Press, 1975.

Notable Editions of *A Christmas Carol*

A Christmas Carol. Frontispiece after John Leech. Leipzig: E. Tauchnitz, 1843.

A Christmas Carol. In Prose. Being a Ghost Story of Christmas. Illustrated by John Leech. London: Chapman and Hall, 1843.

A Christmas Carol. New York: Harper and Bros., 1844.

A Christmas Carol in Prose. Paris: A. and W. Galignani, 1844.

A Christmas Carol in Prose. Edited with an introduction and notes by L. Riechelmann. Leipzig: B. G. Taubner, 1864.

A Christmas Carol. "As condensed by himself for his reading." Frontispiece by Sol Eytinge, Jr. Boston: Ticknor and Fields, 1867.

A Christmas Carol in Prose. Edited with an introduction and notes by W. Sturzen-Becker. Örebro: Abraham Bohlin, 1869.

A Christmas Carol. Edited with an introduction and notes by A. J. Demarest. Boston: Houghton, Mifflin, 1871.

A Christmas Carol in Prose. Edited with an introduction and notes by F. H. Ahn. Mentz: Florian Kupferberg, 1871.

A Christmas Carol. With notes by P. Weeg. Münster: E.C. Brunn, 1872.

A Christmas Carol and The Chimes. Introduction by Henry Morley. London: Cassell, 1886.

A Christmas Carol. Edited with an introduction and notes by Jules Guiraud. Paris: Eugène Belin, 1889.

The Christmas Carol. Facsimile edition of the manuscript. Introduction by Frederic G. Kitton. London: Elliot Stock; New York: Brentano's, 1890.

A Christmas Carol. London: I. Pitman and Sons, 1891.

A Christmas Carol in Prose. Edited by F. Fischer. Berlin: Weidmannsche Buchandlung, 1891.

A Christmas Carol in Prose. With a biographical sketch and notes. Cambridge, Mass.: Houghton, Mifflin, 1893.

A Christmas Carol in Prose. With a biographical sketch and notes in French. Paris: Librarie Charles Poussielgue, 1893.

A Christmas Carol. With notes by Oscar Thiergen. Leipzig: Velhagen and Klasing, 1895.

A Christmas Carol in Prose. Decorations by Samuel Warner. East Aurora, N.Y.: Roycroft Shop, 1902.

A Christmas Carol in Prose. Illustrated by Charles E. Brock. London: J. M. Dent; New York: E. P. Dutton, 1905.

A Christmas Carol. Introduction and notes by E. Gordon Browne. London: Longmans, Green, 1907.

A Christmas Carol in Prose. Illustrated by John Leech and Fred Barnard. Introduction by Sir William P. Treloar. London: Chapman and Hall, 1907.

A Christmas Carol and The Cricket on the Hearth. Introduction and notes by James M. Swain. London and New York: Macmillan, 1908.

A Christmas Carol. Illustrated by Arthur I. Keller. Philadelphia: David McKay, 1914.

A Christmas Carol. Illustrated by Arthur Rackham. London: William Heinemann, 1915.

A Christmas Carol in Prose. With notes by Carol L. Bernhardt. Chicago: Loyola University Press, 1922.

A Christmas Carol. Illustrated by Francis D. Bedford. New York: Macmillan, 1923.

A Christmas Carol in Prose. Introduction by G. K. Chesterton and preface by B. W. Matz. Boston: Charles E. Lauriat, 1924.

A Christmas Carol. Decorations by W. A. Dwiggins. New York: Press of the Woolly Whale, 1930.

A Christmas Carol in Prose. Illustrated by Gordon Ross. Introduction by Stephen Leacock. Boston: Limited Editions Club, 1934.

A Christmas Carol in Prose. Illustrated by Everett Shinn. Introduction by Lionel Barrymore. Philadelphia and Chicago: John C. Winston, 1938.

A Christmas Carol in Prose. Illustrated by Philip Reed. Chicago: Holiday House, 1940.

A Christmas Carol. Illustrated by Fritz Kredel. Mount Vernon, N.Y.: Peter Pauper Press, 1943.

A Christmas Carol. Privately printed facsimile of the annotated copy of the book that was read annually by Alexander Melville Bell and Alexander Graham Bell to their children on Christmas Eve. Illustrated by John Leech. Washington, D.C.: National Geographical Society, 1943.

A Christmas Carol. Illustrated by Ronald Searle. London: Perpetua, 1961.

A Christmas Carol. With special aids prepared by Henry E. Vittum. New York: Bantam Books, 1966.

A Christmas Carol: The Original Manuscript. Facsimile edition of the manuscript in the Pierpont Morgan Library. Preface by Frederick P. Adams Jr. Introduction by Monica Dickens. New York: James H. Heinemann, 1967.

A Christmas Carol: The Public Reading Version.

Introduction and notes by Philip Collins. New York: New York Public Library, 1971.

A Christmas Carol. Illustrated by Michael Foreman. London: Gollanz, 1983.

A Christmas Carol in Prose. Illustrated by Trina Schart Hyman. New York: Holiday House, 1983.

A Christmas Carol. Illustrated by Lisbeth Zwerger. Saxonville, Mass.: Picture Book Studio, 1988.

Lectures: David Copperfield/A Christmas Carol. "Les langues pour tous." Translation and notes by Georges Hermet. Paris: Presses Pocket, 1989.

A Christmas Carol. Illustrated by Roberto Innocenti. New York: Stewart, Tabori and Chang, 1990.

A Christmas Carol. Facsimile edition of the manuscript in the Pierpont Morgan Library. Introduction by John Mortimer. New York: Pierpont Morgan Library; New Haven and London: Yale University Press, 1993.

A Christmas Carol. Illustrated by Quentin Blake. New York: Margaret K. McElderry Books, 1995.

A Christmas Carol and Other Stories. Introduction by John Irving. New York: Modern Library, 1995.

Charles Dickens' A Christmas Carol. Introduction by Dan Malan. Illustrated by Gustave Doré and others. St. Louis: MCE Pub., 1996.

A Christmas Carol, and Other Haunting Tales. New York: Doubleday, 1998.

Notable Editions of *Christmas Books*

Christmas Books. Frontispiece by John Leech. Cheap Edition of the Works of Charles Dickens. London: Chapman and Hall, 1852.

Christmas Books. Title page vignette by Phiz. Library Edition, vol. 22. London: Chapman and Hall, 1859.

Christmas Books. Illustrated by F. O. C. Darley and John Gilbert. New York: James G. Gregory, 1861.

Christmas Carol, and Sketches by Boz. Illustrated by Sol Eytinge Jr. Boston: Ticknor and Fields, 1867.

Christmas Books. The Charles Dickens Edition. London: Chapman and Hall, 1868.

Christmas Books. Illustrated by Edwin A. Abbey. Household Edition. New York: Harper and Bros., 1876.

Christmas Books. Illustrated by Fred Barnard. Household Edition. London: Chapman and Hall, 1877.

Christmas Books. Introduction by Charles Dickens Jr. London: Macmillan, 1892.

Christmas Books. Introduction by Andrew Lang. Gadshill Edition, vol 18. Chapman and Hall, 1897.

Christmas Books. Introduction by Gilbert Keith Chesterton. London: J. M. Dent; New York: E. P. Dutton, 1907.

Christmas Books. Illustrated by Harry Furniss. London: Educational Publishing, 1910.

Christmas Tales. Illustrated by Henry M. Brock. London: George G. Harrap, 1932.

Christmas Books. Illustrated by John Leech and others. The Nonesuch Dickens, vol. 4. London: Nonesuch Press, 1937.

Five Christmas Novels. Illustrated by Reginald Birch. New York: Heritage Club, 1939.

Christmas Books. Introduction by Eleanor Farjeon. Oxford: Oxford University Press, 1954.

The Christmas Books. Edited with an introduction and notes by Michael Slater. 2 vols. Harmondsworth, Eng.: Penguin, 1971.

A Charles Dickens Christmas. Illustrated by Warren Chappell. New York: Oxford University Press, 1976.

Christmas Books. Introduction by Christopher Hibbert. Illustrated by Charles Keeping. London: Folio Society, 1988.

A Christmas Carol and Other Stories. Introduction by John Irving. New York: Modern Library, 1995.

About Charles Dickens

Ackroyd, Peter. *Dickens*. London: Sinclaire-Stevenson, 1990.

———. *Dickens, Public Life and Private Passion*. London: BBC, 2002.

Ainger, Alfred. "Mr. Dickens's Amateur Theatricals: A Reminiscence." *Macmillan's Magazine*, January 1871, pp. 206–15.

Andersen, Hans Christian. *The Diaries of Hans Christian Andersen*. Selected and translated by Patricia L. Conroy and Sven H. Rossel. Seattle and London: University of Washington Press, 1990.

———. "A Visit to Charles Dickens." *Temple Bar*, December 1870, pp. 27–46.

Boll, Ernest. "Charles Dickens and Washington Irving." *Modern Language Quarterly*, December 1944, pp. 453–67.

Bredsdorff, Elias. *Hans Andersen and Charles Dickens, A Friendship and Its Dissolution*. Copenhagen: Rosenkilde and Bogger, 1956.

Bryant, William Cullen. *Letters of William Cullen Bryant*. 6 vols. Edited by William Cullen Bryant II and Thomas Voss. New York: Fordham University Press, 1977–92.

Carlyle, Jane Welsh. *Jane Welsh Carlyle: Letters to Her Family*. Edited by Leonard Huxley. London: John Murray, 1924.

Chesterton, Gilbert Keith. *Charles Dickens*. London: Methuen, 1906.

Clark, Lewis Gaylord. "Charles Dickens." *Harper's New Monthly Magazine,* August 1862, pp. 376–80.

Clayden, P. W. *Rogers and His Contemporaries*. 2 vols. London: Smith, Elder, 1889.

Cockburn, Henry. *The Life of Lord Jeffrey*. 2 vols. Edinburgh: Adam and Charles Black, 1852.

Collins, Philip. "Dickens' Public Readings: The Performer and the Novelist." *Studies in the Novel*, summer 1969, pp. 118–32.

———, ed. *Dickens: Interviews and Recollections*. 2 vols. London: Macmillan, 1981.

———, and Edward Guiliano, eds. *The Annotated Dickens*. New York: Clarkson N. Potter, 1986.

Conway, Moncure D. "Footprints of Charles Dickens." *Harper's New Monthly Magazine*, September 1870, pp. 610–16.

Dana, Richard Henry. *The Journal*. Edited by Richard F. Lucid. Vol. 1. Cambridge, Mass.: Harvard University Press.

Dickens Jr., Charles. "Glimpses of Charles Dickens." *The North American Review*, May and June 1895.

Dickens, Henry Fielding. "A Chat about Charles Dickens." *Harper's Monthly Magazine*, July 1914, pp. 186–93.

———. *My Father As I Knew Him*. London: William Heinemann, 1934.

Dickens, Mamie. *My Father As I Recall Him*. Westminster: Roxburgh Press, 1896.

Dickens, Mary Angela. "A Child's Recollections at Gad's Hill." *The Strand Magazine*, January 1897, pp. 69–74.

The Dickensian, January 1905–current.

Dickens Quarterly, March 1984–current.

Dickens Studies, January 1965–May 1969.

Dickens Studies Annual. Edited by R. B. Partlow and others. Carbondale, Ill.: Southern Illinois University Press, 1970–current.

Dickens Studies Newsletter, March 1970–December 1983.

Dolby, George. *Charles Dickens As I Knew Him: The Story of the Reading Tours 1866–1870*. London: T. Fisher Unwin, 1885.

Duffy, Sir George Gavan. *Conversations with Carlyle*. New York: Charles Scribner's Sons, 1892.

Eliot, George. *The George Eliot Letters*. Edited by Gordon S. Haight. Vol. 2. Oxford: Oxford University Press; New Haven: Yale University Press, 1954.

Fielding, K. J. "Dickens and the Hogarth Scandal." *Nineteenth-Century Fiction*, June 1955, pp. 64–74.

Fields, Annie. *Memories of a Hostess: A Chronicle of Eminent Friendships.* Edited by Mark Antony De Wolfe Howe. Boston: Atlantic Monthly Press, 1922.

Fields, Henry M. *Summer Pictures from Copenhagen to Venice.* New York: Sheldon, 1859.

Fields, James T. *Biographical Notes and Personal Sketches.* Boston: Houghton Mifflin, 1891.

———. "Some Memories of Charles Dickens." *The Atlantic Monthly*, August 1870, pp. 235–45.

———. *Yesterdays with Authors.* Boston: James R. Osgood, 1872.

Fitzgerald, Percy. *The Life of Charles Dickens.* London: Chatto and Windus, 1905.

Forster, John. *Life of Charles Dickens.* 3 vols. London: Chapman and Hall, 1872–74.

Fowler, Lorenzo N. "Phrenological Description of Charles Dickens and Mark Lemon." *Human Nature*, August 1870, pp. 366–69.

Friswell, Laura Hain. *In the Sixties and Seventies.* London: Hutchinson, 1905.

Frith, William Powell. *My Autobiography and Reminiscences.* 2 vols. New York: Harper and Bros., 1888.

Godwin, Parke. *A Biography of William Cullen Bryant.* Vol. 2. New York: Russell and Russell, 1966.

Goodrich, Samuel Griswold. *Recollections of a Lifetime.* 2 vols. New York and Auburn, N.Y.: Miller, Orton and Mulligan, 1856.

Gordon, John D. *Reading for Profit: The Other Career of Charles Dickens.* New York: New York Public Library, 1958.

Hollingshead, John. *My Lifetime.* 2 vols. London: Sampson Low, Marston, 1895.

Hone, Philip. *The Diary of Philip Hone.* 2 vols. Edited by Allan Nivens. New York: Dodd, Mead, 1927.

James, Henry. *Autobiography.* Edited by Frederick W. Dupee. Princeton, N.J.: Princeton University Press, 1983.

———. *Letters.* Edited by Leon Edel. Vol. 1. Cambridge, Mass.: Harvard University Press, 1974.

Jaques, Edward Tyrrell. *Charles Dickens in Chancery.* London and New York: Longmans, Green, 1914.

Johnson, Edgar. *Charles Dickens: His Tragedy and Triumph.* 2 vols. New York: Simon and Schuster, 1952.

Kent, Charles. *Charles Dickens as a Reader.* London: Chapman and Hall, 1872.

Knowles, A. V. "Some Aspects of L. N. Tolstoy's Visit to London in 1861: An Examination of the Evidence." *Slavonic and East European Review*, January 1978, pp. 106–14.

Lester, Charles Edwards. *The Glory and Shame of England.* 2 vols. New York: Harper and Bros., 1841.

Linton, William James. *Threescore and Ten Years, 1820–1890.* New York: Charles Scribner's Sons, 1894.

Longfellow, Henry Wadsworth. *The Letters of Henry Wadsworth Longfellow.* Edited by Andrew Hilen. Vol. 2. Cambridge, Mass.: Harvard University Press, 1966.

Merwe, Pieter van der. *The Spectacular Career of Clarkson Stanfield, 1793–1867.* Newcastle upon Tyne: Tyne and Wear County Council Museums, 1979.

Moss, Sidney Phil. *Charles Dickens' Quarrel with America.* Troy, N.Y.: Whitson Publishing, 1984.

Murray, David Christie. *Recollections.* London: John Long, 1908.

Nivens, Allan, and Milton Halsey Thomas, eds. *The Diary of George Templeton Strong.* 3 vols. New York: Macmillan, 1952.

Pacey, W. C. Desmond. "Washington Irving and Charles Dickens." *American Literature*, January 1945, pp. 332–39.

Patten, Robert L. *Charles Dickens and His Publishers.* Oxford: Clarendon Press, 1978.

Priestley, Lady Eliza. *The Story of a Lifetime.* London: Kegan Paul, 1908.

Putnam, George Washington. "Four Months with Charles Dickens." *The Atlantic Monthly*, October and November 1870, pp. 476–82, 591–99.

Slater, Michael, ed. *Dickens on America and the Americans.* Austin and London: University of Texas Press, 1978.

"Some Plain Words Concerning Mr. Charles Dickens." *The Northern Monthly Magazine*, January 1868, pp. 243–52.

Stirling, Edward. *Old Drury Lane*. 2 vols. London: Chatto and Windus, 1881.

Storey, Gladys. *Dickens and Daughter*. London: Frederick Muller, 1939.

Stott, George. "Charles Dickens." *Contemporary Review*, January 1869, pp. 203–25.

Toole, James L. *The Reminiscences of J. L. Toole*. 2 vols. Edited by Joseph Hatton. London: Hurst and Blackett, 1889.

Trollope, Anthony. "Charles Dickens." *The St. Paul's Magazine*, July 1870, pp. 370–75.

Waddington, Patrick. "Dickens, Pauline Viardot and Turgenev." *New Zealand Slavonic Journal*, no. 1, 1974, pp. 55–73.

Waugh, Arthur. *A Hundred Years of Publishing*. London: Chapman and Hall, 1930.

Wiggin, Kate Douglas. *My Garden of Memory*. Boston and New York: Houghton Mifflin, 1923.

Wilkins, William Glyde. *Dickens in Cartoon and Caricature*. Edited with an introduction by B. W. Matz. Boston: Bibliophile Society, 1924.

Wilson, Angus. *The World of Charles Dickens*. New York: Viking, 1970.

Wilson, James Grant. *Life and Letters of Fitz-Greene Halleck*. New York: D. Appleton, 1869.

Yates, Edmund. *His Recollections and Experiences*. 2 vols. London: Richard Bentley and Son, 1884.

Yeats-Brown, Francis. "Dickens in Genoa." *The Spectator*, September 22, 1928, p. 358.

About Charles Dickens' Work

Aldington, Richard. *Four English Portraits, 1801–1851*. London: Evans Bros., 1948.

Andrews, Malcolm. *Dickens and the Grown-up Child*. London: Macmillan, 1994.

Beresford, Edwin Chancellor. *The London of Charles Dickens*. London: Grant Richards, 1924.

Boll, Ernest. "Charles Dickens and Washington Irving." *Modern Language Quarterly*, December 1944, pp. 453–67.

Bolton, H. Philip. *Dickens Dramatized*. Vol. 1. Boston : G. K. Hall, 1987.

Browning, Elizabeth Barrett, and Robert Browning. *The Brownings' Correspondence*. Edited by Philip Kelley and Ronald Hudson. Vol. 8. Winfield, Kans.: Wedgestone Press, 1990.

Butt, John. *Pope, Dickens, and Others*. Edinburgh: Edinburgh University Press, 1969.

Charles Dickens: An Exhibition to Commemorate the Centenary of His Death. London: Victoria and Albert Museum, 1970.

Chesterton, Gilbert Keith. *Appreciations and Criticisms of the Works of Charles Dickens*. London: J. M. Dent; New York: E. P. Dutton, 1911.

———. *Charles Dickens: A Critical Study*. New York: Dodd, Mead, 1909.

Collins, Philip. "*Carol* Philosophy, Cheerful Views." *Études anglaises*, April–June 1970, pp. 158–67.

———, ed. *Dickens: The Critical Heritage*. London: Routledge and Kegan Paul, 1971.

Davis, Earle. *The Flint and the Flame: The Artistry of Charles Dickens*. Columbia: University of Missouri Press, 1963.

Davis, Paul. *Charles Dickens A to Z*. New York: Checkmark Books, 1998.

Dewey, Orville. "On American Morals and Manners." *Christian Examiner*, March 1844, pp. 250–80.

Emerson, Ralph Waldo. *The Heart of Emerson's Journals*. Edited by Perry Bliss. Boston: Houghton Mifflin, 1928.

Field, Kate. *Pen Photographs of Charles Dickens's Readings*. Boston: James R. Osgood, 1871.

Fields, Henry M. *Summer Pictures from Copenhagen to Venice*. New York: Sheldon, 1859.

Ford, George H., and others. *Dickens Criticism: Past, Present, and Future*. Cambridge, Mass.: A Charles Dickens Reference Center Publication, 1962.

Gissing, George. *Charles Dickens: A Critical Study*. London: Blackie, 1898.

Harbage, Alfred B. *A Kind of Power: The Shakespeare-Dickens Anthology*. Philadelphia: American Philosophical Society, 1975.

Holderness, Graham. "Imagination in *A Christmas Carol*." *Études anglaises*, January–March 1979, pp. 28–45.

Hollingshead, John. "Charles Dickens as a Reader." *The Critic*, September 4, 1858, pp. 537–39.

Horne, Richard Hengist, ed. *A New Spirit of the Age*. London: Harper and Bros., 1844.

Howells, William Dean. *Criticism and Fiction*. New York: Harper and Bros, 1891.

Jackson, Thomas Alfred. *Charles Dickens: The Progress of a Radical*. London: Lawrence and Wishart, 1937.

Jordon, John O., ed. *The Cambridge Companion to Charles Dickens*. Cambridge, Eng.: Cambridge University Press, 2001.

Kitton, Frederic G. *Dickens and His Illustrators*. London: George Routledge, 1899.

Krupskaya, Nadezhda. *Memories of Lenin*. London: Lawrence and Wishart, 1942.

Maurois, André. *Dickens*. Translated by Hamish Miles. London: John Lane, 1934.

Oliphant, Margaret. "Charles Dickens." *Blackwood's Edinburgh Magazine*, June 1871, pp. 673–95.

Orwell, George. *A Collection of Essays*. San Diego: Harcourt, Brace, 1993.

Podeschi, John. *Dickens and Dickensiana*. New Haven: Yale University Library, 1980.

Quiller-Couch, Arthur. *Charles Dickens and Other Victorians*. Cambridge, Eng.: Cambridge University Press, 1925.

Ruskin, John. *The Works of John Ruskin*. Edited by E. T. Cook and Alexander Wedderburn. Vol. 37. London: George Allen; New York: Longmans, Green, 1912, pp. 7, 9–10.

Santayana, George. *Soliloquies in England and Later Soliloquies*. London: Constable, 1922.

Schlicke, Paul, ed. *Oxford Reader's Companion to Dickens*. Oxford: Oxford University Press, 1999.

Slater, Michael, ed. *Dickens 1970*. New York: Stein and Day, 1970.

Stevenson, Robert Louis. *The Letters of Robert Louis Stevenson*. Edited by Sidney Colvin. Vol. 1. New York: Charles Scribner's Sons, 1910.

Stone, Harry. *Dickens and the Invisible World: Fairy Tales, Fantasy, and Novel-Making*. Bloomington, Ind.: Indiana University Press, 1979.

Strong, George Templeton. *The Diary of George Templeton Strong*. 4 vols. Edited by Allen Nivens and Thomas Milton Halsey. New York: Macmillan, 1952.

Swinburne, Algernon Charles. "Charles Dickens." *The Quarterly Review*, July 1902, pp. 20–39.

Thackeray, William Makepeace. *The English Humourists of the Eighteenth Century*. New York: Harper and Bros., 1853.

Tillotson, Kathleen, and others, eds. *Dickens Memorial Lectures 1970*. London: Dickens Fellowship, 1970.

Tomlin, E. E. F., ed. *Charles Dickens 1812–1870: A Centenary Volume*. London: Weidenfeld and Nicolson, 1969.

Wall, Stephen, ed. *Charles Dickens: A Critical Anthology*. Harmondsworth, Eng.: Penguin, 1970.

Wilson, Edmund. *The Wound and the Bow*. Boston: Houghton Mifflin, 1941.

About *A Christmas Carol*

Ambrosino, Salvatore V. "Analysis of Scrooge." *New York State Journal of Medicine*, December 15, 1971, pp. 2884–85.

Anastaplo, George. "Notes from Charles Dickens's *Christmas Carol*." *Interpretation*, January 1978, pp. 52–73.

Calhoun, Philo, and Howell J. Heaney. "Dickens's *Christmas Carol* After a Hundred Years." *The Papers of the Bibliographical Society of America*, October–December 1945, pp. 271–317.

Crowdy, Wallace L. "Some Illustrators of *A Christmas Carol*." *Literature*, December 7, 1901, pp. 1–4.

Dana, Olive E. "The Christmas Carol and Its Author." *The Cottage Hearth*, December 1886, pp. 379–83.

Davis, Paul. *The Lives and Times of Ebenezer Scrooge*. New Haven: Yale University Press, 1990.

Dickens, Cedric C. "A Reading Edition of the *Carol*." *Bookseller*, October 30, 1965, pp. 1016–17.

Fiedler, Fritz. "Dickens' Gebrauch der rymischen Prosa in *Christmas Carol*." *Archiv für das Studium der Neueren Sprachen und Litteraturen*, 1919, pp. 47–50.

———. "Die Vorgeschichte der Hauptgestalten in Dickens' *Christmas Carol*." *Archiv für das Studium der Neueren Sprachen und Litteraturen*, 1924, pp. 60–81.

———. "Wie Dickens das *Christmas Carol* feilte." *Archiv für das Studium der Neueren Sprachen und Litteraturen*, 1922, pp. 37–53.

Gilbert, Elliot L. "The Ceremony of Innocence: Charles Dickens' *A Christmas Carol*." *PMLA*, January 1975, pp. 22–30.

Gimbel, Richard. *Charles Dickens' A Christmas Carol: The Three States of the First Edition*. Princeton, N.J.: Privately printed, 1956.

———. "The Earliest State of the First Edition of Charles Dickens' *A Christmas Carol*." *Princeton University Library Chronicle*, winter 1958, pp. 82–86.

Glancy, Ruth F. "Dickens and Christmas: His Framed-Tale Themes." *Nineteenth-Century Fiction*, June 1980, pp. 53–72.

———. *Dickens's Christmas Books, Christmas Stories, and Other Short Fiction: An Annotated Bibliography*. New York: Garland Publishing, 1985.

Guida, Fred. *A Christmas Carol and Its Adaptations: A Critical Examination of Dickens's Story and Its Productions on Screen and Television*. Foreword by Edward Wagenknecht. Jefferson, N.C.: McFarland, 2000.

Hearn, Michael Patrick. "*A Christmas Carol*: Celebrating the Dickens Classic." *Gourmet*, December 1993, pp. 146, 234–38.

Johnson, Edgar. "Biography of a Classic: *A Christmas Carol*." *Saturday Review*, December 30, 1967, pp. 13, 42.

———. "The *Christmas Carol* and the Economic Man." *American Scholar*, winter 1952, pp. 91–98.

Kitton, Frederic G. "Some Famous Christmas Stories." *The Library Review*, January 1893, pp. 705–17.

Lewis, Donald W. "What Was Wrong with Tiny Tim?" *American Journal of Diseases of Children*, December 1992, pp. 1403–7.

McCaffery, James Manus. "A Kind Word for Ebenezer." *Mensa Bulletin*, December 1881, pp. 18, 20.

Nelson, Roxanne. "The Case of Tiny Tim." *The Washington Post*, December 24, 2002.

Newton, A. Edward. "The Greatest Little Book in the World." *The Atlantic Monthly*, December 1923, pp. 732–38.

Rann, Ernest H. "The Story of Dickens's *Christmas Carol*." *Cassell's Magazine*, December 1907, pp. 75–79.

Rowell, Geoffrey. "Dickens and the Construction of Christmas." *History Today*, December 1993, pp. 17–24.

Sammon, Paul. *The "Christmas Carol" Trivia Book*. New York: Carol Publishing Group, 1994.

Steig, Michael. "Dickens' Excremental Vision." *Victorian Studies*, March 1970, pp. 339–54.

About John Leech

Browne, Edgar. *Phiz and Dickens As They Appeared to Edgar Browne*. London: James Nisbet, 1913.

Cohen, Jane R. *Charles Dickens and His Original Illustrators*. Columbus: Ohio State University Press, 1980.

Dickens, Charles. "Fine Arts: *The Rising Generation* . . . by John Leech." London *Examiner*, December 30, 1848, p. 838.

Frith, William Powell. *John Leech: His Life and Works*. London: R. Bentley and Son, 1891.

Houfe, Simon. *John Leech and the Victorian Scene*. Suffolk, Eng.: Antique Collectors' Club, 1984.

Kitton, Frederic G. *Dickens and His Illustrators*. London: George Redway, 1899.

Ruskin, John. *The Art of England*. New York: John Wiley and Sons, 1884.